The Tortuga Plantation

Blood, Steel, and Empire: Book II

James L. Nelson

Fore Topsail Press
64 Ash Point Road
Harpswell, Maine, 04079

Maps by Chris Boyle

Cover Design by Subtle Touch Creations

ISBN - 979-8-218-53232-1

To my Beloved Victoria Rose Lockard, latest of the Pirate Clan.

PLATE 2

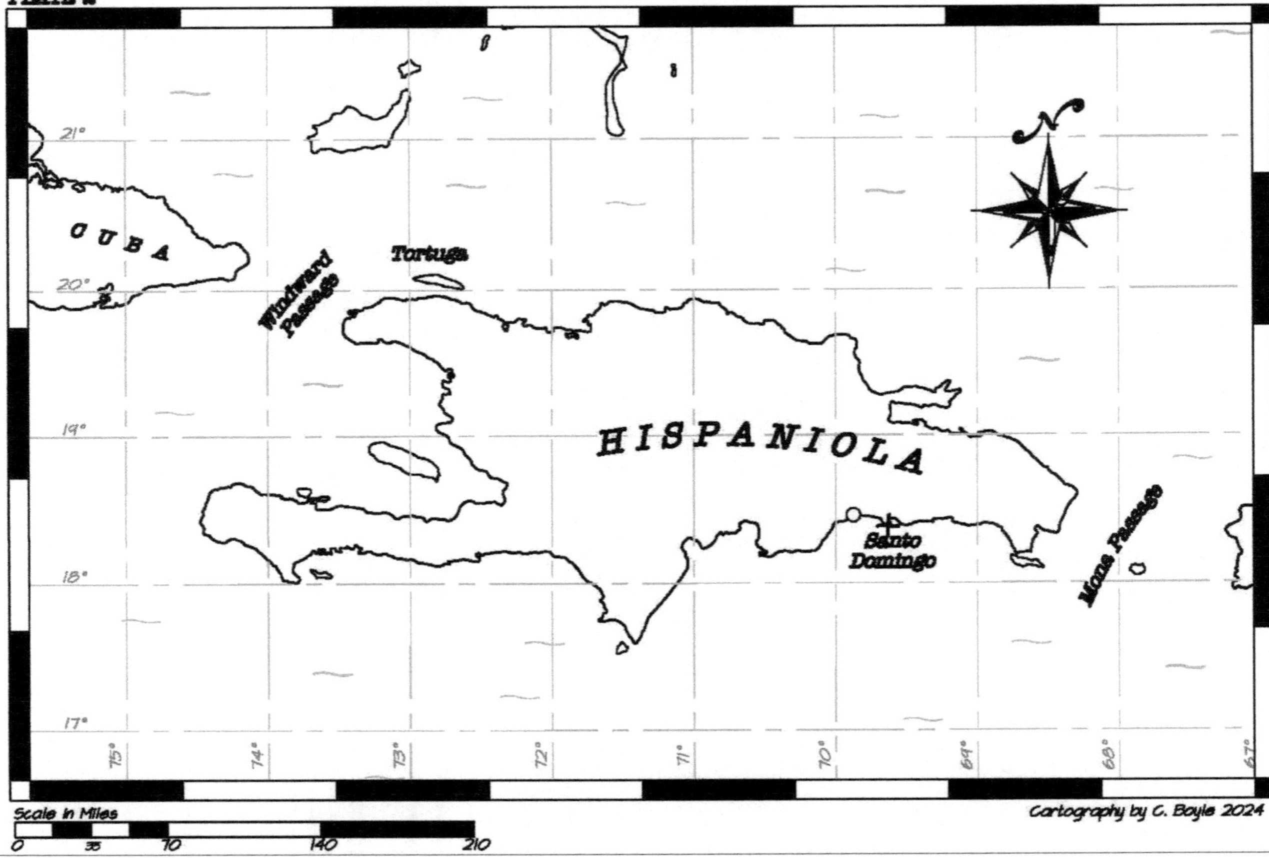
CUBA
Windward Passage
Tortuga
HISPANIOLA
Santo Domingo
Mona Passage
N
21°
20°
19°
18°
17°
75°
74°
73°
72°
71°
70°
69°
68°
67°
Scale in Miles
0
35
70
140
210
Cartography by C. Boyle 2024

PLATE 5

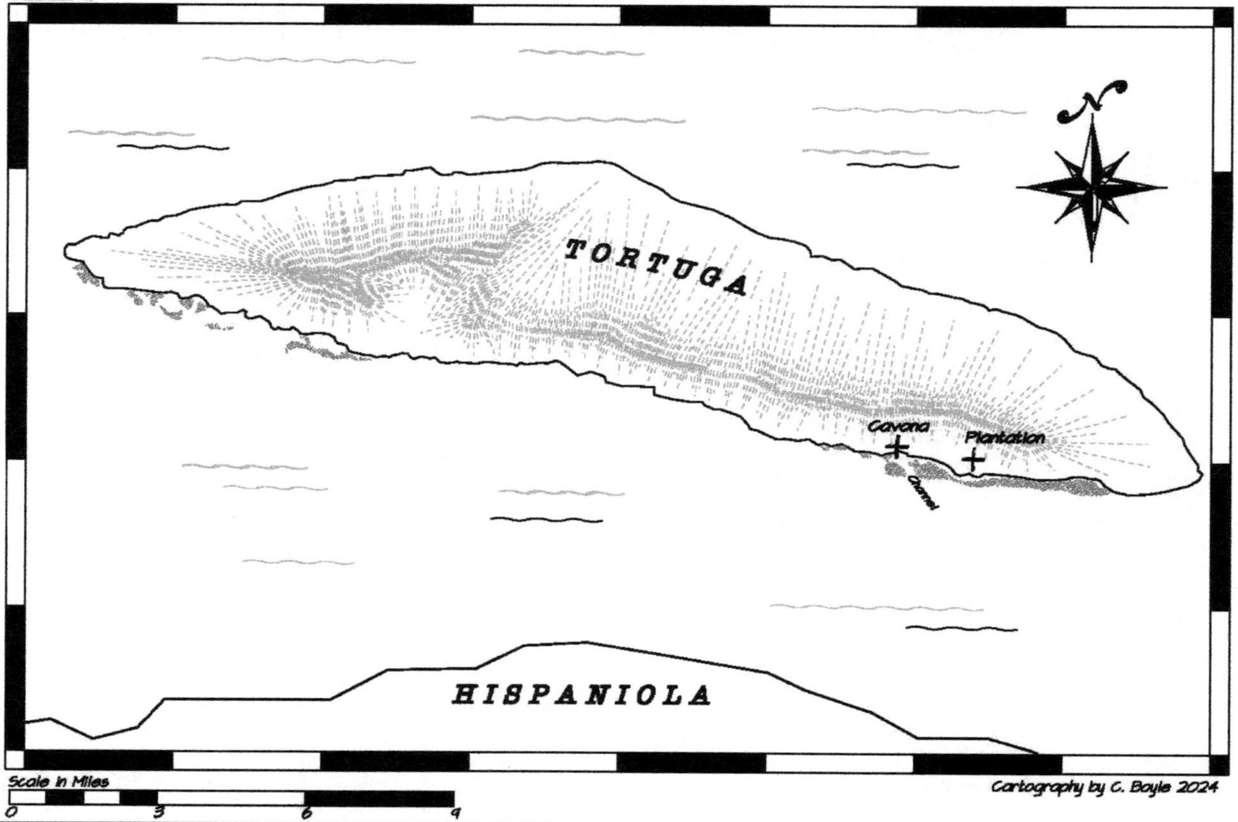
N
TORTUGA
Cavona
Plantation
Channel
HISPANIOLA
Scale in Miles
0
3
6
9
Cartography by C. Boyle 2024

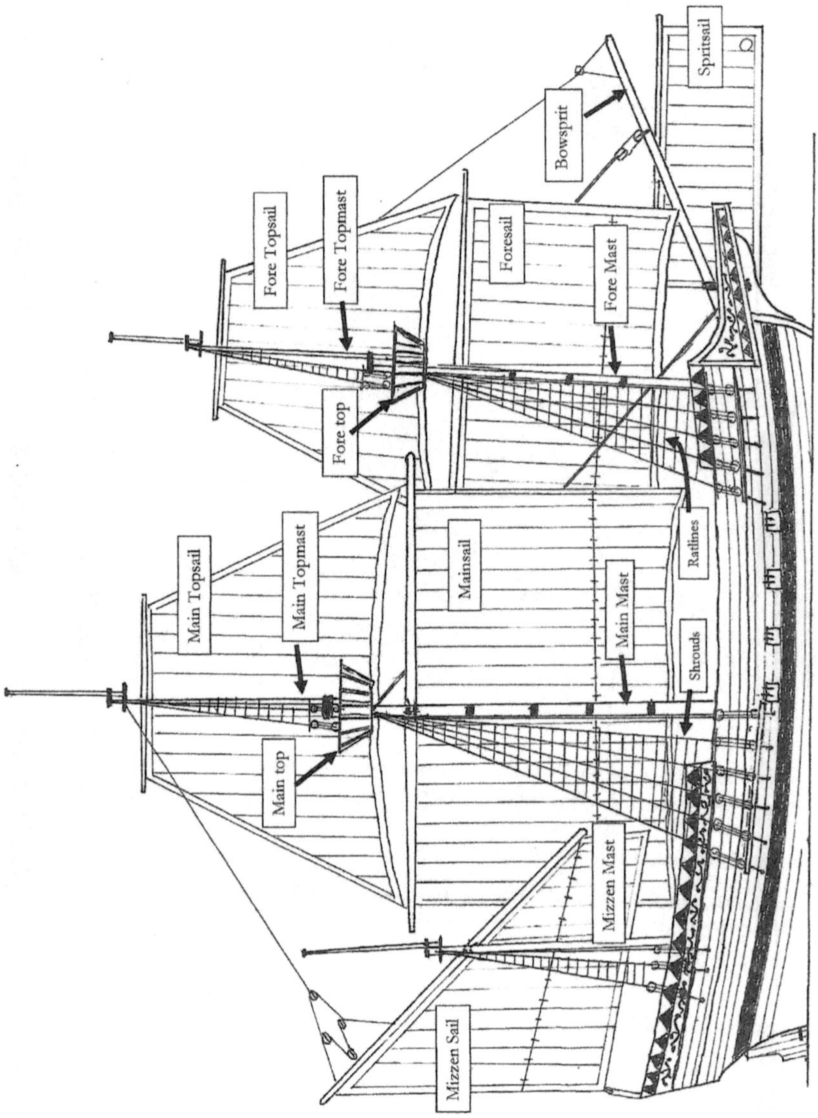

For terminology, see *Glossary*, page 341

Chapter One

Tortuga. *Île de la Tortue.* The Island of the Turtle, rising hump-back from the sea, its great cresting ridge of mountains arching east to west, spilling the impossibly blue water of the Caribbean away on either side. An insignificant heap of rocks and jungle and white beach at the mouth of the Windward Passage between Hispaniola to the south and Cuba to the west—islands of much greater import than that sliver of shell-shaped land.

Tortuga. Ignored, but not entirely. Cristoforo Colombo had set foot there, and given it its name, or at least the name by which the interlopers would know it. In the middle of the second decade of the 17th century, others had arrived, French and English. They came from St. Kitts, where they had been nibbling at the edge of Spain's New World empire, and now looked to plunge into it deeper still.

And because Spain could not protect every corner of the vast territory she claimed, she had not even tried to stop them. The French and English had settled on the island, built a town of sorts, which they called Cayona, and cleared plantations from the jungle.

That, at least, was how Jean-Baptiste LeBoeuf understood it. He had seen Tortuga many times, across the water, from the shores and high country of Hispaniola. Close enough that he could have rowed a periagua there in a day. But he had never actually been to the island.

He stood on the quarterdeck, arms held out straight on either side, his eyes taking the island in. Twenty-five miles, end to end. They were nearly up with the eastern point now, moving into the *Canal de la Tortue*, the five-mile-wide stretch of water between Tortuga and the north coast of Hispaniola.

Turtle… he thought. *Yes, I suppose it looks like a turtle…*

LeBoeuf had seen many turtles over the years, but generally while standing on the deck of a ship, looking down, in which case they did not look like that. One would have to be floating in the water, looking over the surface at the half-submerged creature, for it to look like the island. But LeBoeuf supposed if one were to view a turtle from that angle, it would appear much as Tortuga appeared now.

"You look like an idiot, you know," Henriette said. "I mean, more than usual, you look like an idiot."

LeBoeuf took his eyes from the island and looked over at her. She was leaning against the larboard bulwark, arms folded, lips pressed tight. She was glaring at him. He looked down at the woman kneeling in front of him, the one to his left holding the cloth against his outstretched arm.

The women were wives of the men who had sailed with LeBoeuf from the coast of Hispaniola. At least they called themselves wives. Or most did. They had been imported from the streets of Paris: whores rounded up and sent to civilize the wild men of the West Indies. Henriette had been part of that importation, though she had arrived by a very different route. She had come by way of the king's court, the intriguing of Queen Anne d'Autriche and Cardinal Richelieu. At least by her telling.

The two women crowding around LeBoeuf, it turned out, had skills beyond the ones that had led to their arrest and deportation: they were competent seamstresses, and LeBoeuf was putting those skills to good use. He needed clothes. Not the clothes of a buccaneer, not the patched canvas pants and tired shirt and cassock stained with blood, the rawhide shoes and round canvas hat. He needed the clothes of a gentleman, and happily he had found them in the master's cabin, aboard the ship he had taken from the Spanish just days before.

The clothes, of course, did not fit. LeBoeuf was six-foot-and-some inches tall, his weight in the mid-two hundred pounds—none of it fat. He was not likely to find another man's clothes that fit him. He did find, however, two suits of clothes in a chest below, and now the women were working at turning those two small suits into one large one.

"I don't need to look smart," LeBoeuf said. "I just need to look like Chevalier Philippe Guillemeau de Beaune. Who may be dumb as a stone, for all we know."

"Humph," Henriette said, and she frowned deeper and knitted her brows.

LeBoeuf shook his head in wonder. He was all that stood between her and the buccaneers who manned the ship. If he abandoned her, another man might claim her as his wife. Or several at once. Or they might sell her to the highest bidder. He was the only hope she had of ever seeing her beloved Paris again. She must know that. Yet she seemed not to care. She seemed to have no fear of his casting her aside.

In truth, she seemed to have no fear at all. LeBoeuf found it very hard to reconcile such wanton disregard with her fierce sense for self-preservation, but there it was.

"The whole thing is madness, a waste," Henriette said next. "We could turn around right now and sail for France."

LeBoeuf made no reply. There were actually a hundred reasons why they could not, but he did not try to explain them. He knew why Henriette was so furious, and it had nothing to do with the direction in which they were sailing.

It was the gold. A hurricano had left a ship half-sunk in the bay where their hunting camp had been, and, on taking possession of it, LeBoeuf had discovered a fortune in gold hidden below the deck of the master's cabin. For some reason, Henriette had decided that half of the gold was hers, and LeBoeuf had not disabused her of the notion. He did not care. She was welcome to it.

Unfortunately, the ship had managed to catch fire in the middle of a fight—LeBoeuf never did learn how—and the gold had gone down with the rest. That was the cause of Henriette's fury. Fury not because the gold was lost when the ship went down. It wasn't, really. The ship had sunk in fairly shallow water. They knew where in the wreck it could be found, and a tolerable swimmer (which LeBoeuf was) could have retrieved it with some effort.

But LeBoeuf had not even bothered trying. That was what drove Henriette mad with frustration.

LeBoeuf did his best to ignore her, but he did feel like a bit of an idiot standing there with his arms outstretched like a scarecrow. He opened his mouth to ask if he could lower them when the woman in front stood and said, "Very good. You may take the tunic off, *monsieur*."

LeBoeuf nodded and lifted the half-made garment up over his head. He handed it to the woman, and she and her companion disappeared below. LeBoeuf stretched and let the warm West Indies sun wash over his bare chest and shoulders. It was getting late in the year, not so hot as it was in the summer months, and it felt good to him.

He looked up at the sails. The ship was running with the foresail and fore and main topsails set, the faithful easterly wind betwixt two sheets. They could easily carry more sail, but LeBoeuf did not want to go any faster than he was. He wanted to get a good look at what he was sailing into. He wanted to give the women time to finish his clothes.

He glanced over at Henriette, but she was staring off toward Tortuga, glaring at the island with the same contempt with which she had glared at him. She was lovely, her dark hair tumbling around her shoulders, her flawless skin starting to turn a soft brown in the tropical sun despite all her attempts to keep it the same pearl white it had been when she first arrived.

LeBoeuf wanted to speak. He wanted to tell her the truth, that he did not plan to leave the gold at the bottom of the harbor. That he intended to go back for it. But he had to go back alone, or with a handful of trusted men. If he retrieved that fortune in the company of all the buccaneers—thirty-three men by his count—he would have to share it out with all. Worse, he would have to explain why he had not mentioned it earlier. Blood would likely spill. It often did, he knew, in those circumstances when gold and deception were involved.

LeBoeuf wanted to explain as much to Henriette, but he did not. The past few years had taught him to keep his mouth shut, and he did. It started from necessity, but now it was habit. He was no more inclined to speak than he was to put his hand in a flame. So he stared up at the sails and Henriette glared out at the island. Fury and contempt, it seemed, were as much a part of her as silence was of LeBoeuf.

We are quite a pair… he thought, and then turned to more practical matters. He looked aft at Pierre Le Chasseur, who was at the tiller. Most of the buccaneers had spent time on shipboard in various capacities and had some familiarity with the workings of a sailing vessel, but they were not all seamen, not at all. Le Chasseur, however, was a genuine mariner, which is why LeBoeuf had put him on the helm.

"Bring her head up a bit, we'll close more with the island," LeBoeuf said.

Le Chasseur nodded and said, "Bring her head up." He nudged the tiller to larboard and the bluff bow turned slowly to starboard.

"That's well. Hold her," LeBoeuf said. Le Chasseur nodded again and brought the tiller amidships.

LeBoeuf looked up at the sails. "Forward there," he called along the deck, "brace the sails around to larboard some!"

The men—the crew, the buccaneers—were sprawled around the deck in various positions of relaxation. There was not a lot that needed doing, sailing in those conditions, and the buccaneers were not much inclined to do anything they did not need to do. But they obeyed LeBoeuf's orders, standing and shuffling off to the sides of the ship, casting off and giving desultory tugs on the larboard braces.

They move like they're under water, damn the lot of them, LeBoeuf thought. He was not given to suffering such lethargy in a ship's crew, and even his time among the pig hunters of Hispaniola had not changed that attitude.

Van Loudersong, the Dutchman, whose real name was Van Lauwersoog—too much of a mouthful, for his fellow hunters—came smiling up the ladder to the quarterdeck.

LeBoeuf's hunting dog, which he called Other Dog, lay in the shade of the bulwark. She was a mastiff, a large and powerful beast that moved between frantic activity and near-complete lethargy, and in that way was well-suited to fellowship with the buccaneers. She was in a state of lethargy now, but she stirred a bit and gave a soft growl as Van Loudersong appeared.

"*Calme-toi*," LeBoeuf said. *Calm down.*

Van Loudersong glanced at the dog but did not pause as he stepped onto the quarterdeck and ambled aft. He looked at LeBoeuf and nodded toward the men forward.

"Not so great sailors, eh?" he asked. "No racing to stations and the Devil take the hindermost here, it seems."

LeBoeuf shrugged. "They don't much care to be told what to do."

Van Loudersong nodded and continued to smile. The Dutchman was a sailor of long experience, and unlike the others he did not come from the mudsill of humanity. He had been raised in something akin to wealth, had served as an officer in the Dutch navy, then a privateer, and then at last, a buccaneer, ever in search of greater and greater wealth.

LeBoeuf knew all this because Van Loudersong was always eager to share his life's story, lest anyone think him just another miserable wretch cast up on the shores of the West Indies. To LeBoeuf, who would not even volunteer his real name, it was all very amusing.

Van Loudersong himself was not very amusing. He was smart and he was treacherous and he was always looking for the main chance. His smile and his ingratiating demeanor could hide those qualities from some, but LeBoeuf could see through them as easily as through the startlingly clear water of the Caribbean.

"Well," Van Louderson said, "you'll have no need of sailors and such soon enough, once you have laid claim to your fine plantation on Tortuga."

"Might. Might not," LeBoeuf replied. It was about as chatty as LeBoeuf tended to be.

"Have you thought about what you might do with this ship?" Van Loudersong asked, nodding forward as if to indicate which ship he was referring to. "Once you're settled on the island?"

"I've thought some," LeBoeuf said. Van Loudersong waited for LeBoeuf to say more, and it took him a moment to realize that this was all he meant to say.

"We should talk, you and me," Van Loudersong said, his voice a bit lower now, conspiratorial. "These other fools want nothing more than to drink themselves to death, but you and me, we can see beyond that, eh? I have some thought on how we might use this ship to make us both very rich men."

I'll wager you do, LeBoeuf thought, but he only nodded in reply. Van Loudersong had a small fortune in goods hidden in a cave back on Hispaniola, and he was the only one besides LeBoeuf and Henriette who knew about the sunken gold. LeBoeuf could well imagine he was eager to get his hands on a ship.

"So, what say you? Can we do business?" Van Loudersong asked.

"After I get my plantation," LeBoeuf said. Van Loudersong smiled again and nodded with a knowing look that made LeBoeuf want to slap him. But he checked that impulse: Van Loudersong was decently well regarded by some of the buccaneers, and LeBoeuf knew he would need the help of every man aboard.

Gold was not the only thing LeBoeuf had discovered in the master's cabin of the wrecked ship. There had been a letter patent as well, the grant of a plantation on Tortuga to one Chevalier Philippe Guillemeau de Beaune, given by the King of France himself.

To LeBoeuf, the patent and the ship had been like a drink of cool water to a man dying of thirst. From a shipwrecked life that left him drowning in despair, these things were a line to grasp, a route from pig hunter to ship owner to lord of the manor.

When the ship burned, so burned the last vestige of LeBoeuf's hope. He had sat down on the beach and waited for death to come in like the tide. But Henriette had managed to save the letter patent from the flames, and another ship had come to anchor in the bay and LeBoeuf, incredibly, was given yet another shot at reclaiming his life. He was now aboard his own ship, off to take possession of his plantation. He had no considerations in mind beyond that, and he would allow none to distract him.

"Very well," Van Loudersong said. "After you get your plantation." He nodded and smiled again and LeBoeuf was impressed at how much like a genuine smile the Dutchman was able to manage.

They stood on for another hour or so, closing slowly with the coast of Tortuga. What little LeBoeuf knew about the island he had picked up in conversation with the sailors who bought smoked meat from the buccaneers.

He understood that there were reefs close in to the land, but even a quarter mile off, the water was deep and free of hazards. He understood that Tortuga had only one harbor, and it really wasn't much of a harbor at all, more like an open roadstead, accessible by two different channels through the reefs. Those reefs, he was told, offered some protection from the seas, if not from the wind. Happily, with Hispaniola standing like a wall just five miles to the south, there was not much chance for the wind or seas to build.

Five miles from the eastern point of land LeBoeuf spotted what he imagined was the harbor. He could see a thread of smoke rising up from the trees—a cooking fire most likely—and he thought he could make out a smattering of vessels riding at anchor near the shore. Most seemed to be large periaguas with their single spindly masts, and he might never have noticed them from that distance, save for the fact that two of the vessels appeared to be quite substantial: genuine ships at least as large as the one he commanded.

"Head up a bit more," he said. Le Chasseur acknowledged the order and turned the ship a bit more to starboard.

"Forward there!" LeBoeuf called next. "Clew up that foresail!"

Hands moved to haul away on the lines that would pull up the foremast's lower sail like a curtain. LeBoeuf watched them, considered his next words, then called out, "Van Loudersong! Prithee, would you lay up to the foretop and guide us through the reefs?"

Van Loudersong looked back at LeBoeuf, then up at the round foretop overhead, then back at LeBoeuf, trying, no doubt, to find the real motive behind the request. Then he gave a quick wave and headed up into the shrouds.

Good, good, LeBoeuf thought.

Van Loudersong was a mariner, he would know what to look for. Sending him to the foretop would keep him from plotting with the others, and since the Dutchman clearly wanted to get his hands on the ship, he was much motivated to see it not wrecked on a reef.

As they closed with the shore, LeBoeuf could pick out more of the details there. About a dozen boats of various sizes bobbed at their anchors, and a little farther out the two ships rode quietly at theirs. One was a bit larger than his own vessel, the other about the same size.

The blue-green water ran up to a wide, long, stretch of beach, the sand a brilliant white. There, a fringe of palm trees stood sentry-like, arching slightly toward the sea. Beyond the trees was an acre or so of open ground which seemed to LeBoeuf not so much cleared as beaten down. It formed a road of sorts, with a few structures lining the way, but from that distance he could not tell how many or what sort they were. Cayona. LeBoeuf was sure he had seen less impressive places, but he could not recall when.

Beyond that, for a few miles, the land trended uphill, a patchwork of meadows and fields and jungle, until it rose up to the imposing mountains that formed the crest of the turtle's shell.

"Deck, there!" Van Loudersong called down from the foretop. "Looks to be a reef right ahead, LeBoeuf! Best come up or you'll have her bottom out."

"Very well!" LeBoeuf called back, then to Le Chasseur said, "Come up." He turned forward. "Lay into those braces! Starboard tack!" He wanted to add *you lazy bastards* or *you sheep-biting fools*, the way he would have in the old days, but he bit that last part off. Forward, the men braced the yards around with a lethargy that made LeBoeuf want to lay into them with a belaying pin.

"That's well!" Van Loudersong sung out. "Hold that heading!"

They stood on, moving slowly, which was just as LeBoeuf wanted it. He wondered if there was any current that might be pushing them this way or that. He looked astern to see if the ship was slewing sideways, but the wake was straight and true.

"Billy!" he called forward, and the man who called himself Billy Solent looked aft. He was an Englishman, and a sailor. "Will you see the best bower ready for letting go?"

"*Oui, Monsieur le Capitaine!*" Billy Solent called back in the oddly-accented French he had picked up from his fellow hunters, then started calling for others to bear a hand.

LeBoeuf stepped over to the leeward rail and looked down. The water was astoundingly clear, as if they were sailing through molten glass, and he could see the sand and the occasional coral head on the bottom. The sight amazed him and unnerved him a bit, despite having spent several years sailing the Caribbean. It always seemed to him as if they were about to go hard aground, but he knew from experience they were not.

He looked farther outboard. He could see the edge of the reef now, a couple hundred feet away, a darker patch in the light blue water. Van Loudersong seemed to be piloting them well, and LeBoeuf could only hope he continued to do so.

If we wreck now, we can swim from here, LeBoeuf thought. *At least, I can.*

Soon LeBoeuf could make out more of the anchorage and the shore beyond. Along with the ships and boats at anchor, a dozen others were pulled up onto the shallows where they leaned over at odd angles. He could see there were more buildings on shore than he had first thought, a dozen or so lining the wide dirt road.

"You're through the channel, LeBoeuf!" Van Loudersong called down from the foretop. "We're in the harbor, such that it is!"

"Aye!" LeBoeuf called back. He ran his eyes over the anchorage, calculating how much cable he would need to let out, how much room he would need to swing.

Another cable length or two…

"Clew up that fore topsail! Let go the halyard!" he called forward a minute later, and the fore topsail was hauled up as the yard was lowered away.

"Le Chasseur, round up!"

Behind him, Le Chasseur pushed the tiller over and the ship turned up into the wind and the main topsail, still set, flogged and then pressed back against the mast, stopping the ship dead. LeBoeuf hesitated, just a moment, until he could feel the ship start to gather sternway. The crew, the ship, all were reacting to his spoken word, like they were extensions of himself. It was a familiar sensation, and one that made him profoundly happy.

"Billy! Let go!" he called forward. Billy Solent brought an axe down on the lashings holding the anchor suspended from the cathead and the big iron hook plunged into the water, pulling the thick anchor cable behind it through the hawse pipe.

LeBoeuf looked aloft. He looked at the shoreline, he looked down at the water moving past the hull, swirling stern to bow as the ship made sternway with the main topsail aback.

"That's well! Snub it!" he called and the hands forward stopped the anchor cable from paying out and made it fast to the bits. More hands, at LeBoeuf's urging, headed aloft to stow the fore and main topsails. Soon the ship was riding at anchor as if it had been there a month.

She was called *Trois Frères*—at least she was now. She had been called *Nuestra Señora de Santa Rosa* when LeBoeuf and the others took her from her Spanish crew. *Trois Frères* was the name of the ship that had first wrecked in the bay, the one aboard which they had found the gold and the letter patent, though that ship had also been sailing under Spanish colors with a Spanish name.

There's a lot of damnable intrigue going on here, LeBoeuf thought, though he could only guess at what it might be. And now he meant to insert himself right into the middle of it.

"So, you've reached your paradise, your Tortuga," Henriette said, stepping up beside him, the top of her head level with his mid-chest. "Now what will you do? Go single-handedly lay claim to your great estate?"

"We'll see," LeBoeuf said, and he said no more, though he had already put quite a bit of thought into the problem. From the onset he had made it clear to the others that the ship was his, and he would happily fight any man who thought otherwise. Unsurprisingly, no one objected. They would man the ship, because they feared LeBoeuf and they were as eager as he was to reach Tortuga. But once the buccaneers were ashore, LeBoeuf had no hold over them.

Most of the crew of *Trois Frères*, the erstwhile pig hunters, were crowded at the ship's rail, staring toward the distant shore. LeBoeuf knew well what they were thinking.

Among those buildings, one at least had to be a tavern, or if not a tavern, per se, a place where one might find a drink—rumbullion or brandy or wine, if that was all there was to have—and the men were desperate to get at it. All of their alcohol was lost when the original *Trois Frères* burned, and what little had been found aboard *Santa Rosa* was quickly consumed. They'd had no strong drink in days, and LeBoeuf could already see the unfortunate effect it was having on many of them.

He stepped to the break of the quarterdeck and looked forward. "You fellows, hear me!" he called. The men and women turned and took a few steps aft.

"We'll get a boat in the water directly," LeBoeuf said, "and we'll make for shore." He could see smiles of relief on more than a few faces. "I've never been to Tortuga. Maybe some of you have. But I have it on good authority there's taverns and publick houses ashore that will be glad to take your gold in exchange for drink!"

Smiles faded at that, and eyebrows knit in confusion. A muttering spread through the watching buccaneers. Then a fellow named Lessard spoke up. "We ain't got no gold to speak of," he said.

LeBoeuf put on a look of confusion. "We divided up what we found on the ship here," he said.

"Weren't but a quarter piece of eight per man," another said, which LeBoeuf knew perfectly well. He had personally overseen the hacking up of the few gold pieces they had found in the master's cabin, the better to secure the men's cooperation.

"Won't buy but a mouthful," Lessard said. LeBoeuf could hear the anger and mounting panic in his voice as the others chimed in their agreement.

"You're saying what money you had before, it's gone?" LeBoeuf asked next, yet another question he knew the answer to perfectly well. What little gold they had earned from their hunting had been spent on rum and gunpowder and bullets, and what was left had been stored in bags and sea chests that went down with the first *Trois Frères*.

The buccaneers in the waist looked angry, or sheepish, and desperate, but no one responded to LeBoeuf's question, so LeBoeuf went on.

"You know, I have no more coin than any of you, just my share of what was onboard here. Everything else I had, I lost in the fire." He heard Henriette make a soft snorting sound, an expression of disgust. Unlike the men, she knew just how much that loss amounted to. LeBoeuf ignored her.

"I came here to claim a plantation that I have a letter patent to, you all know that as well," LeBoeuf went on. "I got no notion of what's at the plantation. Don't know if there's even a privy there. But if there's a plantation house at all, there might well be wine or rum or brandy. Food as well. Any man who helps me make my claim to the plantation, well, he's welcome to his share of whatever we find there."

It looked to LeBoeuf as if the sun had broken through the clouds and suddenly come to shine on the faces of the men as they smiled and nodded in their relief. Henriette snorted again, and LeBoeuf thought, *And now I have an army of my own.*

Chapter Two

Las Casas Reales, the Royal Houses in Santo Domingo, Hispaniola, were the physical heart of Spain's New World empire. At least that was how Don Alonso Menéndez de Aviles had come to think of them.

Las Casas were the seat of government, from which flowed order to all the distant strongholds on the islands to leeward and the Spanish Main, to Havana and Maracaibo, Vera Cruz and Panama and all the lesser places. The sea routes from Santo Domingo to those cities were like veins and arteries, reaching out, bringing the blood of the King's rule to the body of the Spanish colonies.

That was Don Alonso's vision of Las Casas Reales, and he kept it to himself. It was ridiculous, and he knew it. But still he could not help but think of that place in that way, as the heart of the West Indies, the hub from which the spokes of empire radiated.

He had been there a little less than a year, and he had come to understand a great deal in that time. The colonial government, he discovered, was not the vibrant, involved, strict but benevolent father that he had imagined it to be when he received his appointment as lieutenant governor. It was not peopled by men who were eager to expand the wealth and might of Spain and grow their own fortunes in the process. It was not a magnet drawing the sharpest metal from Madrid or Toledo or Seville.

Rather, Santo Domingo attracted the sort of men who cherished an office in government because little would be asked of them and little expected. Some, the more ambitious ones, managed to make money with their outside endeavors—a little bribery, a little smuggling—but mostly they were happy to toil in their offices for a few hours per day and collect their salaries and eat the food and enjoy the comforts that Madrid provided.

And that, in turn, was just fine with Madrid. Initiative was not welcome, and had not been since the moment Cristoforo Colombo first returned to Old Spain. The *funcionarios* there did not want anyone besides themselves making decisions for the New World, and since they themselves rarely made decisions, very little direction was given and even less accomplished.

All this Don Alonso had come to understand during his short tenure in office.

And still he harbored his vision of what Spain's New World empire could be, and what it was, and what part he might come to play in it. Five generations had passed since Colombo planted his flag, and in that time Spain's power in the New World had reached its high water mark and begun to recede. Now the French and the English and the Dutch and the buccaneers were all nibbling at the edges of the empire, taking bigger and more audacious bites. But still Don Alonso held fast to his vision.

He considered this as he looked around the ornate, crowded ballroom of Las Casas Reales, the throngs of men clad in silk doublets and trousers, shoes as black and shining as wet paint, brilliant swords of Toledo steel at their sides. The men's wives were on their arms, at least those who, like his own wife, Francisca, had accompanied their husbands across the seas. They, too, were done up in their finest; great confections of silk and velvet and embroidery and lace and hair stacked in piles that took hours to arrange.

Las Casas, where Alonso lived and worked, was generally a sleepy warren of offices and apartments and sundry other rooms, with government officials moving quietly though the whitewashed stucco halls, a monotony broken only on occasion by some affair or other: a ball staged by the governor or the celebration of a feast day such as Navidad or the Feast of Santiago de Compostela.

But things were not sleepy now, and had not been for the past week. Now Las Casas Reales was crowded with men, important men with important business. Now it looked the way Alonso had thought it would from the onset.

Eight days before, Fadrique Álvarez de Toledo y Mendoza, Captain General of King Philip the Fourth's Ocean Sea Navy, commanding the *Armada de Sotavento*, a fleet of twenty great galleons and dozens of lesser ships, had come to anchor under the guns of Santo Domingo. The arrival of Toledo, who had won victories over the Dutch and the Moors, and most recently driven the upstart English and French from the islands of St. Christopher and Nevis, had charged the city with excitement. This night, the night of the governor's welcoming ball, was yet another high-water mark in that flood of enthusiasm.

Alonso moved carefully, maneuvering Francisca through the crowd. His wife paid little attention to where she was stepping, so Alonso tugged her gently this way and that to keep her from bumping into the other guests. Overhead the massive chandeliers threw an uneven light around the big room, so that some areas were brightly lit and some lost in deep shadow. The flames, dancing on the tops of the many candles, poured even more heat into the great hall, which was already stifling from the warm night and the press of bodies.

The buzz of conversation was terrific, but Alonso did not join in, just nodded and smiled as he passed men and women he recognized, or who recognized him, the lieutenant governor, and sought his acknowledgement. Somewhere off at one end of the vast room a quartet was playing, but Alonso could only hear occasional snatches of music. The air was thick and pungent, the scent of perfume and sweat and melting wax moving like a spirit through the crowd.

"My sweet," Don Alonso said to his wife, leaning in close so he could speak as softly as possible. "Let us make our way over there." He nodded toward the far end of the room, where tall windows looked out over the River Ozama. There, Alonso knew, they might get some relief from the heat, and, more importantly, avoid the people they would encounter on their current trajectory.

"Oh, husband, no, I beg you!" Francisca said. "I do so wish to greet Tío Fadrique!"

Tío Fadrique… To Francisca, Captain General Fadrique Álvarez de Toledo was Uncle Fadrique. The great hero of Gibraltar was not actually Francisca's uncle, just a family friend, one close enough that Francisca and her siblings called him *Tío.*

Francisca's father was Don Cristóbal de Seville, a very powerful and well-connected man. Powerful enough to be dear friends with the likes of Toledo. Powerful enough to secure for his son-in-law the post of Lieutenant Governor of His Most Catholic Majesty's colonies in the West Indies.

Alonzo's family was wealthy and well-connected in their own right, but nothing in the order of Francisca's family. Alonso owed his father-in-law a great deal, and he feared him and resented him because of it.

"Well," Alonso said, glancing over to where Fadrique Álvarez de Toledo stood surrounded by the ubiquitous crowd of fawning men and women. "I think Tío Fadrique is quite occupied at the moment."

"Oh, he'll speak with me!" Francisca said. "He'll always find a minute for his *pequeña sobrina*."

"Very well, my sweet," Alonso said, because he knew she was right, and knew she would not be dissuaded. And, as tired as he was of the great, pompous fool, he knew that flaunting his connection to Toledo could only help his reputation.

With a tug on Francisca's arm he changed direction, laying a course for the place where Toledo was making his stand. They had just stepped off in that direction when some minor official, half in his cups, bumped into Alonso's shoulder, which in turn bumped him into Francisca.

Alonso turned on the man, ready to give him a thorough tongue-lashing, but before he could speak, the *funcionario* was bowing and apologizing, near groveling, so Alonso dismissed him with a wave. He liked to see that sort of deference. He was willing to reward it.

They made their way to the outer circle that surrounded Toledo: a silk-clad, bejeweled, perfumed circle made up of some of the most powerful men in the West Indies and their wives, a circle whose combined wealth was likely more than the cumulative worth of every other man in the Greater Antilles. Some of the men—Toledo's senior officers—Alonso did not know, or had only met briefly. The others he knew all too well, and generally looked on them with attitudes running from pity to outright loathing.

The first to notice their approach was Gabriel de Chávez y Osorio, Governor General of Hispaniola, and he called out in his loud, jovial way.

"Ah, Don Alonso! And the beautiful Francisca! Do join us, do join us!"

Alonso nodded his greeting as the circle parted to make way for the newcomers. He could see the resentment on the faces of men whose status was suddenly diminished by the arrival of one more powerful and well-connected.

The mayor was next to greet them. "*Señor* Lieutenant Governor," he said, smiling. "*Señora* Francisca."

Don Nicolás Pérez de Maldonaldo. He was thick of belly and moustache, like the governor-general. In truth they looked very much alike, and Alonso had mistakenly thought they were the same sort of man; jovial, harmless, somewhat comical.

But Alonso had been disabused of that notion, disabused when he realized that Don Nicolás had plundered the illicit goods that he, Alonso, had imported to the West Indies to seed his personal empire. Disabused when Don Nicolás had ordered his men to do unspeakable things to Alonso in retribution for encroaching on the mayor's own illicit trade.

"Mayor Don Nicolás, good evening," Alonso said, nodding in the old man's direction. The mayor was smiling, but his eyes were hard and malicious and left no doubt that his business with Alonso was not done. And that was fine. Alonso was not done with the mayor either. Don Nicolás had spent decades entrenching himself in Hispaniola, and uprooting him would not be so easily accomplished, but Alonso was determined to find the means.

"Tío Fadrique!" Francisca squealed, and all conversation yielded to that meeting, the *conquistador* of St. Kitts and Nevis and the beautiful young wife of the lieutenant governor.

Toledo smiled, a smile partially hidden by his massive moustache, which swept up at the ends in impressive hooks. He wore a silk doublet and voluminous trousers of a purplish hue, intricately embellished with gold lace. Embroidered on the doublet in vivid scarlet thread was the insignia of the Order of Santiago, a cross with fleur-de-lis on the hilt and arms, the lower part resembling the blade of a sword. It was the same insignia that was embroidered on Alonso's tunic, as he, too, was a member of that venerable order.

"My beautiful *sobrina* Francisca!" Toledo gushed. He gave a shallow bow, then snatched up Francisca's hand and kissed her knuckles. He released her hand and turned to the others.

"Can you believe I used to play hide and seek and blind man's bluff with this lovely woman?" he asked, and the governor and the mayor and the others chuckled dutifully.

"Tío Fadrique, you know my husband of course, Don Alonso Menéndez de Aviles, the lieutenant governor here?" She looked up at

Don Alonso and smiled, and Alonso bowed, much deeper that Toledo had done.

"Don Alonso, a pleasure. Have we met?" Toledo asked.

Several times in Spain, you old fool, and we've spoken on five occasions this past week, Alonso thought, but he said only, "I was present at some of the councils you've attended since your arrival. In my office as lieutenant governor."

"Of course, of course," Toledo said, with still no hint of recognition. His eyes flickered down to the insignia on Alonso's doublet but he did not remark on it.

"Perhaps you will recall, Don Fadrique, that when we last spoke I was enquiring about how I might be of help in your plans for Tortuga?" Alonso pushed on. The admiral had been noncommittal, to say the least, during that brief discussion, but Alonso hoped the old fool might be more cooperative with Francisca there.

"Certainly, I recall, Don…Alonso," Toledo said. "At present I…"

There was some rustling behind, some sound unlike the natural ebb and flow of the attendees, and heads turned in that direction. Alonso looked as well, irritated to have his moment with the admiral interrupted, more irritated still to see his personal secretary, Juan Cardero, heading toward him.

Cardero, in his simple and unadorned suit of clothes, looked like some nondescript fish swimming through a school of exotic tropical creatures. There was no chance that someone of his lowly station had been invited to this affair, which meant he was bringing word of something to his master, Don Alonso. The fact that he would interrupt at such a moment meant it was something that could not wait.

"Forgive me, Don Fadrique…gentlemen…my sweet, here is my secretary and I can only guess his business is urgent." With a nod Alonso stepped away from the others and intercepted Cardero as he pushed through the crowd.

"Forgive me, Don Alonso," the secretary said, his voice low, but there's another disturbance. In the tavern district."

The southern end of the city, nearer the mouth of the Rio Ozama, was where the lower sort congregated. It was crowded with taverns and brothels and all manner of disreputable business. There was often trouble in the tavern district, but never before was there anything on the scale there had been in the past week.

"The same sort of trouble as before?" Alonso asked.

"Yes, but worse, Don Alonso. Hundreds."

Alonso frowned. Toledo's fleet carried with it thousands of soldiers and sailors, and the admiral would not consider keeping them confined aboard their ships. They had been given the run of the town: men who had just made the long passage from Spain and had sacked the islands of St. Kitts and Nevis. Their blood was up and they had plunder in their purses, and now they had drink in their bellies. Smoldering passions kept bursting into flames.

"Word has been sent to Delgadillo at the *fortaleza*, Don Alonso," Cardero said. "He and his men can get this in hand, I am certain. You need not leave the ball."

Alonso considered that for a moment, then shook his head. "No, I must see to this myself."

Delgadillo was the captain of the troops garrisoned at Fortaleza Ozama, the chief fortification in Santo Domingo. He was a good man, but Alonso could not bear to have a riot taking place in his city while he stood around making idle chitchat with Don Fadrique and his ilk.

"I thought you would say as much, your grace," Cardero said. "Your horse and your guard are waiting in the courtyard."

"Very good," Alonso said. He frowned deeper and thought, *Damn these men-at-arms, miserable filth, and the sailors…the lot of them!*

This put Alonso in a bind. He was loath to leave the ball and the chance to use his wife to get closer to Don Fadrique. Or worse, to allow the mayor and governor to worm themselves into the good graces of the conquistador in his absence.

On the other hand, the likes of Don Fadrique and those other worthies, and the fawning minor officials swarming like ants, drove Alonso to madness. He could not tolerate their company for long. Here was a chance for some action, the sort that was generally denied him in the monotony of his office. It was a chance to take control of an ugly situation and see it handled right.

That, more than anything, decided it for him. Alonso, unique among the officials at Las Casas Reales, and much to his own surprise, had come to care about Santo Domingo and the role he played in the city's governance. He still meant to use his position to gain personal wealth and power, but if he could bring order to the city as well, so much the better.

"One moment," Alonso said. He turned and in a few steps was back with his wife and the others.

"Forgive me," he said, addressing Francisca. "There is some disturbance in the town and I must see that it is quelled."

"Oh, my darling, must you go?" Francisca pleaded.

"I must, my sweet, forgive me," Alonso said. "With God's grace I'll return shortly." He bowed deep, then straightened and glanced around. He saw worry on Francisca's face, confusion on the face of the governor-general, Don Gabriel. The mayor's face suggested suspicion, and Toledo's a complete lack of interest.

Alonso turned and hurried after Cardero, who was already heading back the way he had come.

To get to Alonso, Cardero had fought his way through the crowd, but now the people parted before the lieutenant governor, who was moving fast with a look of grim determination. Alonso and Cardero did not break stride as the doormen swept the big doors open, and they stepped out of the stifling, brightly lit ballroom into the cool evening air.

The door led out onto the plaza, an acre of smooth, granite bricks that stretched from the front of Las Casas Reales east, and ended at a low wall. On the other side of the wall was a cliff that dropped down to the lower part of the town bordering the river. The plaza was well lit with lanterns hung at regular intervals, and in that light Alonso could see the mounted *guardias,* the six men who made up his own personal guard. They wore tunics and trousers of black and red, and wide-brimmed hats with long white plumes trailing behind. Each was armed with a sword, a dagger, and four pistols. Each was mounted on a fine black horse.

A seventh horse stood at the head of the line, its reins held by a stable boy. Alonso hurried across the plaza and grabbed hold of the saddle, put a foot in the stirrup and swung himself up, adjusting the hang of his sword as he did. Two braces of pistols hung in holsters off the saddles, their brass butts gleaming in the light of the lanterns. Alonso looked down at Cardero.

"Loaded, Don Alonso," he said, and Alonso nodded. He flicked the reins and kicked the horse's flanks and the beast broke into a trot. Alonso heard the sound of the other riders following behind, but did not bother looking back.

They rode quickly down the wide road that ran parallel to the river, the hooves of the horses loud on the cobblestones. Hemming them in on either side was a scattering of fine homes surrounded by high walls, which soon yielded to the open parade-grounds of Fortaleza Ozama to the east. Alonso studied the place as they rode past. The lower windows of the *fortaleza* were blazing with light, but the grounds were dark, and there seemed to be precious little activity there considering that a riot was taking place just a half mile away.

They rode south, and soon they could hear it, even over the clatter of the hooves: shouting and screaming, crashing sounds—wagons being overturned, or heavy objects flung from upper story windows—the occasional report of a musket or pistol.

Alonso had personally intervened in half a dozen such disturbances, but he had never heard anything like this, and it gave him pause as they neared the tavern district.

At the southern end of the city, where the road followed the natural bend of the river, Alonso led his guard west, picking up the pace as the sounds of the riot grew louder and more distinct. Over the tops of the close-packed buildings he could see a bloom of light, and he did not cherish the sight of it, fearing what it might mean.

Two blocks more and they were there. The situation was indeed what Alonso had feared, and worse.

Hundreds of men were jammed in the street, packed together like fish flailing in a great net. Fists and elbows and feet lashed out, punching and kicking left and right; clubs and sticks and bottles rose up at arm's length and slammed down this way and that. Soldiers, sailors, Santo Domingians, even some women, all caught up in a horrible melee.

Alonso could see it all clearly because a tavern on the north side of the street was on fire, and moments away from being fully engulfed. Flames were billowing out of the door and the windows, reaching up the front of the building, and starting to catch the shutters on the upper floor. The smoke was already choking, and Alonso could hear the crackling of the flames over the shouting in the streets. The whole scene was bathed in a strange light: yellow and orange and deep shadow, flaring and dropping away.

En el nombre del Padre y del Hijo y del Espíritu Santo, Alonso thought, making the Sign of the Cross as he reined to a stop and stared at the burning building. A fire like that could easily spread and take out half the city before it was contained. But there was no chance of fighting the blaze, not with many scores of people jamming the street in raucous battle.

Twenty feet away a pistol fired, and in the muzzle flash Alonso saw the back of a man's head blown apart, his arms flung up as he was tossed back into the man behind him. The sight jarred Alonso back into the moment. He looked over the crowd and could see, in the midst of them, a dozen mounted soldiers and at least three riderless horses, bucking and kicking. They were the handful of soldiers from Fortaleza Ozama who had turned out when summoned, or what was left of them. A minute more of that and there would be fewer still.

A dozen men? Alonso thought. There were hundreds of soldiers at the fortaleza, enough to quell this riot quickly. But only a dozen had been sent?

The thought made him furious, but there was no time now to indulge it. Alonso pulled his sword and turned to the *guardias* behind him. "Follow me! Follow me! Forward!" he shouted, then he slammed his heels into the horse's flanks and plunged ahead into the killing mob.

Chapter Three

Alonso's horse, trained for battle, plunged unflinching into the mob, front hooves rising and falling as it charged forward. Alonso held the reins with his left hand and wielded his rapier with his right, twisting it sideways to strike with the flat of the blade as best he could. It was not the sword he would have chosen for that work—had he foreseen this action he would have taken his wide-bladed falchion, better suited for horseback—but he had only the ornate Toledo steel that he had worn to the ball.

The rapier might have been less than ideal, but it was still effective, and between his blade and the horse's hooves Alonso was able to drive the crowd apart as he plunged on, making for the mounted soldiers ahead. Men shoved and stumbled out of the way, or fell screaming at his horse's feet as he continued to urge his mount forward and winnow the crowd with his sword.

"Delgadillo!" he called as he caught sight of the captain, also on horseback, also slashing right and left with his sword. "Delgadillo!"

The captain heard him at last, turned, then jerked his horse's reins to one side, driving the animal closer to where Alonso was wading through the mob.

"We need to get the riders together! Form rank!" Alonso called. He had enough experience with this sort of work to know that only horses could break up a melee such as this, and that would work only if the riders worked together. Some of Delgadillo's men had already been pulled from their mounts, and Alonso doubted they had lived long on the ground. If the horsemen did not act in concert they would all go that way soon enough.

"Yes, *señor*!" Delgadillo replied and began shouting to his men. One by one they heard him and came driving through the mob until they were all within shouting distance.

"Form rank!" Alonso shouted, waving left and right with his sword. "Form up on me! On me!" He turned to the guardias behind him—"Form rank, on me!"—and they moved to obey, pushing their horses into place.

It was no easy task maneuvering into a line abreast, fighting their way through the rioting men at their feet. Alonso could feel the heat coming off the burning tavern, and sometimes a quirk of the breeze would make the smoke roll over them, blotting out everything farther than a few feet away, making the men gag and cough.

He looked to one side, then the other, and saw that the horsemen were as lined up as they were going to get; not an impressive sight, but hopefully effective. The fight was still swirling around them and none of the combatants seemed to be paying the riders any attention, but that would change.

"Forward!" Alonso shouted, waving his rapier and kicking his horse. The animal leapt ahead, lashing with its hooves, charging through the men in its way as they turned, wide-eyed, to look. Mouths opened in screams of panic, men started shoving their way clear.

Along the line, the others advanced as well, their horses, trained as Alonso's was, driving into the crowd. Alonso slashed this way and that with his rapier, smacking anyone within reach with the flat of his blade. He twisted to his right and looked down into the muzzle of a pistol, a soldier holding the gun with a straight arm. Blood was running down the man's face, gleaming in the light, and he seemed to be shouting, but Alonso could not tell.

Alonso jerked his body sideways as the pistol went off with a deafening roar, the muzzle flash bright even against the backdrop of the burning tavern. Alonso felt the bullet pass through his hair and pluck the hat off his head. He twisted back and with no thought, just reflex, he leaned over and lunged, and had the satisfaction of seeing the tip of the rapier pierce the man's throat in a shower of blood.

He pulled the sword free and slashed in the other direction. He looked up, over the horse's head, out over the fighting mob, and what he saw pleased him.

Panic was sweeping through the men under the riders' hooves, and, as they pushed to get clear of the menace, it sent waves of fear radiating out like the heat from the burning tavern. People were starting to flee, to leave off the fight and stagger away, before the warhorses and the sweeping blades were upon them.

Run, you bastardos!

"Push them! Push them!" Alonso shouted, as the riders maintained their relentless advance, keeping good order, holding their line. They were pushing hard enough to keep the panic fresh, but slow enough to give the mob a chance to escape. Because that was the goal: not to trample them, if it could be avoided, but to drive them off.

Alonso felt something thump against his side, like a blow from a fist. He looked down as a cobblestone bounced on the road below, then looked up at the snarling face of the man who had thrown it. Then he watched the snarl turn to fear as the man realized he had made a grave mistake.

Alonso cocked his arm and swung his rapier backhand at the man's face. The man's mouth dropped open, his eyes bugging out, as the lethal steel came whipping around. But Alonso, with many years of practice and perfect control of his blade, was looking only to teach a lesson.

The tip of the rapier hit the stone thrower's cheek just forward of his ear and tore a neat gash from there to the corner of his mouth, a painful wound, but not a fatal one. A wound that would remind the man, for the rest of his life, that an attack on Don Alonso Menéndez de Aviles was never a good idea.

The crowd was thinner now, the horses moving more freely, as more and more people dropped whatever weapons they had and raced away down the street, or through the many side streets and alleys. Some were running, some were limping, and in their wake they left a scattering of motionless forms—heaps of clothing and flesh, some in pools of blood—lying on the cobblestones.

Like Breda, Alonso thought. *It puts me in mind of Breda.*

Alonso had fought with Spinola at the Siege of Breda five years earlier. He had been there when the English column, sent to relieve the city, was driven off. The images of that fight, he knew, would be with him until the grave, and perhaps beyond: the way the enemy would suddenly break and run, as if on some signal, the bloodied English troops racing off as they were cut down by the mounted *lanceros*; the heaps of bodies left strewn on the cold, muddy field. This was like that, writ small.

He pulled his prancing horse to a stop, let it catch its breath, looked around the street. There were knots of rioters still loitering in various places, clear of the horsemen, but the fight was out of them. They just looked on, as if they had no business with the soldiers or the guardias.

Alonso looked across the street at the tavern, where the fire was still building. Flames were gutting out of the second-story windows and lapping up the walls; worse, the building to the left of the tavern was burning as well, the flames having bridged the twenty-foot gap between them and grabbed hold of anything there that would ignite.

*That one's done for...*Alonso thought. There was no stopping the flames now, not with the little time and the few men they had. But that would not be a problem. The second building butted up against a side street, which would serve as a fire break. It was likely that the flames would move no farther. At least in that direction.

To the right of the tavern was a stable: a smaller, less substantial structure, but a more flammable one. If the stable caught fire, the flames could spread from there to the next building and the next, until half the city was engulfed.

Over the sound of the fire Alonso could hear the terrified whinnying of the horses within, the crashing of hooves against wooden stalls. The easterly breeze alone had prevented the stable from going up like a heretic at the stake, but that would not last long. He turned to the other riders.

"We need to pull that stable down! Get it all clear, to stop the fire spreading! Go, get these bastardos standing around and put them to work. If any refuses, shoot them, so the others will understand!"

The riders nodded and raced off. Alonso nudged his mount to a walk and crossed over to the burning tavern, as close as he could get. The heat on his face and hands was terrific. His horse was not pleased to be so close to the inferno, or to hear the cries of his terrified brethren within, and he made it clear, twisting one way and the other, making low, nervous sounds in his throat.

"Easy, easy..." Alonso said, patting the horse's neck.

Behind him he heard shouting, some sort of scuffle, then the report of a single pistol shot, then another. He turned to see what was happening. Two of the bystanders were lying at the feet of the guardias' horses, one thrashing, one lying still. The rest were hurrying across the street, toward him and the burning stable. Behind them, the riders followed like *vaqueros* herding their cattle.

Alonso realized his rapier was still in his hand, and as the crowd approached he waved it and pointed to the stable. "Pull that down!" he shouted. "All of it! The timbers, the straw, get it all out of there!"

The men seemed to pause in their advance, and Alonso saw uncertainty on their faces, and he guessed they were not happy about jumping into that volatile collection of dry wood and straw.

"Go!" Alonso shouted again, but one of the men in the crowd looked up and shouted back.

"Señor! The horses in there, they're mad! They'll trample us all!"

Alonso frowned. He reached for one of his pistols, thinking it was time for yet another lesson in respecting authority, but he hesitated, his fingers resting on the brass butt-plate of the gun. He could hear the horses over the roar of the mounting fire, louder now and more frantic. These men, they might be soldiers or they might be sailors, but they were still just the lowest sort. Real courage could not be expected of them, as it was of a knight of the Order of Santiago.

Without a word Alonso sheathed his sword and swung down from his horse. "Delgadillo! Come with me!" he shouted. The captain dismounted as well and the two of them raced over the thirty feet of cobbled street to the wooden door of the stable.

The heat was tremendous, and the sound of the fire so loud that the scream of the horses could barely be heard, just sharp notes piercing the deep, all-encompassing roar. Alonso paused and turned to Delgadillo.

"We must let the horses out, just let them run!"

Delgadillo nodded. Alonso lifted the iron latch—he could feel the heat through his glove—and swung the door in.

Alonso had never thought much about Hell, but he knew that it could not be too different from what he was seeing now. The flames had already reached the back corner of the stable and were starting to find a foothold, throwing their flickering light around the inside of the building. The sound and the heat that came rolling out of the door hit him like a physical thing.

About half a dozen horses, confined in stalls, were bucking and kicking and slamming against the walls and doors. Their bulging eyes gleamed in the light of the fire, and for the first time Alonso understood how very dangerous this moment was.

But he knew horses, knew them better than he knew nearly anything on earth, and he understood that letting all those terrified animals free in that confined space would be a disaster. He turned to Delgadillo. "Get the stalls to the left, I'll get the right! One after the other, back to front! I'll go first!"

The fire was gaining height toward the back of the stable, and Alonso knew he had to let the horses nearest the flames out first, or there would be no getting them out at all. He pushed past the first stalls, keeping low, keeping away from the doors in case one of the animals kicked its way free. He saw a whip hanging from a nail on a post and grabbed it as he passed.

The heat was so intense that he wanted to scream, but he pressed his lips shut and reached the back of the stable at last. He could see the door on the last stall jerking and bulging as the horse behind it slammed into it in terror. Alonso stepped up quick and lifted the latch, swinging the door open and keeping behind it as he did.

The horse came bounding out, still kicking and bucking, flailing its head and snapping its teeth. Alonso had hoped it would run for the open door at the front of the building, but the beast was clearly too panicked to do anything but leap around in terror.

Alonso stepped out from behind the door. "Yah! Yah! Go!" he shouted, holding his arms up and waving them, but the horse seemed not to notice. He uncoiled the whip, drew it back, and flicked it at the horse's flank. Even through the din he heard the crack of the frayed tip on horseflesh, and that, at last, got the animal's attention.

It reared once more, and once more Alonso flicked the whip, snapping it on the horse's rump. The horse bolted forward, charging for the open door and Alonso turned and waved at Delgadillo.

Delgadillo was at the stall across from Alonso's and he, too, swung the door open and leapt clear. The horse came charging out just as the first had, and like the first it reared and kicked in terror but did not make for the door. Delgadillo stepped up, arms waving.

"No! No! Stay back!" Alonso shouted, but he was too late. The horse lashed out with its hind legs, catching Delgadillo with a hoof and slamming him into the back wall.

Alonso swung the whip and heard it crack, and the second horse raced off. He looked down at the dark heap that was Delgadillo. He wondered if the horse had struck him in the head or chest, if it had killed him with that one powerful blow. But then Delgadillo stirred, and Alonso raced over and helped him to his feet.

"I'm fine, I'm fine," Delgadillo said, which was clearly not true, but Alonso had no more time for him. He took five quick paces forward and swung the next stable door open, then the next. One by one he opened the doors and drove the horses out of the burning building. He used the whip when he needed to, but the horses nearer the front seemed to understand where salvation lay, and they followed their brethren out to the street beyond.

Delgadillo had recovered enough to open the last stall by himself, after which he and Alonso followed the horses through the door. A few coils of rope were hanging from a hook and Alonso grabbed them as they stumbled out into the blessedly fresh and relatively cool night air.

The crowd of men was still there, the mounted horsemen behind them, keeping them from running off. "Go, now!" Alonso shouted. "There are no horses to hurt you now! Pull that stable down, all of it!"

Slowly the men started moving again, skirting around the burning tavern, and a moment later they were plunging into the stable, heaving at the posts that formed the frame of the building, running out with armfuls of straw and dumping it in the streets. Alonso handed the ropes he had rescued to a couple of the horsemen, and they were able to make them fast to the doorframe and use their horses to pull the building down.

Flimsy as the stable seemed, it was no easy job to demolish it, but bit by bit they managed to tear it apart and drag it clear, before the fire could take full control of the wildly combustible material. How long they were at it, Alonso had no notion. Many hours, certainly. Finally, as the last of the timbers was cleared away, the men, one after another, staggered off and dropped in the street, like the dead from the riot, who still lay where they had fallen.

They were mostly done with the stable when the tavern finally collapsed, the whole structure falling in on itself and sending a great cloud of flames and embers and debris high in the air. Alonso was still mounted, watching the flames, Delgadillo beside him, the rest of the horsemen fanned out behind.

Is there no fire brigade? Alonso wondered. It had never occurred to him to ask if anyone in the city was charged with fighting fires. He considered asking Delgadillo if he knew the answer, but did not want to admit his ignorance, so he kept his mouth shut and resolved to find out by other means. If there was no fire brigade, he would see that one was established. He would not have his city burn down because of negligence on his part.

"I think there is no danger from the fire now, señor," Delgadillo said, breaking into Alonso's thoughts. Alonso could see he was right. Both the tavern and the building to its left had collapsed, knocking the flames down when they did, so there was no longer any chance of their spreading. What had once been the stable was now torn down to its component parts and scattered over the two blocks surrounding it.

"Very well," Alonso said, looking around. There was nothing more that needed doing, that he could see. Nothing more that they could do. In the morning he would send work parties to clean up the rest, but for now they were done.

This should not be my concern, he thought. That lazy, duplicitous bastard Don Nicolás Pérez was mayor of the city: he should have been the one answering this crisis.

He is too busy growing rich and fat to do his duty. But we'll see to that as well.

"We're done here. Let us go," Alonso said. He flicked his horse's reins and got the animal underway, though it seemed as tired as he was. Delgadillo rode at his side, the rest following behind.

"Tell me, Delgadillo," Alonso said as they rode. "Why were there but a dozen of your men with you? Out of all the garrison?"

Delgadillo made a grunting noise. "That was all I could gather, Don Alonso. And more than I was supposed to get. Word came to Captain General Sandoval about the riot. He was told to turn out enough men to put it down, I'm all but certain. But he did not."

"Why did he not?"

Delgadillo made the grunting sound again. "I do not know, señor. But I do know this. He said to me that he needed to keep the men at the fortaleza. To protect it. But that was not his decision. The captain general does not make decisions by himself. He is too frightened to do that. He does as the mayor tells him. He's the mayor's man."

The mayor… Alonso thought. They rode in silence for a bit, Alonso turning that over in his head. Word had been sent to Captain General

Sandoval to send troops to quell the riot, but then the mayor had overruled those orders. Why would the mayor do such a thing?

The answer was clear as water. Don Nicolás Pérez de Maldonaldo, mayor of Santo Domingo, was hoping to engineer a disaster. A disaster that could be laid at the feet of Don Alonso.

Alonso, enthusiastic for his new office, and faced with the lethargic neglect of his fellow funcionarios from the governor on down, had taken it upon himself to see to the proper running of Santo Domingo. The lack of initiative galled him, and he understood that the more control he had, the more he would be able to build his own private empire.

But he was late to the hunt. Don Nicolás, fully entrenched, was pulling strings that Alonso could not even see.

Alonso felt a wave of despair come over him. All the plans he had made, all the dreams he had entertained, there seemed no way to make any of it happen. He was helpless, one man against the mayor's hidden forces.

Unless…

"Delgadillo, you say Captain General Sandoval ordered the men to stay at the fortaleza. But you came. And the others came."

"Something had to be done, Don Alonso. And Sandoval is too much of a coward to try and stop me. These others, they are good men. They do as I say."

Alonso nodded, his thoughts racing off down this new track. He had always liked Delgadillo, had found him active and competent. A rarity, indeed: a dependable man.

"You don't answer to the mayor, Delgadillo?" Alonso asked.

"Forgive me, but the mayor does not always have the men's best interests in mind. Mostly, it's his own best interests that concern him. But I'm sorry…I speak too freely."

"No, no, have no fear," Alonso said. "Are there others, others of the men, who feel as you do? Men who might wish to be free of Captain General Sandoval? Who might, perhaps, wish to earn several times the pay they earn now?"

Delgadillo chuckled. "There certainly are, Don Alonso. These men here, and others that I know of. If such a chance were to present itself, they would jump at it."

Then I shall make them jump, Alonso thought. There were possibilities here. Many possibilities.

Chapter Four

Trois Frères was still at anchor the following morning, wind-rode in the easterly trades, with the reef that formed Tortuga's harbor, such as it was, providing adequate shelter from the swells that rolled down between the islands.

LeBoeuf was awake. A few of the women were as well, but no one else. None of the others were motivated to stir at that early hour. Going to sleep sober did not help. In truth, it probably made things worse.

LeBoeuf was wearing a pair of slop trousers, a simple linen shirt. Sailor's clothes. Clothes he had never worn hunting, so they were not stained with blood and soot and tallow such that no amount of washing could ever really get them clean.

Down in the waist, working by first light, the prostitutes-turned-buccaneer-wives were putting the final stitches in LeBoeuf's new suit of clothing. Silk, gold piping, lace, he hoped it would transform him from the pig hunter Jean-Baptiste LeBoeuf into someone else entirely: Chevalier Philippe Guillemeau de Beaune, lord of a thousand-acre plantation, prime growing land, on the French island of Tortuga.

He had even trimmed his unruly beard to make him look more respectable. He considered shaving it down to a moustache and goatee, but rejected the idea. The beard was a disguise; it was not there simply because he was too lazy to shave.

The letter patent was in his hand, that elaborate scroll of paper, signed by the king himself, that bequeathed the land to Chevalier Philippe. Who he was, whether he was alive or dead, LeBoeuf did not know. He knew only that the man no longer had his letter patent. And that he, LeBoeuf, did. And he intended to make good use of it.

He unrolled the paper once again and stared at the neat script, the massive signature and seal of King Louis the Thirteenth. Much of the letter he knew by heart, including the specifics as to where the plantation lay, the boundaries of what would be his estate. Half a league to the east of the "chiefmost harbor of said Island of Tortuga," a mile inland. A thousand acres bordered by a stream to the north, a steep ravine to the west.

What a thousand-acre plantation on the half-savage island of Tortuga looked like, he had no notion. Not much, he did not think.

Tortuga was home to human refuse, men from St. Christopher's and Nevis, English and French, looking for the main chance, or buccaneers such as himself, driven from the north shore of Hispaniola, or others running from one thing or another. But LeBoeuf had nothing, and he did not need much. Whatever this plantation was, he could take it and turn it into something good, given the opportunity. The thought gave him hope, something he had not felt in a long time.

He heard feet on the quarterdeck ladder and he rolled up his scroll and set it down on the binnacle. Other Dog lay in her familiar place by the rail and didn't stir, so LeBoeuf knew it was the women who were working on his suit of clothes. If it had been Henriette, Other Dog would have stood and nuzzled her when she appeared. Henriette was the only one to whom Other Dog showed such affection. Henriette hated it. LeBoeuf wondered if Other Dog did it just to annoy her.

Wily bitch, LeBoeuf thought. He was not sure whom he meant.

"Monsieur LeBoeuf?" The seamstresses reached the quarterdeck and came aft, one holding the doublet, the other the trousers. "I think we're done with your suit, if you would like to try it."

"Thank you," LeBoeuf said, looking down at the clothing. One of the two original suits had been maroon in color, the other gray, but the women had managed to combine them in such a way as to make the two shades look intentional. Or close enough. The clothing would not be so important when it came to laying claim to the plantation. The thirty buccaneers at LeBoeuf's back, their long muskets in hand, would accomplish a great deal more.

LeBoeuf pulled off his shirt, then slipped the doublet over his head and settled it in place. He dropped his slops and stepped into the silk trousers. The women, neither scandalized nor particularly impressed by the sight of him half-naked, helped him pull the trousers up around his waist and hook them to the doublet. LeBoeuf held out his arms to see how the sleeves fit, looked down at the trousers encompassing his legs.

"Well done, *Mesdames*. Very well done," he said, and he meant it. Like most sailors, LeBoeuf could make simple shirts or slop trousers himself, but what the women had done seemed nearly miraculous to him. They curtsied and smiled shyly, which was amusing to LeBoeuf. They didn't seem the sort to be shy.

"I will pay you well for this," LeBoeuf continued. "Once I have something to pay you with." The women smiled and nodded.

"Thank you, monsieur," one said. "Will you take them off now?"

"No, methinks not," LeBoeuf said. "I'll put them to use, once these others stir themselves."

It was another hour or so before the buccaneers began to move, shuffling out onto the channels to relieve themselves, finding what little food they had aboard, drinking water—not at all their drink of choice—to slake their thirst.

Nearly all were showing signs of life by the time Henriette emerged from the cabin which she and LeBoeuf shared, and climbed onto the quarterdeck. Other Dog stood, tongue lolling, and trotted over to have her neck scratched. Henriette cursed the dog in the vilest language but scratched nonetheless. When she finished with Other Dog she looked LeBoeuf up and down. She made no comment about his clothing. No words were needed.

"Today you become lady of a great plantation on Tortuga," LeBoeuf said. "Are you excited?"

Henriette snorted. "Make one of these street whores your great lady. They're more fitted to the part."

LeBoeuf let the words go, let Henriette settle a bit. "We'll return to Hispaniola for what we lost," he said at last, speaking low. "Once we have things in order here."

Henriette frowned and her eyebrows came together, but LeBoeuf could see that his words had struck as intended. The gold they found aboard the previous *Trois Frères* had been Henriette's salvation, her way back to France. Now it lay under twenty feet of clear water: gone but not lost. Holding out hope of retrieving her fortune would secure Henriette's cooperation like nothing else. LeBoeuf understood that.

And he did mean to retrieve the gold. But first, the plantation.

"Very well then," Henriette said, and LeBoeuf could not help but notice the softening in her tone. "I'll play the part you wish."

It was another hour before the thirty or so buccaneers aboard *Trois Frères* were under arms and ready to go, their long muskets primed and loaded, powder horns and shot bags and bandoliers with their twelve powder containers—the "apostles"—hanging in a line across their chests. Their hair was long and tangled, or cut short with their hunting knives. They wore the rough, blood-stained clothes of the *boucaniers*. They were all sober. They were ugly and mean, and LeBoeuf was glad of it. Even he might be frightened by such demi-savages.

He hoped very much that they would find rum or gin at the plantation. If they did not, these men could turn on him just as fast as they had joined him.

There were several boats towing astern of the ship. They pulled each alongside and the men loaded into them, taking up oars and rowing silently for the shore, LeBoeuf's longboat leading the way. They passed the two other ships at anchor, which seemed deserted, save for a single Black man aboard the ship anchored closer in, who watched in silence as they went by.

They pulled through the fleet of smaller boats. Some seemed in good repair, some half-sunk at their anchors. They stood on toward the beach, deserted despite the late morning hour.

The night had been loud, with raucous goings-on: shouting, singing, gun-fire, the occasional scream. Something that sounded like a dog fight. It drove the men aboard *Trois Frères* to distraction: such a bacchanal so close by, and yet inaccessible to them.

But that was over now. The town, what passed for a town, might well have been deserted by the look of it, or wiped out by plague. They could see no movement, no sign of human activity. A few dogs shuffled around the single dirt road. Chickens fluttered here and there. Every once in a while a rooster made its presence known. But beyond that, it was still as the grave.

LeBoeuf's boat ground up on the beach and the men jumped out and pulled it further up onto the white sand. Other Dog was sitting at LeBoeuf's side, and as the boat came to a stop he whispered "*Allez!*" and Other Dog, tongue swinging, leapt up and onto the beach, happy to be free of the confines of the ship.

LeBoeuf stepped out into a foot of water. He turned and beckoned to Henriette, and she stood as well. LeBoeuf scooped her up in his arms and waded ashore. He was wearing silk stockings, now soaked through, and on his feet his old rawhide hunting shoes: the finer pair he had found in the master's cabin could not be made to fit his feet.

One by one the boats came ashore and were hauled up line abreast. LeBoeuf walked up the beach to where the sand melded into the end of the road. Henriette was at his side. The rest followed behind.

He paused for a moment and looked around, rested his hand on the fluted pommel of the fine sword that hung at his side, a familiar and reassuring stance. He could see now that there were more buildings than he had thought: a dozen or so, with narrow alleyways between them. They were mostly two stories, timber-built with plastered walls, whitewashed at some point, in desperate need of refinishing. But substantial. More substantial than LeBoeuf would have guessed.

Potential here… he thought. Tortuga, offspring of St. Kitt's and Nevis, growing sturdy and fast.

He turned and looked behind. The buccaneers were standing in two loose lines, muskets cradled in arms. Faces grim. Alert. They would have been happier if there were people about. As it was, it was unsettling. LeBoeuf knew it, because he felt the same way. He nodded his head in the direction of the town and started walking again. He could not hear the men's feet in the sand, but he trusted they were following him.

They walked up the sloping shore and past the first of the buildings: a warehouse of sorts, it seemed. It was hard to tell. Farther along he could see the shutters on second-story windows swinging open, men and women leaning out, looking down at them.

LeBoeuf imagined that the men behind him were gawking like idiots, but he kept his eyes forward. Doors opened, men wandered out, eyes on the newcomers. Watching. Not eager to interfere. People on Tortuga minded their own business, LeBoeuf suspected. One of the charms of the place.

"And how do you mean to find this grand country estate?" Henriette asked. She spoke softly. Her words had their usual undertone of accusation, but not so pronounced as before.

"It's in the letter patent," LeBoeuf said. "The location. You read it to me."

"Words!" Henriette said, as if their being mere words made them *ipso facto* useless. But she had a point. Translating words on paper to a geographical location was not so clear cut as it may seem.

LeBoeuf looked to his left and right, a casual glance. More men coming out of the various buildings, watching. They leaned on muskets like they were walking sticks, rested hands on pistols hooked to belts. Weapons held at the ready, not aimed at anyone, but conspicuously there.

Best to look like we know what we're about, LeBoeuf thought. They were strangers here. Show fear or hesitancy and the wolf pack would tear you apart. He kept his eyes forward and continued through the town. Just beyond the last building, off to the east, there was a cut through a stand of trees, something between a path and a road.

Half a league to the east of the chiefmost harbor of said Island of Tortuga…

LeBoeuf led the way in that direction, stepping quick as if he knew where he was going. The road might lead to the plantation, or it might dead-end at a festering refuse pile. If he guessed wrong, he would have to turn back and go blundering about looking for the correct path. It would make him ridiculous in the eyes of his men and the eyes of the town. But he threw the dice.

They had followed the quasi-road for a mile or so, through open, rolling county, by the time LeBoeuf dared suspect that he had guessed right. The wide, beaten track ran slowly uphill, through fields of tall dried grasses, past stands of scrubby trees. It was a landscape like Hispaniola, a landscape well known to him and the other pig-hunters.

They passed a few small plantations, some with huts, some with actual houses. Men in ragged clothes working at sundry tasks, hoeing, clearing brush, mending fences. Women tending kitchen gardens, feeding chickens, plucking chickens. They paused in their work to watch the armed men march past, wondering, no doubt, whether or not they should flee. There were fields plowed and planted with some sort of vegetation. LeBoeuf did not know what it was. He did not really know one plant from another.

Reckon I best learn, he thought, as he looked out over the fields and wondered what was growing there.

Van Loudersong, who had fallen in beside LeBoeuf, nodded toward the plantation just downhill of the road. "This fellow, he's well into his tobacco, eh?"

"Reckon," LeBoeuf said, and said nothing more. He would not commit. He wondered if Van Loudersong really knew what the plantings were, or if the Dutchman was just looking to catch him up.

"That plantation, that's not the one you're looking for?"

"No," LeBoeuf said. "Half a league from the town."

He had no way to measure the distance, save for his own instinct for such things, which he knew tended to be damned accurate. He hoped the directions, transcribed on the letter patent in some finely-appointed office in Paris, were just as accurate.

They continued on, and soon LeBoeuf could hear muttering astern. Growing discontent. He wondered how much farther the rogues would follow him. He looked down the road, saw what appeared to be the peak of a tiled roof, just visible over a rise in the distance. Plowed fields stretching off to the eastward.

"This is it," LeBoeuf said, loud enough for all to hear. Another roll of the dice, another chance for humiliation. But this was a plantation, a big one, a thousand acres, maybe. It was half a league from the town. And he had men and arms enough to take it, even if it was not the one indicated in the letter patent.

They were over the rise, coming down the grassy hill toward the house, when they heard the scream. It was high and sharp and loud. Whether it was a man or a woman, they could not tell. LeBoeuf heard the buzz of talk behind him, the rustle of weapons shifting to a more determined grip. He did not alter his pace as he continued down the hill.

The house was two-stories, beam and plaster built like those in the town. Terracotta tiled roof, Spanish style. Probably a nice home once. Now there were wide sections of plaster missing, the wooden lath visible like some gaping, half-healed wound. Tarpaulins were stretched unenthusiastically over parts of the roof where the tiles were gone. The structure was probably not that old, but it did not take long in that climate for nature to reclaim her own.

Another scream, but they were close enough now to hear the crack of the whip that proceeded it, and the sobbing that followed. LeBoeuf led the men onto the patch of trampled dirt that circled the house and then around the side of the structure. There was a scattering of outbuildings beyond, a well, a fenced-in sty, a couple of bored pigs lying in the shade. A sorry-looking wagon of the sort you might use to bring produce to market, or the condemned to the gallows.

Midway between the house and the sty, forty feet away in the middle of a wide lawn, a pole standing upright and a man, shirtless, half-hanging from manacles made fast near the top. His back was glistening with blood. Dark lacerations, left in the wake of the whip's end, ran down at a sharp angle from high on his right shoulder.

The man holding the whip, a cat o' nine tails, stood with his back to LeBoeuf, running the bloody strands through his fingers. Untangling them. He wore a linen doublet and trousers, once dark blue, now well-faded. A wide hat on his head, a feather pointing aft.

He was not alone. A dozen others stood in a rough line; men, grim-faced, and women, some of whom were crying loudly. They wore servants' clothes, field hands' clothes, faded and patched and torn. Their ages were hard to guess. No older than twenty, mostly, but they were worn down, beaten down, and that made their years hard to judge.

Ten feet behind the man with the whip stood a man in canvas trousers—well patched—and a leather jerkin. LeBoeuf could see him in profile. He was holding a musket, port arms, a whip on his belt. He had the look of an overseer about him: tough and merciless.

The man lowered the cat o' nine tails to his side, ready to draw it back again. He looked over at the servants standing in line, now staring open-mouthed at the armed men who had just appeared. The man turned quick, following their gaze, and the other man, the overseer, did as well. LeBoeuf could see that the whip hanging from the overseer's belt was not a cat o' nine tails, but a bullwhip, black and coiled like a snake. The first man wore a moustache; the overseer's face was thick with beard, his eyes small and mean-looking.

The man with the cat o' nine tails scowled and took a step in LeBoeuf's direction. He seemed more angry at the interruption than surprised or frightened by this armed column. LeBoeuf was impressed.

"Who the devil are you?" he demanded. He spoke French. His eyes moved over LeBoeuf, feet to head, then over to Henriette. Then toward the men behind them.

The overseer, too, took a step in their direction, but he did not bring his musket to bear on them. One bullet to the buccaneers' thirty; he probably did not care to give those men cause to shoot.

LeBoeuf stopped ten feet short of the men. "Le Chasseur, Levasseur, get that sorry bastard down from the post," he called over his shoulder.

"Avast there, belay that, don't you interfere in my business, you poxed sons of whores!" the man with the moustache shouted. Le Chasseur and Levasseur ignored him, unhitched the manacles, let the bleeding man drop to the ground. The one with the moustache said nothing more, gave no orders to his overseer. In the face of the buccaneers, there was little he could do but sputter.

"I am Chevalier Philippe Guillemeau de Beaune," LeBoeuf said, giving the tiniest nod of his head, then nodding toward Henriette. "My wife," he added. "And you, sir, are?"

"Pierre Lepers, if it is any business of yours. *Capitaine* Pierre Lepers," the man spit, then added, in a doubtful tone, "*Chevalier*."

"Capitaine," LeBoeuf said, looking around. "I do believe this is my plantation."

"You're…you're…" Lepers could get no more than the one word out.

"By gift of His Most Christian Majesty, Louis the Thirteenth," LeBoeuf said. He spoke in the tones of the court, of the Tuileries, not the hunting camp of the buccaneers. He spoke in a voice that conveyed boredom with the entire thing, and an unwillingness to argue with the likes of Pierre Lepers. He glanced at Henriette, and she was looking at him the way she might look at a monkey that suddenly spoke in fluent French.

LeBoeuf held up the letter patent, partially unrolled, all but stuck it in Lepers' face. "This is a letter patent, signed by the king. It bequeaths this plantation to me. You may read it for yourself, if you wish, but be quick about it."

Lepers looked at the letter and scowled. He showed no interest in reading it, even if he could, which was not clear.

"I don't give one damn if you have…" Lepers began but LeBoeuf did not allow him to continue.

"Who is this man?" he asked, nodding toward the bleeding man half sitting at the base of the post.

"He…he's…" Lepers sputtered, before his voice gained some traction. "He's my servant, bought and paid for, bought fair and honest, and I'll damned well do as I please with him."

LeBoeuf nodded. He looked at the overseer and at the other ragged servants, still in a line. He wondered how many of them had been flogged. Most, he suspected. Or abused in some other manner.

They were not slaves. They were people bound over for servitude, for three years most likely, in exchange for passage to the West Indies, and land and tools of their own when their time was up.

But often as not, their time was never up. Masters would sell them off to someone else, oblige them for another three years. They would work them into the grave. They would beat them without mercy, sometimes to wring more labor from them, sometimes simply because they enjoyed it. LeBoeuf had seen it often enough since venturing to that part of the world.

"These people, they are mine now," LeBoeuf said. He had a pistol thrust into his belt, a lovely ornate thing he had found in the master's cabin, and he rested his palm on the butt.

"You son of a whore," Lepers said, and he and the overseer, still mute and scowling, took a step forward. "You don't frighten me. And no letter gives you the right to take my property."

"It does," LeBoeuf said. "And I will. But I will pay you for the servants."

"Pay me? Very well then, pay me. Let me see your gold."

"I'll pay you when my first crop is in and sold," LeBoeuf said.

Lepers sputtered some more, the spittle actually flying from his lips as he tried to speak. "Ha! Rich *chevalier*, my ass!" he managed to get out before Henriette cut him off.

"This?" she said in a tone of outraged disgust, glaring up at LeBoeuf. "This is your great plantation? You took me from a *manoir* in Paris to this? This is what the king thinks is some fine gift for your service? You, a chevalier?"

"His Most Christian Majesty was doubtless led to believe it a finer plantation than it is," LeBoeuf said, impressed with Henriette's timing, and the outrage she could muster.

"No doubt," Henriette said, sounding very doubtful indeed. "And now you waste your time arguing with this…this…person?" She waved her hand at Lepers in a stunning display of contempt.

"Now you listen to me, you *bâtarde,* and your little whore, I'll have none of this!" Lepers shouted. His face was turning red. The overseer lowered his musket, just a few inches, but the threat was clear. LeBoeuf heard some of his men shuffling behind him.

They have balls, these two, I'll give them that, LeBoeuf thought. *I have thirty armed men, and still they threaten and call me bâtarde.*

"*Chevalier,* so you call yourself…" Lepers growled. "I am not some fool to be kicked around. I am a man of consequence, captain in his Majesty's navy! Appointed to command by Richelieu himself!"

His Majesty's navy…

LeBoeuf felt a breath of panic waft over him. He stood straighter and lowered the letter patent. A second—no more—and then his mind was back, his thoughts steady.

It was too late. Lepers saw the hesitancy. He frowned, squinted, shut his mouth, and looked closely at LeBoeuf's face.

"You may gather your things and be gone…" LeBoeuf continued, resuming the bluster. But even as the words were tumbling out he saw the flicker in Lepers' expression, the pieces falling into place.

Merde…

LeBoeuf wrapped his fingers around the butt of his pistol and pulled it free. It was primed and loaded, the wheel cocked, but it was mostly there for show. He had never fired it, had no idea if it would work, but it was worth a chance. He raised it, leveled it, found the trigger, as Lepers swung the cat o' nine tails around.

The tails of the whip hit the gun and LeBoeuf's arm hard enough to knock them aside. Flame erupted from the muzzle, the gun jerked in LeBoeuf's hand, and the bullet missed Lepers's head by inches. Behind him, the overseer swept his gun around, ready to blow LeBoeuf away at point blank range, and damn the consequences.

The muzzle was coming level with LeBoeuf's chest when Other Dog bolted forward, a blur of brown and black, two steps, and then she was airborne. The overseer screamed, a truncated sound that turned to a choking gasp as Other Dog sunk her teeth into the man's neck.

They went down together as LeBoeuf lunged toward Lepers and Lepers took a step back, swinging the whip as he did. LeBoeuf raised his arm, twisted sideways to shield Henriette and his own face from the wicked tails.

LeBoeuf had his back to Lepers for all of three seconds, no more, but that was all Lepers needed. He dropped the whip, spun around, and raced off as LeBoeuf straightened and threw the pistol aside.

"Shoot him!" LeBoeuf shouted to the men behind him. "Shoot that son of a bitch!"

The buccaneers were hunters, accustomed to taking down fleeing prey with their long muskets. Dropping Lepers would have presented no challenge at all. But the entire exchange, from pistol shot to Other Dog's attack to LeBoeuf's order, had happened so quickly that they were taken fully by surprise. By the time they even realized what LeBoeuf had called on them to do, Lepers was halfway to the line of servants, who were still watching, motionless and dumbstruck.

"Shoot him!" LeBoeuf called again, furious that he did not have his own musket in hand. He heard the sound of weapons coming to firing position, flintlocks snapping in place. But Lepers, no fool, had reached the servants, slammed through their line, and was still running, with the servants now between him and the buccaneers.

"Get out of the way!" LeBoeuf shouted at the servants, waving his arms. "Get out of the way!" But they just stared at him and did not move.

"Shoot those sorry bastards?" LeBoeuf heard one of his men ask. LeBoeuf hesitated, then his better angel spoke.

"No, don't shoot the servants! Clean shot!" But there was no clean shot.

"Other Dog, allez, allez!" he shouted, pointing at the fleeing Lepers, but Other Dog and the overseer were still at it, rolling on the ground as the man kicked and pounded and tried to fight the beast off.

LeBoeuf looked up. Lepers was charging off past the pigsty and around one of the outbuildings, which further shielded him from the guns. He was fast; faster than LeBoeuf would have guessed. Well-motivated. LeBoeuf considered telling his men to chase after him, but that was pointless. Lepers was too far ahead, probably knew the land around there too well to be caught.

The buccaneers came running up on either side of LeBoeuf, looking for a place from which they might take a shot. Some stood, some took a knee, their muskets aimed at the spot where Lepers had disappeared. Levasseur fired. D'Anton did as well. LeBoeuf could not see what they were shooting at. Whatever it was, they did not hit it. He could see that on their faces.

Then it was over. Lepers was gone. The men upended their muskets, rested the butts on the ground. LeBoeuf looked down at Other Dog. She was sitting on her haunches, tongue lolling, her muzzle drenched in blood. The overseer lay sprawled in front of her, eyes wide, his neck, or what was left of it, a shredded mess. Henriette made a gagging sound and turned away.

Van Loudersong wandered up to LeBoeuf's side. "What was that about, *Chevalier*?"

"I didn't like the look of that one," LeBoeuf said, nodding in the direction in which Lepers had run. "Methinks he'll give us trouble."

"Didn't like his look?" Van Loudersong chuckled. "Well, I'll be sure to keep myself as pretty as ever I can."

LeBoeuf stepped away. He did not care to speak with Van Loudersong just then.

The man who had been manacled to the post was standing now, hunched over a bit against the pain. "You," LeBoeuf said. "Why were you being flogged?"

The man met LeBoeuf's eye. There was defiance there, and uncertainty. A bit of fear. "Master said I was stealing," he said at last.

"Were you?"

The man glared at LeBoeuf, then spit on the ground. "No. Don't matter. That whore's son, he just likes to use the whip."

LeBoeuf nodded. There would be time to straighten all that out. "Is there food in the house?" he asked next. "And drink? Rum? Gin?"

The man looked at him and glanced at the crowd of men behind him, dangerous-looking and heavily armed. He looked back at LeBoeuf. "Yes. A goodly store. Of all that."

LeBoeuf nodded again. Felt a wave of relief. The first he had felt in some time. His men would not turn on him. At least not immediately.

Chapter Five

Don Nicolás Pérez de Maldonaldo, mayor of Santo Domingo, sighed and heaved himself to his feet. His office, an expansive affair in the heart of Las Casas Reales, was largely deserted, save for a single scrivener hunched over a tall desk and scratching away. The hour was late, the windows that looked out over the courtyard were black.

The whore's son has waited long enough, Don Nicolás thought. He adjusted his doublet, laid a hand on the hilt of the dagger hanging from his belt. It was worn ornamentally, but that did not mean it was not a practical weapon. He had used it before. He had used it to teach a lesson, to emphasis a point. He did not think he would need to use it again.

Several doors led in and out, and Don Nicolás left through a side entrance. He walked down the long hall, heels clicking on the polished tile underfoot. Near the end of the hall he came to another door, lifted the latch, and stepped inside.

This was the office of his secretary, but his secretary was not there. On Don Nicolás's instructions he had escorted the visitor to the office, and then made himself scarce. The only one in the room was Carlos Hernández, who was seated in a high-backed chair at the far end, his legs crossed. He wore a studied look of boredom.

"You found your way to the servants' entrance," Don Nicolás said.

"I did."

Hernández was accustomed to arriving at Las Casas Reales through the front door, but Don Nicolás had instructed him to come by the less visible route. He did not want it known that he was meeting with Hernández. He did not want Hernández to think he was still welcome to enter the way respectable people did.

Don Nicolás grabbed another high-backed chair, swung it close and sat so he was facing Hernández, with just a few feet between them. The two men looked into each other's eyes, silent, assessing.

Hernández gave nothing away. He rarely did, not for as long as Don Nicolás had known him, since the two men had started doing business together a score of years earlier. It was one of the qualities that made Hernández so very good at what he did.

We'll see what's behind those eyes…

"Show me," Don Nicolás said, and he was certain he saw a flicker then, a hint of something other than calm. Humiliation? Anger? Fear? It should have been all three. That was Don Nicolás's intention.

Slowly, Hernández reached thumb and forefinger into a silk purse hanging from his belt. He pulled out an odd-shaped scrap, an inch or two long, black and shriveled. It might have been old leather or a dried piece of meat. He held it up, and when Don Nicolás nodded, Hernández returned it to his purse.

It was, in fact, a piece of Hernández's left ear. Most of his left ear. Just a few months earlier Don Nicolás had sliced it off with the dagger he wore on his belt. He had told Hernández that he wished to see it every time they met. A reminder to be truthful. A reminder not to cross the mayor of Santo Domingo. Hernández knew better than to forget either thing.

Carlos Hernández was an interesting and important link in the great chain of being that was Santo Domingo. He was a merchant, a warehouse owner, an importer. As such, he was one of the lower sort, one of the occupants of the lower town that skirted the river. A man of little visible consequence.

But Hernández was not a fool, as so many of that sort were. He was not lazy, or blind to opportunity. He had used his cunning to take over a great deal of Santo Domingo's trade and amassed considerable wealth and power as a result. Just how much wealth Hernández had, Don Nicolás did not know. Unlike the men in Don Nicolás's world, Hernández did not take every opportunity to flaunt his riches. Better not to attract the attention that the trappings of money could garner.

Don Nicolás Pérez de Maldonaldo had been mayor of Santo Domingo for more than two decades, and had been doing business with Hernández for nearly as long. There was money to be made in legal trade, and vastly more to be had in skirting the law. The government in Madrid had long ago declared Spain the only legal exporter to the New World, but Spain could not possibly supply all that was needed. This set up a huge demand and a lucrative market for nearly everything that anyone could send to the West Indies. But in the case of any nation other than Spain, such activity was called smuggling. One could be hanged for doing it.

From the time of his arrival on Hispaniola, Don Nicolás wanted to get his hands on the smuggling trade, but he did not want to get them dirty in the process. That was why his partnership with Carlos Hernández had worked out so beautifully. The mayor provided capital and official cover, he saw to it that snooping bureaucrats snooped in other directions. And Hernández handled those things for which a man might end up on the gallows.

Beautiful. Except lately it seemed Hernández had been less than forthright, less than honest. The upstart pup Don Alonso Menéndez de Aviles, lieutenant governor, appeared to have ambitions as well. He was ignorant of the ways of Santo Domingo, and not half as clever as he thought himself, but he had wealth and he had influence, that those things could pose a problem.

Worse, Don Nicolás had caught a whiff of Hernández working with Alonso, a hint that Hernández might be helping the pup. That sort of disloyalty could not be ignored. It was why he had cut off Hernández's ear, why he made him carry the ear with him and show it whenever they met. To remind the man that Don Nicolás Pérez de Maldonaldo ruled in Santo Domingo, and that forgetting that fact could be dangerous indeed.

"Tell me of Toledo's troubles," Don Nicolás said next. He had heard rumors. He knew Hernández would know the truth of it.

"The purser on Don Toledo's flagship, he oversees the victualling of all the fleet," Hernández said. His voice was even, as if the ritual with the ear had not happened. "This information I get from his secretary. It seems the dockyard in Seville cheated them, which is hardly a surprise. They just discovered that a thousand or so casks of beef are rotten, unfit even for the soldiers and sailors to eat. As you know, Toledo is in great haste to sail, but he cannot. Not until he has replaced those stores."

Don Nicolás nodded. *Interesting.* His mind began to work through various problems.

"Toledo has gold, no doubt, to pay for what he needs," the mayor said. "And he will pay well."

"He does," Hernández said, "and he will. I've done some minor business with the fleet so far. They've been…generous. A few small gratuities in the right hands, and they'll pay whatever price one asks for supplies."

Minor business, Don Nicolás thought. He could just imagine. Rope, sailcloth, brandy, gunpowder, tobacco, whores, Hernández had no doubt supplied it all, and grown richer still in doing so. But a thousand casks of beef, that was beyond even Hernández's capability. Instead, Hernández had set this lovely opportunity in front of him, laid it at his feet like an offering. Which, no doubt it was. An offering. An apology.

"I can see what you're thinking, your grace," Hernández said before Don Nicolás could speak. "Believe me, I thought it as well, which is why I brought this you. But how we can take advantage of it, I don't know. A thousand casks of beef? There's nothing close to that in any of the storehouses I know of, and to butcher and salt down that much would take longer than Toledo cares to wait."

"A problem, yes," Don Nicolás said.

There was little salted beef in Santo Domingo because there was little need for it. *Ranchos* surrounded the city, and cattle literally ran wild in the hills. Dried meat could be had from the *boucaniers* who inhabited the north coast, though their numbers were dwindling as they were driven away. Small supplies of salted provisions were kept on hand to sell to ships calling at that the port, but coming up with a thousand casks in just a few days was beyond the capacity of the local suppliers.

Or perhaps not.

"How much do you have on hand?" Don Nicolás asked.

Hernández shrugged. "Five score casks? That's the most I ever keep at the ready."

"And the stores we liberated from the pup, Don Alonso? Most of that should still be in your warehouse."

"Yes, Don Nicolás. The finer things, the silks and the olives and such, most of that has been sold. The casks of salt beef, those remain. But there's no more than a few hundred."

"Very well," Don Nicolás said, and he was quiet for a moment, staring off at a place over Hernández's shoulder, pondering the situation. There was risk in what he was considering, but the potential profit was huge. Too huge to ignore. He looked back at Hernández, who was waiting, expressionless, for him to continue.

"I can get the balance of the provisions Toledo needs."

"*Señor?*"

"It can be had. I can get it," Don Nicolás said. "Tell the purser's secretary it will be delivered in a few days' time. You figure out the highest price the man is willing to pay and that's what the price will be. I want that in writing, and when he pays, I want all the money brought to me. Every *real.* From that I will give you ten percent for your efforts."

Hernández gave a slow nod of the head. "Very good, señor."

"You can find your way out? Through the kitchen?"

"I can."

Don Nicolás stood, the meeting at an end.

By midmorning the next day, Don Nicolás was back at his desk in his own, more sumptuous office. The scrivener was back at it, or, for all Don Nicolás knew, had never left. His personal secretary, a man named Barros, was there as well, and servants were coming in and out: the usual thrum of activity that seemed to go on whenever the mayor was there during the day.

I wonder if these lazy bastards are so active when I'm not here?

If not, that would account for why so little seemed to get done: Don Nicolás was often absent from his office.

He took a sip of chocolate and set the cup down on its saucer. He looked at the array of papers spread out in front of him and nearly sighed. He would have to give some attention to all of them, but not just now. He had something more pressing on his mind.

"Barros," he said. The secretary looked up from his desk. He always had a wary look about him, like a small dog that did not know, one minute to the next, if it was going to get a treat or a beating.

"Señor?"

Don Nicolás meant next to tell Barros to send for Captain General Sandoval, but before he could speak, the mayor's undersecretary, who was stationed just outside the office door—and whose name Don Nicolás could not recall—hurried in, bowed in front of Don Nicolás's desk, and said, "My pardon, your grace, but his excellency Captain General Sandoval is here, and he wishes to speak with you."

Don Nicolás frowned. An odd coincidence, and he did not care for coincidence. What's more, Sandoval would never have come unbidden if it was not something of great importance, and Don Nicolás did not care for those things, either. But this at least would save him the bother of having to wait for his summons to reach Sandoval at Fortaleza Ozama and for Sandoval to hurry over to Las Casas Reales.

"Very good," Don Nicolás said. "Send him in. And the lot of you, leave us in private."

Without a word, Barros and the scrivener and the servant who was clearing away the remnants of breakfast grabbed up what they were doing and hurried out the door. A moment later Captain General Sandoval stepped in, ushered by the undersecretary, who closed the door behind him.

"Captain, come in, come in. Sit," Don Nicolás said, gesturing to the chair in front of his desk. Sandoval was wearing a burgundy-colored tunic and breeches, a long rapier at his side. In his hands he held his hat, its long feather jutting off to the side. He was working the wide brim nervously in his fingers, back and forth, making the feather wave as if there was a breeze blowing through the room.

"Thank you, your grace," Sandoval said, sitting. He moved to set his hat on the desk, hesitated, then set it on the floor.

What would this sorry cur do in the face of an enemy, when he is so frightened just facing me? Don Nicolás thought, but he smiled and said in as friendly a tone as he could muster, "To what do I owe the great pleasure of your visit, Captain General?"

"It is this guard, your grace. The new guard. Are you aware of it?"

"New guard?" Don Nicolás shook his head. "I know nothing of this."

"Well, it's Delgadillo. Captain Delgadillo. He's organizing it. But the orders came from the governor's office. Official orders, with the governor's seal."

"Orders for what?" Don Nicolás was struggling to remain patient. It would not help to get the Captain General any more flustered.

"He is putting together a new guard. A Governor's Guard, he said. Delgadillo said, that is. One hundred hand-picked men. They're to be specially outfitted, and they will not answer to me. They'll be at the governor's beck and call."

"The governor?" That did not seem right. Gabriel de Chávez y Osorio was not an active or ambitious man. He was not the sort to show such initiative. What's more, Don Nicolás made a point of keeping close to the man, maintaining a friendship, seeing to it that he knew whatever the governor was about. He considered it part of his function as mayor. And it was, to some degree. But more importantly, it allowed him to see opportunities, and potential threats to his own business.

"Yes, your grace. The orders came from the governor's office."

"So you said. The governor's office? Was the governor's name on these orders?"

Sandoval frowned and looked away, as if trying to picture the orders. He looked back. "I don't recall his signature," he said. "But the orders were clear. Captain Delgadillo was to have whatever men he chose, to the number of one hundred. And the governor's seal was on it. Of that I am quite certain."

Alonso Menéndez de Aviles…the little pup…the cur… This had to be his work. Don Nicolás was not the only one in government who understood that the governor paid little attention to what was taking place, that a great deal could be done under the fat man's nose.

"To what end are they doing this?" Don Nicolás asked. "What's the point of it?"

Sandoval shook his head. "I do not know, your grace. All that Delgadillo would say was that in these dangerous times the governor wishes to have a more numerous guard, one made of the most active and trustworthy men. Which, of course, strips me of the best under my command, leaving but the dregs. I have no notion of what any of this means, but I thought I had best alert you."

"Yes, and well done," Don Nicolás said. "But let's not concern ourselves with this. I'll look into it, see if I can get your men back."

There was no point in discussing this with a powerless fool like Sandoval. There were clearly machinations going on that were far above the soldier's ability to understand, nor was the captain general of the garrison in a position to do anything of use.

But there was one area where Sandoval could be very helpful indeed.

"I'm glad you've come, Captain General," Don Nicolás continued. "Not just for bringing me this important news, but for another matter I wish to discuss."

"Yes, your grace, what can I do?"

"As you know, Admiral Toledo is very eager to be underway. But now he's run into a problem. It seems some incompetence in Seville has led to his fleet being supplied with rotten provisions. A thousand casks of salt beef, all spoiled."

Sandoval shook his head in disgust. "Just what you'd expect of those corrupt dockyard bastards. They are as bad as the Jews."

"Indeed. And I think it is our sacred duty to do what we can to help. I've seen to rounding up all the salt provisions that can be found in Santo Domingo, but it's not enough."

"A thousand casks? I should think not."

"But see here. It's my understanding that there is at least that much stored at Fortaleza Ozama."

"Well, certainly," Sandoval said. "We're a fortaleza, a garrison. It's essential that we be self-sufficient. Ready to stand against siege and the like."

"Of course, of course. But there's little chance of anyone laying siege to you in, say, the next month. And in that time you can certainly resupply the fortaleza."

"Are you saying…?"

"We must allow the fleet to take the salt provisions stored at the fortaleza. We'll be doing the great Toledo a favor he will not soon forget. And, between you and me, I'll be happy to see his soldiers and sailors on their way."

"A man can't walk the streets these days without being accosted by the brutes."

"You speak God's truth. Not to mention the rioting, the drunkenness. An unholy situation. So what do you say? Can I count on you to help in this matter?"

"You mean to sell these stores to the fleet, Don Nicolás?"

"Sell? No, no. Sell to a man such as Toledo, doing the work of His Most Catholic Majesty? No, we'll offer the provisions as a token of our esteem. I'll be grateful for your help. And Captain General Toledo will be very grateful, indeed. And I'll make certain that knows to whom he should direct his gratitude."

Don Nicolás gave a sly nod in Sandoval's direction. He watched Sandoval's expression change from suspicion and unease to smug contentment.

"Of course, Don Nicolás, I'm most please to come to your aid. And that of the great Toledo."

"Ah, the great Toledo!" Don Nicolás said. "Indeed, he's a great man. And like all great men, he has enemies. There are those who would like to see him fail."

Sandoval frowned. "There are?"

"Oh, yes! I won't name names, but there is one young man, recently come to us, and quite high up in the government, that I fear might well be a snake in the grass. But you let me worry about that. My point is, we must keep this arrangement about the salt beef to ourselves. Let no one know, lest Toledo's enemies find some means to interfere and keep the *conquistador* from getting to sea."

"Of course, Don Nicolás. No word will leave my lips. Shall I have my men begin to move the casks today?"

"No. No need for that," Don Nicolás said. "It would be a waste to set your men-at-arms to such a menial task. I have men enough for the work. I'll send them by. Would that be convenient?"

"Certainly."

"Of course, there are arrangements to be made, a great deal of things to sort out. It might be a day or two. It might be quite late at night before my men can come for the provisions."

"I'll be sure to alert the guards to be on the lookout for them, and to show them where the stores are to be found."

"Excellent, excellent!" Don Nicolás said. He put his hands on his desk and pushed himself to his feet, smiling broadly under his thick moustache. Sandoval stood as well. He was also smiling, and his face showed relief: relief that he had said the right things, reacted the right way. Won the approval of Mayor Don Nicolás Pérez de Maldonaldo.

"Everything else goes well at Fortaleza Ozama?" Don Nicolás said, stepping around his desk and steering Sandoval toward the door. "Besides this unfortunate business with the Governor's Guard, nothing else in which I might be of assistance?"

"No, nothing, Don Nicolás," Sandoval said. "Everything else is in order."

"Good, good to hear it. I know the garrison is well-led." Don Nicolás leaned over and pulled the door open. "Now you go and see to the arrangements we made, and remember, not a word to anyone."

"Of course, Don Nicolás, not a word!"

With that, the mayor gave him a nod and a gentle push out the door. Then he leaned into the hallway and called, "Barros! Get in here!"

He turned and headed back to his desk. Behind him he heard the secretary's shoes hurrying over the tile. It was good that Barros was hurrying. There was indeed much to do, many arrangements to make. A great deal of money to be wrung out of Toledo's cursed fleet.

Chapter Six

Henriette was running out of patience. So was Van Loudersong. And they were not making much effort to hide that fact. In Henriette's case it was mostly just annoying, but Van Loudersong was a genuine threat. LeBoeuf was not sure what to do.

For three weeks Jean-Baptiste LeBoeuf, the ersatz Chevalier Philippe Guillemeau de Beaune, reveled in his new home, his Tortuga plantation. Three weeks, and then it all started spiraling down to Hell. But for LeBoeuf, who was not an optimistic man, that was about the best he would have hoped for.

His tenure on this new land had not started well: the overseer dead, his throat ripped out. Other Dog sitting happily on her haunches, proud of her effort. Henriette gagging. Lepers, who LeBoeuf did not know, or did not remember, and who might be a genuine problem, run off. Servants terrified.

There were many things he could do wrong at that moment, when he took ownership of the place. He knew it. And he knew the worst would be to show any sort of weakness or indecision.

The servants were staring open-mouthed at him and the other buccaneers, too shocked or too beaten down to react beyond that. LeBoeuf pointed at two of the women standing in the line, the oldest of the lot, it seemed, though he doubted they were even twenty-five years of age.

"Come here," he said, softening his voice as best he could.

The women hesitated. LeBoeuf wondered if they spoke French. Servants on Tortuga, they might have been French, or English, or even Dutch for that matter. But after a pause the two moved hesitantly toward him.

LeBoeuf turned and gestured toward the handful of the buccaneers' wives who stood near the back of the column and they, too, hurried over to him.

"You two," he said to the plantation servants, "take these women and show them where the food and drink is found, and help them set out supper for my men. Have you and the other servants eaten today?"

The women shook their heads.

"Yesterday?"

"Some," one of the women offered.

"Then set out food for the servants as well." He turned to the man who had been flogged, who was making an effort to stand straighter, to hide the pain. "What's your name?"

"Vassy."

"Anyone else here who should worry us, Vassy?"

The man shook his head. "It was just Lepers. And that pile of horse shit," he said, nodding toward the overseer's corpse.

LeBoeuf called for some of the other servants, the men, to approach, and they did. He gestured toward the corpse on the ground. "Take this one and bury him."

The men shuffled their feet, glanced around, frowned. No one moved to obey.

"Don't reckon any want to do him that honor," Vassy offered.

"Then throw him in the brush and leave him for the crows," LeBoeuf said and that was greeted with more enthusiasm. They grabbed up the dead man's legs and arms and lifted him, his head lolling, showing off Other Dog's good work to its full advantage.

"Throw him to leeward, mind you, and a cable or two distant," LeBoeuf called as they hauled the dead man away. He turned back to Vassy. "Know anything about growing tobacco?"

Vassy nodded slowly. "I was on Nevis, three years, on a tobacco plantation. Indenture was supposed to be up, but the bastard I was indentured to, he sold me to Lepers and I ended up here. Been working tobacco…five years now. So yes, I know something about it."

"Anyone here know more than you?"

"Don't think so. The others, they sort of looked to me to take charge of such things." He said it in a matter-of-fact way, such that LeBoeuf guessed he was telling the truth. He wondered if that was the real reason Lepers had shackled him to the post. Lepers, if he had indeed been a naval captain, likely did not know much about tobacco farming, and he might resent anyone who did.

"We'll find out how much you know," LeBoeuf said. "For now, put your shirt on, if you can, and get the others inside. The women are setting out food and drink."

"Inside?" Vassy asked. He frowned, nodded toward the big house. "Inside there?"

"That's where the food is, ain't it?"

Vassy nodded, and LeBoeuf could see him rethinking the entire situation; then he bent over, snatched up his shirt, and called for the others to follow him. LeBoeuf turned to the buccaneers.

"And now, we eat."

And eat they did. For the next few days LeBoeuf let the buccaneers take their leisure, a regular cycle of feasting, drinking, sleeping. They roasted a pig over a big open fire in the yard and breeched kegs of rum and brandy. LeBoeuf discovered, to his relief, that there was enough food and drink on the plantation that even those men could not deplete it all in that time. He did not know why Lepers had felt the need to stockpile so much, but he was grateful to the man for doing so.

The laborers got no such feast days. LeBoeuf gathered them together, told them he had purchased their indentures. He did not know how long any of them had served, he explained, so he considered their time to be up, and they were free to go. Or stay.

If they stayed, they could continue working as they had, and once the crops were in and sold, he would pay them. The choice was theirs.

But it was not really a choice, and he knew it. The freed men and women had nowhere to go, and no means of getting there. For the men, it was stay and work, or leave and hope they could eke out some existence wherever they washed up. For the women, the most likely end was a brothel in Cayona. LeBoeuf was not surprised when they all decided to stay.

They were wary at first, as well they might be. The buccaneers who had overrun the plantation were a frightening lot, unpredictable and half wild. They ate and drank with abandon, fired their weapons, fought with one another on occasion and slept where they dropped. The men of the plantation avoided them; the women all but hid. But as the days went passed, and none of the servants were brutalized or raped or killed, the former indentures became more comfortable with the new order of things.

It was two days after taking the plantation that LeBoeuf and Vassy went to inspect the tobacco crop. The sun was up, but it had not been for long. The air was cool, the light golden on the trees and the hills. They crossed the open ground around the big house and walked out toward the spread of cultivated fields, with Other Dog maintaining station on LeBoeuf's flank. Their feet left trails through the dew on the grass. The breeze was pungent with the smell of the jungle and the warming earth and the nearby sea.

Dear God…this is magnificent, LeBoeuf thought.

Tortuga was not so different from Hispaniola, he knew. The land, the fauna. It was he who was different. His eyes were open. He was awake.

"This twenty acres, this is all in tobacco," Vassy said, indicating with a sweep of his arm the fields stretched out before them. "Oronoco. Good quality, I'd warrant. Not the finest, but good."

"Hmm," LeBoeuf said, looking out over the rows and rows of massive leaves standing shoulder-high and stretching away to the east. "What needs doing just now, to tend the crop?"

LeBoeuf did not care to sound ignorant, but he had no way of sounding knowledgeable on the subject. To him, tobacco came in a tight brown plug to be broken up and stuffed into a pipe. He was not sure he had ever seen it growing out of the ground.

"Not much," Vassy said. "The plants have all been topped, which I did mostly myself, since you have to know your business to do that. A couple of the others, they helped, to be sure."

"Topped?"

"We trim the tops off, once we have the number of leaves we want. With the thumbnail and forefinger." Vassy held up his hand, demonstrated the snipping motion. "We've been suckering them all along, which is taking off the shoots we don't want. I keep the field hands weeding and worming. That's it, for now. A month or so we'll be ready to harvest, and then the real work will commence."

"I see," LeBoeuf said. What he saw was that tobacco cultivation did not require nearly as much effort as, say, making hay or hunting wild pigs. Good money for little labor. No wonder it was so favored in the West Indies.

"Very good, then," he said to Vassy, giving him a bit of smile, which he knew was all but hidden by his beard. "Keep them at it."

The tobacco fields seemed to be in tolerably good shape, the main house less so. It was two stories high and solidly built of timber framing, but in great need of repair. The walls were thick daub, whitewashed at one time, over wattle slats. LeBoeuf knew this because sections of wall had crumbled away, revealing their construction. Each of the windows was flanked by heavy wooden shutters that retained only vestiges of their original dark green paint.

The front door opened onto a foyer with a staircase directly ahead, and the kitchen farther back down a hallway. Sitting rooms flanked the hall on either side, and a dining room made up the rest of the lower floor.

There were four bedchambers on the second floor, and LeBoeuf took great care when mounting the stairs to reach them. He placed each foot as close to the outer edge of the treads as he could, certain the partially-rotted boards would collapse under his weight if he stepped in the center. Once he and Henriette had surveyed the rooms, Henriette claimed the largest for her and LeBoeuf. She made clear to all that the other three were not available for use.

For all the work it needed, there was little that LeBoeuf could do to set the house to rights, at least not immediately. The servants had all the work they could manage, and the buccaneers showed no interest in labor. Free of having to hunt and smoke pigs to earn their daily bread, they were making the most of their situation, eating their way through LeBoeuf's storehouse and drinking to insensibility.

LeBoeuf figured on giving them a full week of that before he put a stop to it. He reckoned that was a fair exchange for the help they had given him in laying claim to the plantation. But a week was several days longer than Henriette was willing to tolerate.

She had taken easily to her role as lady of the manor. Abrasive and mule-like as she could be, she had a unique ability to accept her circumstances and prosper in them, even as she complained every painful inch of the way. So it seemed on the Tortuga plantation.

Once she accepted the fact that the plantation house was her home, for the near future at least, she set about taking dominion over it. Like a general commanding troops in the field, she set the servant women to work cleaning, mending, organizing and sorting. When one of the buccaneers dropped to the floor, unconscious, the women would drag him out of doors and deposit him on the ground, or

Henriette would beat him awake with a stick until he was able to crawl away.

It was five days after Henriette and LeBoeuf moved into the big bedchamber above stairs that Henriette's ebbing patience hit the low water mark. LeBoeuf, honestly, was surprised it had taken that long. For some time he had been bracing for the outburst, and he wondered if this forbearance represented some sort of dulling of her hard edge. But he need not have worried.

"These pig-hunters must go," she announced that morning. "We'll be eating tobacco soon, the way they are running through the stores."

LeBoeuf was standing in front of the big, open window in the bedchamber, staring down at the land below, just as he did at the start of every day. Both the house and the master bedchamber were well-positioned: the window looked out over the bulk of the plantation off to the east, the rows of tobacco plants, the stands of palm trees and pines beyond that, the mountains that made up the center of the island. He could even glimpse the quartz glitter of the ocean to the south.

Beautiful…damned, damned beautiful…

Some men hated the West Indies. They hated the heat and the jungle and the mosquitos and the disease and the Spaniards. LeBoeuf had no love for those things either. But he could see beyond them. He could see the great profusion of life, the fecundity of a tropical world. He could see the beauty in the palms and the white sands and the water like tinted glass.

He had marveled at it all, when circumstances brought him there from old France. For all the nightmare his life had become in that place, he did not blame the West Indies, and he did not love it less. Most of his years had been spent in a ship's fetid, cramped space, beating around the frigid gray waters of the North Atlantic, or in the tight-packed cities of the Old World. This new world, this Caribbean, might well have been some virgin land conjured up in a dream.

"Forgive me, what did you say?" LeBoeuf asked. He did not take his eyes from the plantation spread out below him.

"The pig hunters? The ones who are now dead drunk below stairs? Or eating our food? And puking all over the sitting room, most like."

Our food… LeBoeuf thought. He wondered when everything that was his had become Henriette's as well. Once he had taken Henriette from the villain who was auctioning her off, he supposed. Once he had given her the freedom of his miserable domain. Once she realized he did not care enough to object to such presumption.

"What of them?" LeBoeuf asked. His eyes were on the fields of tobacco, and he was reveling in the lovely symmetry of the rows juxtaposed with the chaotic profusion of the plants. He could see Vassy and a few others were already at work, though he was not sure what they were about.

"Damn your eyes," Henriette said, "will you mind me?" He felt something bump against his back and fall clattering to the floor and he realized she had thrown a tankard at him.

"Yes, of course, my sweet angel," LeBoeuf said, turning to look at her.

She was still in bed, propped up on a few pillows piled against the headboard. The bed was lovely, a four-poster. The gauzy fabric, draped around the sides to ward off mosquitoes, was pulled back now. The frame was well-built, LeBoeuf had been happy to find. A man of his bulk needed a well-built bed, and this one stood solid, even when he and Henriette tested its limits.

"You must do something about the rogues who are eating through our food and drink," Henriette said. "You may consider them your fellows, but they're doing you no good now. We'll all starve if they keep this up. And that includes the servants, who you coddle so dearly."

"The moveable feast ends today," LeBoeuf said. "That was my intention." It was not, actually, and Henriette probably knew it, but she let the lie pass unremarked.

"What do you mean to do?"

"I'll give them a choice. Same choice I gave the indentured servants. They may stay and work, or they may go."

"Hmph," Henriette said, and folded her arms across her chest. "I suppose that's the best I can hope for."

"This island is beautiful, but it's a dangerous place," LeBoeuf said. "The West Indies are dangerous. There's much to be said for the company of armed fellows such as these. They're well-proven in a fight, as you've seen."

"Hmph," Henriette said again. It was her usual response when she could think of nothing else to say. LeBoeuf took one last look out the window, then found his trousers—faded, patched canvas now, not silk—and pulled them on.

"There's another matter," Henriette said before LeBoeuf could grab his cassock and disappear. He knew what was coming, and hoped to avoid it, but he could see he would not.

"And what is that?" LeBoeuf asked, but Henriette was glaring at him, arms still folded, lips pursed.

"Yes, yes, I know," LeBoeuf said.

It was the gold, the fortune they had left behind on Hispaniola. The gold that had gone down with LeBoeuf's former ship. Henriette had brought the subject up so often that she no longer had to speak to make her argument.

"There's a great deal to be settled here on the plantation," LeBoeuf explained. Again. "The gold's not going anywhere. I'll be off for it the moment I have the chance."

"You say it's not going anywhere, but that whore's son Van Loudersong knows it's there, and you can't keep him away forever."

"Van Loudersong isn't going anywhere either," LeBoeuf said. "He has no means of getting back to Hispaniola."

He spoke with all the assurance he could muster, but in truth he knew that Van Loudersong might be a problem. There was no chance that Henriette would take the gold for herself and run off with it. Not because she felt any sort of moral obligation—LeBoeuf did not think that even crossed her mind—but simply because she could not sail to Hispaniola and salvage the riches on her own, and she had no other men she could trust to help her.

Van Loudersong, however, could most certainly find a ship or a boat, and he could find the men. He could recover the riches and disappear into the Caribbean. And that was very much a problem, because LeBoeuf needed the gold himself.

Tobacco planting could be a profitable affair, but it would be some time before LeBoeuf realized any return from his crop. Until then, he would need to purchase food, and stores, and powder, and shot, and enough rum and brandy to keep his men happy—all the things necessary to maintain the Tortuga plantation and keep it running.

Van Loudersong had mentioned the gold to LeBoeuf on more than a few occasions. He had reminded LeBoeuf of their agreement to split it up in exchange for his not telling the others of its existence.

LeBoeuf in turn had given Van Loudersong just enough reassurance to keep him satisfied.

But that was before. The Dutchman had not mentioned the gold again, not for some time. And that made LeBoeuf suspicious. It made him wonder what the man was up to. So he had some of his more trusted men—D'Anton, Levesque, Le Chasseur, who hated Van Loudersong—keep a constant watch on the Dutchman and see that he did not wander off the plantation. LeBoeuf was starting to consider just shooting the son of a bitch and being done with it, but he was not sure how that would sit with the others.

"That gold…" Henriette continued, but this time there was a different note to her voice. Vulnerable and afraid. She paused, swallowed, tried again. "That gold is my only way back to France. You know that."

LeBoeuf nodded. He wondered if she was acting. If so, she was doing a magnificent job, enough that he felt genuinely moved.

I'm a fool, he thought.

"We'll get the gold, I promise you, if it's within my earthly power to do so," he said, and he tried to sound reassuring. Henriette pressed her lips together and nodded. What she was thinking, LeBoeuf could not guess.

He sighed, pulled on his cassock, and bid her goodbye. He did not forget his other promise to her: the buccaneers' movable feast would end that day.

It was close to midday before the bulk of the men were sober enough to listen to LeBoeuf's pronouncements. Once they were, he gathered them together in the dooryard and explained the situation. He pointed out that the food and drink did not flow from some sort of cornucopia, that it would run out eventually. He explained that getting more would involve work, and that meant growing or harvesting tobacco, or tending livestock, or any of the many other things that needed doing to keep the plantation going.

And if working on the plantation was of no interest, there was always pig hunting on Hispaniola. The choice was theirs.

Once again, LeBoeuf had a pretty good notion of which they would choose, and once again he was right. The thought of going back to hunting and smoking wild pigs held no appeal, and the loss of their camp and their boucans and their packs of hunting dogs put that life even farther out of reach.

Comparatively, life on the Tortuga plantation was pretty idyllic, even if it did involve a little labor. So, grudgingly, with sore heads and bleary eyes, the buccaneers agreed to stay and work.

The work that LeBoeuf put them to was not particularly onerous. Vassy and his men had the tobacco fields well in hand, so LeBoeuf set some of the buccaneers to repairing the house, and some to repairing the tobacco barn. Some he sent into the mountains to hunt wild pigs, which were not so numerous as on Hispaniola, but numerous enough that he could feed his men with them and slow down the depletion of the plantation's stores.

The pig hunting was a success, and, to LeBoeuf's surprise, the rest of the work was as well. The walls and roof of the big house were repaired, the shutters painted, the tobacco barn, with its missing boards and doors half fallen off, brought back to life. Henriette even stopped haranguing him about the feckless buccaneers lounging their days away.

LeBoeuf found it all very pleasing. The Tortuga plantation, a near wreck when he claimed it, was starting to revive.

But still, like a pebble in his shoe, the thought of the gold he had left behind was a constant irritant. Every day for three weeks after taking the plantation from Lepers, LeBoeuf wrestled with the question of how to retrieve it without having to share it out with Van Loudersong, and without having his own men turn on him for keeping it secret.

And for three weeks, no answer came. Then, finally, he was done thinking about it. The days on the plantation had settled into routine. LeBoeuf's men were keeping careful watch over Van Loudersong, and the Dutchman seemed to be behaving himself. It was time to go.

"This will cheer you, my sweet," LeBoeuf said to Henriette, as he stood at the window of their bedchamber, looking out over another flawless morning. It annoyed her when he called her, *my sweet*, he knew: perversely, this was why he did it

"What will cheer me, you great ox?" Henriette asked. LeBoeuf could hear the sleep in her voice. She was not an early riser. "I can't imagine what you could say that would cheer me."

"The gold. On Hispaniola. I'm going to go fetch it." He heard the rustle of bedclothes as Henriette sat up. He did not look at her, but he could picture her perfectly well: propped up on one arm, lips pursed in a bit of a frown, eyebrows knitted as she tried to guess how serious he was.

"Today?" she asked.

"Tomorrow. We'll sail on the tide. Today I'll make the arrangements."

"How do you mean to do it?"

"I'll take five men I trust. We'll go in the ship's longboat. That's all I need. It has oars and a sailing rig, and the harbor's not so far off. Pierre Le Chasseur can see to the men here while I'm gone. Vassy will oversee the servants. You can run the house."

He turned and looked at her. She was sitting up now, fully awake, with an eagerness close to hunger on her face that he did not think he had seen before. And then her eyebrows came together and she frowned.

"What of Van Loudersong?"

"I'll take him with me, keep him from talking to the others here. Mind you," he added, giving Henriette a bit of a smile, "an open boat trip like this can be dangerous. Who knows what might befall him?"

With that, he left the bedchamber and stepped out onto the landing at the head of the stairs. Other Dog, banned by Henriette from the bedchamber itself, was waiting there as she always was, and she leapt up and rubbed against LeBoeuf and received a good scratch on her neck.

"You do know you're a hunting dog, right?" he said. "I should not treat you like some lady's pet the way I do."

The two of them stepped from the house into the cool of the morning. The servants were already hard at work, and a few of the buccaneers were moving about, but only a few.

LeBoeuf's mind was already working through logistics: who would he take with him in the boat, what food would they need, what gear would be required to retrieve the gold? He saw Levesque standing by a rain barrel, scooping water with a ladle and pouring it over his head, and he made his way over to him.

"'Morrow, Levesque," he said. Levesque nodded. His eyes were red and bleary, and water was streaming from his beard.

LeBoeuf looked around. "Where's Van Loudersong?" He imagined that the Dutchman was still in his tent. He, like most of them, was not wont to turn out early.

"Gone off," Levesque said. "Off hunting. With Huet and Boylan."

"Off hunting? Damn it, I told you and the others to keep your damned eyes on him."

"Didn't have to. Huet and Boylan are watching him. While they hunt. I told them."

Son of a bitch! LeBoeuf thought. This was not good. Van Loudersong had never shown any interest in hunting before, not since leaving Hispaniola.

"When did they leave?"

"A little after daybreak."

Son of a bitch, LeBoeuf thought again.

Van Loudersong had set up a makeshift tent, as had most of the men after Henriette banished them from the plantation house. LeBoeuf walked quickly across the grounds to where it stood. He flung the flap open, stepped inside, and looked around the dim interior.

A pile of straw lay to one side, but there were no blankets on it. Van Loudersong's musket and bandolier were gone, which was only to be expected. But the Dutchman's pistols were gone as well, weapons that were useless for hunting, as was his sword and the haversack he used to carry the rest of his personal goods. In fact, none of Van Loudersong's things were there. LeBoeuf shook his head in disgust and backed out of the tent.

Levesque was standing there, watching curiously.

"Go wake D'Anton and Genet and Wilson, tell them to get their muskets and meet me by the big house," LeBoeuf said, as he hurried back across the grounds to the house. He raced up the stairs and into the bedchamber where Henriette was sitting on the edge of the bed, combing her hair.

"What the devil?" she said. "You startled me! And get that filthy beast out of here!" Other Dog had taken the opportunity to follow LeBoeuf into the forbidden room.

"Sorry, my sweet," LeBoeuf said, not even looking in her direction as he snatched up his musket and bandolier and headed back for the door.

"What's acting? Is there trouble?" Henriette demanded.

"Nothing, nothing, all is well," LeBoeuf called over his shoulder as he hurried down the stairs.

"If all's well, then close the damned door, you great beast!" Henriette called after him, but he did not reply. He hurried out the door and was gratified to see D'Anton and Genet and Wilson waiting with muskets ready. Those three were the best hunters among the buccaneers, the most able to move fast over the rough terrain. If anything, LeBoeuf would slow them down, but even so he was not willing to stay behind.

"Van Loudersong went off hunting with Boylan and Huet this morrow, and now we have to go hunt for them," he explained.

"Why?" Genet asked.

"Because I don't trust that Dutch whore's son." LeBoeuf hefted his musket and led the way north, to the head of the trail that the hunters used to take them into the high country beyond.

They hiked for miles, LeBoeuf moving as fast as he could at a pace that he could maintain, the others easily keeping pace with him. They were all streaming sweat and red in the face as they moved uphill, nearly always uphill.

Other Dog, bored with the slow-moving men, would run ahead and disappear into the brush, only to reappear sometime later. Whether she was hunting for Van Loudersong and the others or not, LeBoeuf did not know, but he doubted it. She was not trained for such things. More likely she was following the scent of pigs or some other creature of interest.

They kept at it for a couple of hours before LeBoeuf called a halt. They found some shade to sit in and took up their water flasks and drank the warm but welcome liquid. Other Dog was nowhere to be seen, and had not been seen for some time. There was no sound save for those of the island: insects, birds, animals in the undergrowth.

And then, barking. It was hard to judge how far off it was, but they could hear that it was loud and emphatic. Other Dog had found something, and now she was calling out.

Merde…

LeBoeuf had a pretty good notion of what this was all about. He stood and gestured to the others, but they were already getting to their feet, muskets in hand. The four men headed off again, up the track worn by the passage of hunters and hunted. They moved quickly, and the sound of Other Dog's barking came louder as they closed the distance.

They came out from a stand of trees onto a patch of open ground. Other Dog was there, barking, but she stopped when she caught sight of them. On either side of her, two men, sprawled out motionless on the ground.

LeBoeuf and the others lowered their muskets and thumbed the hammers back to the cocked position. They moved forward cautiously, eyes searching, but they could see nothing save for trees and grass and sky.

They stopped where the men lay and looked down at last, and LeBoeuf saw pretty much what he expected to see. Boylan was lying face down, arms flung wide. Huet was on his back. His eyes were open. Both men's shirts were holed and soaked with blood, the cloth charred from the muzzle flash of a pistol fired from inches away.

"Damn his eyes," LeBoeuf said, softly. "Damn him to Hell."

Two of his men murdered, their bodies left for the scavengers. But Boylan and Huet's problems, at least, were at an end. LeBoeuf's had just begun.

Chapter Seven

There was considerable work to be done, many arrangements to be made, but Don Alonso Menéndez de Aviles was undaunted. Quite the opposite. He was on fire. He could see the possibilities.

He swung his legs off the edge of the bed, feet down on the soft rug that covered the tile floor. Outside the windows he could just see the first hints of dawn.

"Dear husband…you're leaving me at this hour? Again? Won't you at least breakfast with me?" Francisca was still in bed, still in the embrace of the great down mattress, all but buried under the sumptuous silk bedclothes. Her voice was sleepy, her words mumbled.

"No, my love, no breakfast for me, I fear." Alonso spoke softly, kindly. "Much to do."

"But this is all so unusual," Francisca said, her voice growing stronger as she came more awake. "You were never up at this hour before."

"Oh, I know. But with your Tío Fadrique here, it makes my work many times harder. All the considerations that go along with seeing the fleet supplied, the sailors and soldiers kept in order. I wish it weren't so, but it is."

"Of course," Francisca said, as if she was only now coming to understand this, as if Alonso had not told her the same thing half a dozen times already. Though in truth, Alonso's newfound activity had little to do with Tío Fadrique. Tío Fadrique could be damned, for all Alonso cared.

It was this new venture that animated him. The Governor's Guard. One hundred of the best men, picked by Delgadillo, trained by Delgadillo. Supplied, housed, outfitted, and paid by Don Alonso Menéndez. Loyal to Don Alonso Menéndez, and ready to do as he ordered.

Los Cien. The One Hundred.

The first spark had come in the aftermath of the stable fire. Out of all the garrison at Fortaleza Ozama, only a dozen men had come when needed. More would have answered the call if the lazy, corrupt, Sandoval, the mayor's marionette, had allowed it. That was what Delgadillo had said

It made Alonso think: what if he had a core of such men at his personal disposal? Good men, reliable men? Men whose pay—the miserable pay of a soldier in the ranks—he augmented to the point where they would be desperate to remain loyal? What could he do with such a force?

It was like dawn, like the sun coming suddenly bright over the horizon.

Alonso had felt like a whipped dog ever since Don Nicolás Pérez, mayor of Santo Domingo, had played him for a fool, but he had hidden his despair well. He had hidden it from Francisca, who in any case was so focused on prayers and confession and Mass and renovating her chapel, that she tended not to notice much else. He hid it from the governor, Don Gabriel de Chávez y Osorio, who tended to be equally oblivious. He hid it by seeming to throw himself into his duties, to take extra interest in overseeing those parts of the government that came under his purview, and some that did not.

But in truth he had felt like an idiot, felt as if he had been stripped clean. Thoughts of the dreams he had entertained and the plans he had made when first appointed mocked him. He had sailed from old Spain with no understanding of the entrenched power and deep-seated duplicity he would meet in the New World. And once it had revealed itself, he felt small and vulnerable beside it. Pathetic.

But that had changed the moment he conceived of the One Hundred. It was a glowing ember, a spark that could start a conflagration. He suddenly understood, with a flash of insight, that this was what he lacked: the power to enforce.

He could develop all the plans he liked, scheme and arrange and conspire, but unless he had force enough to see those plans carried out, he was a child in a world of adults.

No more.

The door to the bedchamber opened and Francisca's lady's maid, Gabriella, came sweeping in. She was carrying a silver tray with cups and a carafe of chocolate—Alonso's morning ritual—which she set down on a table near the windows.

"Thank you, Gabriella," Alonso said. He could smell her scent as she passed, a scent he knew well. A scent he often feared might cling to him after he and Gabriella made furtive love, but if it had, Francisca had never seemed to notice.

Gabriella curtsied and for a moment her eyes met Alonso's and lingered there and Alonso felt an instant stirring. Gabriella was young and lovely to look at and skilled in many things, not all of them related to her work as a lady's maid.

Francisca, to be sure, was beautiful as well, and Alonso was not at all averse to making love to her, not the least because he very much wanted a son. On occasion he could manage a spontaneous bedding, but generally, making love to his wife meant going to Mass first, and then considerable prayer with Father Pedro, the young Benedictine who served as Francisca's personal priest. Alonso found it all fairly off-putting. Bedding Gabriella required no such preliminaries.

"I had hoped you might go to confession and Mass with me this morning," Francisca persisted, once Gabriella had left.

"That sounds wonderful, but, alas, I must get a head start on the day. So much to do! But I promise I'll go to confession this afternoon." That, of course, was a lie, one to be added to the many things he would eventually have to confess.

Alonso poured a cup of chocolate and then made his way from the bedchamber to his own dressing room where his manservant waited to dress him. He stood patiently as doublet and trousers and silk stockings and garters were all put carefully on his person. He thought of Gabriella and how nice it would be if it was her hands on him now, and that thought made him happy. And then he thought of the One Hundred and how that was all coming to fruition and that made him happier still.

The sun was just up, the light pouring through the many windows of Las Casas Reales, as Alonso made his way from his apartment to his office, one floor below. He was alone at that hour; he would not make his secretary, Juan Cardero, come to work so early. Nor did he particularly want him there. He preferred to have that time to himself.

There were papers on the desk left over from the day before, and others that had been placed there after he retired to his apartment the previous evening. Some were business for the lieutenant governor, including the usual complaints from the local *rancheros*, or reports of smuggling in Havana, or requests for various licenses; the drudgery at the heart of his high office.

But most had to do with the new Governor's Guard: requisitions for horses and weapons that waited his review and signature, reports on the progress being made on quarters for the men, notes from Delgadillo concerning various matters. These he gathered together, the rest he pushed aside.

There was also a note, several days old, from the secretary of Governor General Gabriel de Chávez y Osorio.

> *To Don Alonso Menéndez de Aviles, knight of the Order of Santiago, Lieutenant Governor of Hispaniola and His most Catholic Majesty's territories in the West Indies: His grace, Gabriel de Chávez y Osorio, Governor General of Hispaniola and His most Catholic Majesty's territories in the West Indies, requests I send word to you regarding information he has received of late concerning the formation of a new guard of men, allegedly known as the Governor's Guard, of which he has not been informed. His Grace begs the honor of your presence as soon as is convenient to your grace, the lieutenant governor, so that you might further enlighten him in this matter.*

Of which he has not been informed…

He seemed to know about it now, despite Alonso's attempt to keep this business out of sight for the time being, which meant someone was doing some informing. And Alonso had a fair idea who it was. The mayor, Don Nicolás, had eyes and ears everywhere, including those that belonged to Captain General Sandoval who commanded the garrison at Fortaleza Ozama.

There was no possibility of forming the guard without Sandoval's knowledge. Indeed, Alonso had written to the man, under the seal of the governor's office, directing him to allow Delgadillo to select the One Hundred. Alonso knew that word would get to the mayor, who might not fully understand what was going on, but would sense a threat. And Don Nicolás could be very persuasive in dealing with his old friend the governor general.

There was no avoiding it. He would have to confront Don Gabriel eventually. He just hoped to have as much in place as he could before that moment arrived.

The note called for a meeting "as soon as is convenient," which Alonso knew was the governor's polite way of saying "immediately." And to be sure, when Alonso had first assumed his office, that was how he would have responded. But he had been lieutenant governor for close to a year now, and had a much better sense for how these things worked. He understood that "immediately" was more flexible than one might think.

Alonso had directed Cardero to send a series of excuses and promises to the governor general's secretary, assuring him of Alonso's imminent compliance, once he had attended to this or that crisis. So far it had worked. But the reprieve was just about up.

No matter, Alonso thought. He was nearly ready to meet with the governor. Just a few more details to set in place. He placed a fresh sheet of paper down on the desk and dipped a quill in his inkstand.

My dear Governor General, I beg your forgiveness in my not replying to you sooner with regards to the matter of the new Governor's Guard. I fear I have been quite consumed with…

He paused. What had he been consumed with? Helping get Toledo's fleet to sea, of course, but he needed something more. An outbreak of yellow fever in Maracaibo, that should do it. Don Gabriel would not think it strange he had not been informed, and he would not care enough to inquire of anyone.

> *I fear I have been quite consumed with the demands of Captain General Toledo's fleet, as well as the recent outbreak of yellow fever in Maracaibo and the numerous requests for relief that have of late been forwarded to me. But as you well know, the crisis there seems largely in hand now, with thanks to God and to your Grace's bold leadership in this matter. If it would be convenient I would be most honored to call on your Grace after Vespers this evening…*

Alonso read over the words and nodded his approval. The governor general could hardly object to Alonso's taking time for evening prayers, and putting the old man off until then should leave enough time to finish up the last of the details. Alonso folded the note, sealed it with the seal of the lieutenant governor's office, and rang for a servant to deliver it to the governor general.

He looked out the window. It was not too long past sunrise, which meant it would be hours before Don Gabriel even read the reply.

Perfect…

Don Alonso plunged into the stack of papers before him, reading, signing, making notes in margins. Juan Cardero arrived soon after and they set about the work of the lieutenant governor's office, but Alonso only half paid attention to that business. It was not foremost in his thoughts, not at all.

Delgadillo arrived a little after noon, just about the time that Alonso, losing patience, was preparing to send someone out to find him. Delgadillo looked calm, as he always did, self-assured and confident, and that helped assuage Alonso's mounting anxiety.

"All's well?" Alonso asked, even as Delgadillo was bowing his greeting.

"Very well, your grace. Will you walk with me and see?"

The two men took their leave of the office. Delgadillo escorted Alonso across the courtyard to the rear areas of Las Casas Reales, where the more prosaic work of that sprawling institution took place; the kitchens, the workshops, the servants' quarters. There, Alonso had ordered a former storage area converted to a barracks for the One Hundred. The workmen, now finished, had done a fine job building out the rooms for officers and men, installing tables and benches and a fireplace at the far end. The air was still thick with the smell of fresh-cut wood and newly applied paint.

Alonso and Delgadillo toured the stables where the horses for the Governor's Guard were housed, and Alonso, a far better judge of horseflesh than of carpentry, could see that the animals were everything he might have wished. Delgadillo showed him tack and weapons and clothing, and all of it more than met with Alonso's approval.

"You've done well," Alonso said.

"Thank you, your grace," Delgadillo said. "I wish I could take more credit, but it was your…largess…that's made this possible. But it's my honor to help as I can." He was silent for a moment, looking down the line of stables. "This will be a good thing," he added.

"It will," Alonso agreed. "Which is why we must see that it happens. I'm meeting with the governor general after Vespers. You'll be ready?"

"I will, Don Alonso. Do not worry."

But of course, Alonso did worry. He worried that this entire thing, this vision that had buoyed him beyond what he could have anticipated, would be torn from his grasp. He worried that the mayor, Don Nicolás, had undermined the effort in ways he could not see.

If Don Nicolás knew that Alonso was behind the Governor's Guard he would try to stop it, even if he did not fully grasp Alonso's intent. The mayor had considerable influence with Governor General Don Gabriel, who was capricious, indecisive, and easily swayed. With a single word, the mayor could make all of Don Alonso's plans disappear like a whiff of smoke.

Alonso had made a tactical decision to not inform the governor of his plans until all were in place. Now he worried that that had been a mistake.

He did not go to Vespers, which he never intended to do, but when it was over he made his way to the governor's office. His stomach was roiling and his palms sweating as he stepped through the big door and into the outer room where the governor's secretary kept vigil.

"Ah, Don Alonso," the secretary said, standing and giving a shallow bow. "Pray, go right in. His grace is waiting for you."

Alonso nodded as he walked past and into the governor general's splendid inner office. Don Gabriel was behind the desk, the remnants of dinner spread out before him, a napkin tucked under his chin.

Seems you didn't attend Vespers either, Alonso thought as he gave a short, quick bow.

"Don Alonso, my hard-working young man, come in, come it!" Don Gabriel said, tugging the napkin free and tossing it aside. His greeting was friendly, effusive, and, Alonso imagined, genuine. He did not think the governor general had enough guile for it to be otherwise, though he had misjudged men that way in the past.

Don Gabriel looked for a moment as if he meant to stand, but then changed his mind and gestured to a chair on the other side of his desk. "Sit, my boy, sit," he said, and Alonso sat.

"Indications are that Toledo will sail soon," Alonso said. "A few days hence, or such is what his people are reporting to me."

He wanted to start this meeting with words that would cheer the governor general, and none would cheer him more than that. Don Gabriel wanted desperately to see Toledo and his thousands of soldiers and sailors on their way, and no longer creating a massive headache for Santo Domingo. The feeling was shared by nearly everyone, with the possible exception of the tavern keepers and the whores, but even they had to be growing weary, Alonso imagined.

"Let us hope, let us hope," Don Gabriel said. "But see here, what I wish to speak to you about is this Governor's Guard I hear tell of…"

Alonso nodded. Don Gabriel was not going to be sidetracked, which meant the mayor had indeed been whispering in his ear, and not in any minor way. Alonso fixed his most ingratiating smile on his face.

"It was presumptuous of me, I know, to call it the 'Governor's Guard,' without leave from you. I pray you'll forgive me. I meant it as an honor to you. And a gift."

"A gift?"

"Indeed, a gift. A gift to lead to the better running of Santo Domingo, and the greater glory of Don Gabriel de Chávez y Osorio, governor general."

"Well, I…," Don Gabriel began, then sputtered out and then began again. "Indeed. But the thing of it is, Don Alonso, I'm not entirely certain what it is that you're about."

Alonso nodded. "Of course. Again, forgive me. I wanted all in place before I presented this to you. A gift is not much of a gift if it is but half done. You see, after that last disturbance, the one in which the tavern burned down, and the stable as well, I realized that there is no force in Santo Domingo that might be relied on, truly relied on, in such an emergency."

"We have the garrison," Don Gabriel protested. "Captain General Sandoval's troops who are at the ready."

Sandoval…lazy swine, the mayor's lickspittle, Alonso thought, though the smile did not fade from his face.

"Captain General Sandoval is a good man, to be sure. Most able. But he's pulled in so many directions. Keeping order in Santo Domingo, that's only one concern of many for him. So I thought, what if we had a hundred handpicked men? Each trained and properly outfitted and ready to answer directly to the governor general? Ready at a moment's notice? What an impression they might make on the people, and what good work they could do in keeping the peace. The Governor's Guard!"

"The Governor's Guard…" Don Gabriel was warming to the idea, Alonso could see it.

"Of course, nothing such as this could be established without your approval," Alonso continued, "but I wished to make a start of it. Captain Delgadillo, he has the training and supervising of the guard, and I believe he's working them now in the rear courtyard. Would you care to see what it is I have in mind?"

"Now?" Don Gabriel said, and Alonso saw him take a furtive glance at the bottle of brandy on the sideboard. "Well, yes, certainly. I do believe I can spare a moment."

The two men left the governor general's office, made their way down the wide staircase to the lower floor, then out the big doors and across the courtyard. This was the fine, paved courtyard that fronted Las Casas Reales and looked out over the river, not the rear courtyard bordered by the servants' quarters and now the barracks of the Governor's Guard, where the mounted troops would be drilling.

The last of the daylight was disappearing in the west, and there was not much to see beyond the flare of the lanterns and torches that lined the way. Behind them, the windows in the façade of Las Casas Reales, set in regular intervals, glowed with the light of the chandeliers that hung from the rooms' high ceilings, the many candles sparked to life by the servants who attended them.

The evening was cool, but not cold—early autumn in the West Indies—as the two men made their way around the far buildings toward the rear courtyard. They could hear the drilling long before they could see it; the pounding hooves of a hundred horses, the clash of steel on steel as a hundred blades parried each other. There was no shouting, no sounds of chaos or lack of discipline. It was as orderly as such a thing could be, like a battle of mounted troops, all of whom had taken vows of silence.

They stepped through the archway into the rear courtyard, ringed with lanterns that illuminated the open, hard-packed ground. The sight was just what Alonso had hoped it would be, just what he had counted on Delgadillo providing. The hundred men of the

Governor's Guard, mounted on their fine horses, whirled around one another, blades working in practice battle. They were dressed in black tunics and breeches, wide-brimmed hats on their heads. They wore black capes that swirled dramatically as they maneuvered their horses around in mock combat. The air was filled with the sharp sound of clashing blades.

"My dear Lord…" Don Gabriel said as they stopped and watched from under the arch. Alonso glanced at the old man. He was not certain how to interpret that.

"They make quite a sight, do they not?"

"They do, indeed…." Don Gabriel took a step closer, his eyes moving over the courtyard. "Very impressive…."

Alonso felt himself relax. That was the reaction he was looking for.

"But see here," Don Gabriel said next, and there was a shift in his tone. Suspicion. Concern. "The horses, the swords, the clothing…that's a damned sight of money that went into this. Where did this come from, exactly?"

"Forgive me, Don Gabriel, I hope you won't be cross with me," Alonso said. "It was my desire to do you honor with this guard, for all the kindness you've shown to me and to Francisca since we have arrived here. So I've paid for all of this from my own purse."

"Your own…you undertook all this expense?"

"I did, yes," Alonso said. In truth, the money came from Francisca, or more correctly, Francisca's father, but marriage had happily erased such distinctions. "And if this is pleasing to you, I'll be happy to undertake the maintenance of the Guard. As long as you deem it worthwhile."

Before Don Gabriel could reply, Delgadillo, who was overseeing the training, trotted over to where they stood. From his saddle he bowed and said, "Your Excellency Governor General, you do us a great honor visiting us during our little drill. Might you care to inspect the men, Excellency?"

"Well, they seem quite occupied," Don Gabriel began, but before he could protest further, Delgadillo turned to the courtyard and shouted, "Governor's Guard! Form up by rank!"

There seemed to be no surprise among the men at this sudden shift of orders, no protest or confusion. Delgadillo's words were still echoing off the walls as the riders broke off their drill, sheathed their swords, and reined their horses over to form up, four lines abreast. It was like a trick, like an elaborate court dance: one moment they were at each other, hammer and tongs, and the next they were in perfect order, one behind the other, sitting straight in their saddles, eyes forward.

Don Gabriel nodded.

"Come, my dear Governor General, let us inspect," Alonso said and he led Don Gabriel forward, past the ranks of horsemen sitting statue-still on their mounts. Don Gabriel ran his eyes over them as they passed, over the glittering tack and the black clothing, the boots that glinted in the torchlight, and he continued to nod. It appeared the Governor's Guard was making just the impression Alonso had hoped it would.

And yet, as they reached the end of the line of horsemen, Alonso felt Don Gabriel's attitude shift, his enthusiasm wane.

"Yes, yes, this is all very impressive," he said. "And I'm honored you would take on such an expense. But I'm not entirely sure we need such a thing. It might provoke jealousies with the other men in the garrison, do you see? And there's the question of who's to have charge of these men. I'm just not so sure about all this."

It was clear enough to Alonso what was happening. Don Gabriel had first been awed by the Guard's display, as he was meant to be. But that reaction was wearing off now, and he was recalling all the objections that the mayor, Don Nicolás, had whispered in his ear. Don Gabriel might be speaking, but it was the mayor's words that were coming out.

Don Nicolás was cunning, and he was persuasive, and he and Don Gabriel were friends of old. When the mayor whispered, Don Gabriel paid close attention.

"Of course, I understand your concerns," Alonso began. He was mustering his counterarguments when he heard it, far off: the sound of hooves on cobblestones, a horse riding hard. He paused, cocked his ear.

"What?" Don Gabriel asked. The old man's hearing was not so sharp anymore.

"Rider," Alonso said. "Someone riding fast."

Soon Don Gabriel could hear it as well, and he frowned as the rider came closer. It was unusual for someone to be riding that hard within the confines of the city, even more so within the borders of Las Casas Reales. It rarely signaled good news.

They heard the horse moving under the archway, the rider reining back to a walk, and a moment later he appeared in the courtyard. He looked hurriedly side to side, saw Alonso and Don Gabriel, and approached.

"Your Excellency! Señor Lieutenant Governor!" he called. He was winded but doing his best to speak calmly and clear.

"Hold there, hold," Don Gabriel interrupted. "I can well guess what you have to say. There's a riot, down at the tavern district, am I right in that?" This sort of thing had gone from rarity to near daily occurrence.

The rider, flushed and sweating, nodded.

"Damn them, the lot of them, the miserable rogues and thieves!" Don Gabriel spat. It was getting tiresome.

"Damn them, indeed," Don Alonso said. "But mind you, señor, this is the very thing I had in mind when first I thought of the Governor's Guard. When trouble breaks out, as it will, you have right on hand the very best men, ready to go. Shall we ride to the sound of the guns? See what good these men might do?"

There was little chance that Alonso, a newcomer half the mayor's age, could, with words alone, convince the governor general of the benefits of the Governor's Guard. But seeing those men in action, that was a different matter entirely.

Chapter Eight

Once again, Captain Delgadillo's voice echoed around the rear courtyard. "Governor's Guard! Form up by file!"

The horsemen, who had been waiting in their four ranks of twenty-five horses, line abreast, shifted with parade-like precision, and a moment later they were in two long columns, fifty horses long and two wide.

They were just settling into place when the stable boys came hurrying out, leading mounts for Alonso and the governor general, Don Gabriel. They led the horses over to the granite step set in place to help a rider mount, and first Alonso and then Don Gabriel swung himself up into the saddle. One of the boys handed a sword up to Don Gabriel, and then to Alonso.

"Is all well, Your Excellency?" Alonso asked as Don Gabriel settled into his saddle and the stable boys placed his feet in the stirrups. "Do you want for anything?"

"No, no," Don Gabriel said. He slipped the baldric over his shoulder and adjusted the hang of the sword. Alonso could see the gleam in his eye, could hear the crackle of enthusiasm in his voice. Earlier, the governor general had been reluctant to leave his office and his bottle of brandy. But Alonso knew that Don Gabriel was a campaigner of old, that he had seen hard fighting against the English and the Dutch in his younger days, leading battalions of mounted *lanceros* and pikemen in the field; he could sense that that spirit was stirring to life again.

Don Gabriel flicked his reins and walked his horse over to where Delgadillo stood at the head of the column. Alonso followed behind.

"Your Excellency," Delgadillo said, "mayhaps it would be prudent for you and Don Alonso to come behind the column. We have no notion of what we're riding into."

"Nonsense," Don Gabriel said. "This is the Governor's Guard. A man does not lead from behind."

Delgadillo's eyes flickered over to Alonso, looking for confirmation, and Alonso gave the subtlest nod of his head.

"Captain Delgadillo, lead on!" Don Gabriel called.

"As you wish, Your Excellency," Delgadillo said, a smile playing on his stoic face. He half-turned in his saddle and called, "Governor's Guard, move out!"

They rode through the archway and into the courtyard of Las Casas Reales. The hour was not late and there were dozens of people milling about: government officials of various importance and their wives, high-ranking officers from Toledo's fleet, civilians of wealth and high standing who were passing through that part of the world. Alonso was happy they were there to witness this. He understood how impressive a sight the Governor's Guard made, riding off to quell trouble in the streets.

He hoped that the whore's son mayor was watching and seeing as well.

They reached the far end of the courtyard and moved out onto the streets of Santo Domingo, and since there was much less chance of trampling anyone of importance there they increased their pace from a walk to a quick trot. It was like riding down a narrow canyon, with the walls of the more opulent houses rising up on the right-hand side, the various shops and other businesses on the left, back to the river. The way was lit here and there with lanterns hanging on gateposts, but Alonso would have been fine even with virtually no light at all. It was, by now, all very familiar to him.

They continued south, leaving the more affluent area behind and making for that part of the city where the riotous sort congregated. Alonso was eager to pick up the pace, to gallop into the fight—but he glanced over at Don Gabriel and he could see the governor general was sweating, his mouth open, his face red.

"Captain Delgadillo!" Alonso called, then paused as he gasped dramatically for breath. "Pray, might we slow the pace a bit? I fear I'm having a hard time of it tonight."

Delgadillo raised and arm and slowed his horse and Alonso and the governor general did as well. Behind them they heard the One Hundred matching their pace.

"I'm sorry," Alonso said. "The work of a lieutenant governor makes me unfit for such things."

"Of course, Don Alonso," Delgadillo said. "Better this way. We don't want to go racing into the Good Lord knows what."

They continued on at a walk and Alonso heard the governor general's breathing return to normal, and finally Don Gabriel said, "Whatever's taking place, I think I can hear it from here."

And indeed they could: the now-familiar sound of rioting in the streets, the shouting, the screams, the sharp crack of things breaking, the crash of carts and such overturned. But Alonso could not smell smoke, and could not hear the sound of any significant blaze, and that was a hopeful thing.

They rode past the remains of the stable where Alonso and Delgadillo had freed the horses from the fire. That structure, and the tavern that once stood beside it, were still nothing more than blackened heaps of debris between the still-standing buildings. They continued up the street another block until they reached the fighting, the swarm of brawling men choking the road, flailing away at one another and plundering the taverns on either side. Half-dressed women leaned out from upper-story windows, shouting and pelting the mob below with whatever they had on hand: basins, night-jars, candlesticks, lanterns. They seemed to have no purpose in mind that Alonso could tell, beyond adding to the chaos.

"Ah, these dogs! Sheep-biting rogues! Let's be at them!" Don Gabriel shouted. He pulled his sword from its scabbard and raised it high. The man's blood was up, his old passions reawakened.

"To be certain, Your Excellency," Delgadillo said. "But pray, let us put some of our training to the test." Before Don Gabriel could reply, Delgadillo called in a voice that cut through the sound of the mob, "Governor's Guard! Wedge formation!"

Once again the horsemen moved out of their lines and reformed, fifty riders on one side of Delgadillo, Don Gabriel, and Alonso, fifty on the other, spread out like an arrow with the men in the center as the point. Swords were drawn.

Ahead of them, the riot continued unabated, arms and fists swinging, clubs, pikes, chairs, even a dead dog, flailing in every direction. The noise was terrific, like some lower level of Hell. No one seemed to have noticed the Governor's Guard, or if they had, they did not care. No one in Santo Domingo expected order to be enforced in any meaningful way.

"If you must strike, use the flats of your swords!" Delgadillo shouted. "On me!" He kicked his spurs into the flanks of his horse and the animal moved forward, stepping high, threatening to trample anyone in its path. To their right and left the rest of the guards moved as well, and Alonso and Don Gabriel moved with them.

The last time Alonso and Delgadillo had done such work, the flames from the burning tavern had illuminated the fighting mob. There was no fire now, thankfully, but that left most of the street in darkness, the rioters a barely visible, struggling mass, like fish in a net, just below the surface, indistinctly seen.

Delgadillo leaned forward and swung his sword backhand, the flat of the blade catching the nearest man on the back of the head and sending him stumbling into the next. The man looked up—Alonso could just make out his face in the uncertain light—and the anger turned to panic as he saw the mounted guard looming over him, and the others spread out behind. He shouted, as much a scream as a shout, turned and pushed away from the swinging sword and the deadly hooves of the horse.

Don Gabriel and Alonso were riding side by side, directly behind Delgadillo and the others. Alonso had not missed the way Delgadillo skillfully put himself and his men between the governor and the fighting mob, though Don Gabriel, in his enthusiasm, seemed not to have noticed. Now, as Delgadillo lashed out at the rioters, Don Gabriel laughed out loud and shouted, "Ha, ha, run you *bastardo*!"

The frightened bastardo, if such he was, was indeed running. And more than that, he was half-climbing over anyone in front of him as he tried desperately to get clear, and his panicked flight was getting attention. Others in the mob, directly in the path of the guard, were looking up now, shouting in terror, turning and running. The massive, high-stepping horses, the riders in black, swords drawn, were having just the right effect, sending just the right message with their relentless advance.

"Here, let me at 'em! Clear the way!" Don Gabriel shouted, spurring his horse forward in an effort to get around Delgadillo's right side. But as he advanced, Delgadillo swerved to the right, blocking his way again. Delgadillo turned in his saddle, looked back at Don Gabriel with an apologetic expression.

"Forgive me, Excellency!" he shouted. "I didn't see you there! I'm hemmed in here by the mob, but I'll try to let you through!" He turned back to the human flotsam under his horse's hooves, the soldiers and sailors and local trash, and he swung his sword and pushed his horse forward and made no attempt to get out of Don Gabriel's way.

The Governor's Guard, in their wedge formation, were driving forward down the center of the street, step by step, pushing the rioters before them. And with each step the rioters were losing interest in the fight. At the fringes of the crowd people were breaking off and fleeing down alleys and pushing their way into the taverns or down the side streets. Flight was their chief concern now.

Alonso shook his head and smiled. He thought back to his last time in those streets, him and the half dozen men who Sandoval allowed to come help quell that riot. It had been a close thing. He and Delgadillo and the others had put a stop to the fight, but they could just as easily have been killed.

This time it was so very different.

Something bounced off Alonso's shoulder and he looked down in time to see a basin smash against the cobblestones at his feet. He looked up. A woman wearing nothing but a loose shift was leaning out a second story window, arm still extended from having thrown the heavy ceramic. Her eyes met Alonso's and they held one another for a moment, then she made an obscene gesture and retreated back into the room.

Whore… Alonso thought. He considered leading men into the brothel and dragging her out of there, but dismissed the thought. It was not important.

Beside him, Don Gabriel gave a shout like a triumphant cry and spurred his horse, which leapt forward. Delgadillo had shifted to one side, leaving an opening for the governor general, and he was taking advantage of it, plunging into the fight.

Delgadillo, damn your eyes, Alonso thought. He was not happy to see Don Gabriel coming to grips with the rioters. If something happened to the old man, he, Alonso, would take the blame.

But Don Gabriel did not seem much concerned for his safety as he charged past Delgadillo, shouting, waving his sword, the disintegrating mob fleeing before him. And as he did, Alonso realized that Delgadillo had timed the thing perfectly. There was no fight left in the rioters. They were just trying to escape. Don Gabriel was getting the action he craved, at very little risk to his person.

"Guard! Forward!" Delgadillo shouted, waving his sword and urging his horse on, surging ahead from their walking pace to something more like a trot. The guard followed, shouting and cursing and swinging swords, just as Delgadillo, just as Don Gabriel, was doing.

That was enough to break up the last vestiges of the riot. There were no more than two or three score people left in the streets and now they turned and fled as quickly as they could, disappearing into the dark. Above their heads the women withdrew from their window perches, pulling shutters closed behind them.

And then, only the Governor's Guard remained. The riders abandoned their wedge formation and patrolled the perimeter of the area, peering down alleyways and into taverns, looking for any threat. Don Gabriel, who had charged off down the road in pursuit of the rioters, now came riding back, reining in with a flourish beside Alonso and Delgadillo.

The light from a nearby lantern fell on his face, which was red and glistening with sweat. His thick moustache did not hide the wide grin of delight he wore. "Well, I guess we showed those dogs, did we not?" he said, before anyone else could speak. "Sent them running like the rats they are, no?"

"We did, Excellency," Delgadillo said. "You did. Well done, there, driving the last of them off."

Don Gabriel gave a shrug, a self-deprecating gesture, but his grin did not fade. "And this Governor's Guard, damnation, but you've trained them well, Captain! Very well! As good as any of the king's mounted troops that I've seen."

"You do me great honor, Excellency," Delgadillo said.

Don Gabriel turned to Alonso. "My boy, I'll be honest with you…I had my doubts about this whole thing, I did. There were some who said it was all a waste of time and money, a bad idea. Me, I was not certain. But seeing them tonight, seeing how they can keep the peace, well, damn my eyes, I wish we had put this Governor's Guard in place a dozen years ago!"

"Thank you, Don Gabriel," Alonso said. "It makes me very happy to hear that." And it did.

It was late the next day, after his regular business was concluded, that Alonso found himself once again in the newly-built barracks of the Governor's Guard, seated in the room that served as Captain Delgadillo's office. It was a small room, much smaller than Francisca's closet in their apartment in Las Casas Reales. But it was private, and that was the important thing.

Adjoining the office was Delgadillo's bedchamber, which was the full extent of the captain's suite of rooms. As intolerably confining as Alonso might have found it, he understood that this space was cleaner, newer, and altogether superior to the captain's former quarters at Fortaleza Ozama. The same was true of the quarters for all the men of the Governor's Guard. Better quarters, better food, easier duty, far better pay: none of those men were likely to betray Alonso and risk losing that.

The new barracks served another purpose as well, one that Alonso had not even considered: it made an ideal place for him to conduct clandestine meetings. It was far safer and more convenient than sneaking into town, and even though it was part of Las Casas Reales, no one of any importance would see him there, because only servants and people of that stature ever wandered over to that part of the compound. Perfect.

Sitting across from him now was the ubiquitous Carlos Hernández, exactly the sort of man with whom Alonso did not wish to be seen, but just the sort he needed for his endeavors. Delgadillo was not there. He had gladly vacated the rooms at Alonso's request.

"That was well done, Hernández," Alonso said. "Last night."

Hernández shrugged. "It's the easiest thing in the world these days, to start a riot in Santo Domingo. Pay a sailor to spit in the face of a soldier, and there you are."

"Still, it was well done. The timing was perfect. The governor general was impressed. Very impressed."

"I'm pleased to hear it, señor."

Alonso nodded. "You should be. Don Gabriel's enthusiasm will serve us well. Now, you have news for me?"

"I do," Hernández said. "It concerns Toledo's fleet."

Hernández was sitting with his legs crossed, a glass of brandy held loosely in one hand, a look—his usual look—of nonchalance on his face. Alonso wondered how he himself might adopt such a look, and make it seem as authentic as Hernández did.

Still, as unperturbable as Hernández might appear, Alonso knew there was a lot roiling under the surface. There had to be. The way he let his hair fall unbound over his ears and onto his shoulders, rather than in a queue, as he used to wear it, suggested as much.

The mayor, Don Nicolás Pérez, had sliced off the top of Hernández's left ear. He had done it to remind Hernández that Don Nicolás was not a man to be trifled with. Rumor had it that he made Hernández carry the severed part with him and display it whenever the two met.

Don Nicolás had done it to instill fear and loyalty in Carlos Hernández's heart. Alonso suspected the gesture had done neither. Which was why Hernández was meeting with him now.

"Toledo's fleet?" Alonso said. "Go on."

"It seems they found that much of their stores of salt beef are rotten," Hernández continued. "Probably rotten when it was loaded aboard in Spain. So bad it cannot even be fed to sailors or soldiers."

"How much beef?"

"A thousand casks, that's what the purser's secretary told me."

"A thousand casks…" Alonso said. "That is a great deal of beef."

"It is," Hernández agreed. "And Toledo is desperate. He would pay whatever he had to for more. He would not hesitate." Alonso could see that Hernández was being coy.

"I have no doubt," Alonso said. "But who in Santo Domingo could get that much salt beef? And as quickly as Toledo wants it?"

"Apparently Don Nicolás can, señor," Hernández said. "He's promised to provide it. How that's possible, I don't know. But he says that he can."

"I see," Alonso said. This was all very interesting. Not so much about Toledo's need for supplies; Alonso had heard that rumor already, from other sources. Hernández was a font of information when it suited him, but Alonso had learned through hard use that he could not rely on Hernández alone, so he had cultivated other channels. Now, between Delgadillo, and his secretary, Juan Cardero, and his wife's maid Gabriella, and sundry others to whom he showed generosity, the news came flowing in.

Still, of all of them, Carlos Hernández was the most knowledgeable, the most well-connected. He was not just an observer: he was a player. And as such, he would not be telling

Alonso this if he did not think there was some mutual benefit to be had.

"You don't know where Don Nicolás means to get a thousand casks of beef?" Alonso asked.

"Some he already has on hand," Hernández said. "Some is what he stole from you. But that's only a small part of it. Where the rest is to come from, I do not know."

Alonso looked into Hernández's eyes, wondering if that was true. He himself had heard talk of the storerooms of Fortaleza Ozama being emptied out, and if he had heard that, then Hernández certainly had as well. But Hernández's expression gave nothing away, and in truth it did not matter if Hernández was lying or not. It did not matter to either man where the beef came from, just what became of it.

"If you're not involved in procuring these thousand casks," Alonso said, "what part do you play in all this?"

"I play a very small part, Don Alonso. A go-between. I'm warehousing what Don Nicolás procures, making arrangements with Toledo's purser. Disposing of the rotten stores. That's it."

"I understand," Alonso said. And of course, he did. He understood that the mayor had tapped Hernández for this role because he needed someone who would not ask questions, who would do as he was told, and do it competently. A man like Hernández, whom Don Nicolás figured he had frightened into remaining loyal.

"Just now, Don Nicolás doesn't want anyone to know of his involvement," Hernández continued. "But once he has supplied the fleet, then he'll make certain that the great Admiral Toledo knows who helped him in this crisis. It's very much to any man's advantage to do a favor for Fadrique Álvarez de Toledo y Mendoza, Captain General of the Ocean Sea Navy."

Alonso nodded as his thoughts whirled off in various directions. There was opportunity here. He could see it. Hernández could see it, which was why the man was telling him this. But whatever Hernández was thinking, he would not just come out and say it. That was not how he played these things.

"It must be very concerning to you," Alonso said, "having care of these stores that are so important, both to Don Nicolás and Admiral

Toledo. A thousand casks of beef? That's a lot to protect, and you with just a handful of men in your employ."

Hernández shook his head slowly. "That's not a concern. Sure I have only a few men to help me out. But Don Nicolás is taking no chances. He's seeing that the warehouse is well protected. He has *El Cinco* watching the stores, and they have a few score men with them. Hard men. Don Nicolás is most anxious that nothing happens to that salt beef."

"So it would seem," Alonso said. "It seems no one will be interfering with Don Nicolás's plans."

"I don't see how it would be possible," Hernández said, and a hint of a smile played across his otherwise expressionless face. "To effect anything against Don Nicolás, a man would need…oh…I should think at least a hundred men. Loyal and well-armed."

Chapter Nine

Benjamin Graves saw the man come through the door of the inn and he knew things were about to change. He did not know why. He did not even know who the man was, or if his business was with him and Maja. But something in his gut told him a change was coming. And he had a mariner's gut. He trusted it.

They were staying at an inn called the The Tuileries, the finest establishment of its kind on all of Tortuga. Graves figured the name was meant to be funny. He was pretty sure the king of France would not tolerate his privy, or even his stables, becoming as nasty as the Tortuga Tuileries were. But that was the point. The men and women of Tortuga, Graves had come to understand, seemed to revel in bending over and showing their collective arses to the rest of the world. If the king of France could have his Tuileries, so could they.

They had been there for a month, he and Maja and the men of *Charles Rex*. Maybe two months. Graves could not recall. The days seemed to blend together. Since they had arrived, Graves had done little beyond drinking and whoring and overseeing some minor work on *Charles Rex* while he waited for Maja to make a decision as to what they would do next. And Maja did not seem in danger of making a decision soon.

Only one thing of interest had happened since their arrival, and that had been three or four weeks earlier. It started in the early morning with Maja's toe in Benjamin Graves's gut. Familiar, infuriating. It was the toe in the gut that woke Benjamin Graves on so many mornings. It woke him the day that the strangers came ashore.

Prodding, prodding, Graves grunted and swatted at the tormenting foot, but failed to make contact. And then the toe was there again, sharp and insistent. Graves groaned and opened his eyes.

Maja was standing beside his bed, his dark face expressionless, carved out of some tropical hardwood.

"Son of a bitch…" Graves muttered, once more swatting and missing, as Maja nimbly pulled his foot out of the way.

It didn't even make sense that Maja would wake him like that. It was one thing if he was lying on a ship's deck; in that case it was reasonable enough that Maja would use his foot to poke him awake. But Graves was lying in a bed. Maja had to cock his leg like some sort of deranged heron just to reach him.

But Graves understood the truth of it, perfectly well. The toe annoyed him to no end. Maja knew it, and enjoyed it.

Graves propped himself up on his elbow. "What the bloody hell…?" he muttered. He remembered that he had gone to bed with some whore named Betty or Becky or some such. Maybe Nancy. A reasonably pretty young thing, as good as he was like to find on Tortuga. He craned his neck to see if she was still there, but she was gone.

Stole my purse and left me the pox, no doubt, Graves thought.

"Get up," Maja said. "Come see this."

Graves swung his legs over the edge of the bed. His head was throbbing, his mouth bitter-tasting and dry as straw. There was a bottle of rumbullion on the small table by the bed, an inch of the blessed liquid left at the bottom. Graves snatched it up, tilted it back, felt the warm curative running down his throat.

He stood, somewhat restored, pulled his shirt over his head, pulled his trousers up over his shirt, and followed Maja out of the small room. He stumbled down the hall with its flaking plaster walls and splintered floors and down the narrow stairs to the tavern room below.

Maja led Graves over to a big, glassless window that looked out onto the dusty street. Men and women were crowded around, but they moved aside as Maja approached. More people were gathered just outside the door, and across the road.

The Tuileries, like most of the dozen or so taverns and brothels, and the even less legitimate businesses in Tortuga, had large windows and doors which were nearly always open. The light coming in, the warm trade winds blowing through, made the tavern room seem less awful than those of England or the Continent or Santo Domingo. Even if the sun revealed more than Graves cared to see, the smell of tobacco smoke and rum and unwashed men and vomit was mostly carried off by the sea breeze.

"Look there," Maja said, stopping a few feet back from the window, where he was still mostly lost in shadow. He nodded down the road toward the harbor, a hundred yards away. A boat had pulled up on shore, a dozen men and what appeared to be a woman and a dog had come up onto the beach. More boats were pulling in behind.

"They're from that ship that came to anchor yesterday," Graves said. "What of it?" People were always coming and going on Tortuga. Some stopped for a day or so. Some stayed longer. Some stayed until they died from disease or drink, their bodies buried in the sandy soil if they had friends, tossed out into the tall brush that bordered the town if they did not.

"Watch," Maja said.

Graves watched. One by one the boats came ashore and the men spilled out, and when they were all ashore the men formed up in a loose column behind some big son of a bitch who seemed to be in charge. The woman stood on one side of him, the dog on the other.

They made their way up the beach to the wide road that ran through town. The men were armed with the long muskets of the hunters of Hispaniola, and in the tavern and across the street the watchers were armed as well. They held their weapons easy, rested the butts on the ground or cradled them in their arms. But they were ready for a fight, and they made certain that it was obvious.

Graves's eyes were on the man leading the band. He was even bigger than Graves had first thought. His beard was thick and untended, like a hedge in need of clipping, his hair long and tied back in a queue. He wore no hat, but his clothes were not those of a buccaneer. They were something fancier than that: silk or fine linen by the look of them. A gentleman's clothes, though there was something not quite right about them.

A sword hung at the man's side, its hilt glinting in the sun. Silk stockings stretched tight over massive calves. And the shoes—rawhide. A hunter's shoes.

"Odd looking bugger," Graves observed. "What the devil is he wearing?"

"Don't recognize him?" Maja asked.

Graves frowned. "Should I?"

"Same villain we fought aboard that ship. At anchor at Hispaniola."

Graves stared at the man as he approached, and thought back. It had only been a week or so, but the memories were smoky and dim. For all the smuggling and privateering and such that Benjamin Graves had done, he was not very used to pitched battle. Even in the midst of it he found it hard to keep his thoughts straight. Since then, the images had become even less clear, as if they were sinking in muddy water.

But he remembered now. A big man, but fast, and good with a sword. Surprising. Him and Maja going at it, hammer and tongs. The wicked slash he had given Maja across the gut. Maja dropping the big man with his *boutou*, his native club.

"I thought you killed that bastard."

"Me too," Maja said. "I guess he don't kill easy."

They watched the column move up the road, as did everyone else alive and awake in the town. The big man walked with determination, eyes forward. He did not look around. The men behind him were more curious, staring this way and that, but they did not waver in their advance. Graves could feel the tension rippling through the men in the tavern.

"What do you reckon they want?" Graves asked. It was a stupid question, but he could not help himself.

"We'll see," Maja said.

But Maja was wrong. They did not discover what the newcomers were after, only that it had nothing to do with Cayona. The ad hoc column marched right on past, beyond the north end of the town, then veered off onto a road that ran east into the hills. They did not return.

At first, the men in town kept their weapons handy, more so than usual, in case this potentially dangerous crew reappeared. But they never did. There was some speculation as to who those men and the one woman were, but no one had any notion beyond guesses, and no one was going to track them down and ask. People on Tortuga minded their own business. It was what drew a certain type to that place.

They learned more three days later, after the newly arrived crew had marched through town and disappeared to the east. That was when Capitaine Pierre Lepers came staggering into The Tuileries, filthy, his clothes torn. He had a story to tell, and was eager to tell it, concerning how the strangers had arrived at what he fancied was his plantation, had killed his overseer, driven him off, and taken possession of the place. How he had been hiding in the jungle ever since. Now, he was looking for help to take it back

It was an interesting tale, but Lepers was not well regarded among the people of Cayona, so no one much cared about his plight, or was much inclined to render aid. Lepers had, himself, stolen the plantation from its previous owner, and he enjoyed using the lash on his servants a bit too much. When in town, he made himself uniquely obnoxious in the taverns and brothels; quite a feat in that company. And even if Lepers had been well-loved, the men of Tortuga were not inclined to offer help to anyone if it was not to their own immediate benefit.

Eventually Lepers gave up trying to recruit allies for his vendetta and took to drinking instead. He kept that up for a day or so, until all his coin and anything else of value that he owned, including his shoes, were gone, and he was thrown bodily from the tavern.

It had been three weeks, as far as Graves could recall, since the newcomers arrived and Lepers had come crawling into The Tuileries, and not much had happened since then. But now, as this new fellow came in the door, Graves had a sense that things might once again get interesting.

"Here, we know this one?" Graves asked Maja, jerking his head toward the front of the tavern room where the man had just stepped through the door. He and Maja were sitting at their familiar table, near the back of the room. A few of Maja's pirates were seated there as well.

Maja turned his head and looked. The man had paused just inside the door and was looking around the room. He wore rawhide shoes and wide canvas trousers and a jerkin that might have been a decent garment at one time. A belt was around his waist, a hunting knife in a crude leather sheath. He held a long musket and wore the Apostles dangling from a bandolier slung over one shoulder, a haversack and bedroll over the other. On his head, a wide hat with a jaunty feather.

His beard was shaved to a goatee and moustache, but he had several day's growth on his cheeks. He looked as if he had been living in the jungle for a while.

"Don't know him," Maja said. Graves grunted. The man stepped over to the bar, leaned in and spoke to the tavern keeper, and the tavern keeper pointed directly at Maja and Graves. The newcomer nodded, crossed the crowded room, heading in their direction.

Now we'll see, Graves thought. He looked into his tankard, pretended to be unaware of the man's approach. The man stopped at the table, looked around, then down at Graves.

"You, sir, are master of the ship in the harbor?"

Graves looked up and held the man's eyes for a moment before answering. "More than one ship in the harbor," he said.

"Not the one with the red and yellow chevrons that arrived a few weeks past. I mean the one that was at anchor before that." His English was decent, his accent was Dutch, his words spoken as if he was a man of some breeding, not the sort of lowborn cur one generally found in that place.

Every damned sort of whore's son comes through here, Graves thought. He glanced over at Maja. Graves was most certainly not master of *Charles Rex*, not anymore. First mate? Sailing master? He didn't know what he was. And he was never sure what Maja wanted him to be.

Maja met his eye, gave him a slight nod of the head, so Graves looked up at the Dutchman and said, "Aye, I'm he."

"Ah, then, might I join you? Have a word?" the Dutchman asked.

"You have coin to buy us drink?" Graves asked.

The Dutchman hesitated, just a beat, before replying.

"Of course." He turned and waved to the servant girl, indicated the table, then leaned his musket against a chair, pulled up another, and sat.

"My name is Hendrick Van Lauwersoog," he said, and smiled. "A name you English cannot pronounce, I know, so you may call me Van Loudersong, as the others do."

Graves nodded. He looked anxiously over at the servant girl and saw she was indeed bringing more brandy. He relaxed a bit. "So, what's your business with us, Van Loudersong?"

"It's a long tale, and I won't bore you with the lot of it," Van Loudersong said.

"Good. Pray don't," Graves said.

Van Loudersong frowned slightly, apparently displeased with the interruption. "I arrived here a few weeks past, aboard that other ship in the harbor. We came from the north coast of Hispaniola, where we had a boucanier camp."

"Saw the lot of you come ashore," Graves said. He recalled Maja pointing them out as they landed, the crew of the ship they had attacked on Hispaniola. An odd situation indeed: he and Maja and this Van Loudersong had been on opposite sides of a bloody and desperate fight, and Van Loudersong did not even know it.

"Heard you took over a plantation to the east of here," Graves added.

"That's right. Not me. This great villain called LeBoeuf, who fancies himself chief of that lot. But that's no matter, not to our business."

Our business? Graves thought. *Do we have business now?*

Van Loudersong took a long drink and continued. "The late hurricano destroyed our camp. We had nothing when we left. Save for one thing, which LeBoeuf left behind. And that's a great fortune in gold. Well-hidden. And still there."

That got Graves's attention, but not as much as Van Loudersong seemed to think it might. Graves had heard that sort of thing often enough, had even acted on such information in the past. And he had not a widow's mite to show for it.

"Why would he leave such a thing behind?" Graves asked.

"Because he couldn't retrieve it in secret," Van Loudersong said, "not where it's hidden. No one else in our company knew about it. Had he retrieved it under the eyes of those other rogues, he would have had to share it out with them. Worse, the others would like have killed him for trying to keep it secret."

"But you know of it?" Graves asked. He did not try to hide his skepticism.

"It was only by accident that I discovered it. No one else knows. Right now, LeBoeuf seems to put great stock in his plantation, but I have no doubt he means to soon go back for the gold. And then an opportunity is lost."

Graves took another long drink. No point in asking why the Dutchman was telling him all this; it was pretty clear where he was heading. So Graves asked another question, to which he also knew the answer.

"You know where the gold is," Graves said. "Why don't you go fetch it?"

"I don't have a ship," Van Loudersong said. "I don't have men. I might go in a piragua, or a longboat, but I'd be damned vulnerable, do you see? But you have a ship, well-armed and manned, by the looks of it."

Graves nodded. "That we do," he said. "But if we join company, then you'll needs share the gold with me and my men. A damned lot less of it for you."

"True," Van Loudersong said. "But more than if I simply let LeBoeuf take it all. Besides, I have other goods hidden nearby. Trade goods. Worth quite a bit if I fetch those as well."

"And you think we won't just knock you on the head and take your share?" Graves asked. "And your goods?"

Van Loudersong smiled. "You might. But it's hardly worth it, for…what? A twentieth share, split among your men? No, I don't think you'd do that. You look to be men of honor."

At that Graves laughed out loud, and thought, *You're as slick as a herring, aren't you?*

"There's no point in my lying about this," Van Loudersong continued. "If I were to lead you there, and you found this was all a tall tale, then I *would* expect you to knock me on the head."

Graves was silent as he considered the logic of that argument. There were any number of reasons why this would likely all come to nothing, but he did not think the Dutchman was lying to them. As Van Loudersong said, there was no reason for him to lie. At least none that Graves could see.

"Well, this might be of interest to us," Graves said. "And it might not. Let me seek the council of my partner."

"And who, sir, is your partner?" Van Loudersong asked.

"Why, this fellow right here," Graves said, nodding toward Maja. He almost laughed again, to see the look of surprise on the Dutchman's face.

Graves knew Van Loudersong's type: haughty and superior, with an air like they were forever doing the world a favor. That sort rarely thought of anyone as their equal.

And here was Maja, with his patched and sun-bleached linen shirt and leather jerkin, his head bound in a red cloth, his wide feet bare. He wore a necklace comprised of multiple strands of beads and small shells and sharp animal teeth; a savage's necklace, as Van Loudersong would see it. And that aside, Maja's dark skin, his obvious mixed race, would be enough for Van Loudersong to dismiss the man as little more than an indentured servant, or a slave.

And now Van Loudersong's plans hinged on Maja's yes or no. It was genuinely amusing.

"Maja, what say you?" Graves asked. Maja, as was his wont, stared at him silently. Then stared at Van Loudersong. Then finally he spoke.

"How did this LeBoeuf, this boucanier, come by such a fortune? And why was he still hunting pigs if he had it?" Graves could hear the doubt in Maja's voice.

"The hurricano drove a ship aground on the beach where we had our camp," Van Loudersong explained. "LeBoeuf found the gold onboard. He did not tell anyone."

"And how did he come to lose it?"

"The ship caught on fire and burned. LeBoeuf left the gold behind because, as I said, he dared not tell the others it was there. But the ship sunk in just fifteen feet of water, or so. Easy to salvage."

At that, Graves looked over at Maja and their eyes met. Graves could practically read Maja's thoughts: they were the same as his own. Don Alonso Menéndez had sent them to recover a ship that had wrecked on Hispaniola's north shore. He did not tell them why it was of such value, but a hidden fortune in gold would explain it. It must have been aboard even as they were fighting LeBoeuf and Van Loudersong and the rest. And the fact that the ship had burned to the waterline would explain why the gold had not been removed.

"How far off is this place?" Maja asked.

"Half a day's sail, with the right slant of wind," Van Loudersong said. His voice was respectful, his arrogance well-hidden. "But it's to windward, so it could be two or three days to beat there.

Well, damn my eyes, Graves thought. Half a day's sail to the east would indeed put them right where Alonso's ship had burned. This was sounding more and more plausible.

"If you agree to this venture we should set sail…immediately," Van Loudersong added. "Next tide."

"Why?" Maja asked.

"LeBoeuf, the one who took the plantation? Who claims the gold for himself? He commands the other ship anchored here, and he commands about thirty rogues," Van Loudersong explained. "They're a sorry lot, but they're dangerous as well. I've been with them in a fight and I know they're not to be trifled with." He drank again, and continued.

"LeBoeuf's been hunting me since I left his company, and he's likely keeping an eye on the harbor. He'll guess I'm looking for means to go after this gold, and he'll try to stop me, and anyone who's joined with me, or he'll make every effort to get it first."

"And you think we're not his equal? You think he'll kill us all?" Maja asked.

Van Loudersong smiled. "I think it would be better if we did not find out, one way or another. Better to fetch this fortune without spilling blood."

Graves nodded. He could not disagree. He turned to Maja. "Well?"

Maja was silent again, staring at Van Loudersong until Van Loudersong began to shuffle a bit under his inscrutable gaze. Then Maja said, "We'd best be off, then. Next tide."

Chapter Ten

Van Loudersong was bound for Cayona, LeBoeuf was sure of it. On all of Tortuga there was no other place he could go that would do him any good. But he was not stupid enough to go there directly. LeBoeuf was sure of that as well.

Still, he had to prepare for any possibility. He sent Levasseur off to Cayona to keep watch for the man. Levasseur was reasonably intelligent, able to stay mostly sober, and unlikely to stand out. He also sent teams of hunters off into the hills to try to run Van Loudersong to earth. He joined in on the hunt himself, with Other Dog at his side.

It was no use. Van Loudersong was not stupid, and he was not without skill when it came to hunting, or to avoiding those who hunted him. After three days LeBoeuf called it off. They would not find Van Loudersong. They would have to wait until Van Loudersong came to them.

The next day he did. Or at least he came to Cayona. Levasseur arrived back at the plantation, red-faced, sweating, breathing hard. He had been sitting in a dark corner of a tavern when the Dutchman appeared, and fell into discussion with a group of men, an Englishman and some villainous-looking savage and sundry other piratical sorts.

LeBoeuf named off five men to come with him, the five he considered his most reliable. He reckoned five was about right. Walk into town with his entire company under arms, and he might get a bigger reaction from the folks there than he wanted. He did not need a misunderstanding leading to a pitched battle against men with whom he had no quarrel.

But if he walked into town by himself, or with too few men, then he might not accomplish what he meant to do, which was to hunt Van Loudersong down and kill him. He did not know if Van

Loudersong had managed to find any friends on Tortuga, but if he had, LeBoeuf might need some friends of his own to help do the job.

"Le Chasseur, Genet, get your weapons," LeBoeuf said, once he had heard what Levasseur had to report. "D'Anton, Steen, Billy Solent, you lot, under arms and meet me in the dooryard. No time to waste."

And, indeed, no time was wasted. Five minutes later the men were gathered with muskets in hand and bandoliers over their shoulders, and LeBoeuf joined them, similarly armed. He gestured for Vassy.

"I should be back directly," LeBoeuf said. "Keep the field hands at their work. Henriette will see to the house servants." He looked at the rest of the buccaneers, who were all gathered around now.

"I'll send for you lot if I need you," he said. "Keep your weapons at hand and be ready to move." With that he turned and headed off down the road toward the town, Other Dog at his side, the five buccaneers falling in behind.

LeBoeuf had traveled that road only once, when he and his men first marched to the plantation. He had not left his holding since taking possession of the place—there had been no need for him to leave—and he was happy for that. After half a lifetime of perpetual motion, he was content to stop for a bit, in a place he loved on first sight. But he knew his settled life would come to an end eventually. It always did. And now it had, less than a month later.

They covered a couple of miles quickly, with no grumbling or complaining from the men. Former pig-hunters, they were well used to moving fast over rough ground, loaded down with weapons and shot and supplies. Now they were walking on a road, such that it was, and it was not terribly taxing, even at the pace they were moving. But LeBoeuf had to remind himself that his stride was half again as long as the others; they might not complain, but that did not mean keeping pace with him was easy.

He stopped at a place where the palm trees arched together overhead and cast shade over a long stretch of the road. "Rest a moment," he said. "Have a drink."

The others stopped as well. They were red-faced and sheened with sweat. Some leaned on muskets, some sat. They wore bottles of water, or whatever liquid they preferred, in slings over their shoulders and now they uncorked them and drank deep. They were silent for a moment, listening to the call of the birds in the trees and the rustle of creatures in the brush. LeBoeuf knew that the silence would not last. He knew what was coming.

"So, LeBoeuf," Pierre Le Chasseur said. "There's been some talk, the past few days. None of us much liked Van Loudersong, and we reckon he knew it. But if he wanted to leave the plantation, why didn't he just leave? Why kill Boylan and Huet? I know you had us keeping an eye on him for some reason, but did he have to kill them two?"

LeBoeuf sighed. He looked from man to man. "Well, *messieurs*, I didn't want to tell you this…hoped I wouldn't have to. You know that I feared Van Loudersong was going to try to raise men against us. But it turned out his treachery was greater than that. Much greater." He let that sink in, let the curiosity build, before he continued.

"Just found it out myself," he said. "How I found out…it doesn't matter. But it seems that ship we had, the one that burned? There was a fortune in gold onboard. Hidden down below the deck. Van Loudersong found it when he was sneaking around. Never told anyone. I think he meant to wait until we got to Tortuga, until everyone was ashore, then go back aboard by himself and fetch it out. Run off with it. Whoever attacked us, back on Hispaniola, they were probably looking for the gold, too. But, of course, everything changed when the ship burned."

He paused again, let the men drink that in. He didn't want to drown them in revelations. Heads were nodding. A mad story, but it was all believable. It all made sense.

"So, Van Loudersong got other ideas, after the ship went down?" Genet speculated.

"Exactly," LeBoeuf said. "He figured he could get the gold out of the wreck, I'll warrant, but not with all of us there. If we were there, we'd know he'd been holding out on us, and that would go hard on him."

"Sure would," Le Chasseur said. "We'd cut his throat, we found out he'd been keeping that gold from us."

"As well you should," LeBoeuf agreed. "I just discovered this a few days ago. Told Van Loudersong we'd go back for the gold and share it out among the whole company. And he agreed. But he must have known I was keeping an eye on him, so he killed Boylan and Huet and run off. My guess…he's gone to find some men in town to help him get back to Hispaniola, and they'll fetch the gold out of the wreck and disappear."

This, LeBoeuf could see, had struck the right note, and it redoubled the men's desire to butcher Van Loudersong. It also meant that if he, LeBoeuf, managed to salvage the gold, he would have to share it out with the lot of them, but so be it. Anything was better than letting that murderous bastard Dutchman get it.

Le Chasseur shouldered his musket. "We'd best move on," he said, and the others nodded and made ready to resume the march.

LeBoeuf took one last swallow of water then held the bottle for Other Dog to take a drink. "And you," he warned the dog, "no ripping out any throats I do not tell you to rip out." He corked the bottle, rested his musket on his shoulder and led the way west.

They could smell the town well before they reached it: hints of wood smoke and garbage and jakes, cooked meat and tobacco smoke swirling through the pungent smell of the jungle and the warm earth. LeBoeuf instinctively took his musket from his shoulder and cradled it in his arms. He had no idea what they might encounter.

They came out of the jungle at last and onto the single road that ran through the town and down to the beach and the harbor beyond. The last time they had come that way, there had been scores of people turned out on the street and the porches and in the windows, many with arms ready, watching them suspiciously as they marched past. But they were not there now. There was hardly anyone to be seen now.

A few laborers were working at various tasks, none with much enthusiasm. A woman pushed a barrow full of washing. A few drunks were propped against walls or sprawled out in the street. They might have been alive or dead, it was hard to tell. There were stray dogs and pigs wandering around, at least as numerous as the people.

But the town was not deserted. They could hear voices and bits of music and shouting from the few taverns along the way, a man and a woman yelling at one another from an upper story window, another couple loudly copulating. Buccaneer Eden.

"Come," LeBoeuf said. He led them down the road, and they came to a tavern with a low porch and a big window looking into the tavern room. There was no glass, and LeBoeuf wondered if it had been built that way, or if the glass had been smashed out. A chair or a patron thrown through it, perhaps.

There was a sign hanging over the door, a wooden sign painted with a crown and a fleur-de-lis, though it took LeBoeuf a moment to figure out what it was. Above the crown was the name of the tavern: The Tuileries.

LeBoeuf smiled. Delusions of grandeur or a good sense of humor, he did not know which. Either way, it was amusing. He knew the Tuileries in Paris, and though it had been a few years, he did not remember them looking much like this.

But this was where Levasseur had reported seeing Van Loudersong. He had not been able to read the name, but he described the sign accurately enough.

LeBoeuf stepped into the tavern. It was the sort of room he had entered a hundred times before. Dimly lit, a low ceiling with smoke hanging below blackened beams, a smattering of tables and chairs. A score of men, perhaps, drinking and smoking, some women serving drinks or plying their trade. It might have been a tavern in France or England, save for the big, open window that allowed the fresh, island breeze to blow some of the fetid air away, and let in sunlight that managed to work its way half into the room.

LeBoeuf looked around. The bar was to his right, against the north wall, an ugly, bulldog-faced gentleman behind it. LeBoeuf took him to be the tavern keeper. He crossed the room, leaned half over the bar.

"I'm looking for a Dutchman, might have been in here today or yesterday, middling height, wears a moustache and goatee." As he spoke he placed a silver *real* on the bar and slid it toward the man.

The tavern keeper's eyes did not leave LeBoeuf as he picked up the coin. "Yesterday," he said. "Evening time."

"Still here?"

The tavern keeper shook his head and said no more, inviting LeBoeuf to place another *real* on the bar. Instead, LeBoeuf leaned his musket against the bar and placed his hands palms down on the wood. Beside him, Other Dog made a low, guttural sound, and the tavern keeper found his voice again.

"Left this morning, with that savage Maja. And Graves. And that crew." LeBoeuf frowned and his eyebrows came together, and the tavern keeper continued. "They're off that ship down in the harbor. Not the one with the red and yellow chevrons, the one with the wales and tops painted blue. One that's been there a while."

"They went back aboard their ship?" LeBoeuf asked.

"Meant to sail on the tide, I heard," the tavern keeper said, and his tone suggested that he did not plan to give much more away for free. "Might be underway now."

Merde, LeBoeuf thought. He nodded, took his leave of the tavern keeper. He stepped outside, blinking in the sun. "Come on," he said to his men.

He led them down the road toward the harbor. He forced himself not to run. He could see that the water was well up on the sand and knew it was near the top of the tide. He could see his own ship, still riding at anchor a few cable lengths off.

And, to his great relief, he could see the other ship as well, also still at anchor. There was a boat alongside, but from there LeBoeuf could see no activity onboard.

He and the five buccaneers stopped at the water's edge and looked out. "Haven't sailed yet," Le Chasseur observed.

"No," LeBoeuf said, and just as the word left his mouth they saw the ship's fore topsail come spilling off the yard, falling in great heaps of gray canvas as it was loosened off in preparation for setting.

"Damn my eyes!" LeBoeuf said out loud. He turned to D'Anton, whom he reckoned was the fastest runner among them. "Back to the plantation with you. Get all the men under arms, get them down here, fast as you can. Understand?"

D'Anton nodded, turned, and raced off.

The boats LeBoeuf and the others had brought from Hispaniola were still pulled up on the beach. LeBoeuf hurried over to the longboat and put his musket in the sternsheets. The other four put their guns in the boat as well, and they all grabbed onto the gunnel and dragged the boat toward the water. Other Dog took a noble leap and came down in the bottom of the boat, then found her feet and barked at the men to pull harder.

The boat reached the water and floated free. LeBoeuf jumped in and the others did the same. Forward, the men grabbed the oars and dropped them in the tholes. They backed the boat away from the beach and LeBoeuf grabbed the tiller.

"Make way!" LeBoeuf said and the men pulled together as LeBoeuf pushed the tiller over. The boat swung away from the beach, its bow toward the ship at anchor, and LeBoeuf thought, *Now what the devil do I do?*

He could not simply stand on the beach and watch Van Loudersong sail off. That much, at least, he understood. But he had put no thought into how he might stop him. There had been no time to think. So he tried to clear his mind and think now.

Don't know that Van Loudersong is even aboard…

He had assumed that the ship was sailing to Hispaniola with Van Loudersong on board, but he did not know that for certain. So there was the first task: find out if the Dutchman was actually there. And if he was, LeBoeuf would figure what to do next, and then next after that.

Through the creaking of the oars in the tholes, LeBoeuf could hear the faint clacking sound of capstan pawls falling into place as the last of the ship's anchor cable was hauled aboard. He could see the foreyard and the fore topsail yard bracing around, the fore topsail sheeted home, the yard jerking its way up the topmast. The sail fluttered and filled and the ship began to gather way. Ponderously, barely moving, but certainly underway.

Damn it all! LeBoeuf thought. He turned to the buccaneers at the oars. "Pull! They're making sail!"

The men leaned farther aft, grunted as they pulled with greater strength. LeBoeuf felt the boat gather speed. Other Dog was trembling, but she recognized that this was a hunt, and that meant silence, hard as it was.

Stroke by stroke the longboat gained on the ship, but LeBoeuf knew that could not last. The ship's foresail fell like a curtain as the clewlines and buntlines were let go. The sheets were tallied aft, the sail bellied and filled, and the ship's speed increased visibly. She was fighting the last of the flood tide, which was slowing her down, but she would still walk away from the longboat as her sails were set.

The main topsail, cast loose, tumbled into the main top. LeBoeuf wanted to tell the men to pull harder, but he held his tongue. They were pulling as hard as they could. He pushed the tiller over, edging the boat closer to the ship as they closed the gap. One hundred feet away, and LeBoeuf could read the name on the transom: *Charles Rex.*

English, he thought, but he could see no significance in that fact. As Spain's grip on the New World loosened, every other seagoing nation was starting to infiltrate. He shifted his eyes up to the rail. There were a few men leaning on it, looking aft. They did not seem overly concerned about the five buccaneers overtaking them. Nor should they have been.

Overhead the main topsail was sheeted home and the yard began its ascent, but LeBoeuf's eyes remained on the men at the rail. One had dark skin; not dark like an African, but more like a Taino, a native of the Caribbean islands. One was white, heavy-set, with a thick, dark beard. The third was Van Loudersong.

"Son of a whore," LeBoeuf said softly, then, louder, to his men, "There's that damned Dutchman, sure enough."

Three more strokes and they were past the transom and alongside the quarterdeck, LeBoeuf looking up at Van Louderson and the others, fifteen feet above and forty feet away. He was still thinking of what he might say, but Van Loudersong beat him to it.

"LeBoeuf!" he called, and he did not try to hide the amusement in his voice. "You dumb ox! Five paces behind, as usual!"

"I see you've found some friends," LeBoeuf called back. "Not an easy thing for you. They'll cut your throat when they find there's no gold!"

"Ha!" Van Loudersong laughed. "A valiant try! But where might it have gone? None knew of it but you and me, and it's well for you the others did not know you were holding out on them."

"You reckon I'd leave it where it was? Knowing a rat such as you was after it? I sent someone to fetch it weeks ago!"

He was improvising, speaking the words as they came to him, but he saw the first shadow of doubt cross Van Loudersong's face. They had been speaking French, their only shared language as far as LeBoeuf knew. He wondered if the others, the master of the ship and the dark one, could understand. He took his eyes from Van Loudersong, looked closer at the other two, the dark man and the bearded man.

Damn my eyes… he thought. The dark skin, the red cloth bound around his head, the leather jerkin. It had been nighttime, with the flames of the burning ship casting light and shadow over the deck, but still LeBoeuf was sure: there stood the man he had fought back on Hispaniola, the man with the cutlass and that wicked native club. The man who had laid him out, nearly cracked his head open.

Thought I killed that son of a bitch, LeBoeuf thought. *Apparently not.*

He hesitated, considered his next move. He did not care to give secrets away, to reveal anything about himself, but he would not shake Van Loudersong with bluffing alone. His best play, his only play, was to stop the others from helping him.

"You there!" he called in English. "I hope you have not put your trust in this murdering Dutchman!"

He saw Van Loudersong straighten in surprise, shocked to discover that LeBoeuf spoke English. Van Loudersong had always considered LeBoeuf a blockhead, and LeBoeuf had never tried to disabuse him of that. Van Loudersong was probably surprised that LeBoeuf could speak his own native French, never mind a second language.

"Van Loudersong thinks there's gold on Hispaniola, but there's not," LeBoeuf continued. "I sent my men for it weeks back. It's gone."

The bearded man and the Taino looked at one another, then looked back at LeBoeuf. They did not reply. Van Loudersong had more of a reaction.

"That's enough from you, you dumb ox," he called back in French. He took two steps forward to where a swivel gun, a falconet, was mounted on the rail. He grabbed hold of the gun's monkey tail and swung the barrel around until it was aimed directly at LeBoeuf. From someplace below the bulwark he produced a linstock with glowing match wound around the end.

Bâtarde! LeBoeuf thought. Van Loudersong had made ready for them, made ready to blast them with langrage—shards of iron—from ten yards away. He gripped the tiller tighter, eyes on Van Loudersong. He heard Le Chasseur shout, "Oh, you whore monger Dutch villain!"

Van Loudersong raised the linstock, brought the match down to the falconet's touchhole, and LeBoeuf jerked the tiller over. The longboat slewed hard to larboard just as the gun fired, sharp and loud, and the langrage tore up the water where, a second before, the boat's stern had been.

LeBoeuf heard Van Loudersong curse loudly. He kept the tiller hard over, swinging the boat around, full circle, until it was once again on the same course as the ship. The men at the oars were pulling hard, straining to keep up. They would not be able to maintain that pace for long.

On the ship's quarterdeck, Van Loudersong and the heavy man were swabbing out the falconet. LeBoeuf let go of the tiller and stood, feet wide, and snatched up his musket. He pulled the lock back and brought the weapon to his shoulder and swung the muzzle in their direction.

The heavy man saw him first, and with a shout he ducked behind the bulwark. Van Loudersong was right behind him, and the Taino next. LeBoeuf continued to train the musket around. As much as he would have liked to take any of those three out, they were not his target.

Aft of the mizzenmast he saw him, the helmsman, just visible from the shoulders up. A hard shot in the best of circumstances, harder still when shooting from a moving boat at a small target on a moving ship. But LeBoeuf had put hundreds of bullets through that gun and he knew its idiosyncrasies. He rested his finger on the trigger and sighted the end of the muzzle a little above and to the left of the man's head. He felt the longboat roll under him, lifting the muzzle from the target. Then it paused and rolled back and LeBoeuf pulled the trigger.

The musket slammed against his shoulder in that familiar way and his sight was lost in the cloud of gray smoke from the muzzle and the pan. His eyes were on the ship as his hands instinctively dropped the butt of the gun and grabbed up one of the apostles. He could not see if he had hit the helmsman or not, but he could see that the man was no longer at the helm and the ship was turning fast to starboard, the wind pushing the bow down.

LeBoeuf poured powder down the muzzle, fished a ball from his pouch and jammed it in after, his eyes still on the ship. He saw the heavy man with the beard appear where the helmsman had been. He was leaning toward the starboard side and LeBoeuf guessed he was trying to push the tiller over, with the helmsman lying dead or wounded on the deck.

Without looking, without even thinking of what he was doing, LeBoeuf pulled the rammer out from under the muzzle of his musket. He jammed a paper wadding in and rammed it home, dropped the rammer and shouldered the weapon.

The ship was turning back up into the wind, responding to the heavy man's efforts at the helm. LeBoeuf leveled the musket and waited as the boat rolled back. The heavy man looked over at LeBoeuf and LeBoeuf saw him drop from sight in the same instant that he pulled the trigger.

"Damn!" LeBoeuf cried in frustration. The smoke blew clear and the heavy man was not there. LeBoeuf did not know if he had hit him, but he suspected he had not.

And then he realized that it did not matter. The ship was turning again, the tiller abandoned. And then it stopped. The entire vessel seemed to shudder, the masts bending forward, the sails rippling as the bow ran hard up on a sandbar. It was just past high water and the tide was falling. They would not be going anywhere for a while.

LeBoeuf smiled. He set his musket down, sat, and grabbed the tiller. "Pray, slow it down afore you lot drop dead," he said and the rowers sighed as they slowed their pace. He pushed the tiller over and swung the bow away from the stranded ship. He kept turning until the boat was headed toward his own ship, riding at anchor a cable-length off.

Chapter Eleven

There were various roads in and out of Fortaleza Ozama, but only one that the wagon was likely to take. It ran through a little-used gate in the north end of the wall, tucked in near the corner closest to the river side. A gate for supplies, or servants, or laborers, or whatever else was best hidden from view.

Captain Delgadillo knew it well, so he placed himself and his men a quarter mile outside the gate, on the battered road that led from the fortaleza downhill to the lower town, the warehouses and docks. If a wagon was coming, it would come that way. Many already had over the past few nights, he was certain of it. His only concern was that he was too late, that the last of them had already come and gone.

A bell rang out, far off, a sound as familiar to Delgadillo as his own voice: the bell at Fortaleza Ozama ringing out midnight. It was a sound that normally would give him comfort, as it meant that all was well. But this night it meant only that time was moving along, and no wagon had yet come down the road.

He heard one of his men grunting in the dark, and Delgadillo knew the man was thinking just what Delgadillo was thinking... *Where is it?* It irritated him, and he almost called for silence, but he stopped himself. These men knew better than to make any noise louder than a grunt, and snapping at them would just reveal his own concerns.

And then he heard it: the creak of hinges, the clap of hooves on cobblestones. Far enough off and faint enough that he never would have picked it up had the hour not been so late, the night so quiet. He heard a rustling among his men as they caught the sound as well, and their nerves, which had grown dull, sharpened up again.

More creaking, the gates closing, and at the same time the renewed clatter of hooves, and now ironbound wheels moving along. Delgadillo felt the odd sensation of both relief and tension spreading over him. He reached down and laid a palm on the butt of the pistol thrust in his belt.

"Stand ready, men," he said, his voice barely audible, even to himself. His muted speech was an unnecessary precaution. The driver would barely hear a cannon blast over the sound of his horse and wagon. There was a rustling, like a breeze in branches, which Delgadillo knew was his men, hidden in the dark, putting hands on weapons, assuming a more ready stance. They were not certain what they would face, but they were ready for it, whatever it would be. Or so they hoped.

Delgadillo reached down to grab the edge of his cape and toss it back over his shoulder, a now habitual gesture, but his hand found nothing. Only then did he recall he was not wearing the cape, or any of the clothing he had become accustomed to. The doublet, the trousers, the sword, all were back in the new barracks at Las Casas Reales.

Instead he wore his fatigue clothing: loose breeches and a linen shirt, a simple leather jerkin over that, a brimless cloth cap on his head. No different from the dress of any of the hundreds of men who labored along the river's edge. His men, now unseen in the dark, were dressed the same.

Delgadillo closed his eyes and listened. The wagon was coming nearer, no question. He had guessed right as to the road it would take. And there was only one wagon, he was fairly sure. Four horses, as he had expected, pulling a big wagon with a heavy load. If there were other men in addition to the driver, he could not tell, but he had to assume there were.

The sharp clack of hooves and the deep rumble grew louder, blotting out what other faint sounds could be heard in the night. Delgadillo lifted the scrap of canvas that was covering the shuttered lantern at his feet and held the lantern at waist height. He pulled the pistol from his belt. In the bit of light leaking out around the lantern's closed door he checked that it was cocked.

He saw it, finally, in the light of the quarter moon: the team of four, the dark bulk of the wagon pulling behind. He could see shadows alongside which he took to be men walking beside the wagon. Armed men, he had to imagine. Five on the side he could see, so he guessed there was another five on the other.

Wait…wait… His thoughts were directed at his own men, but he did not dare give them voice.

Ten more feet and then Delgadillo stepped out from the trees and into the center of the road. He unshuttered the lantern and lifted it high, high enough that the light would gleam off the polished wheellock of the pistol he held leveled up at the driver.

"Hold!" Delgadillo called, more than loud enough to be heard over the hooves and the wheels. He heard the driver yell, "Ha!" and could just see him hauling back on the reins. One of the men walking beside the wagon called out, "What, ho?" Delgadillo heard weapons coming to hand.

Then there was more movement, a shuffling confusion as his own men stepped out of the dark. They had been positioned farther up the road, and had stood fast as the wagon rolled past the places where they were concealed. Now they came forward, knives and pistols all but pressing against the guards surrounding the wagon.

"Easy! Stand easy! No call for any to get hurt!" Delgadillo said, all but shouting. He took a step forward, raised the lantern a bit higher. He meant what he said, most sincerely. These men were soldiers from Fortaleza Ozama. His fellows. He reckoned he knew many of them. He did not want harm to come to any.

There was a pause, a moment of quiet, the only sound the restless motion and soft whinnying of the horses. Then Delgadillo said, "Weapons down, the lot of you! We won't ask again." He listened. He heard the grunt of men complying, of weapons being lowered. No one seemed inclined to resist. No surprise: this wagon was not something a man would willingly lay down his life to protect.

"Delgadillo?" It was the voice of the driver, up on the wagon's seat. Delgadillo stepped forward, lifted the lantern higher, and let the light fall on the man's face.

"Sánchez," Delgadillo said. "Good day to you." Delgadillo and Sánchez had been three years together in the same battalion. Sánchez was a decent enough man, a decent enough soldier. The sort who would remain in the ranks until he was killed by yellow fever, or sent as an old and broken man back to Spain.

"What in the name of God are you about?" Sánchez asked. There was more curiosity than anger in his voice, more surprise than outrage.

"I might ask the same about you," Delgadillo said. "Where are you taking this wagon, and at such an hour? The good people of Santo Domingo are trying to sleep, and you making such a racket."

"Taking this load of barrels to some poxed warehouse in lower town," Sánchez said. "Taking it now because I was told to take it now. And if you mean to steal it, I give you my blessing. A score of casks of salt beef? You'll make your fortune."

And that was all that Sánchez knew about what he was doing and why, Delgadillo was sure of it. There was no reason for Sánchez to know more, no reason for him to question his orders, unusual as they might have been, or even care why they were given. Caring was well above Sánchez's station in the great scheme of things.

"Steal these barrels?" Delgadillo said. "No, not at all. In truth, we've come to assist you in getting them to where they want to go."

"Is that what you've done? Damned strange way to go about it, hiding in the dark, coming out with guns loaded."

"I know, I know," Delgadillo said. "But it's true." He slipped the pistol back into his belt, then shut the door to the lantern. The darkness closed in again, and Delgadillo paused for a moment as his eyes adjusted. Then he walked past the horses and pulled himself up on the seat beside Sánchez.

"Listen here, the lot of you," Delgadillo called, half turning to address the men beside the wagon. "We're off to the warehouse, just as before. Nothing's changed, save that me and my men are with you. And you'll keep your mouths shut about that. Do so, and there's gold in it for you. Don't, and there's a bullet in the head. Understand?"

He waited. He heard grunting, which he figured was all the acknowledgement he was going to get, but it was enough.

"Now, I'll thank you all to dump the priming out of your pans. And you may go ahead, Sánchez. On your way."

They rolled on downhill for another quarter mile or so, and again there was nothing to hear above the sound of the horses and the wagon wheels. They could see pinpricks of light ahead of them, lower down; lanterns burning in the warehouse district, or along the docks. To the east, a smattering of lights marked where men stood deck watch on the ships that lay at anchor in the river, ships ranging from the massive galleons of Toledo's fleet to the sloops and brigantines that carried goods around the islands of the West Indies.

Delgadillo looked off to his left. A smaller road ran off at a sharp angle, back up toward the upper part of Santo Domingo. It was a road he had been looking for. He let the wagon drive on past before he said, "Hold up, Sánchez. Stop here."

Sánchez threw him a look—irritation, confusion—but he reined the horses back and pulled the lever for the brake and the wagon lurched to a stop. Delgadillo hopped down from the seat, walked back to where the two roads met, and gave two sharp whistles. He waited, no more than a few seconds, and received a third whistle in reply. That was followed by a snap of reins and the sound of another team of horses, another wagon, gathering way.

Delgadillo stepped aside, and a moment later this second wagon, nearly identical to the first, came rolling out of the dark. Like the wagon that Sánchez was driving, this wagon's bed was loaded with casks standing end-on. Unlike Sánchez's load, and invisible to anyone standing on the road, the casks were empty, their upper ends open to the sky.

"Very well," Delgadillo said. "Governor's Guard, off you go." With that, the men who had come with Delgadillo, twenty in all, climbed up onto the bed of the second wagon and onto the barrels. They stepped carefully, one barrel to the next, and then each man eased himself down into one of the empty casks. A few minutes, no more, and they were all secured and hidden from view.

"Remember what I said," Delgadillo spoke in a loud whisper to Sánchez's men who were still gathered around the wagon. "Gold for the man who keeps his mouth shut. A bullet for him who doesn't."

There was more grunting, and then nothing else. Delgadillo climbed back up on the seat beside Sánchez. He was not much worried about any of these men speaking out of turn. Like Sánchez, they were just doing what they were told to do. They had no notion of what was going on, and they had little enough interest. They had heard *gold* and *bullet*, and that would be enough to keep them in line.

"On your way now, Sánchez," Delgadillo said.

"Where to?"

"I told you…we're here to help you in your work. So wherever you were told to bring these casks, bring them there."

Sánchez frowned and shook his head. Then he released the brake and flicked the reins and once again the wagon rolled away downhill, this time with the rumble and clatter of the second wagon joining in the chorus.

The road began to flatten out as they neared the lower part of the town, and soon they were rolling past buildings on either side, mostly warehouses, hastily built of wooden planks or cheap brick. In between those, the odd tavern that catered to the sailors just off the ships, as well as chandleries, sailmakers, coopers, smiths, and the like. It was a grimy, ugly, dangerous section of the city. And, at the same time, it was the junction between Santo Domingo and the rest of the world, the sluice gate through which the great wealth of the capital flowed in and out.

Delgadillo and Sánchez did not speak as they rolled along down the narrow streets, which were all but deserted. Delgadillo's senses were sharp, ears listening for any sounds over the wagons' rumble, eyes searching the dark. He could catch only the odd glimpse of some figure or other moving through the shadows. He wondered who they were, what business they had at that hour. He wondered if they were there because of Sánchez and his wagon, or if they were involved in some other nefarious activity. Not that it mattered.

"Here we are," Sánchez said, nodding toward a warehouse that stood on their right. It was larger than most, its long front wall featureless, save for five sets of sliding doors, each big enough for a wagon to pass, and evenly spaced down the length of the building.

"Good," Delgadillo said. He knew the building; one of the warehouses belonging to Carlos Hernández, a merchant of dubious reputation. It was where Delgadillo had been told the wagon was heading. It seemed that Sánchez was not trying some clever ruse.

The wagon rolled past the first two doors, then Sánchez brought it to a stop just short of the third, and Delgadillo saw that they were not alone. A dozen men seemed to materialize out of the shadows, stepping out into the street, but still keeping their distance. Watching.

"Now what?" Delgadillo asked.

"Now, if they don't kill you, we go to work. You remember how to work, right?"

"I think so."

"Good," Sánchez said. "But they'll probably kill you."

One of those who had emerged from the shadows studied the wagon for a moment, looking it up and down. Apparently satisfied, he stepped over to the warehouse door and banged hard on it with his open hand; three quick strikes, a pause, then a fourth. From the other side of the door they heard a bolt sliding free.

The warehouse door rumbled as it slid open, rolling on iron wheels on an overhead track. There were lanterns lit inside, making pools of light in the cavernous space that fell on stacks of barrels and crates and bundles. Delgadillo remained seated, glancing around, fighting the urge to stand so he could better see what was happening. The men who had appeared in the street were not coming any closer. Everything seemed to be suspended and waiting.

Then Delgadillo heard footsteps from inside the warehouse, just one man at first, then others. Someone carrying a lantern stepped out through the door. The light from the lantern spilled over the warehouse wall and the road and the horses, and the man holding it lifted it high, looking up at Delgadillo and Sánchez on the wagon's seat. There was a pistol in his belt, what looked to be the hilt of a cutlass at his waist. His face, illuminated from the side by the uncertain light, looked ugly, harsh, animal-like.

For a long moment the man did not speak, just looked up at Sánchez, then over at Delgadillo, then back at Sánchez. Delgadillo recognized the man. He did not know his name, but he knew him as one of El Cinco. The Five. They did brutal work for whoever paid them the most, which just then was rumored to be the mayor, Don Nicolás Pérez de Maldonaldo. They did whatever they were told. They did not hesitate and they did not ask questions.

"Who's this?" the man asked Sánchez, jerking his head in Delgadillo's direction.

"Help," Sánchez said. He nodded toward the pistol in Delgadillo's belt. "Protection."

"Why're there two wagons?"

"They couldn't fit the lot of it in one," Sánchez said. "I was told it all had to come tonight."

Delgadillo remained expressionless as he thought, *You'll be well paid for that, my friend.* He was not sure why Sánchez was lying for him. He probably saw it as the option least likely to get him killed. And that was fine.

The man with the lantern turned to the others who had followed him out of the warehouse. "See what's in that other wagon," he said.

More footsteps on the cobbles, men moving around, then, a moment later, a voice called out, "Beef casks. Twenty, or so. That's what it looks to be."

The one with the lantern looked back at Delgadillo and Sánchez, his ugly face unreadable. Then he jerked his head toward the open door. "Very well," he said. "In you go."

Sánchez did not reply, just flicked the reins and hauled them over to one side and directed his team through the door and into the big, open space beyond. Delgadillo heard the second wagon rolling in behind. He heard the door rumble shut on its iron wheels.

Here we go, Delgadillo thought.

Sánchez, unbidden, dropped the reins, stood and climbed down from the wagon's seat. Delgadillo imagined that Sánchez had done this many times over the past week or so, that he and the ugly one with the lantern had their routine well established. No wonder the man had been suspicious when a second wagon appeared. He probably did not care for any change in the way things were done.

Delgadillo stood as well, climbed down, and found himself face to face with the ugly man. That part of the warehouse, meant for off-loading it seemed, was better lit than the rest, a half dozen lanterns hanging around, but still the ugly man held his lantern up and moved it closer to Delgadillo's face, squinting as he studied it. It was possible the man would recognize him, just as he had recognized the man, but Delgadillo could see nothing in his expression that suggested that he did.

A second man, one whom Delgadillo recognized as another of El Cinco, stepped up. The ugly one handed his lantern off to the man, his eyes never leaving Delgadillo.

"You recognize this miserable whore's son?" the ugly man said. The second man took a step closer, raised the lantern again. For a long moment he was silent, peering at Delgadillo.

"Maybe," the man said. "Not sure."

"He's from the garrison," Sánchez offered from the other side of the wagon. "The captain general said we needed more men. Like I said."

The ugly one did not respond and he did not look away. He rested his palm on the butt of the pistol stuck in his belt. "Give me your gun," he said.

Delgadillo shook his head. "I'm here to protect the cargo."

"Protecting's our job," the ugly one said. He pulled his own pistol free from his belt and held it, muzzle down, at his side. Not an immediate threat, but something close. "Now, give me your gun."

For a moment Delgadillo and the man just stared at one another. Then Delgadillo reached slowly for the pistol in his belt. He saw the muscles in the ugly one's arm twitch. The man did not know what Delgadillo meant to do, and neither did Delgadillo. He wrapped his fingers around the butt of the gun, keeping them far from the trigger, presenting no threat, just a man ready to hand a weapon over.

He heard a shout behind him, a thump, a man stumbling, another shout. "Bastards!" someone screamed and a pistol fired, loud like a cannon blast in the quiet and confined space.

Delgadillo's men, hidden in the barrels, had been found out.

The ugly man's head jerked over in the direction of the sound, his eyes wide in surprise, despite his admirable self-control. His arm began to bend, the pistol coming up from his side. He was a second too slow. Delgadillo's pistol was free, level, and Delgadillo shot the man in the chest.

Chapter Twelve

Delgadillo's arm jerked up with the recoil of his gun, the blast sounding abnormally loud in his ears. The ugly man's face registered shocked surprise, just for an instant, just for the length of time it took for the primer to ignite and for the gun to fire. Then he was flung backward, arms out. The horses in the traces whinnied loud in fright and stomped and thrashed their heads, but they did not bolt.

Somewhere behind him, Delgadillo heard Sánchez shout, "*En el nombre de Dios*!" He caught a glimpse of him diving to the floor and out of sight, but he did not turn and look. Rather, he flung his pistol at the second man, the one holding the lantern, and drew the sword from the scabbard at his side. Not his fine, new Governor's Guard sword—it was a cruder affair, but just as effective.

He took a step toward the man, bringing the sword back to deliver a slashing blow, but the man swung the lantern in an arc and flung it at Delgadillo. Delgadillo flinched and the lantern bounced off his upper arm and fell clattering to the floor, and by the time he turned back the man was ten feet away, racing for the cover of a nearby stack of casks.

There were footsteps behind him and Delgadillo swung around, sword up, but it was his own men, the Governor's Guard, who had been hidden in the barrels. The plan had been for them to remain undiscovered until Delgadillo gave the word, but it had not worked out that way. And so it was with such things.

"How many are there?" Delgadillo asked, as his men formed up around him.

"Don't know," came the only answer. "We killed two. Saw a half dozen run off."

Delgadillo nodded. It was silent in the big warehouse, suddenly and perversely silent, as if Delgadillo and his men were the only ones there, as if the others had vanished in the night. Which would be a grand thing, but Delgadillo did not think he and his men would get off so easily.

"Where'd they go?" another asked, his voice just above a whisper. That was the question. What the answer was, no one knew. Delgadillo cocked his head, listening. He could hear nothing, but his nerves were crackling like burning brush. He felt the threat hanging in the air.

"Let's get back, between the wagons," Delgadillo said, returning his sword to its scabbard. He had expected that the men guarding the warehouse would make a headlong rush at them. He had been hoping they would, because he felt certain the Governor's Guards' training and discipline would give them a big advantage in a standup fight such as that. But apparently the warehouse men were not going to do them that favor.

Behind him he heard the shuffling of feet as his men started to back away, looking for shelter between the wagons. The warehouse guards had pistols, that was certain, and they might have muskets as well. If so, they could take their time picking off Delgadillo's men, like birds in a tree, sheltered by the ample cover the warehouse offered. It's what Delgadillo would have done.

The man beside Delgadillo moved back, and then Delgadillo followed, his eyes searching the warehouse as he did. Thirty feet away stood a wall of casks, stacked four high. To the left of that and farther back were crates of some sort. Some areas were illuminated and others in deep shadow, where the light from the intermittent lanterns did not reach.

Delgadillo stepped around behind the wagon where his men were gathered. Sánchez and his men were there as well, and Sánchez glared at Delgadillo as he joined them.

"You came to help, you say?" Sánchez said. "Maybe we have different ideas of help."

"I didn't say who I was helping," Delgadillo said. "Are your men armed?"

"Some cutlasses. Some pistols," Sánchez said.

"Good. You better join with us in this fight. Those bastards out there," he nodded toward the warehouse, "don't think you're on their side. They'll show you no mercy." Sánchez grunted, but he did not reply.

Delgadillo heard a scurrying sound, feet moving on the stone floor somewhere off in the dark. It was proof at last that he and his men were not alone in the warehouse. Then he heard more sounds off to his left. One of his men turned sharply, looking behind them.

"They're circling around us," he said.

The villains…damn them…

To Delgadillo's right, from one of the dark corners of the warehouse, a muzzle flashed, a blast of light and smoke and noise. The man beside Delgadillo pitched forward, mouth and eyes wide with surprise, arms flailing out as if he was trying to break his fall. Delgadillo saw the torn fabric of his shirt, the bloody wound in his back.

It was a deadly shot. It was, apparently, a signal as well. The warehouse seemed to explode with small arms fire. The crack and flash of the guns came from the floor level and higher up, where men had climbed up onto stacks of casks and crates to shoot down on Delgadillo and Sánchez's men.

"Under the wagons! Under the wagons!" Delgadillo shouted, and men leapt to the floor, shuffling under the beds of the loaded wagons, shrinking from the gunfire. Three of Delgadillo's men were down, and two of Sánchez's, and of those only two were still moving.

Delgadillo was the last down, a bullet buzzing past his ear as he crouched and slid behind the wagon's wheel, the wagon that Sánchez had been driving. His men were shooting now, leaning out from under the wagons with pistols extended, firing where they saw the flashes of light because they could see no other targets at which to aim.

Damn me for a fool, Delgadillo thought.

He had not considered that the men guarding the warehouse would put up so vigorous and organized a defense: a stupid and needless mistake. And now he and his men were trapped, an island of wagons and horses, well-lit and surrounded by an enemy they could not see.

Bullets made cracking sounds as they bounced off the stone floor and thumping sounds as they hit the sides of the wagons and the barrels stacked in the beds. One of Delgadillo's men shouted and dropped the pistol he had been aiming as a bullet ripped through his shoulder. The gun hit the floor and fired uselessly as the man pulled back, one hand clapped on the wound, blood running out from between his fingers.

The heavy, ironbound wheels of the wagons ground back and forth on the warehouse floor as the horses tugged and pulled at their traces. The animals were on the edge of panic, and it seemed a miracle to Delgadillo that they had not bolted yet. He reckoned it was just a matter of minutes, or less, and then he and his men would be fully exposed, if they were not first crushed under the wheels.

And that gave Delgadillo the first genuine idea he had had since the gunfire began.

"All of you, under the other wagon! Go, go!" he called to the men crouched around him, but they just looked at him, confused, uncertain. He pointed to the second wagon, the one behind them. "Go! Under that wagon! Go, quick!"

With that they seemed to understand. One after another they shuffled to the back of the bed, then flung themselves across the open space, keeping low, sheltering behind the frightened horses, then under the second wagon. Finally, Delgadillo alone remained under Sánchez's wagon.

He moved in a deep crouch, tucking in behind the front wheel, peering out between the spokes. The flashes of gunfire from the dark places reminded him of fireflies on a summer night, but the sound of the bullets striking, the wounded moaning and pleading, the terrified horses, seemed more like Hell itself.

He turned to the second wagon, where the rest of the men were sheltering now, and shouted, "When the casks come down, you move!" He did not wait to see if they understood: if they didn't, they soon would. He made the Sign of the Cross, then swung himself around the wagon wheel and stood.

A bullet smacked into the side of the wagon a foot in front of him, making a jagged hole in the plank, but he was committed now. He raced forward, six steps, and clambered up into the driver's seat. The *pistoleros* hidden in the dark had seen him, and the bullets buzzed around his head and made thumping sounds in the wood. He felt a hot slash across his arm, like a cut from a razor, where a bullet grazed his flesh, leaving a long tear in his shirt and a brilliant red wound he could see through the cloth.

He grabbed up the reins and held them in his left hand. He reached around with his right for the hilt of his sword. The terrified horses would need only the slightest prodding to break and run, and he reckoned the point of a sword should do it. But he never found out.

Even as his fingers wrapped around the leather-bound hilt, a bullet slammed into the rump of the left lead horse, opening a bloody gash, then hit the right horse as it passed. Both animals reared, as much as their harnesses would allow, screaming and kicking, then came down and bolted forward. Delgadillo was flung sideways into the seat and just managed to keep hold of the reins as the panic spread to the wheel horses, and the four of them charged ahead, the only thing they could do.

"Ah…you dumb bastards!" Delgadillo shouted, struggling to get upright again. This was what he wanted the horses to do, but on his command, not theirs. He pushed himself halfway up, saw the great stack of casks just ahead and to the right, and he hauled the reins hard over.

Whether he had any control over the terrified animals, or whether they were well beyond that, he could not tell, but he pulled hard and kept pulling. The lead horses veered off, turning to the right, toward the wall of casks. Delgadillo did not know if they were responding to the reins or to their own blind panic, and he did not care. They were going where he wanted them to go.

Five steps, no more, and the lead horse and wheel horse on the right-hand side brushed by the stack of casks with inches to spare. Delgadillo dropped the reins and pressed his feet down and braced himself as the corner of the wagon slammed into the lower tier of casks. The wagon skittered off sideways, dragging the horses with it, and Delgadillo had a glimpse of the barrels crashing down, rolling and tumbling, and behind them, a dozen or more men, the pistoleros, scattering like roaches.

The warehouse was filled with thunderous noise: the rumble and crash of the falling casks, the grinding of the wagon wheels on the stone floor, the scream of the terrified horses, the scream of the warehouse guards as the barrels rolled down on them, the crack of pistols and muskets, the shouts of men as they reacted to this sudden turn.

Delgadillo braced himself again as the wagon continued to slide sideways, spinning to the left as it careened off the casks. It slammed into the stack of crates on the other side and the impact flung him across the seat. The crates, stacked fifteen feet high, went toppling over, flying in every direction and shattering into hundreds of wooden slats. Delgadillo flung his arms over his head as the remains of the crates and their contents rained down on him.

The horses, more panicked than ever, continued their terrified flight, but now the wagon's wheels were tangled up in shattered wood, and the wagon began to tilt as it rode over the debris. Delgadillo clawed at the seat, trying to right himself, trying to get clear before the wagon rolled over and crushed him underneath. He pulled himself halfway up, wedged a foot against the floor, and that was as far as he got before the wagon turned sideways and came crashing down.

For a confused instant Delgadillo had the odd sensation of being weightless, and he was not sure why. Then his shoulder hit the stone floor and the pain exploded through his upper body and he knew he had been thrown clear of the wagon. He felt himself tumbling along, felt the floor shaking as the casks, spilling out of the wagon's bed, came rolling past, and even through the shock and the pain he wondered if one of them would roll right over him and crush him underneath.

He stopped rolling and lay still for a moment. When he was sure he had sustained no major injuries he got his hands under him, pushed himself up to a half-sitting position, and looked around.

The horses were bucking and kicking and pulling, but they could not budge the overturned wagon, tangled as it was in broken crates and barrels. In front of him, the once neatly stacked wall of casks was now a chaotic jumble. A handful of the warehouse guards lay sprawled on the floor where they had been knocked down like pins in a game of bowls. Others were still standing, pistols or swords in hand. They seemed stunned, bracing themselves as Delgadillo's men came charging up and over the pile of casks, or racing around the debris, shouting, swords out.

Delgadillo groaned as he forced himself to his feet and pulled the sword from its scabbard. He took a step forward just as the first of his men fell on the first of the warehouse guards, sword on sword, the ring of blades adding yet another sound to the great din.

He heard steps to his right and he turned as a figure raced out of the shadows, a cutlass in one hand, a massive knife like a short sword in the other. Delgadillo recognized him; he was one of El Cinco, the one who had run off when Delgadillo had shot the first man. But he was not running away now.

The cutlass was up, over the man's head, and it came down at Delgadillo in an awkward, slashing stroke, but even as Delgadillo parried the attack he knew that that was not the blade to worry about. He stepped back just as the long knife came sweeping around. He felt the point slice through the cloth of his jerkin. An inch closer and he would have been disemboweled.

Delgadillo felt something else as he stepped back—a shooting, stabbing pain up his leg, some injury from his tumble, unnoticed until now. He clenched his teeth, tried to push the pain back even as he lunged forward, the point of his sword driving for the other man's chest.

The big knife came swinging around again. It connected with Delgadillo's blade and knocked it out of line, an inch shy of Delgadillo running the man through. The man took a step closer—he favored the knife, Delgadillo could see that—and stabbed upward. Delgadillo grabbed his wrist with his left hand, and with his right he slammed the knuckle-guard of his sword into the man's face, sending him staggering back. The blood was flowing from his nose even before he had regained his footing.

The man reached up and touched his broken nose, which was a mistake. Delgadillo took two quick steps and lunged. He would have skewered the man had his knee not half-buckled as he went forward. The man jumped back, knocked Delgadillo's sword aside with his knife, then stepped in with his cutlass for the counterattack.

It was an awkward move, and the man's last. Delgadillo swatted the cutlass aside and extended his sword, not so much running the man through as letting him run onto the blade, which he did. His eyes went wide, blood erupting from his mouth and joining that running down from his nose. Delgadillo pulled the blade free and turned away. He heard the man's body thud against the stone floor but he did not watch him fall.

There was still fighting going on beyond the collapsed stack of casks, his men and the warehouse guards. Some were fighting in the pools of light from the lanterns, others seemed like mere shadows, battling it out in the darker corners. But it was tapering off. The falling mountain of casks had sent the guards into confusion, and Delgadillo's men, pouncing at just the right moment, had swept them away. But they would not get off that easily, Delgadillo was all but certain of that.

There must be more of them, Delgadillo thought, more men guarding the warehouse than just the ones he could see now. The mayor, he understood, had taken little chance with his precious casks of beef. They were too hard to come by, the payout—in terms of gold and Toledo's gratitude—too great to risk, so he had made certain they were well-guarded.

Delgadillo looked off into the darker recesses of the warehouse and saw that was right. A hundred feet away, coming out from behind the shelter of another row of casks, from the place where they had been firing on the two wagons, were another twenty men at least. They might have been unsure what was happening, but now they seemed ready to join the fight.

"Governor's Guards!" Delgadillo shouted. "Governor's Guards! Stand ready, there's more of them!" He pointed with his sword toward this new threat, and those of his men who were not still fighting turned and looked, first at him, and then at where he was pointing.

"Form rank! Form rank!" Delgadillo shouted. His men had to stand together and meet this new onslaught as a unit, not each man to himself. He started limping toward them as they hurried to make a half-circle, forming up shoulder to shoulder, a human redoubt, swords in their right hands, the shorter *main-gauche* in the left.

The warehouse guards, those who had just emerged from their cover, were racing toward the fight, clambering over the tumble of casks or hurrying around the scattered pile. Delgadillo reached his men just as the first of them came at the line, cutlass swinging. It was a wild and undisciplined attack, and a sword thrust from one of Delgadillo's men ended it quickly.

The rest of the mayor's men did not attack in such a fashion. They came on as a group—by design or accident it was not clear—but they rolled up on Delgadillo's men like a massive wave, weapons swinging, screaming as they advanced. There was no discipline, no coordination, but there was fury and there was power and numbers and those things were nearly overwhelming. Delgadillo's men parried and stabbed and stepped back against the attack. One fell, then another.

"Hold fast! Cut them down, cut the villains down!" Delgadillo shouted. He was working his sword as hard as ever he had, fending off their attacks: a sword from the left, a long knife from the right, even a fist from the man directly in front of him, which Delgadillo countered with a blow from his knuckle-guard and a lunge with his sword as the man staggered back. He did not know how long his men could stand against that onslaught. Not much longer, he thought.

Behind them, over the din of the fight, he heard another sound, one he had heard earlier: the squeal of the iron wheels from which the warehouse doors hung, followed by the rumble of the door sliding open. He heard the clatter of shoes on stone, felt a waft of cool air coming in from the street.

What new devils are these? he wondered. He had seen a handful of men lurking in the alleys as they approached the warehouse, and he suspected there were many more who had remained unseen. If they were joining the fight now, then it would be over very quickly indeed.

He slashed at the man in front of him, forcing him back, then took the moment's reprieve to glance behind. He could see men moving in the dark, charging through the shadowy places, hurrying toward them. He caught the flash of steel in lantern light.

He turned back to the fight: a knife, inches shy of eviscerating him. Delgadillo slammed his knuckle-guard down on the blade. "Behind you!" he shouted, "Behind you!" but he knew his men could not turn and look. That would be instant death.

The footsteps were close now, coming up behind. Delgadillo tensed for a blade in the back, but no blade came. Instead, the newcomers rushed in from the left and right, slamming into the flanks of the warehouse guards' disorganized line, cutting them down where they stood.

These men, like Delgadillo's, were dressed in laborer's clothes, but Delgadillo knew now who they were: they were the rest of the Governor's Guard. The warehouse men broke and ran before them. They raced off into the dark, throwing weapons away as they ran. The Governor's men pursued them in their flight for twenty or thirty feet before abandoning the effort.

One of those who had just arrived turned now and faced Delgadillo. He wore leather breeches and a wool doublet that gaped open across the chest from a rent in the fabric, a clean tear that looked as if it had been delivered by a sharp blade. There was a smear of blood on his cheek and a constellation of dark spots—also blood, most likely—on his clothing.

"Don Alonso," Delgadillo said, giving a respectful nod of the head.

"Captain," Don Alonso said. He looked around the warehouse, his eyes moving over the heaps of casks, the overturned wagon, the horses standing quiet now, exhausted, the dead and wounded men strewn about. "A bit of excitement?"

"More than I'd reckoned on."

Alonso nodded. "Us as well. A damned sight more men guarding the streets than I had thought. Which is why we were so late. You have my apologies."

"Thank you, Don Alonso, but there's no need to apologize," Delgadillo said. "We underestimated the mayor. Didn't appreciate how eager he would be to protect his investment."

That was their plan from the start, and it had nearly worked. Delgadillo and his handful of men would gain entry to the warehouse by way of the wagons, and once in, Alonso would lead the rest of the Governor's Guard in from the street. They had dared hope that if they timed the thing just right, and if the warehouse was not heavily guarded, then they could take the mayor's casks like taking an egg from a hen. No fighting, no one killed.

Such was the way of plans. Alonso and his men had been so late in arriving that Delgadillo had started to despair of their showing up at all.

"No, we did not appreciate that," Alonso agreed. "But clearly he's worried. Which will make this whole thing all the sweeter."

Delgadillo turned to the others. "Whoever of you isn't hurt, off with you and round up those whore's sons who ran off. Make a sweep right through this place. And take care—they might have some fight left in them."

Some of the men nodded. Some who were loading pistols, or binding wounds, or looting the dead warehouse men, took a moment to finish the job. Then they moved off carefully, spreading out, eyes everywhere, a human net looking to catch the mayor's fish. And as they did, Carlos Hernández appeared from behind the remaining crates.

He stepped with care through the field of debris, looking around at the destruction that had been wrought on his warehouse. His expression did not change as he took in the toppled wagon, the smashed crates, the tumble of casks, the pools of blood on the stone floor.

"I did not count on a Holy War happening in my building, *señores*," he said, moving closer to Delgadillo and Alonso.

"And we did not count on so many of the mayor's men being here," Alonso said. He did not try to hide the accusation in his voice.

Hernández shrugged. "There were not so many this afternoon. The mayor doubled the guard this evening. Tripled it, perhaps."

"Why would he do such a thing?" Alonso demanded.

"I don't know, señor. Perhaps he's growing nervous. He's promised Toledo he'll provide all the salt beef the fleet needs, and tomorrow the great admiral will send his boats to collect it. Perhaps the mayor is afraid of anything happening at this late hour to ruin his plans."

"Strange, that he would think such a thing. Could he have had some hint about plots unfolding?" Again Alonso made the accusation clear as a pistol shot.

"There is no one who is taking a greater risk with this business than me, señor," Hernández said, sounding both servile and outraged. "Don Nicolás cannot see you hanged, as he can me. And he will, if I'm found out. I'm the one who opened the door for you, just this moment."

Alonso made a grunting sound and said nothing more. Delgadillo did not know what to think. To him, Hernández's protest sounded entirely sincere, but then Hernández was a crafty one.

What I think does not matter in the least.

"We don't have much time, señor, and we have much to do," Hernández said next, as if that last exchange had never happened. "When your men are back we must be at it."

"When my men are back, we'll set the prisoners to it," Alonso said. "Now, what among this is what we need?"

"These casks here," Hernández said, indicating the jumble of casks that Delgadillo had knocked down with the runaway wagon, "these are the new stores, the ones Don Nicolás has collected. The rotten meat that the admiral's purser sent over, that's at the far end of the warehouse, nearest to the docks."

"Good, good," Alonso said. He, too, seemed to have forgotten his suspicions of a moment before. From the other end of the warehouse they heard footsteps, and the Governor's Guard reappeared, driving the mayor's men—the erstwhile protectors of Don Nicolás's most precious stores of salted beef—before them, like *vaqueros* driving cattle.

"Here we are," Alonso said. "Let us get to work."

Chapter Thirteen

LeBoeuf brought the boat alongside his ship and Billy Solent grabbed the chains with the boat hook. LeBoeuf gave Other Dog a boost up the boarding steps and scrambled up behind. Billy tossed him the bow line and he made it fast and the others climbed up behind him.

"I didn't know you spoke English," Billy Solent said in English.

"I don't," LeBoeuf said in French.

"Heard you speak English," Billy said.

"Thought I was speaking Dutch," LeBoeuf said.

Billy Solent looked at him as if trying to decide whether LeBoeuf was as dim-witted as he seemed or if he was just acting that way. LeBoeuf did not let him ponder long.

"Come along, we have to keep those bastards on the sandbar. Tide's falling. If they're not off in an hour, they're there for the next twelve."

The other ship, Van Loudersong's ship, was about six hundred feet away. LeBoeuf could see men climbing down into the boat tied alongside, and he had no doubt they meant to set a kedge anchor astern and try to haul the ship off the sand. And he meant to discourage that activity.

He considered the relative positions of the two ships. They were both pointing generally south, held in place by the last of the incoming tide. *Charles Rex* was astern of LeBoeuf's ship and off her starboard quarter.

LeBoeuf's ship, the former Spanish ship, as yet unnamed, was flush-decked, save for a quarterdeck raised four feet. On the main deck she carried bastard culverings, cannons firing seven-pound shot, eight per side. It was possible that the aftermost gun on the starboard would bear on *Charles Rex* if they could train it around far enough. But it would be close.

"We'll see what we can do with this," LeBoeuf said, pointing to the aft gun, starboard side. "Get it cleared away. You know the use of such ordnance?"

The four men nodded their heads.

"Good. Let's be at it."

This would not have been a tall order aboard a ship better prepared. But the buccaneers were not prepared. The vessel had not long been theirs, and they had done nothing with the guns, save to sit on them occasionally. Rammers, sponges, ladles, powder, shot, wadding, match all had to be found. Le Chasseur and Genet fell to casting off the breechings that held the gun lashed in place, while the rest of them went below and rummaged around for the gear and supplies they needed.

Powder was discovered in a small magazine all but hidden behind the cables on the cable tier. Rammers, sponges, and the other necessities were found forward, by the manger, on top of a stack of old sails. The minutes wasted in searching drove LeBoeuf nearly to madness, but eventually men and gear were all assembled on the weather deck.

They could find no powder cartridges made up, so LeBoeuf ladled loose powder down the barrel of the gun. Le Chasseur rammed a wadding after that and Billy Solent selected the roundest shot and stuck that in next. When all was ready they grabbed onto the train tackles and hauled away, two men per side, straining to run the three thousand pound gun out the gunport. LeBoeuf leaned over and sighted down the barrel.

"Get those handspikes here, train it right around, all the way around."

Genet and Steen stepped up, jammed their spikes in the deck and leaned into them. Inch by inch the bastard culvering was levered around until it was trained as far aft as it would go, its muzzle pointing to some place beyond *Rex*'s transom.

"Good, good," LeBoeuf said. He snatched up a powder horn and spilled powder into the touchhole. Le Chasseur had managed to get the match on the linstock lit and he handed it to LeBoeuf, who continued sighting down the barrel.

Through the gunport LeBoeuf could see *Charles Rex*'s boat. It was under the transom and they were lowering the kedge anchor down to it. A cable from the anchor ring was run through the transom window.

What, just getting the kedge aboard now? LeBoeuf thought. That was not very handily done, which told LeBoeuf the other ship was poorly manned, either in numbers or skill. Good to know.

Six hundred feet away, the men in *Charles Rex*'s boat settled the kedge anchor on the davits astern and lower their oars into the tholes. They would row the anchor out astern of the ship, drop it, and then others aboard the ship would heave away on the capstan, hauling the anchor cable in. If they were lucky, they would drag the ship off the sand before the falling tide left them stuck until the next high water.

And, in rowing the anchor out, the boat would pass right through LeBoeuf's line of fire. He had one shot, because once the boat had gone past, the gun would not train far enough around to reach it again.

"Stand clear," LeBoeuf said, hunched over the gun. He grabbed the quoin and pulled it out an inch, raising the elevation of the barrel. He had never fired this gun, had no idea what it would do. A hit would take a damned lot of good fortune.

The boat was making way now. LeBoeuf pressed his lips together and waited. A second for the priming to burn, a second for the gun to fire and the ball to traverse the distance, it all had to be accounted for.

Still hunched over, LeBoeuf saw that the bow of the boat was now passing directly in front of the gun. He straightened and brought the match down on the touchhole. The powder fizzled and smoked and sparked, and then the gun went off with a great roar, leaping back against its breechings, missing LeBoeuf's toes by inches.

LeBoeuf did not see the gun pass his toes. His eyes were on the boat, a cable length away. He saw the dark streak of the flying shot, saw the oars in disarray as the surprised rowers lost their stroke. He saw the plume of water shoot up as the round shot landed fifty feet beyond the boat and twenty feet to the right.

Merde, LeBoeuf thought. That was his one shot, and it was not even close.

"Load it again?" Le Chasseur asked.

"Yes," LeBoeuf said, not because he had any hope of getting another shot to bear, but to keep the men busy while he thought of what to do next. As they fell to swabbing out the barrel and ladling more powder in, he stepped back and looked astern. The *Rex*'s boat was struggling against the weight of the cable as they hauled the kedge out far enough to drop. Once the anchor was down they would start heaving on the capstan, but they would not have much time.

LeBoeuf stepped over to the bulwark, pulled a spare belaying pin from the pinrail, and tossed it overboard. The pin landed with a splash ten feet away, bobbed up and down and then stopped, floating motionless, not moving in or out with the tide. Slack water.

He turned to the others who were just running the loaded gun back out. "The lot of you, start loading the guns on the larboard side. Load them all, starting aft and moving forward."

Looks of confusion, glances at the starboard battery, but then the men were moving, racing across the deck and casting off the breechings on the two aftermost guns. They did not ask what LeBoeuf had in mind, and LeBoeuf did not know if they had guessed, nor did he care. They were doing as he told them. That was all that mattered.

He hurried aft. The brails that held the lateen mizzen sail up were tied off near the base of the mizzen mast. He loosened them off and let them go and the triangular sail dropped and hung from the yard, rippling and flogging in the breeze. LeBoeuf grabbed onto the sheet, hauled it tight, and the sail quieted down as the wind caught and filled it.

The four-man gun crew had finished with the aftermost guns and moved on to the next two forward, working with admirable speed. LeBoeuf looked astern. The boat was fifty feet from the other ship, nearly in place to drop the kedge.

"It's slack water," LeBoeuf explained as the men worked at the guns. "Tide's not holding us, so this easterly wind will swing us around, and these guns to larboard will come to bear as we turn. We'll get one shot from each as we swing past."

He saw heads nodding as the men realized what he had in mind. The wind and the turning tide would swing the ship through one hundred and eighty degrees, swinging the larboard battery past *Charles Rex*. That was their chance.

"Here we go," LeBoeuf said, as the pressure of the wind in the sail started pushing the ship around. He grabbed the linstock and ran aft to the aftermost gun. No need to train it around, the ship would do that, but the elevation had to be right. He sighted over the barrel. He recalled that his first effort had put the shot too high, so he levered the breech end of the barrel up and pushed the quoin in to lower the muzzle.

The ship was turning now, very slowly. It was agonizing, but it would give LeBoeuf more time to lay each gun. He could see *Charles Rex*'s longboat, nearly in place to drop the kedge, and he could see it would be under his gun presently. He stepped clear of the recoil and sighted down the barrel, through the gunport.

He could see only water at first, and the beach and jungle beyond, sweeping slowly past. And then the boat was there, coming into view. LeBoeuf waited a second more, waited until the muzzle was even with the bow of the boat, then drove the match down into the priming powder.

He straightened as the priming flared, and looked out over the bulwark as the gun blasted away. He saw the ball skipping across the water, making a series of small splashes as it flew directly at the longboat. Then he saw it take one last splash, right into the side of a small wave, and it was gone.

Too low, LeBoeuf thought, and he raced to the next gun. He leaned over, adjusted the quoin. The ship was turning faster now, and LeBoeuf did not have the gun exactly where he wanted it when he saw the longboat over the barrel.

No more time, he thought. He stepped aside, put the match into the priming. Once again the gun roared and leapt back against its breeching. LeBoeuf's eyes were on the longboat. He did not see the flight of the shot that time, did not see it fall. But he did see a goodly part of the midsection disappear, like a sorcerer's trick, as the ball struck and plowed on through. Two of the rowers amidships simply vanished, blown out the far side of the boat, and the remaining men froze in surprise and panic.

The heavy anchor cable hung dripping in a great arc from the stern of the ship to the kedge anchor hanging from the boat's transom. With the pull of the oars suddenly gone, the weight of the cable began dragging the boat backwards through the water, losing every foot of distance the rowers had so painfully made. LeBoeuf could see the oars flailing like the limbs of some wounded sea creature.

And then the stern end of the boat was dragged under by the weight of the anchor and the water flooding in. The boat disappeared, leaving the crew clinging like wrack to the cable.

"Ha! You got them, LeBoeuf!" Le Chasseur called, loud with delight. "Good shooting!" The others were smiling as well. Pleased with themselves.

"You men did good, serving the guns," LeBoeuf said. "Fast."

The compliment was sincere. It was no mean task to load and run out a gun with a dead weight of well over a ton, particularly for a short-handed gun crew that had not drilled together. LeBoeuf wondered if any of these rogues were former men-of-war's men. He knew nothing about their origins, just as they knew nothing about his. It was part of the appeal of the buccaneers.

"Shall we keep it up?" Le Chasseur asked. Firing great guns was always amusing, but there was nothing like doing real hurt to inspire further action.

LeBoeuf, however, had already considered that question. Even if the guns would bear on the stranded ship, a bastard culvering could not do enough damage at that range to make it worth using up the powder and shot. Whatever Spaniard had supplied their ship, he had not been overly generous with either.

"No," LeBoeuf said. "We'll save our powder until we can engage them on the morrow. I sure as damnation am not done with Van Loudersong."

That decision made, there was nothing left but the waiting. LeBoeuf was used to that. Waiting was always part of this sort of thing: waiting for wind or tide, waiting to see if an enemy would appear where you thought they would, waiting for a fight to commence. The waiting was always the worst of it. Save for death, or grievous wounding.

LeBoeuf had a pretty good idea of how things would play out if the night went as expected, and oddly enough, it did. The tide ran out and the sun set and the two ships remained where they were, enemies staring warily at one another across six hundred feet of water.

In the dark hours, the people on Van Loudersong's ship manned another boat, retrieved the kedge anchor and set it again, ready to haul the vessel off when the water rose. LeBoeuf and the others could hear it all, coming over the water: the clack of the capstan, the creak of the oars in the tholes, the hushed call of men trying not to be heard. Just as LeBoeuf had guessed.

There was no moon, and the men in the distant boat carried no lantern, because a lantern meant a target for the guns that had already claimed one boat and two men at least. There was some discussion among the buccaneers about shooting at them anyway, or attacking from a boat of their own, but LeBoeuf shut that down. Shooting was a waste, and the boat was too risky. One lucky blast with the falconet, and LeBoeuf's entire crew was gone. As it was, if D'Anton and the rest of the men did not make it back before the other ship was free of the sand, there would be little they could do except wave to Van Loudersong as he sailed away.

LeBoeuf set a watch, three turns of the glass for each man, but he was not too confident about their vigilance. They had managed to find some wine onboard, and had put enough down their throats to dull their senses, but it did not really matter. Other Dog was standing watch as well, and her eyes and ears were better than even the most alert and sober human watch-stander.

Sure enough, it was sometime in the middle of the second watch, with Steen keeping the deck, when Other Dog began to growl, low and menacing, and pace back and forth, staring out the gunports into the dark.

LeBoeuf was instantly awake, as was Steen, who had dozed off. LeBoeuf hushed the dog and listened. He could hear nothing, but that was neither here nor there. He trusted Other Dog's senses far more than his own.

"Up, up!" he called to the others. "To arms!" They had been sleeping with their loaded muskets beside them, and now they jumped to their feet and rested the guns on the bulwark, pointing out into the dark. A moment later they could hear it: the splash of oar blades in the water, the creak of the looms. LeBoeuf relaxed a bit. It was not Van Loudersong. The Dutchman would have known to muffle the oars.

A moment later a voice called from out over the water. "LeBoeuf! It's D'Anton! I'm with the others!" There was no mistaking the man's voice, his French heavy with the accent of Africa's Ivory Coast.

"Good, good! Come alongside, the lot of you!" LeBoeuf called, and the rest lowered their guns as the first of the boats materialized out of the dark. One by one the boats ran up to the boarding steps and the men climbed aboard, until all thirty or so were gathered on the deck. It was a reassuring sight. They were tough men, good in a fight. Armed and motivated.

"Here's how it stands," LeBoeuf said to the assembled company. "Van Loudersong's found some confederates who have a ship. It's stuck hard on a sandbar just now. You passed it in the dark. Next high water they'll float free and be off to fetch the gold that should be ours. D'Anton told you of Van Loudersong's treachery?"

Heads nodded. Men scowled.

"Well, we'll put a stop to it," LeBoeuf said. "Turn of the tide."

"Why not attack now?" someone asked. "In the boats?"

LeBoeuf shook his head. "Don't know how many are aboard that ship. Anyway, you can be sure they've made ready for us. Great guns loaded with grape. Falconets. A couple of lucky shots and we're done for."

Those words struck home, as LeBoeuf thought they might. These men would be happy to fight, but not so happy to be ripped apart by grapeshot, so there was no more talk of a night attack. The new arrivals found places on the deck to sleep, snug beside their muskets; Other Dog resumed her patrol, and the bulk of the night passed with tranquil calm.

There was just a hint of dawn when LeBoeuf began to nudge men awake. Across the water he could make out the vague shape of Van Loudersong's ship. Or he thought he could. But he could certainly hear activity there, the unmistakable sound of men taking up on a capstan.

"You men, get aloft, loosen off the topsails!" he said, loud enough to be heard, emphatic enough to be obeyed. Groaning, grumbling, the men stood and shuffled off to the shrouds and made their way aloft. They were bound to complain, but they had turned in relatively sober, so it was not so bad.

By the time the men came down from aloft the light was spreading over the water, the island of Tortuga a dark wall to the north, the harbor blueish-gray. Van Loudersong's ship was moving, inching its way astern, the kedge anchor cable rising up out of the sea as the men heaved the capstan around. LeBoeuf could not tell if the vessel was floating yet, but if not, it would be soon.

His own ship was lying stern to Van Loudersong's. High water, LeBoeuf guessed, and the tide just turning now. The wind was from the east, as it usually was, and blowing an easy eight knots. Perfect.

"Any here know how to rig the messenger on the capstan?" LeBoeuf asked.

Billy Solent raised his hand, as did Le Chasseur and a few others who LeBoeuf had reckoned were proper seamen, so he set them to it. When that was done, the less useful hands were put on the capstan bars and the nippers, short lines used to temporarily lash the cable to the messenger. The men with more salt water in their blood were set to the sheets and braces.

"Should we load the great guns first?" Le Chasseur asked. He was standing amidships, the starboard foresheet in hand.

"No," LeBoeuf said. He was not in the habit of explaining himself, and Le Chasseur could be God's own pain in the ass, but he went so far as to add, "We'll head for open water first. Too much chance of running aground here. Heave away on the capstan!"

Forward, the men began to walk the capstan around, and the ship began its slow progress ahead as it was hauled up to the anchor. Billy Solent, leaning over the bow, yelled "Short rope!" as the ship approached the spot where the anchor had been dropped, and then, "Up and under!" when they were right over it. He said the words in French, for LeBoeuf's benefit, and they were not quite the right words, but LeBoeuf knew what he meant.

"Sheet home the topsails! Hands to the halyards!" LeBoeuf called and the clews of the two topsails were hauled out and the yards hoisted up the topmasts. The sails flogged until the yards were braced around, and then they filled and the ship heeled a bit and began to make headway, with the warm trade wind on the larboard quarter.

LeBoeuf looked astern. Van Loudersong's ship was free of the sand and setting sail as well, fore and main topsails.

Sea room, LeBoeuf thought.

They had to get clear of the sandbars so they would have room to maneuver, room to fight. Half a mile from shore would be enough, but they could not do battle among the shallows and the coral heads. He did not know how well-trained or able the crew of Van Loudersong's ship was, but until shown otherwise he had to assume they were better than the buccaneers.

LeBoeuf did know, of course, that it was not really Van Loudersong's ship. He guessed it belonged to the heavy, bearded man who had taken the helm after LeBoeuf shot the helmsman. Or perhaps he was just the ship's master. The dark man with the red head cloth had been aft on the quarterdeck as well, but what role he played, LeBoeuf could not guess.

There was more that LeBoeuf did not know. He did not know who the heavy man was, or, more importantly, if he had friends on Tortuga. If he did, there was no saying how many of his fellows might come out to help if LeBoeuf fought him too close to shore.

They needed sea room.

"Let's get the great guns loaded!" LeBoeuf called down the deck. "Le Chasseur, Levesque, Lessard, Billy Solent, pick gun crews and take charge of two guns each, one larboard, one starboard. Get them ready for action. Anyone else who knows the use of guns, join in. The rest, stand by the ropes! Steen, take the tiller!"

The Dutchman, Joost Steen, who seemed to have familiarity with such things, took the tiller from LeBoeuf. The rest scrambled to their various places, and fell to loading the guns or carrying up more powder or shot, or finding the ropes they would need to haul when the time came.

LeBoeuf could see the sandbars lurking beneath the surface as they slipped past, the dark shapes of the coral heads. He was sorry to not have Van Loudersong aloft this time. The man might be a lying villain and a murderous bastard, but he had proved himself a good seaman, and for that LeBoeuf could forgive a lot.

A lot, but not everything. And that morning LeBoeuf meant to offer Van Loudersong no forgiveness.

The last of the sandbars passed astern and LeBoeuf felt himself relax. There was only open water ahead, or so he was fairly certain. Van Loudersong's ship was in their wake, and half a mile behind.

Soon…

One by one the great guns were hauled up to their gunports, loaded and ready. LeBoeuf looked out over the open water ahead, Hispaniola in the distance. He looked astern. Van Loudersong's ship was gathering way. He turned his head into the wind, felt the breeze on his face.

"Set the foresail!" he called, and with a little prompting the hands at the foresail gear let go the clewlines and buntlines and martnets and the sail dropped and filled as it was sheeted home. LeBoeuf felt the ship surging forward underfoot, felt it heel a bit farther over.

They stood on south, with the wind on the larboard beam, then bore up to work to windward of Van Loudersong's ship. The yards were braced sharp up, the larboard tack hove taut as the ship drove as nearly upwind as she could. Once Van Loudersong's ship was clear of the shallows, LeBoeuf meant to turn and swoop down on her like a bird of prey.

For nearly one turn of the glass they stood on like that, Van Loudersong's ship creeping through the shallows and coral heads, LeBoeuf's sailing almost directly away from them as if trying to flee. LeBoeuf's eyes were everywhere: on Van Loudersong's ship, aloft at the set of his sails, looking down the length of his deck at the men standing ready at the guns and the lines, out to windward at the ripples marking the wind on the water.

"We're going to come about!" LeBoeuf shouted down the deck. "Billy Solent, take charge of the foremast! Le Chasseur, the main! Genet, come aft and get ready to back this mizzen when I give the word!"

It was time to turn, to charge down on Van Loudersong, but tacking was a tricky business and LeBoeuf was not certain his crew was familiar enough with the evolution to pull it off.

Reckon we'll see.

"Steen, put your helm alee," LeBoeuf called. The Dutchman pushed the tiller over and the ship's bow swung up into the wind. The weather leeches of the sails began to flog and LeBoeuf called, "Mainsail, haul!" The yards swung around and the ship, slowly, gracefully, swung her bow through the wind. Another ship might have failed to make the turn in that light air, but LeBoeuf knew this ship was a handy one, and he once again expressed his quiet gratitude for that.

They turned, almost a complete circle, until they were heading back the way they had come. LeBoeuf nodded his head slightly.

Perfect…

They were running down on Van Loudersong's ship, and would cross her bow just as she was coming clear of the submerged near-shore hazards and into open water. They would rake her fore and aft while the other ship was unable to maneuver in the channel. One broadside and, with any luck, they might cripple Van Loudersong's ship entirely.

"What cheer, mates, stand ready on the starboard battery!" LeBoeuf called. "We'll pass them by, and you fire as you bear!"

Men waved. They smiled. They looked through the gunports at the enemy with whom they were closing. Enjoying themselves.

LeBoeuf put a hand on the rail and looked aloft, and then looked across the water at Van Loudersong's ship. It felt…familiar. Like being in a home in which one spent many years, but thought never to see again.

An armed vessel, great guns charged, running down on an enemy at least as powerful. And he, LeBoeuf, on the quarterdeck, and all of it moving to his spoken word. Glory, perhaps, or death, just a few broadsides away.

LeBoeuf took a deep breath and, despite himself, he smiled.

Chapter Fourteen

Don Nicolás Pérez de Maldonaldo, mayor of Santo Domingo, woke just after sunrise in a buoyant and optimistic mood. It was an odd, almost foreign sensation. The feeling did not leave him as he climbed ponderously from his bed, nor did it when his servant brought him his breakfast of cold roast beef and eggs, roasted onions, warm bread right from the oven, butter and small beer. He still felt optimistic when he finished the last of the meal and called for his manservant to attend to him, his horse made ready, and his mounted guard assembled.

He was optimistic, but not unreservedly so. His optimism was tempered with a vague and ill-defined concern.

You worry too damned much, you miserable old bastard, he thought. And it was true. He did worry a lot. And he was rewarded for that worry with success in his various ventures, and with never being found out in those things that might reflect badly on him. His peace of mind was simply the price he paid for success.

That's why we have confession, he mused. Not that he would ever confess the worst of his transgressions, in those rare times when he did seek reconciliation.

Don Nicolás's manservant, who had been poised behind the bedchamber door, hurried in at his master's summons to help him into the doublet and trousers laid out on the bed. The doublet was silk, the trousers were silk, and they sported a tolerable amount of embroidery, but they were not his finest. His finest were not appropriate for this business. He would not be in the rarified halls of Las Casas Reales. He would be in the meaner parts of Santo Domingo. And he wished to look humble, but not too humble, at his moment of triumph.

"Hurry it up, you damned fool," Don Nicolás growled as the manservant scooped up the tunic.

"Yes, Excellency," the man said. "If Your Excellency could just lift his arms…"

Don Nicolás lifted his arms. Worry was draped like a thin veil over his optimism. There had been no word from Carlos Hernández, and that niggling fact poked at him. To be sure, there was no reason why there should have been word: he had never instructed Hernández to notify him when all was in place, which might have been an oversight on his part. If things were not in place, if something had gone amiss, he would expect Hernández to alert him. Which he had not.

Hernández, damn his eyes, he knows better than to make a hash of this. I'll have the son of a bitch's other ear if he fails me or crosses me again.

Don Nicolás looked down at his manservant and scowled in irritation. The fool was having some difficulty getting the trousers hooked to the doublet. His hands seemed to be shaking. Don Nicolás smacked him hard on the side of the head, not so much for the man's clumsiness, but more as a way to ease his own tension. The manservant's head jerked to the side but he did not lose his grip on the hook and eye. He was used to working through sundry kicks and cuffings.

Three days earlier, Don Nicolás had made his promise to Fadrique Álvarez de Toledo y Mendoza, Captain General of King Philip the Fourth's Ocean Sea Navy. It was at an official function, organized to discuss the upcoming expedition to Tortuga, and what might be done to expedite the campaign, which was a matter of great concern. Toledo wanted to be on his way, and everyone in Santo Domingo, from the governor general, Gabriel de Chávez y Osorio, to the meanest beggar, was desperate to see him and his soldiers and sailors gone.

It was at that assembly that Toledo, or, actually, Toledo's purser, revealed the crisis: a majority of the Armada de Sotavento's remaining salt beef was inedible. A thousand casks, a supply that would take weeks to replace. Toledo himself said a few words, and his anger and frustration were palpable.

It was then that Don Nicolás had stepped up and assured them that he could do the impossible and provide what they needed in just a few days' time. He had explanations as to how he could accomplish this all laid out and ready, but no one asked. They were too grateful or too uninterested to bother, but Don Nicolás felt like Moses, summoning manna from heaven.

The upstart pup Don Alonso had been there, of course, and Don Nicolás had taken particular delight in the crestfallen look that had crossed the little rodent's face. Alonso the lickspittle, making his pathetic attempts to get into the admiral's good graces, even suggesting he might take part in the attack on Tortuga.

Toledo, apparently, was an old friend of Alonso's father-in-law, even something of an uncle to Alonso's wife, though Don Nicolás wondered if there wasn't something more unsavory going on there. Toledo, the old buggerer. But there was no indication that Alonso would be joining the expedition. All of his groveling seemed to have been for naught.

As he thought of Alonso, Don Nicolás's good mood began to dim, crowded out by loathing. It was not that he considered Alonso a threat; he did not. Alonso was a boy, a silly upstart. He, Don Nicolás, had all but crushed him underfoot. And he would continue crushing until the pup was reduced to dust and had blown away.

It was Alonso's effrontery that so offended Don Nicolás. To show up in Santo Domingo and think he could snatch away even a part of what Don Nicolás had built over three decades—the smuggling, the privateering, the slaving, the bribes, wealth pouring into his coffers from a dozen, two, three dozen directions—it galled Don Nicolás to no end. And the thought that the upstart pup might succeed, even to some small degree, was intolerable.

By the time he was dressed, sword buckled around his waist, brilliantly polished boots pulled on, Don Nicolás was in a thoroughly foul mood. To calm himself he imagined watching the casks of beef ferried out to the fleet, his plan accomplished. He imagined some official function at which Toledo would thank him for coming to the Armada de Sotavento's rescue, at which time the admiral would bestow some favor on Don Nicolás, his humble servant.

He envisioned the moment when the admiral's purser handed over small chests of gold as payment for the beef. Ample payment. Even if Don Nicolás had invested money to acquire the stores, the profits would have been substantial, given the inflated price he was asking. As it was, selling beef he had acquired for free, the earnings would be far beyond substantial.

Those thoughts cheered Don Nicolás up a bit as he made his way out of his bedchamber and into his apartment's outer rooms. His secretary stood by the door, dutifully fidgeting, and likely had been there for some time. The man knew better than to be late.

"Good morning, Your Excellency," the secretary said, giving a shallow bow.

"Hmm," Don Nicolás said. "Any word?"

The secretary straightened. He looked confused. "Word, Excellency? From whom?"

"Anyone," Don Nicolás snapped. "Hernández? One of the Five?"

"No, Excellency. Were we waiting on word?"

Idiot, Don Nicolás thought, but he did not pursue it. "You sent sufficient men down to guard the warehouse?" he asked instead. "Not just the Five, and that lot?"

"Oh, yes, Excellency!" the secretary said, happy to know the correct answer. "A dozen at your first request, and another thirty when you sent word after Compline last night."

"Hmm," Don Nicolás said again.

He had taken great care to protect his investment and see that nothing went amiss. Hernández had assured him he had men enough to protect the stores, but Don Nicolás wasn't going to trust his word alone. As the first of the casks began to make their way to Hernández's warehouse, Don Nicolás sent the Five, with half a dozen others, to keep an eye on things. The Five were brutes, and like brutes they responded to the most basic motivations—money, lust. That was why Don Nicolás trusted them.

But he did not trust them entirely, and he was not sure that just a handful of men were enough. With each passing day, with each wagonload of casks, the weight of the promise he made to Toledo seemed to grow heavier, his concern more acute. He ordered his secretary to find another dozen armed men to join the first in protecting the warehouse. Then, the night before, with everything nearly in place, he called for thirty more. He would take no chances, not with this.

"Very well," Don Nicolás said. There was nothing for it now. The die was cast, the Rubicon crossed. He swept out of the apartment without another word, made his way down the wide steps to the lower floor. The doormen opened the big doors for him as he approached, and he stepped out into the courtyard of Las Casas Reales.

The air was warm in the morning sun, a light breeze blowing in off the river. Don Nicolás was pleased to see that his horse was waiting, and with it a dozen mounted soldiers from Fortaleza Ozama, courtesy of Captain General Sandoval, to serve as escorts.

Don Nicolás crossed the courtyard to where his horse stood by the mounting step, two stable hands in attendance. He surveyed the soldiers, sitting their horses in a loose formation. They must have been among Sandoval's best—the man would have known better than to send anything less—and they looked decent enough. At least they did not look as ridiculous as the lickspittle Alonso's make-believe Swiss Guard, his toy soldiers, this Governor's Guard.

Try as he might, Nicolás had failed to kill the Governor's Guard in its infancy. It was no mystery what Alonso had in mind: an armed force he could use as he wished. Don Nicolás had already made an effort to infiltrate the Guard, looking for one or more of the men who might provide him with information in exchange for gold. No takers so far, but it should not be long. In the meantime, he could see that the whole thing was just a bit of foolishness, and no real concern of his.

Still, it too made him uncomfortable when he thought on it.

He climbed up onto the mounting step and swung his leg over the horse, adjusting his sword. The stable boys took hold of his boots and put his feet in the stirrups. Don Nicolás turned the horse so he was facing the corporal leading the six-man guard.

"Come along, follow me," he said. "And try not to look like a covey of fishmongers."

He reined his horse around, walking it across the courtyard and out into the city of Santo Domingo. The streets were crowded at that time of the morning, with everyone going about their business, but they stepped aside for Don Nicolás's horse in a way that he found particularly satisfying. Most of the people recognized him, of course. For those who did not, his clothes, his sword, his handsome mount with its gleaming saddle and tack, were enough to indicate that he was someone to whom they should yield. For those too dim to understand that, there were the mounted soldiers following behind.

The area grew less affluent as they rode south, the buildings and streets in worse repair, the crowds a meaner breed. Don Nicolás turned toward the river and followed the road down to the lower town, where the warehouses and chandleries and sailmakers were located, where the taverns and brothels catered to the lowest sort, the sailors and soldiers come right off the ships. It was here that the mounted troops served as more than just a way to impress the mob. In that part of Santo Domingo, a gentleman such as Don Nicolás required real protection.

He rode through the narrow streets, littered with sundry garbage, shattered crates and broken barrel staves and bottles, the contents of chamber pots. He came at last to the largest of the warehouses owned by Carlos Hernández, a place that Don Nicolás knew better than he was willing to admit. A half dozen men were milling around, armed with cutlasses and clubs and long knives. They looked like cutthroats, and might have given Don Nicolás pause had they not been in his employ.

Two of them stepped up and took the reins of his horse and held it as he dismounted. Don Nicolás did not recognize any of them, but that was no surprise. His secretary had been rounding up every mercenary he could find to stand watch over the warehouse. Of all these men, the Five were the only ones that he might know, and most likely he would not recognize any of them, either.

Another of the unnamed villains slid the warehouse door partway open and Don Nicolás stepped through. The mounted guard from Fortaleza Ozama, now dismounted, followed behind as he made his way through the cavernous space, with its stacks of casks and crates and bales and bundles.

On the building's far side, the river side, where the big doors opened onto the docks that jutted out into the water, he could hear a buzz of activity, the thump and grind of casks being moved, men calling orders, the squeal of ropes in blocks. He felt his optimism come seeping back in. An hour or two's effort on the part of the dock workers and the sailors and Don Nicolás would be a considerably wealthier and more influential man.

He skirted around a great stack of crates that blocked his view, and found himself looking through one of the big riverside doors, out to the dock and the river beyond. Hundreds and hundreds of casks were lined up in the warehouse and along the dock—salt beef for the fleet—and dozens of men were rolling and tipping and heaving them out where they could be lowered into the boats.

Don Nicolás looked out at the river. The great Armada de Sotavento lay at anchor, the massive galleons and the lesser ships. Between them and the shore a swarm of boats were pulling for the docks, coming to collect up the bounty that Don Nicolás had provided.

"Ah, Don Nicolás!" a voice called out, and Carlos Hernández appeared from the crowd, followed by Admiral Toledo's purser. Hernández gave a shallow bow, and nodding toward the dock and the activity there said, "As you can see, señor, all is in order."

Don Nicolás gave a nod. "I see, yes. Good."

"Don Nicolás," the purser said, sounding far less ingratiating than Hernández. "What brings you here, señor?"

"This is important to me, all of this," Don Nicolás said, indicating with a sweep of his hand the hundreds of casks standing in wait. "It was my effort that got this here, as you well know, and I mean to see it carried through, with never a problem."

"I see," the purser said, and he did not sound as impressed with Don Nicolás's diligence as Don Nicolás hoped he would. "Very well, then. We're moving the first of the casks out onto the dock. The flagship is sending its boats now."

The purser turned and walked back toward the open door and the dock beyond, and Don Nicolás and Hernández followed behind. "There's been no problems?" Don Nicolás asked as they walked.

"None, señor," Hernández said. "Some drunkenness among the men sent to guard the warehouse, but no more than you would expect."

Don Nicolás looked around at the men shifting the barrels. He saw no faces that he recognized, but he did not really expect he would. The Five had likely made themselves scarce when the more respectable sort arrived, and the rest were not the kind of men Don Nicolás was likely to have contact with, outside of watching them dangle from ropes at a public execution.

It was a cloudless morning, perfect, the sunshine warm on their faces as they walked out toward the end of the dock, past the rows and rows of casks, standing like soldiers in ranks. The top of each beef barrel was branded with a **BQ**, encircled by a design that looked to be a crown of some sort. Don Nicolás had no idea what that could be: most likely the mark of whatever victualer had salted down and sold the meat initially. It did not matter. He did not care where it came from, only where it was going.

They were nearing the end of the dock when Don Nicolás saw, to his great displeasure, that Don Alonso was there as well, in conversation with someone who seemed to be an officer from Toledo's fleet. Don Nicolás frowned. He tried to keep the surge of anger in check.

"Don Nicolás," Alonso said, courteous as ever, transparent, as he pretended to just notice the mayor. "Good morrow, señor. A big day…all of your efforts come to fruition at last."

"Indeed," Don Nicolás said. He did not trust himself to say more, at least not to Alonso. The flagship's longboat, thirty-five feet long, painted a brilliant white, trimmed in red and gold, and manned by twenty sailors at the oars, was just drawing up to the dock. Don Nicolás turned to the purser. "Shall we get this business moving along?"

"Yes, we will," the purser said. "But first, I think it would be prudent that we inspect the beef, do you see? Just to be certain all is in order. I'm sure the admiral would agree."

Don Nicolás felt his anger flare anew, and he was certain that his face was flushing red. "Inspect?" he said. "What are you insinuating, señor purser?"

"Insinuating? No, no, nothing at all," the purser said, but he did not seem to be trying too hard to sound sincere. "It's just that, there are always men looking to defraud. You are not one of them, obviously, but there's the chance that you yourself were defrauded. As I was, in Seville, when I took on the cargo of rotten meat."

"Yes, well…" Don Nicolás began, then stopped. He was about to say *You were a fool to take on those spoiled stores*, but that would just bolster the purser's argument for inspecting the casks. "Certainly, then," Don Nicolás said instead. "But let's get on with it."

The purser nodded to one of the dockworkers, standing by with hammer and chisel. The man stepped up to the nearest cask and began to knock the hoops off with well-placed strokes. Don Nicolás felt a growing unease in his stomach, and he told himself to stop being ridiculous.

There's not a thing wrong with this beef, I know it. Sandoval had assured him it had been no more than a few months in storage after being salted down. Salt beef did not go rotten in a few months.

The two upper hoops came off the barrel and the man worked his chisel in around the barrel head, loosening it up, then tilting it and pulling it free. The morning air was suddenly filled with the putrid and gut-turning smell of rotten meat. The man with the chisel turned quickly away, cursing as he did, a look of disgust on his face.

"Dear Lord!" the purser said, putting a hand to his mouth and nose and taking a step back. The stench filled Don Nicolás's head and made his stomach twist, but he was too shocked and uncertain and angry to react beyond that.

Alonso, of all of them, approached the barrel, leaned over it and looked down, then backed away, shaking his head. It made Don Nicolás wild with fury and he fought to keep his expression neutral.

"Of course, there's bound to be at least one bad one," Don Nicolás said. He spoke normally, not letting his tone reflect his rising anger and the sick feeling in his stomach, which was only partially due to the nauseating odor. "Out of a thousand damned casks there's bound to be one bad one."

"Of course," Alonso said. "Of course. One would only expect it." Don Nicolás wanted to slap the little bastard, and even more so when he added, "Let us pick another, at random, and we'll see. I'm sure it's just the one. Señor purser, will you choose?"

"Yes, of course," the purser said, and he walked slowly down the row of barrels, looking them over as if he could tell anything about their contents from such an inspection. The man with the hammer and chisel followed behind, and Don Nicolás and Alonso followed behind him.

The purser stopped at a barrel a third of the way down the line. He pointed toward it and stepped back, and the man with the hammer and chisel set to work. A minute later the barrel head came free, and they were again met by the vile smell of putrid meat.

"I wonder if some fraud has not been committed against you, Don Nicolás," the purser said, and while his words suggested a belief in the mayor's innocence, his tone did not.

"Fraud?" Don Nicolás nearly shouted. "Damn my eyes, yes, there's some fraud going on here, that much is clear."

But who was committing that fraud he did not know. First among his suspects was the purser, who might be hoping to avoid paying for what Don Nicolás had provided so he could pocket some or all of the gold earmarked for the beef. It was the purser, after all, who had chosen which casks to open, and that choice might not have been random.

"See here, I don't know what's going on, but it cannot be that all of this meat is spoiled," Don Nicolás continued. He turned to the man with the hammer and chisel and pointed to a random cask farther down the line. "You. Open that one, and be quick about it."

The man nodded and hurried over to the cask which Don Nicolás had indicated, and tapped away with the hammer. Don Nicolás glanced over at Alonso and the purser. He looked for some sign of concern that they were about to be found out, but they were watching, expressionless, with arms folded. He wanted to punch them each, square in their lying, disinterested faces.

He heard the man with the hammer gasp. He smelled the rotten meat even before he turned to examine the cask.

"Well, Don Nicolás, it seems you, too, have been the victim of some scoundrel, just as we were in Seville," the purser said. "I feared it was too much to hope for, that such a supply as we needed could be had so quickly."

"No, damn your eyes, this is not right!" Don Nicolás said, barely able to get the words out. "The rotten beef that came from the fleet, it must have been mixed up with what I provided. Where the devil is that little bastard Hernández?" Hernández, he realized, seemed to have made himself scarce.

"These are not the casks that came from the fleet, I assure you," the purser said. "The brand that's burned into them, it's entirely different. One does not erase a brand."

"'Different brand,' we'll see about that," Don Nicolás said. He turned to the man with the hammer and a couple of laborers who were standing nearby, watching the fun. "You there…" He pointed to an unopened cask. "Turn that over, let us see what's on the bottom of that."

The three men grabbed the cask and lowered it onto its side, then spun it around to reveal the bottom. The same brand was stamped at the end, the **BQ**, encircled by a shape like a crown.

"The casks from Seville bore an altogether different brand," the purser said. "Forgive me, Don Nicolás, but clearly you have been defrauded by some rascal whom you trusted." His tone suggested that he was done discussing the matter.

"Yes, wherever did you get this salt beef, Don Nicolás?" Alonso asked. The words were like a poke with a dagger. Nicolás looked sharply at Alonso, tried to fathom what was at the bottom of that question. It sounded innocent, mostly, but not entirely. There was a hint of something else. Knowledge? Accusation?

"The casks come from various sources," Don Nicolás said, as calm as he could manage. "Men I was led to believe I could trust. Hernández! Where is that son of a whore Hernández?"

"Forgive me, Don Nicolás," the purser said, "but I must leave you to sort this out yourself. As unpleasant as this discovery may be for you, I must now go inform Admiral Toledo that he will not have the supplies he needs. And that will be far less pleasant than this has been, I can assure you."

Alonso cleared his throat softly. "Actually, señor purser, I believe I can be of some assistance in this matter."

"Assistance? How?"

"I believe I can supply the salt beef you need."

"A thousand casks?" The purser did not hide his skepticism.

"No easy task, to be sure," Alonso said. "But looking here and there, I'm quite certain I can gather up what you need. And soon, I should think. The *rancheros* in this district, they have a great deal of official business with me. It's in their interest to help."

"Well," the purser said, "if you were to do so, I would be most grateful. Most grateful, indeed. And I know the admiral would share my gratitude."

Don Nicolás felt his eyes go wide, his mouth fall open, at the gut-punch of those words. He looked over at Don Alonso, whose expression still gave nothing away. Then Alonso looked over at him, their eyes met, and just the hint of a smirk played across his face.

Chapter Fifteen

Benjamin Graves did not have a good feeling about any of it.

He did not like the ease with which that big son of a whore put a bullet right through his helmsman's head, even while standing in a pitching boat. He did not like the way this LeBoeuf killed two others and shattered the longboat with what may or may not have been a lucky shot.

He did not like the way the big son of a whore (which was what Graves had dubbed the man) set sail and made for open water. He had assumed LeBoeuf would attack them there in the harbor at Tortuga, in which case Graves would have found some means to run him up onto a coral head and sail away. But he had not given Graves the chance.

Graves did not like the way Van Loudersong seemed unable to shut his mouth, or understand that he was not in command. The Dutchman was, at that moment, instructing Graves on the safest passage out of the harbor.

Another word, I pray you. Another word and I'll gag you with a damned belaying pin, Graves thought. But he knew he would not, because he knew that any gagging with belaying pins was Maja's decision, not his.

"Damned fine navigating you're doing there, damned fine," Graves said, cutting the man off in mid-sentence. Forward, hands were still stamping the capstan around. Inch by painful inch *Charles Rex* was moving astern, the sand's grip on her bow loosening with every bit of anchor cable they hauled in.

"Forgive me, I must have a word with the captain general, here," Graves said, nodding toward Maja who was standing by the rail aft and staring out at the other ship. His body, as usual, was motionless, his face without expression.

"Yes, yes," Van Loudersong said, irritably. He did not like being cut off, Graves had learned, and he did not like that a man such as Maja—dark-skinned, of uncertain race, dressed like some luckless buccaneer—had any authority at all, much less complete authority over the workings of the ship. Consulting with Maja was one way of irritating the man, and Graves enjoyed that.

"Maja," Graves said, ambling aft. He spoke soft enough that Van Loudersong would not hear.

Maja turned his head. He blinked slowly, in that raptor way of his, but his expression did not change.

"See here," Graves said. "I have little faith in this Dutchman and his tales of gold. Let's come to anchor again and forget this folly."

Maja stared at Graves a moment before replying. "What ho? Afraid?"

"Afraid to waste my time on a fool's errand," Graves said. "Better we throw this Dutchman overboard and be done with this."

"No," Maja said. His tone made clear he was done talking, but Graves ignored it.

"I've seen plenty of this Dutchman's sort. Him and his gold. It will all turn out to be a pile of horse dropping, you mark me."

Maja was silent again, longer this time. "Don't care about the Dutchman, and I don't care about the gold," he said at last. The two men glared at one another, and then the ship shifted below them, pitching slightly, fore and aft, as the bow slid free of the sand.

"We're off the sand," Maja said. "Go sail the ship."

And that was an end to it. Further discussion was pointless.

Graves sighed. He understood what was acting here. At long last, he understood. This had nothing to do with the Dutchman or the gold on Hispaniola.

It might have at first, and laying hands on that gold might still be a fine thing, but it was not about that. Maja wanted to kill the big son of a whore. He thought he had killed him before, and he was wrong, and he did not like that. This LeBoeuf had given Maja a wicked wound, and Maja did not like that, either. And now he had killed three of Maja's men and driven the ship aground.

In Maja's mind, LeBoeuf had to go. That was what this was about. And Graves would have to see it through. He turned and walked forward.

A bit of smuggling, that's all I'm looking to do, Graves thought. *Some smuggling, some privateering, if the odds is good. Why must I be tangled up in this?*

But of course the ship and the men were Maja's, and without Maja he had nothing, and nowhere to go. Graves felt very sorry for himself. And justifiably so.

"No need to get the boat aboard," Van Loudersong said as Graves resumed his place at the weather rail. "You'll just want it towing astern again, once the fighting starts. Best to just leave it for now."

Graves balled his fists and waited until the urge to strike Van Loudersong passed, then he turned and faced the man.

"How about we do this?" Graves said. "What say I put you in the boat, and you may have command of it and do as you will? Go fight that big son of a whore by yourself."

Van Loudersong frowned. He seemed unsure of how to reply, so he said nothing. Instead, he looked outboard to where LeBoeuf's ship was setting sail and gathering way, and Graves did his best to ignore him.

"Hands to the topsail sheets, hands to the braces!" he called and the men moved quickly to those stations. They were a tolerable crew, about forty men, and well-practiced enough in seafaring to do what was needed. They might have been more adept at cutting purses, or throats, than handling sails, but they were good enough mariners to work *Charles Rex*.

"Haul away your sheets, you lubberly bastards!" Graves shouted. "Haul your halyards! Haul away!"

The yards rose up the topmasts, foot by foot, and the men braced them around and the ship gathered way. Graves ordered the foresail set, and the gun crews to load and run out the guns.

He looked off to the south. The other ship, the big son of a whore's ship, was sailing close-hauled on a larboard tack, making off to the east as quick as they could.

"See there?" Van Loudersong said. Graves knew the Dutchman would not be able to keep his mouth shut for long. "LeBoeuf's heading off for the coast of Hispaniola, making a race of it. His ship is quick, and handy in stays. She'll have the legs on you, I'll warrant."

Graves sighed again. "No, he ain't," he said. "He's getting to weather of us, then he'll turn and run down on us, try to rake us as he passes."

Van Loudersong frowned again. Apparently that had not occurred to him.

"Perhaps," he said at last.

"Bear up a bit," Graves said to the helmsman. "Steady there, steady on."

Charles Rex heeled to starboard and her speed built, and Graves looked over the side and watched the coral heads and sandbars move past under the startlingly clear water.

Miserable place, miserable excuse for a harbor, he thought. He was going into some kind of bloody business, and he was not feeling too kindly disposed to anything. He did not like bloody business. He did not like people firing round shot at him.

To the east, LeBoeuf had tacked around, just as Graves knew he would, and was settling down on the new course, running down wind to cross *Charles Rex*'s bow.

You timed that just right, didn't you, you sheep-biter, Graves thought. He could see that LeBoeuf had judged it well. He had tacked at just the right moment to put his ship near *Charles Rex* just as *Charles Rex* was finding open water, but before Graves had room to maneuver. At least, that was what he reckoned.

"Ortiz!" Graves shouted down the deck. "How stand the great guns?"

"Loaded and run out!" Ortiz called back, waving. *Charles Rex* carried only minions, firing four-pound shot, and only eight of those. Less firepower than LeBoeuf's ship, he was certain. But get close enough, and aim well enough, and even those could do some real hurt.

"Get the men to the starboard battery, we'll fire those guns first!" Graves called back. He saw Van Loudersong straighten, and could feel the man was about to speak. LeBoeuf's ship was on their larboard side; the starboard battery was pointing at open water.

Graves looked over at the Dutchman and scowled, and Van Loudersong's open mouth shut again as he leaned back against the rail. Graves looked down the deck. Men were at the starboard battery, men were at the ropes, standing ready. He looked out to windward, where LeBoeuf's ship was charging down on them.

Are you a very good mariner, or a very lucky one? he thought. LeBoeuf's ship would cross *Charles Rex*'s bow just as *Rex* was coming clear of the channel. His great guns would fire their rounds down the full length of *Charles Rex*'s deck. The carnage could be terrific. Graves felt his stomach twist.

"You men at the braces, stand ready, mark my words closely, and jump to it when I say!" This was going to be a near thing, what he had in mind, but better than passively taking fire, like a bird sitting on a branch.

Only a few hundred feet separated the two ships now, and LeBoeuf's ship was driving along nicely in the breeze. A handy vessel, indeed. Graves could see that. But *Charles Rex* was handy too, and Graves meant to take advantage of it.

"You men on the starboard battery, when we turn, you fire as you bear!" Graves called. "You'll fire from forward aft. The very bloody second you fire, you get to reloading, quick, like the devil's biting your arse. Just don't blow your bloody arms off."

The men at the guns looked back at him and some nodded and some did not. They were calm, ready. Eager, even.

These cutthroat whores' sons, they love this business, Graves thought, and he felt his stomach twisting up further.

Two hundred feet separated *Charles Rex* from LeBoeuf's ship, their courses at right angles to one another. LeBoeuf's guns could easily hit *Charles Rex* even now, but Graves was certain he was holding his fire, waiting until he was up with *Rex*'s vulnerable bow.

Graves glanced over the windward side. He could see the hump of a sandbar, submerged, just twenty feet away, the last hazard they had to clear before reaching open water. But LeBoeuf would be firing into them well before that.

"Hands at the braces, stand ready!" Graves shouted. "Starboard battery, stand ready! Helmsman, helm's alee!"

Without hesitation the man at the helm pushed the tiller over and *Charles Rex*'s bow swung to larboard, turning up into the wind. Graves heard Van Loudersong gasp, and in the corner of his eye he saw him straighten and take a step toward him.

"Are you mad?" the Dutchman sputtered. "There's a sandbar there, damn your eyes!"

Graves heard Van Loudersong speak, but the words passed through his head unheeded. Yes, there was a sandbar there, and yes he was mad. But the tide was near its height and they were near the outer end of the bar and Graves was all but certain that there was water enough below them to do what he was doing.

The bow swung past LeBoeuf's ship, turning up into the wind, but Graves's eyes were on *Charles Rex*'s sails now. Seconds would spell the difference between success and disaster as he balanced the forces of wind on canvas, and all of Graves's mind was concentrated on that evolution. When LeBoeuf fired his first gun, and the round shot tore through the starboard bow, leaving a great jagged hole in the bulwark, Graves hardly registered the fact.

"Foreyards, brace them around, brace them around! Lively, now!" The luffs of the sails were starting to shiver as they turned edge-into the wind. Forward, the men heaved on the braces, on the tacks and sheets, and the yards came swinging around, the sails pressed back against the mast as the wind caught them on the front side, checking *Charles Rex*'s swing.

"Aft there, sheet the mizzen to windward, as hard over as ever you can!"

The forward-most minion fired into LeBoeuf's ship, and in the same instant LeBoeuf fired back, but again Graves hardly noticed. He was part of the ship now; he could feel her motion through the water, he could sense the opposing forces on the sails, he understood the hesitation in her fabric which he felt underfoot.

He pulled his eyes from the sails, looked to starboard. LeBoeuf's ship was right alongside and sailing past, with *Charles Rex* stopped nearly dead in the water, when *Rex*'s second and third guns fired. Graves could actually see the big son of a whore on the quarterdeck, standing motionless, watching. The fourth gun in LeBoeuf's broadside went off, and in the same instant Graves heard the scream of the shot flying past and he flinched at the sound.

That's bigger than a damned minion, he thought. His own aftermost gun fired and he saw the bulwark near LeBoeuf's quarterdeck blow apart and thought for certain he saw LeBoeuf flinch, which made him smile. The men on Graves's forward-most gun were already reloading.

And that was all the thought he could give to guns and such. He looked aloft again. The foresails were still fully aback, the mainsails flogging.

"Shift your helm! Put it right over!" Graves called to the helmsman. "Let that mizzen sheet fly, just let it go!"

The helmsman pushed the tiller over, the mizzen sail began to bang loudly as the sheet was let go and the wind spilled from the canvas. Graves felt the ship shudder a little underfoot, so slightly that anyone less attuned to the vessel would never have felt it. For a second it seemed as if *Charles Rex* was hanging trapped between wind and sea. And then, slowly, the bow began to fall off, turning back to starboard as LeBoeuf's ship sailed past, presenting its thin transom to Graves's battery of guns.

"Shoot that whore's son as we pass him by!" Graves shouted forward. "Ha, ha! Right up his arse!" He was smiling now, laughing with a giddy delight. Then he thought about the sandbar, and how close he had just come to running aground, and the delight was replaced with a sense of relief so profound he thought he might puke.

Guess there was enough water after all, he thought. Then, as the reality of his having pulled it off settled in, he thought, *Damn my eyes, I'm good at this.*

The forward-most gun fired, and the rail around LeBoeuf's transom blew apart, but Graves could not see what other damage the ball might have done on its journey down LeBoeuf's deck. Quite a bit, he hoped. He wondered how long LeBoeuf would be willing to take that abuse.

"Well done."

It was Maja, who seemed to have appeared out of thin air at Graves's side.

"Thank'ee," Graves said. "Now we'll play cat and mouse until he tires, or we manage to shoot something of import away." The second gun went off, but Graves saw no damage done.

"No," Maja said. "You run us into him. We'll board him."

"Board him?" Graves said, taking is eyes from LeBoeuf's ship, looking at Maja. "Why in all Hell would we…"

"Does he have bigger guns that we do? More of them?"

"Yes, but that don't mean…"

"Do we have more men than he does?"

"How in Hell should I know that?" Graves demanded.

"We have more men," Maja said. "We board."

"Son of a bitch!" Graves said, an expression of frustration, not directed at Maja *per se.* He knew Maja was right. In a ship-to-ship duel, LeBoeuf certainly had the advantage in firepower. And he knew that Maja wanted to come to grips with the big son of a whore. Kill him face to face. Actually do it this time.

And he knew that he, Benjamin Graves, was much happier in this duel of seamanship. And that he was not going to get his way.

He looked off to starboard. "Oh, damn your eyes!" he shouted, and this time the words were directed at LeBoeuf, but they might have been for Maja as well, for distracting him, even for those few seconds.

LeBoeuf had put his helm down and was turning, coming around to bring his ship broadside to broadside with *Charles Rex*, where his bigger guns would tear them apart.

"Stand ready for stays!" Graves called. He would tack, turn *Charles Rex* away from LeBoeuf's ship, spin around in a full circle and get astern of him once more. He had to stay clear of those guns.

"What are you doing?" Maja asked.

"We're coming about, getting away from this whore's son before he does for us."

"No," Maja said, as calm as if he was refusing another tankard in a tavern. He nodded toward LeBoeuf's ship. "Run aboard him. We're going over the rail."

LeBoeuf fired again, the round shot hitting the number two gun starboard side with a great clanging sound, like a broken church bell. The barrel upended, hung vertical for a moment, then crashed to the deck.

There it is, Graves thought, scowling. Maja was right. LeBoeuf had just proved as much. It was time to act. Put the helm to weather, *Charles Rex* would spin like a top and slam into LeBoeuf, and Maja's screaming lunatics would pour onto the Frenchman's deck.

"Fine, fine, as you wish!" Graves said. "Forward there, stand by to board! Helmsman, helm's a'weather!"

Maja's men cheered. They were ready to go. The helmsman pushed the tiller over and the bow began swinging wildly to leeward, *Charles Rex* driving at LeBoeuf's ship. Graves clenched his teeth to prevent himself from vomiting on Maja's feet.

Chapter Sixteen

That was well done, LeBoeuf thought grudgingly, even as he tried to tamp down his fury. *And how shall I respond?*

Of course he was furious. Mostly with himself. His well-thought-out maneuver, well executed, had been blown all to Hell because his enemy did not do what he expected him to do. He had seen this before. Many times. But that did not make it more palatable.

Price of hubris, LeBoeuf thought.

He had been a hundred feet short of crossing Van Loudersong's bow and firing his bastard culverings right down the length of the Dutchman's deck, when Van Loudersong's ship flew up into the wind, presenting not her bow but her starboard broadside to LeBoeuf's battery.

"Damn your eyes, I'll do for you yet," LeBoeuf said out loud, as he saw the enemy make his move. Whoever was driving the other ship had deprived LeBoeuf of his raking fire, but he could still give them a good pounding. "Forward there, fire as you bear!"

Starboard side, forward, the first gun went off, and in the same instant Van Loudersong's ship fired back. A section of the bulwark blew apart. One of the buccaneers staggered, a splinter a foot long jutting from his shoulder. But he yanked it out, threw it aside, and once more took up the train tackle he had been holding.

Just forward of where LeBoeuf stood by the helm, Other Dog growled, barked once, then continued her patrol, side to side. She had been doing this since they first got underway. She could sense there was something of import happening—a hunt, but unlike any she had ever witnessed—and she was not sure what to do.

"Be calm, you'll get your chance," LeBoeuf reassured her, but she did not seem mollified.

LeBoeuf looked over at Van Loudersong's ship and thought, *You miserable toad, you scabbed whoremonger.*

The second gun went off and a shroud on the mainmast parted as the shot flew past. Forward, his own guns replied: two, three, leaping in against the breechings, tearing away railings aboard the other ship, but doing no worse damage than that.

The two ships were close, less than a hundred feet apart. LeBoeuf could see Van Loudersong aft, and the heavy man with the beard, and he wondered which of them was giving the orders. The dark man with the red headcloth was there as well, but farther aft, leaning against the rail, watching, apparently, and nothing more.

You're going to run hard aground on that sandbar, you whoremonger, I know it.

Wishful thinking, perhaps. LeBoeuf knew that as well. But if they did go aground, he would enjoy laying off their quarter and slowly pounding them into flotsam.

Van Loudersong's aftermost gun fired. The bulwark just forward of LeBoeuf exploded into its component parts, and LeBoeuf jerked in surprise. He cursed himself for a fool, but the cursing was cut short by a scream, piercing and desperate. On the larboard side a man named Rioux was down, thrashing, a two-foot shard of wood jutting from his chest, his shoulder a bloody wreck where the ball had apparently clipped him.

"Someone see to this one!" LeBoeuf called forward, and a couple of men hurried aft.

Van Loudersong's ship was astern now, LeBoeuf's running past it, downwind. The Dutchman, or whoever was driving that ship, had rounded up right over the sandbar, right where LeBoeuf thought there would never be water enough for so deep a vessel to pass. Now they were stopped dead, and they might be hanging bow to wind, or they might be aground. A moment more and the answer would be clear.

We'll see directly if you're clever, or if you're a fool.

And then LeBoeuf had his answer.

God's teeth!

With her foresails aback, Van Loudersong's ship started turning slowly to starboard. She was not caught bow to wind, she was not aground. Whoever was driving her, Van Loudersong or the bearded one, he had made a very daring move indeed, and had executed it well.

LeBoeuf smiled, a grim smile, and nodded his head. This fight would not be won so easily, he could see that.

He turned and looked forward. A gun crew was running the last of the bastard culverings out the gunport: all guns loaded and ready for the next act. But how would that act play out? The other ship was now upwind of them, thanks to LeBoeuf's hubris. They were crossing LeBoeuf's stern, and that would not do.

"Ready at the braces!" LeBoeuf shouted. "Ready to brace up, larboard tack! Steen, bear up!" Then, to himself, he said, "We'll get right alongside this bastard, blow him to the Devil."

Steen was just starting his reply when the other ship fired. LeBoeuf was knocked forward in a great hail of splinters and shards from the transom's planks and rail. He staggered and dropped to his hands and knees. He could feel a hundred points of pain on his back and legs, but he could not tell if they were from the impact of the splinters or if the wooden daggers had been driven into his flesh. He reached behind and swept his hand over his cassock, but he felt only cloth.

Something pushed against him—he could not imagine what—and then he realized it was Other Dog, sticking her worried muzzle into his side.

"I'm fine, I'm fine," LeBoeuf said, as he struggled to his feet. "Steen! Bear up!"

Steen did not answer. LeBoeuf turned, looked aft. The tiller was unmanned, what was left of Steen was jammed against the binnacle. Direct hit: the round shot likely had not slowed at all as it tore the man apart.

LeBoeuf staggered aft and grabbed the tiller, pushing it over to starboard. His foot slipped in the wash of blood and he adjusted his stance.

"Forward there! Brace up, larboard tack!"

The men at the braces heaved away, the yards swung round. LeBoeuf scanned the deck, looking for any other damage the round shot had left behind. He saw nothing at first, and then he did. Five feet up the mainmast, a nasty, splintered section was torn away, as if some mad giant had taken a bite from the wood.

Merde…

That might be a problem. Or it might not. They would not know either way until disaster came knocking.

He looked over the larboard side just as the other ship fired again. He heard the shot scream by but did not see it strike.

Those are not big guns, LeBoeuf thought. He doubted they were as big as his own. *Broadside to broadside, we'll beat them to kindling.*

LeBoeuf's number two gun went off, the six-pound ball striking the muzzle of one of Van Loudersong's guns, point blank range, with a clang they could hear even through ears dulled by gunfire. LeBoeuf saw the gun upended, half a ton of iron airborne, then heard it crash to the deck.

That should give them pause…

The two ships were sailing nearly parallel to one another, but not for long, LeBoeuf imagined. Whoever was driving Van Loudersong's ship would know better than to trade broadside for broadside with LeBoeuf's heavier ordnance. He would turn; either away from LeBoeuf's ship, or toward it.

It was toward it. No sooner had the gun upended than the other ship put her helm up, turning hard downwind, swinging directly at LeBoeuf's larboard side.

Boarding, LeBoeuf thought.

They would try to slam into LeBoeuf's ship and board. He may have the bigger guns, but the other ship had the bigger crew. They were not fools; they would use that advantage, swarm over the side, turn this into a bloody fight on the deck.

Methinks not.

Number three gun fired but LeBoeuf did not bother looking to see what damage the shot had done. His eyes were on the bow of the other ship as it swung toward them, its bowsprit pointing like a boney finger. If LeBoeuf did nothing, they would hit just aft of the main channel.

"Shall we dance?" LeBoeuf said out loud as he pushed the tiller to leeward and his ship began to slew to larboard, turning toward Van Loudersong's ship. If he had timed it right, Van Loudersong's bowsprit would swing right past. If he had not, they would collide, and Van Loudersong would get what he wished for.

"Forward there! Leave off with the great guns! Take up your muskets! Levasseur, come take this helm!"

Men scrambled. The sails flogged as the ship turned up into the wind. Levasseur ran aft and took the tiller from LeBoeuf.

The two ships were turning in opposite directions, Van Loudersong's ship trying to run into LeBoeuf's stern or foul the main shrouds, LeBoeuf trying to duck clear.

This will be a damned close thing, LeBoeuf thought, and then the end of Van Loudersong's bowsprit hit the shrouds with enough force that he felt the deck shudder, and the two ship were locked together. Already men were gathering in the bow of Van Loudersong's ship, ready to race up the bowsprit and into the shrouds.

Allez, allez! he thought. He hoped they would be stupid enough to launch their attack. And they were.

Half a dozen men led the way. They leapt onto the bowsprit of Van Loudersong's ship, one after the other, and raced upward, one hand gripping the manropes, the other holding cutlasses or swords or pistols. They were an ugly, piratical looking bunch, but they seemed not to understand whom they were attacking.

It might have been a deadly assault, but to the buccaneers, accustomed to dropping wild pigs with their long muskets at ten times that distance, it was little more than a game. They waited, waited, until the first man was reaching for the main shrouds, and then they let loose. The volley swept the attackers away like wind in dried leaves. Most fell writhing into the sea, some tangled in the rigging as they kicked out their life. Those near the base of the spar fell back into the beakhead.

Another five or so were mounting the end of the bowsprit, ready to follow their shipmates out, but before the smoke had even cleared they leapt back aboard Van Loudersong's ship and disappeared behind the bulwark. They would not try that again.

But the danger was not past. The two ships were swinging together, pivoting on the bowsprit thrust between the two aftermost main shrouds. If they came side to side, Van Loudersong's rogues would be able to pour over the rails, fore and aft, and it would be a different story.

"Cut those shrouds away, cut them away!" LeBoeuf called, pointing at the place where the bowsprit was caught firm. A half dozen of the buccaneers raced to the base of the shrouds, one with an ax, the others brandishing cutlasses. They hacked at the lanyards that held the shrouds in place, hard as iron bars under the pressure, and bit by bit the strands came apart.

Muskets appeared over the bow of Van Loudersong's ship, bullets buzzing across the deck, but the buccaneers responded before LeBoeuf could even call an order. Half a dozen small arms went off at once, the volley punctuated by a scream from the other ship as the buccaneers kept up their fire.

The lanyard on the aftermost shroud parted under a final blow, and the next after that, and suddenly the bowsprit was free of the rig. Van Loudersong's ship, checked in its motion, began turning again. LeBoeuf looked up at the sails, on his ship and the other, and he calculated, on some gut level, the pressures of wind and tide on canvas and wood.

He turned and ran aft. When they had shot the transom away the mizzen sheet had gone with it, and now the sail was flogging and useless. LeBoeuf grabbed what was left of the sheet and heaved it out to windward, forcing the sail to scoop the wind, driving the stern of his ship around.

He grunted with the strain and leaned into the pull, craning his neck to see what was happening. The stern of his ship was swinging to starboard, opening up the gap between the two, and the wind was driving Van Loudersong's ship down past him.

"Man the larboard great guns! Fire as you bear!" he called, loud as he could with the strain of heaving on the sheet. Forward, men raced to the guns, and two came running aft and relieved him of the rope. He stepped away, called again for the men manning the larboard battery to let loose.

The two ships were broadside to broadside now, and both their batteries went off at once. The great gush of smoke that filled the space between them was blinding, the sound of the cumulative blast, the crush of wood, the scream of round shot deafening.

LeBoeuf tried to peer through the smoke, to see what hurt they might have done, but he could see nothing. He looked up as the wind began to whip the smoke away. He thought he saw Van Loudersong's foremast leaning a bit to one side, but he could not be certain. He kept his eyes on the mast as the ship sailed by.

Yes, yes, he thought. He was certain now. The mast was leaning to starboard. And just as he was sure of what he was seeing, he saw it start to collapse, like a tree finally cut through at the base. It leaned farther, and farther still, gathering momentum, then went completely by the board, tumbling half over the side in a great tangle of sail and rope and shattered spars. Fore and aft, the buccaneers cheered.

LeBoeuf turned his attention to his own ship, his own rig. "Levasseur, put the helm down!" he called. They were still turning up into the wind, the sails coming aback. A moment more and they would be in irons, caught with their bow pointing into the wind, but with any luck their momentum would carry them around onto the other tack.

Levasseur grunted as he pushed the tiller over. LeBoeuf looked aloft. The main topsail was still set, and the foresail as well. He could not see the fore topsail, which was hidden from view by the main. He stepped forward and looked up.

Damn my eyes…

The topsail had collapsed and LeBoeuf guessed that the halyard had been shot through, causing the yard to fall. That was not going to help get the bow through the wind. In fact, they were already stopped dead, caught in irons, unable to move.

"Set the spritsail!" LeBoeuf called, pointing forward. The spritsail, a square sail slung under the bowsprit, had not been set that morning, but now LeBoeuf hoped it would help turn the bow away from the wind, get the ship moving again.

Forward, hands let go of the clewlines and the buntlines and sheeted the spritsail home. It dropped and flogged and men hauled on the braces until the wind caught it and filled it out. LeBoeuf sighted along the bowsprit, out toward the distant shore of Hispaniola. Nothing. The ship was as motionless as if she was aground.

Then, slowly, she began to turn. The spritsail, full and aback, began to push the bow over to leeward. Inch by inch the horizon moved past as the bow swung around. LeBoeuf was just feeling a vague and fragile sense of relief when he saw the shrouds hanging slack.

The main shrouds. Larboard side. The heavy cables that stopped the mast from falling over. The two forward-most seemed unhurt, but they also seemed loose, and held in place by the ratlines alone. LeBoeuf frowned. He raced over to the larboard rail and looked over the side. The forward end of the channel, to which the shrouds were attached, was a shattered wreck. Van Loudersong's final broadside had turned it into kindling, leaving the ends of the shrouds hanging limp.

That's not good, LeBoeuf thought.

The two shrouds aft were already loose, the lanyards having been cut away to free Van Loudersong's bowsprit. That meant that the mainmast, already badly wounded, was supported by the one remaining shroud alone.

"Let go the main topsail halyard! Just let it go, and clew up the sail! Now! *Now!*" LeBoeuf called. The pressure on the sail was building as the ship turned downwind, and that in turn was putting enormous pressure on the single shroud.

Hands raced to the halyard, raced to the clewlines. LeBoeuf heard the shroud groan as the pressure built. He could see it quivering under the load. Le Chasseur whipped the end of the halyard off its belaying pin just as the chainplate holding that last shroud to the hull tore free with a wrenching, tearing sound.

Le Chasseur let go the halyard and the main topsail yard slid down the mast, but it was too late. The entire works—lower mast, main top, topmast, flagpole, main yard, topsail yard, and all attendant sails and gear—leaned over to the starboard side as if taking its cue from Van Loudersong's foremast. The yards twisted as the braces were drawn tight. The mainstay stretched tight and popped and strained with the enormous weight.

LeBoeuf watched, tightlipped and silent. His men were clear of the danger, as clear as they were going to get. There was nothing else to say, and no force on earth that could stop the rig from going over.

The mast buckled at the point where Van Loudersong's round shot had taken its bite, and then went slowly over the side. It hit the water with a great splash, and then another as the fore topmast and topsail yard came down as well.

The butt of the mast came to rest on top of the bulwark, which was partially smashed under its weight. The shattered end, sticking up at a steep angle, seemed to nod up and down as the ship rolled under it. From there, the wreckage reached out a hundred feet from the side of the ship.

"Cut that all away!" LeBoeuf called. "Cut it free and shove it overboard!" There was no time to try salvaging any of it. They could sail with the foresail alone, or they could tow the ship with the boats, if need be. But they did not have the luxury of time. Van

Loudersong's ship was still nearby. They were still in the middle of a fight.

The men fell on the rigging with axes and cutlasses. LeBoeuf looked over at Van Loudersong's ship. It was a couple hundred feet downwind now, turning slowly in the current, the men struggling to cut their own wreckage free. LeBoeuf might have beaten them to pulp if his downed mainmast was not draped over the great guns.

We'll see to Van Loudersong later, LeBoeuf thought. The first order was to get the ship underway, and do it before Van Loudersong. They had the weather gauge now. They could destroy the others at their leisure.

While the men hacked away at the shrouds and the mainstay and backstays, LeBoeuf drew his big hunting knife and went at the braces and sheets and sundry running rigging that was keeping the mast bound to the ship. Line by line he cut them clean and tossed them aside. Forward, one of the shrouds parted, and with a groan and a shudder the mast slid another five feet farther overboard before it caught up again.

Come on, come on, LeBoeuf thought, but he kept his mouth shut. He could see the men were working as fast as they could. The starboard main sheet was bar-taut so he crossed the deck and brought his knife down on the inch-thick line. Two slashes with the razor-sharp blade and the line parted with a pop and whipped off forward.

LeBoeuf glanced off to windward, a reflex, deeply engrained. He froze, motionless, still holding the now-forgotten knife in front of him.

What the devil is that? he thought.

But he knew what it was. Ships. A dozen at least, likely more. They must have come up unnoticed while he was fighting Van Loudersong. They were perhaps three miles off, and running down with all sail set.

Merde…

He turned quick and looked off to the west, to leeward. Van Loudersong's men were making progress, but he had no thought for them. He was looking instead at the horizon. If he and his men could clear the wreckage quickly, and get underway with the foresail, spritsail and mizzen, there might still be a chance they could sail free.

But there was not. There was no chance. Because there were more sails to the west. Not as many, and not as large: frigates, most likely, more nimble ships, able to beat to windward. They would seal up the back door between Tortuga and Hispaniola.

LeBoeuf felt his heart sink as he watched the ships to leeward, sailing with their tacks aboard, closing the distance with each mile made good. He could see no flags flying, nor any sign of where this fleet was from. But he knew. In those waters, there was only one nation that could possibly deploy that much naval power.

The Spanish had arrived.

Chapter Seventeen

It had been two weeks since the action in Hernández's warehouse, and still, when Don Alonso Menéndez thought on it, he could only shake his head in wonder. It had been the longest night of his life; the most dangerous, the most tenuous, and the most exhausting. He had risked everything, including his position, his fortune, and his very life. And the morning had brought with it his greatest triumph.

He had worked out the plan with Delgadillo and Carlos Hernández. The hard part, they figured, would be simply getting into the warehouse. The mayor had El Cinco standing guard, which would not have been a problem—hard as they might be, they were just five men. But Don Nicolás apparently realized that five was not enough, so he sent more men to guard the place. And then more.

And even if all those guards surrounding the warehouse could be eliminated, the building itself was like a fortress. Hernández had built it that way, knowing it was meant to keep valuable goods safe in the most dangerous part of a dangerous city. With the mayor's men standing guard inside as well as out, there would be no easy way to breach the walls. Unless the men on the inside opened the door for them.

It was Delgadillo's idea to intercept the wagon and use it as a means of getting into the place. Alonso thought of the second wagon, once it was clear that just getting Delgadillo in by himself was not going to be enough. The second wagon would put twenty of the One Hundred inside the warehouse, enough to start the festivities. The remainder would be with Alonso, ready to attack the men on the outside, then come to the assistance of Delgadillo and the others. Simple.

Hernández had not much cared for any of it. The risks were great, the chances of success less so. But he kept his objections to a minimum, and Alonso could guess why. He hated Don Nicolás with a passion like white-hot iron. And worse, he was more and more under Don Nicolás's thumb. For all his secret wealth and influence, Carlos Hernández could not free himself from a man as powerful as the mayor, not without an ally who was equally well-placed. Alonso was Hernández's only way out from under.

Things had not gone entirely as planned. That was hardly a surprise to anyone, least of all Don Alonso, who had seen battle at Breda and the Siege of Groenlo and knew how quickly military actions large or small could fall apart. What did surprise him, when he and his men came to the aide of Delgadillo and the others, was how hard the fighting had been. Don Nicolás, it seemed, had sent even more men to guard the warehouse than Hernández had reported. The mayor was taking no chances. And when Alonso and the One Hundred fell on them, they fought like demons.

The fight played out with pistols and swords and knives and pikes, and it raged through the streets. It took place in dark alleys and dirty, cobbled roads, a confused and bloody affair. Alonso had suffered a few wounds, minor things. He killed three men that he knew of. Six of his own men were wounded and two killed. A handful of the mayor's men had run or limped off. The rest were rounded up and held prisoner.

With the fight over, and the mayor's dead tossed into the river on the ebbing tide, the hard work began. A thousand casks of perfectly good salt beef, the stores that Don Nicolás had pilfered from various places, were found lined up in the warehouse, ready to be turned over to Admiral Toledo's purser. One by one they were tilted on their sides and rolled to a far corner of the building where they would not be seen. In their place went the thousand casks of rotten beef that the purser had sent ashore days earlier.

One cask looks like another, but the brands burned into them, the supplier's marks, do not. Each of the casks from the fleet was branded with the letters **EC**, but Delgadillo had already arranged for new brands to be made, ones that would overlay the **EC**, change the letters to **BQ**, and add the outline of a crown for good measure.

They worked all through the night, rebranding each barrel, top and bottom. When they were done, it seemed to all appearances that the casks that had come from Seville were different casks entirely. Admiral Toledo's purser never questioned it. Of course, Alonso paid him a substantial amount to limit his curiosity, and to express shock and outrage when it was discovered that Don Nicolás was trying to sell rotten beef to the fleet.

The profit Don Alonso made selling Don Nicolás's salt beef was considerable, even after Alonso offered, as a gesture of patriotism and good will, to sell it at a much lower price than Don Nicolás had. He was quite satisfied with the money and the praise. But none of it came close to the joy he felt at seeing Don Nicolás's impotent rage, a fury so profound that it seemed as if the man's head might blow apart like a petard. Don Nicolás, Alonso was certain, knew exactly what had taken place, and there was not a thing he could do about it. It was wonderful.

Ten days had passed since then, and Don Alonso had not seen Don Nicolás once during that time. Nor had anyone with whom Don Alonso spoke. The consensus, repeated in pitying tones around Las Casas Reales, was that Don Nicolás had been the victim of some nefarious supplier who sold him rotten stores which he unwittingly had tried to sell to Toledo's fleet.

At least, that was what everyone said. It was not at all what anyone believed. What everyone believed was that the mayor, whose corruption was well know, had tried to swindle Toledo's purser and had been caught in the act. Don Nicolás, robbed of the huge profit he stood to gain, his illicit plan publicly found out, knew that his reputation was tattered, if not destroyed, and he was making himself scarce.

Alonso had not stopped with the casks of beef. The three surviving members of El Cinco, and those of the mayor's men who had been taken prisoner, were turned over to Admiral Toledo's flag captain as hands for the galleons' crews—a thing they needed almost as much as they needed food—which stripped Don Nicolás of his muscle. Don Alonso Menéndez de Aviles, a fellow knight, with Toledo, of the Order of Santiago, was a hero in the eyes of the Admiral. He found the whole thing delightful.

These things he considered as he leaned on the quarterdeck rail of the massive *Nuestra Señora de Seville*, Toledo's flagship, looking out to the northwest. Beside him stood Captain Delgadillo. The island of Tortuga, humpbacked and green, lay stretched out before them off the starboard bow.

Behind them, and inboard, stood the admiral himself, the cock of the walk, with his sycophantic officers like hens gathered around him and clucking away. Don Alonso was no stranger to fawning, and was not in the least adverse to the practice, but even he could not stomach the spittle-licking that went on around the great man.

"I wonder what's acting there," Delgadillo said. He was not referring to the discussion Toledo was having with his men. They had been watching two ships, several miles ahead, apparently engaged in battle. They could see them spinning around one another, like slow, silent dancers. They could hear no gunfire so far away, not over the sound of the wind and the creaking of the ship and the simpering of Toledo's entourage, but they could see jets of smoke erupting between the two vessels. Both men had seen great guns fired often enough to recognize it, even from that distance.

"I wonder," Alonso said. "These miserable pirates contending for supremacy, I suppose."

Toledo and the other men on the quarterdeck were also aware of the battle. The lookouts had reported it sometime back. But they showed no interest, did not even bother to glance forward and see what was happening. In their minds, the Armada de Sotavento was so powerful, so able to roll over any resistance, that there was no point in even acknowledging such things. And they were probably right.

But Alonso and Delgadillo were more curious than that, leaning over the rail and watching the action. The ships seemed to have doled out some real punishment to one another; it was hard to tell from that distance, but each appeared to have lost a mast. Alonso knew little of naval warfare, but he guessed that the two vessels would now come together, the crew of one ship would board the other, and they would fight it out in that manner. That seemed reasonable.

"It seems, Don Alonso, the curs have not even noticed the Armada de Sotavento," Delgadillo said. He sounded amused.

"Good. The blind dogs, they'll get quite the surprise when they do."

They watched for some time more, until the ships, like amputees with their missing masts, seemed to abandon the fight and turn their bows toward the shore. Soon it was clear that they were both aground and no doubt being abandoned by their crews.

"I think they've seen us now," Alonso observed.

He was sorry to see the ships doing such damage to each other. They would both soon be prizes of the Armada, and though Alonso was not clear on how the plunder would be shared out, he hoped to get a piece of it, however little it might be.

The money Alonso made selling the salt beef was delightful, the pain he brought to Don Nicolás even better. But his greatest prize, which he was now enjoying, was securing for himself a place in the upcoming attack on Tortuga.

Even after his noble gestures toward the fleet, it had taken some effort: a word in the admiral's ear from the purser, and from Governor General Gabriel de Chávez y Osorio, and, perhaps most important, a few words from his wife to her Tío Fadrique. Finally, Alonso and the Governor's Guard had been asked to take part in the capture of the island. Their actual role was ill-defined, but then, there did not seem to be a very impressive level of organization in any of the land or naval forces. And that was fine with Alonso.

His plans for Tortuga were twofold. First, he intended to take part in the fighting, and to distinguish himself if he could. Second, and of greater importance, he would lay claim, at last, to his Tortuga plantation.

The plantation had been a year and a half in the planning: a letter patent secured through the court of France, a false owner put in place to lay claim to the land, gold sent out with the man to make a proper establishment. Alonso had been working on this since he first secured the lieutenant governorship of Hispaniola.

There was a fortune to be made in the New World. Smuggling, illicit trade, privateering. Alonso meant to outstrip his father and even his father-in-law in wealth and prestige. But there was only so much that could be done in Santo Domingo, under the eyes of the governor and the mayor and the *real audiencia.*

No, to really bring his plans to fruition he needed another place, in a lawless country, where he could run his business unimpeded.

Tortuga. Just a bit over four hundred miles from Santo Domingo, mostly downwind sailing, an uncivilized outpost, claimed by France but peopled by the human refuse who drifted around the West Indies. No one asked questions there. It was perfect. The Tortuga plantation had been central to Alonso's plans, at least until a hurricano swept the islands, wrecked the ship he had sent to set up the plantation, and nearly killed Alonso himself in the process.

The plantation, he thought, had been snatched from his grasp. And then Toledo, *Tío Fadrique*, arrived at Santo Domingo with plans to sail to Tortuga, drive the vermin out, and lay claim to the island for Spain, which was the rightful possessor of all the West Indies. And Alonso felt his hope kindle again.

He heard some talk behind him, loud, in the cadence of orders, words passed from mouth to mouth. Then one of the ship's officers (Alonso did not know what his actual position in the hierarchy was) stepped to the break of the quarterdeck and called out, "Clew up your t'gan's'ls! Hands aloft to stow! Boatswain, a man with the lead in the chains!"

Alonso, no sailor, did not know what any of that meant, save that it suggested something was finally happening. They had been underway for six days now. For the first four of those days, after setting out from Santo Domingo, they had struggled to make good the two hundred and fifty miles to windward they needed to get around the eastern end of Hispaniola. But once they rounded Cabo Engaño at the far end of the island, they turned northwest, and then west, with the wind right astern and steady.

After that, the sails seemed to need no adjusting, none of the hauling and pulling and racing up and down the rigging that Alonso associated with mariners' work. They just rolled along in the warm breeze, the entire Armada de Sotavento and the dozens of smaller ships that accompanied it. It was quite dull, really. When Tortuga hove into sight it peaked Alonso's interest for a while. After that, the distant fight between the two ships had offered some minor diversion. But now, at last, something of consequence seemed to be happening.

A few dozen men swung themselves up onto the thick, black shrouds and began to hurry aloft, *to stow*, Alonso guessed. At the ship's rails others took hold of sundry lines and hauled away. Alonso, as he often did, marveled at how they could find the precise ropes they needed out of the seemingly chaotic jumble that ran down from aloft. Sailors, in his opinion, were a generally stupid breed, and it seemed incredible that they could master such things.

Forward, a man had climbed onto the little platform that jutted out from the side of the ship and, squeezing between the shrouds, he swung a vaguely conical piece of lead on the end of a rope, then flung it out ahead of the ship, letting the rope pay out through his fingers.

All this activity Alonso found interesting for a moment or so, before it settled back into dullness once again.

"Well, sure this is a good omen," Delgadillo said hopefully. "Sure this must mean we'll come to grips with an enemy soon."

"By all that is holy, I pray you're right," Alonso said. Six days at sea and already he thought he would go mad. He wondered how the mariners could endure the monotony of it all.

It's no surprise these dogs are all drinkers and sodomites, he thought. *What else is a man to do?*

For some time their hopes remained high, sure that this new business meant a quick end to the monotony, but eventually those hopes grew dull as well. Alonso watched, surreptitiously, anxiously, as a few of the officers conferred amongst themselves, then with the captain of *Nuestra Señora de Seville*, then with Toledo, and then once more amongst themselves. There was a great deal of pointing and waving of arms, and Alonso did not think any of it was going to make him happy.

Soon the conferring and arm-waving was done, and once again orders were shouted out along the deck. Men grabbed onto the various ropes and hauled the few sails still set up to the yards and the flagship lost what little way she had. Another call from the quarterdeck, and forward the massive anchor, hanging from a short arm jutting out over the side of the ship, dropped from sight. Alonso heard the splash, saw the spray of water flying up beyond the ship.

"What is going on?" he asked the officer with whom he had spoken earlier. "We've anchored?"

"The tide is low now, and flooding, your grace," the officer explained. His tone was friendly, and not patronizing, and somehow Alonso found that even more annoying. "Water's too low for us to get in close to shore, and with the flood tide there's too much danger of being swept in. So we wait."

"Wait? For how long?"

"The morning should bring us the tides we need."

Alonso closed his eyes, let his immense irritation settle a bit. He opened his eyes. The officer was still standing there, waiting patiently to answer Alonso's next question. Alonso wanted to strike him.

"Very well," Alonso replied. There was not much else for him to say.

Chapter Eighteen

LeBoeuf allowed himself half a minute, no more, to consider the approaching Spaniards and to curse their existence. Then he turned back to his more immediate concerns.

Lessard was standing on the ship's rail, amidships, ax held over his head. He brought it down on a backstay that was lying over the rail. The tarred rope—the last thing tethering the wreckage to the ship—burst apart, and mast, yards, sails, topmast and rigging all slid, with a chorus of wrenching and snapping, off the rail and into the sea.

The men stepped back. They lowered their axes and cutlasses. They grinned at one another, proud of what they had accomplished. LeBoeuf immediately stomped on the embers of their pleasure.

"Listen here," he called down the deck. "There are sails to weather and to lee. They could be but the Spaniards, come to drive us from Tortuga."

For a moment no one spoke, no one moved. They stared back at LeBoeuf as if he had just shouted some complete gibberish. Then it occurred to them to look for themselves, which they did, swiveling to east and west. And then they all started talking, cursing, shouting at once.

"We'll get ashore, set up what defense we can," LeBoeuf called next, his voice, like a thunderclap, rolling over the swarm of noise. "Brace the yards up, starboard tack! Le Chasseur, come take the helm! Billy Solent, get some men and find a means to sheet this mizzen home!"

Shocked, stunned as the men were, LeBoeuf's commanding voice brought them back. They scattered, some to the braces, some to the bowlines. Billy Solent and a couple of the others hurried aft. Le Chasseur grabbed onto the tiller and shifted it amidships.

The foreyard came swinging around as the men hauled the lee braces. The foresail snapped and filled. LeBoeuf looked to the east, and though he was not looking for the Spanish fleet he could not help but steal a glance in that direction. He let his eyes linger a bit, felt a curse building in his gut, then turned his attention to the shoreline.

They were well to leeward now of the channels that led to the harbor of Cayona, such as it was. There was no chance that they could work their way to windward with their crippled ship. The best they could do was sail straight at the island, see how close they could get.

"Put your helm down," he said to Le Chasseur. Le Chasseur pushed the tiller over, and the wind in the foresail and the spritsail helped push the bow around. LeBoeuf could feel the ship start to gather way.

"That's well. Make your heading there."

Behind him, Billy Solent and his gang managed to tame the mizzen sheet and pull it home and the mizzen sail filled as well. LeBoeuf took a step aft, looked back at the ship's wake. They were moving now, the string of boats they were towing astern following behind. Two of the boats had taken hits from Van Loudersong's broadsides and were little more than floating wreckage. But the rest seemed intact, and they would be enough to get the men ashore.

To the west, and a half a mile or so away, Van Loudersong's men had managed to clear their fallen foremast; LeBoeuf could see it floating free. Their mizzen and spritsail were still set, and they were setting the mainsail now, getting underway as LeBoeuf had done.

They must have seen the Spaniards.

The men on that ship would be no more pleased about this new development than LeBoeuf and his crew were.

"LeBoeuf!" D'Anton was standing at the forward most of the great guns, a linstock in his hand. "You want we fire at these bastards, we pass by?" He nodded toward Van Loudersong's ship, which would be directly under their guns very soon.

"No," LeBoeuf called. "Leave them be."

D'Anton frowned and hesitated a moment. It seemed a plum opportunity. Even at that range they might have done terrific hurt with the bastard culverings, well laid. Maybe even sunk the whores' sons.

But LeBoeuf had no stomach for firing on Van Loudersong just then, and he hoped Van Loudersong felt the same. He was more concerned with avoiding further damage to his own ship, or worse, the boats, than he was with meting out punishment to the Dutchman. There would be time for that later. Perhaps.

LeBoeuf's eyes were on Van Loudersong's ship as it passed within the arc of their broadside. He waited for the familiar, silent, puff of smoke, followed a beat later by the blast of the gun and the whistle of the shot passing overhead. Or the concussion of the shot striking the hull. But he could see no sign that Van Loudersong's men were manning their battery, and no guns fired as they passed.

It does seem a shame.

Other Dog was on the prowl, pacing fore and aft. She paused, stared out a gunport at the other ship, growled.

"I know, I know," LeBoeuf said.

Then they were past, and LeBoeuf's broadside would no longer bear on Van Loudersong's ship. The guns had all remained silent. The men on that other ship, like LeBoeuf and his crew, had greater concerns now.

LeBoeuf looked down the deck, but the foresail blocked his view of everything beyond the bow. "Steady as she goes," he said to Le Chasseur, then hurried forward, past the foremast, and up onto the heel of the bowsprit.

Directly ahead of them, and a couple miles off, was Tortuga: the fringe of white beach lining the shore, the bulwark of palms and vegetation just inland of that, and the dark green jungle marching up the slopes to the mountainous country to the north.

But the land was not LeBoeuf's concern, not yet. It was the water that concerned him now; chiefly, how much water there was under their keel. He looked out over the sea's surface, clear as glass and aquamarine, a color that continued to astound him even after all his years in the West Indies. Darker up ahead, with a lighter stretch close off the larboard bow a couple hundred feet away.

"Le Chasseur!" he called down the deck. "Come up a bit!"

The light patches warned of sandbars at various depths below the surface, and LeBoeuf did not care to find out how deep this one was. They were making about three or four knots, a respectable speed given that they had only three sails, and enough to get them well stuck if they ran aground.

They were sailing straight at the island; they would run aground eventually, but LeBoeuf hoped to get much closer than they were before that happened.

He heard Le Chasseur's muffled reply. He kept his eyes on the lighter patch of water. A moment later the ship reacted to the shift of the helm, turning slightly more to windward, away from the shallow water.

"That's well! Make that your heading!"

He watched the sandbar pass down the larboard side. He could see now the water was thin over the sand, and he wondered if he had adjusted course enough. He felt himself tense, waiting for the bump, the slight jolt of momentum checked. But there was nothing, and a moment later the sandbar was astern.

Ahead, nothing more, nothing but the lovely blue-green sea right up to the brilliant white beach. LeBoeuf stepped down from the bowsprit and made his way aft.

"Collect up your gear!" he called to the men as he passed. "Firelocks, anything you want to bring with you. We'll get as close to shore as we can, then take the boats directly. I don't reckon we'll set foot on this ship again."

The men turned to collecting up what they had, slinging bandoliers and powder horns and haversacks over their shoulders. There was not much aboard the ship worth saving, beyond what the men had brought. LeBoeuf had figured that the ship, left at anchor, would be ransacked eventually, so he had taken everything worth having with him before heading off to claim the Tortuga plantation.

He stopped by the tiller and leaned on the weather rail. To leeward, Van Loudersong's ship was underway with their oddly unbalanced rig of spritsail, main, main topsail, and mizzen. They were also making directly for the island, and LeBoeuf imagined they were having trouble just keeping their ship on some kind of proper heading. There was no chance they would be attacking anytime soon.

LeBoeuf looked up at the sails, he looked over the side, he looked forward at the shores of Tortuga. They were closing with the island, moving as fast as their damaged ship was going to sail, and it was only a question of how close they might get.

Minutes passed—five, ten—and the details of the island grew more distinct.

"We're getting damn close," Le Chasseur said. "Surprised we ain't run aground yet. You reckon we'll get much closer?"

"No," LeBoeuf said, and just as the word left his mouth they felt the slight jar of the ship plowing its keel into the soft sand ten feet below the waterline. The vessel came to a stop so gently that LeBoeuf was not even certain they were aground until he looked over the side and saw that the water was no longer flowing past.

"Reckon you can let go of the tiller now," he said to Le Chasseur. He turned forward, and in a voice that could be heard fore and aft, he said, "That's as far as we get, *Messieurs*. Get the boats alongside."

Le Chasseur and a few others cast off the tow line and pulled the boats around the ship's side. The two that had been reduced to driftwood were left to float away; the others were hauled up one at a time to the bottom of the boarding steps. The buccaneers gathered at the gangway, and with them two canvas bundles containing the earthly remains of Rioux and Steen. The blood, soaking through the cloth, looked black, like spilled tar.

"Load the boats up, but don't overload them," LeBoeuf said. "Can't take the lot of us in one run, regardless."

One by one the men climbed down into the succession of boats, moving awkwardly with muskets in hand and sundry gear hanging from belts around their shoulders, until roughly half the ship's company was embarked. They took up the oars, or took their place on the center thwarts.

On deck, D'Anton and Billy Solent grabbed up first Steen, then Rioux, and passed them down to the men below, and once the bodies were laid on the floorboards the little armada pulled for the beach. There, most of the men climbed out, wrestling the canvas bundles after them, and the few remaining aboard pulled back to the grounded ship.

Once again the boats came up under the boarding steps, and the men still aboard climbed down and found a place. LeBoeuf came last, grabbing up his musket and stepping over to the gangway, Other Dog at his heels. He paused and rested his musket on the bulwark.

"Your turn," he said to Other Dog, who was looking up at him with tongue lolling. LeBoeuf leaned over, gathered the dog up, and lifted her in his arms, likely the only man aboard who could have carried the mastiff that way.

He took two steps down the boarding ladder, the panting dog against his chest, and called, "Stand from under!" Then he tossed Other Dog the remaining distance as the men in the boat leapt clear of the falling beast. Other Dog hit the bottom with a thud and sent the boat rocking violently as the men struggled to retain their seats.

Maybe I shouldn't have done that, LeBoeuf thought, but the boat settled and did not swamp, so he climbed back to the deck, retrieved his musket, then climbed back down, getting into the boat more carefully than Other Dog had.

They pulled through the clear, clear water for the beach, one hundred yards away. To the west, and several miles off, LeBoeuf could see the Spanish frigates coming about as they clawed their way to windward. They may have been handier than the big galleons, but no square-rigged ship could make much progress that way, sailing tack on tack, and it would take them some time to reach Cayona. Longer than the galleons which were running downwind, certainly.

Van Loudersong's ship was only half a mile away, and like LeBoeuf's it was also aground, the men pulling the boats around. They had struck well to the west of LeBoeuf's ship, which meant the two crews would not come face to face on the beach. Just as well. LeBoeuf was content to fight one battle at a time

LeBoeuf's boat, last in line, ground up on the sand ten feet short of dry land. The men forward leapt over the gunnels and started pulling it closer. Other Dog leapt out as well, with a great splash that showered them all, and charged up the sand.

LeBoeuf stood, hopped over the gunwale and waded ashore. The entire company, thirty or so men, were gathered there. Some were sitting, some were leaning on their muskets. Most had bottles of some sort, from which they were refreshing themselves. A few were tossing the last shovelfuls of sand onto the graves they had dug for Rioux and Steen up near the tree line.

Good place to spend eternity, LeBoeuf thought. *Warm, at least.* Of course, where Steen and Rioux and likely all the buccaneers were bound would be warm enough.

"Let's pull these boats into the trees, hide them as best as we can," LeBoeuf said. Men nodded, corked their bottles. They leaned their muskets on the driftwood logs cast up on the sand and marched down to the edge of the water.

LeBoeuf was not sure why he had given that order. He had put no thought into it. He had first considered smashing the boats to deprive the Spaniards of them, but on impulse decided to keep them hidden instead.

Des options, toujours des options. One never knew.

The men hauled the various boats up the beach and into the tree line, where they were quickly lost in the deep vegetation.

"Good," LeBoeuf said. "Let's go." They took up their muskets again and headed east along the beach, walking close to the edge of the water where the sand was firm. Other Dog kept mostly at LeBoeuf's side, on occasion running off and charging through the shallow water when she could no longer endure the pace of her human companions.

To the south, and a few miles across the water, the rugged mountains of Hispaniola stood out dark against the blue sky, the mounds of white cloud. LeBoeuf looked at the distant island as he walked, then allowed his eyes to wander east to where the fleet of Spanish galleons was rolling down under pyramids of white sail.

They were still several miles away, still an hour at least from reaching the roadstead off Cayona. A few hours, more like. The great beasts, with their fifteen feet or more of draft, would reduce sail and feel their way into the shallower water as they approached Tortuga.

He tried to count the ships, but he could not, as some were obscured by others. He could see ten for certain. He silently cursed them, again; cursed the Spaniards, cursed the whole wicked world in general. Then he turned his eyes to the white sand, the green trees, and kept on walking.

They had come ashore about a mile west of Cayona, and LeBoeuf figured to march his men back to the town and see what was acting. A majority of the good citizens were likely drunk, he imagined, but some at least must have seen the Spaniards in the offing and perhaps started preparing for their arrival. If there was nothing happening at Cayona, he would lead his men back to the plantation and see about making a stand there.

Damned Spaniards…mayhaps they'll stay in Cayona, not dare wander too far afield…

It was possible, certainly, but LeBoeuf doubted it. As inept as the Spaniards were at administering what they conquered, they were pretty thorough when it came to the conquering part. And by the looks of the fleet, they would be arriving with men enough to do whatever they wished.

A quarter mile shy of Cayona, the buccaneers could hear some sort of activity; the thud of some heavy thing dropped on something else, banging, like a maul on iron, shouting. The occasional musket shot. Singing.

"What the devil is going on there?" Levesque asked.

"I hope they're building a gallows to welcome the Spaniards," Levasseur said. "That's the welcome I'd give them."

LeBoeuf did not offer an opinion. He could not imagine what was going on. And he was not optimistic.

They came at last around a wooded point of land and found themselves back where they had started the day before, on the beach at the end of the road that led up to the town of Cayona. But this time they were not alone. Nearly all of the town, it seemed, was there, and most were directing their energy toward a single project: the construction of an ad hoc wooden rampart where the beach met the road.

The wall was about ten feet high and fifty feet long. From the look of it, the people had torn down some of the more dilapidated buildings and used the component parts to build their defenses. They had also used driftwood logs, an old wagon, some broken bits of furniture and anything else, apparently, that was solid and unwanted.

A dozen men were climbing along the top of the rampart. They were hefting various objects handed up to them and securing them as directed by the engineer of the operation, who was standing near the center of the wall, pointing here and there, calling out orders. LeBoeuf recognized him as the tavern keep at The Tuileries. The unofficial mayor of Cayona.

LeBoeuf stopped where he was and the men behind him stopped as well. He sighed a deep sigh and shook his head. He did not want to do this. He did not want to be part of this, any of it.

He wanted to go back to his plantation. He wanted to lay down on the warm earth and he wanted Henriette to lay down beside him and he wanted to let all of the worry and the consideration and the anger drain away into the fecund soil. And he wanted to stay there, with the hot sun beating down on him, and he wanted to never move again.

But that was not to be. LeBoeuf had ample experience and training and God-given ability that would benefit those hapless folks on the wall. Worse, he was possessed by some spirit that would not let him walk away, would not let him ignore all this, not, at least, without making some effort to stop the folly.

He sighed again and continued on toward the seaward side of the wall.

"Halloa, there," he called up to the tavern keeper above.

The tavern keeper looked down at LeBoeuf, frowned, and said, "You're the one was fighting Maja and that lot today. We watched that. Damned bit of entertainment."

"Maja?" LeBoeuf said. "Van Loudersong. I was fighting Van Loudersong."

"Who?"

"The Dutchman. Van Loudersong."

"Oh! No, not the Dutchman. He was with them. But it was Maja. And Graves."

LeBoeuf frowned. "Who's Maja?"

"The Taino fellow. Always wears that red cloth on his head. Mean bastard. It's his ship, his men. But Graves, he's master. Does the actual sailing."

Maja and Graves… LeBoeuf thought. So it was not Van Loudersong he was grappling with. It was this Graves bastard—the fat one with the beard, most like. He was the one who had put up such a fight. Interesting. But it was of no importance, not then.

"What have you got going on here?" LeBoeuf asked, nodding toward the wall.

"Fortification," the tavern keeper said, and there was a touch of pride in his voice. "Spanish fleet's in the offing. They'll be here soon enough, and won't they be surprised when they see what's waiting for them."

LeBoeuf nodded. He looked up and down the length of the makeshift barricade. The other men on top of the wall, and some on the ground, were taking advantage of the mayor's distraction to have a rest and listen in.

"Impressive," LeBoeuf said. "But the Spaniards, they won't come ashore, not at first. They'll work their way in close, come to anchor as near-on to the beach as ever they can get. A couple hundred yards, I'd reckon. Then they'll rig springs to their cables, swing their ships broadside to, and they'll open up with their great guns. Those galleons, they're heavy armed. Demi-cannons, most like. Thirty-pound shot. They'll lay waste to all of this before they even launch a boat."

That statement was greeted with silence. No one seemed sure what to say. Then the tavern keeper spoke.

"You know what the Spaniards are going to do?" His tone was skeptical. Annoyed. LeBoeuf imagined that the wall had been his idea.

"No," LeBoeuf said. "I don't know. I just know what they usually do. What I would expect them to do. It's no matter."

There was silence again after that. Then one of the other men spoke.

"So you…your men…you won't stand and fight with us?"

"We won't stand in front of the Spaniards' demi-cannons, no," LeBoeuf said. "I've seen what a thirty-pound round shot can do. Don't care to see it again. We'll go into the jungle, let them fire as much as they please. Then, when they start sending men ashore, when they can't fire their great guns for fear of hitting their own soldiers, then we'll come out and fight."

LeBoeuf waited for someone to reply, but no one did, so he shouldered his musket, turned to his men, and said, "Let us away."

He headed off around the far end of the wall, where more people were gathered, a hundred or more at least. The entire citizenry of Cayona, it seemed. They stood still and watched the buccaneers march past in their loose order.

LeBoeuf kept eyes ahead as he walked up the sandy road to the now deserted town, the gathering of mismatched buildings that lined the way. He could hear the soft footfalls of his men following behind. Like him, they still wore the rawhide shoes of the pig hunters of Hispaniola, and they made little sound as they walked.

The jungle? he thought. That was his plan: retreat into the jungle, let the Spaniards blast away, then come out and catch them as they made for shore. The buccaneers, accustomed to firing fast and accurately, could do great slaughter among the surprised invaders.

But to what end? If the others in Cayona remained at their silly wall and allowed themselves to be blow into their component parts, what good could LeBoeuf and his thirty men do? They might kill a hundred out of the thousand men-at-arms the Spaniards would put on the beach. Of what use was that?

Better to head off to the plantation, set up a defense on land that he cared about.

He heard something else behind him, farther behind, a shuffling, rattling, clanking, murmuring. He did not turn around. He knew what it was. The people of Cayona, the people at the wall, were following him now. They believed him. They would look to him to lead. They would follow him into the jungle.

LeBoeuf frowned. He had spoken up because he could not bear to see those people pointlessly slaughtered by the Spaniards, as so many others had been, since Cristoforo Colombo had first stumbled into the New World. He had not promised to lead them—a subtle distinction they did not, and would not, see.

The price of my folly, he thought. And he did not think about it anymore.

Chapter Nineteen

The morning was well along by the time the massive *Nuestra Señora de Seville* was moving again, making her ponderous way along Tortuga's southern coast. Alonso had spent a largely sleepless night in the tiny closet that the sailors called a cabin, finally drifting off as dawn approached and waking again to the chaotic sound of the men preparing to weigh anchor.

He dressed quickly and hurried topside, fearful that he would still be in bed as the flagship finally made her way into shore and came to grips with the enemy. He reached the quarterdeck, found an unobtrusive place by the rail, and waited.

Two hours later, the ship was underway.

As the island of Tortuga passed slowly down the starboard side of the ship, Alonso took the opportunity to study it more closely: thick with jungle in some parts, more barren in others, rising up to steep, mountainous country on the north side. He could see no signs of civilization, no towns or plantations or much of anything else. In that way it was little different from most of the West Indies he had seen, which admittedly was not much.

Lost in his contemplation of the island, Alonso did not see the officer once again step up to the quarterdeck rail, and he jumped when the man shouted, "Every man to your charge! In with the foresail and mainsail! Make ready, all!"

Those dozen or so words sent the entire ship's company, more than four hundred men, racing off in every direction. Ropes were cast loose and hauled away, the sails let to flog as they were drawn up to the yards. Lashings on the great guns were untied, the guns hauled inboard for loading, the various tools for that purpose taken down from where they were stowed. Ship's boys appeared with cartridges of gunpowder. It seemed for all the world that the ship was being made ready for a fight, but Alonso could see no one with whom they might do battle.

He looked aft. Admiral Toledo and his coven were standing amidships, engaged in some animated discussion. Alonso did not want to interrupt, certainly not to ask a question that might indicate ignorance. But the officer who had been giving the orders was standing off to one side, watching the activity forward, and since he was certainly Alonso's inferior, Alonso felt more comfortable addressing him. He stepped over to the man and joined him in watching the sailors at work.

"Pray tell, are we making ready for some sea fight?" Alonso asked, nodding toward the men in the waist busily loading the great guns.

"I should think not, your grace," the officer said. "No ships hereabouts to give us battle. But these rogues ashore might have set up some defense, do you see? We'll work in as close as ever we can and we'll do what hurt we can to them before we set our men on the beach."

"Ah, I see," Alonso said. Of course, it made perfect sense. Lay waste to the vermin before sending the soldiers in. No reason to toss away the lives of men-at-arms. They were not easily replaced, what with the West Indies being so far from Spain.

"Captain Delgadillo," Alonso called next, "see that our men are under arms and ready to go ashore. We'll be on the beach directly."

Delgadillo hurried below to get the men moving and Alonso continued to watch, with interest, as the men prepared the ship for battle. Chains were run aloft, apparently to keep the heavy, lower yards from crashing down to the deck, fire buckets set out near the guns, sand spread for traction. The ship's boats, stored in the waist, were hoisted one at a time and set over the side. It all seemed a bit much to Alonso, given that their only enemy was a gaggle of pirates with small arms, but he figured the ship's officers had only one way of doing things, and this was it.

The sailors were just finishing with their preparations when Delgadillo appeared in the waist, below the quarterdeck. Behind him came the One Hundred, and they spread out in the space where the boats had been. They wore their black tunics and tall boots, but now they were outfitted with crested helmets as well, and breastplates, and muskets that were too awkward to carry when they were on horseback. They looked good; an elite troop.

The officer with whom Alonso had spoken earlier stepped up by his side. "Forgive me, your grace," he said, nodding toward the waist. "These are your men?"

"Yes," Alonso said. He waited for the praise he was sure would come next.

"I have no doubt they'll do us great service, señor," the officer said, "once we are ashore. But I fear they will be in my men's way, gathered in the waist as they are."

"These are the finest fighting men," Alonso protested. "They should be the first ashore. Should I speak with Admiral Toledo on this matter?"

Alonso reckoned that a mention of the Admiral, which suggested that he, Alonso, held particular sway with the great man, would make the officer more pliant, but it seemed not to work that way.

"I'm certain the admiral will want your men to take the lead," the officer said, "once we're ready to go ashore. But that will be some time from now, I fear."

Alonso looked past the bow. They were a third of the way down the length of the island, and the ship had already turned a bit north, closing with the land. It seemed to Alonso that they would be going ashore quite soon. Sail in close, fire a few cannons, and off they go.

At the same time, he knew there was much about this sort of thing he did not understand. He did not care to countermand his order to Delgadillo, but even less did he want to lose an argument with an officer of Toledo's flagship. Either way he risked appearing ignorant. He considered which would be the lesser of two embarrassments.

"Very well." He stepped up to the rail of the quarterdeck. "Captain Delgadillo, pray take these men below and await my further orders." He tried to sound as if this was his intention all along, and, good subordinate that Delgadillo was, he did not question it.

Nuestra Señora de Seville continued to close with the Tortuga coast, the rest of the Armada de Sotavento following in her wake. Alonso felt the surge of energy that came with going into action, the tension in his limbs and shoulders. That feeling had been absent for some time, since he gave up the military life for marriage and domestic peace. It had returned with the action he had seen in Santo Domingo, putting down riots, leading the One Hundred, and raiding

Hernández's warehouse. And now here it was again, and he relished it.

And then, an hour later, it was gone. The flagship's officer had not lied: they were in no immediate danger of going ashore and coming to grips with an enemy.

Yard by agonizing yard, barely drifting under her fore topsail alone, *Nuestra Señora de Seville* crept toward the island. The man with the weighted line was back, calling out numbers that Alonso realized were the depth of water under the ship, and men aloft reported in urgent tones about this or that reef or sandbar to larboard or starboard.

Seems to be quite a lot of concern about running the ship aground, Alonso thought. They were approaching the island like an old man, blind and lame, feeling his way along a broken path.

The whole thing was agonizing. Alonso had spent enough time campaigning to know that waiting was a big part of it, but at least on land he usually had some notion of what was going on, why the wait was necessary. Now, he could only watch and wonder.

Then, finally, to his relief, something happened. With a few shouted orders the ship made a final turn, the fore topsail was hauled up, and the massive anchor was let fall into the clear water. The largest of the ship's boats was pulled alongside and a gang of sailors climbed down into it. Alonso hoped that meant the first of the men-at-arms—his men—would be going ashore. But instead, a heavy rope from the stern was lowered into the boat and the sailors brought it forward and made it fast to the anchor cable. Why they did that, he did not know, and he was not going to ask.

The ship had come to anchor a couple hundred yards from the beach. Beyond the stretch of white sand, Alonso could see that the ground had been cleared, or beaten flat, by the people who had come ashore at that place. There seemed to be a cluster of buildings a bit farther inland, where the sand turned into a road, or perhaps a wide path.

Between the edge of the water and the start of the road there was a wall of sorts, some ad hoc defense that seemed to have been set up against the coming invasion. Alonso could only smile at the sight of it. *Pathetic.* He could not imagine what the people who built it thought it would accomplish. He hoped very much they were hunkered down behind it at that moment. The broadsides that the fleet was about to unleash would make short work of the lot of them.

One by one the other galleons drew in astern of *Nuestra Señora de Seville* and anchored, and they too ran ropes from their sterns to their anchor cables. As they did, the sailors on *Señora de Seville* began to heave the capstan around. The line from the stern rose dripping from the water and the ship began to swing slowly to starboard, until her broadside was indeed broadside to the shore.

Oh, indeed, I see it now! Alonso thought. The rope allowed them to turn the ship and bring more of the great guns to bear.

He did not know how long it had been since he ordered Delgadillo and his men below. Hours, certainly. It felt like days. He looked up at the sun. There seemed to be plenty of daylight left, anyway, so that at least was encouraging.

Once again, the ship's officer stepped to the quarterdeck rail and looked down into the waist. There were four great guns on either side mounted there, and more in the fo'c'sle forward and on the quarterdeck, aft. Those guns were *canons perro*, firing twenty-four-pound shot. The big guns, fifteen per side, demi-cannons firing thirty-pound shot, were on the gundeck below, hidden from Alonso's sight.

On the starboard side, the landward side, the guns were manned by crews of eight men each, all of whom looked up eagerly at the quarterdeck. Alonso assumed that the larger guns below were similarly loaded and manned.

"Take care with your aim, and fire as you will!" the officer called. "Pass the word to the gundeck!"

In the quiet, the order rang out as it was repeated around the ship's deck and then below. The gunners, it seemed, had already taken care with their aim, or they simply ignored the officer's order. Either way, in the instant after the word was passed, the entire broadside went off as one.

Alonso was staggered. The noise was like a physical thing, like some invisible force slamming into him. The galleon, which had seemed stable as a granite ledge, shuddered underfoot and rolled a bit to larboard. An impenetrable wall of smoke erupted from the muzzles, blotting out everything beyond the ship's rails.

Impressive, Alonso thought, his ears suddenly ringing and dulled. He was no stranger to the fire of great guns, but he was accustomed to ordnance laid out in a long line on open ground, not bunched together behind wooden walls. When guns were fired in the field, the earth did not move and shake the way the galleon did.

Nuestra Señora de Seville's opening salvo was cue for the other ships, and one by one they too opened up on the shore. The trade wind swept the smoke clear and Alonso could see the damage their single broadside had done, and the further hurt the other ships were doling out.

The makeshift wall was nearly gone, blown into its many parts and scattered far up the beach. If there had been anyone hunkered down behind it, they were likewise only bits and pieces now. There were a few smaller vessels at anchor closer in, and a number of boats on the beach, which had been mostly reduced to flotsam. There appeared to be holes in the walls of some of the buildings farther inland, and sections of roofs missing, but it was too far for Alonso to tell for certain.

In the waist the men were reloading the guns, going through each step with an admirable precision, and one by one, in more ragged order, each was run out and fired again. On the gundeck below, the demi-cannons added their deeper boom to the rolling sound, and from the other ships more guns roared out like answering calls. Onshore the debris jumped, the boats were torn apart, spouts of sand shot skyward as the round shot plowed up the ground.

No one could stand up to that, Alonso thought. *There'll be no one ashore left to fight.* And with that thought he recalled his determination to be the first on the beach, to lead his men to the forefront of any potential glory. The one ship's officer had promised him that place of honor, but Alonso was not certain the man had the authority to make such a promise.

He pushed himself away from the rail and walked aft, as casually as he could manage, to where Toledo was watching the action, still surrounded by his officers and sundry toadies. Glances were shot Alonso's way as he approached, but the men parted to allow him through. They knew who he was. Word had gone around the flagship that Don Alonso Menéndez de Aviles enjoyed some special status with Toledo.

"Señor Admiral," Alonso said, giving a shallow bow. "A most impressive display, your grace."

"Hmm," Toledo said, noncommittal. "Thank you…Don Alonso." There was a hitch before he spoke Alonso's name, which he had clearly forgotten, but happily recalled at the last moment.

"Your grace, I have brought a hundred handpicked men with me, the finest of men-at-arms. I wonder if…." He paused as three guns went off at once, then continued. He was speaking loudly, he could tell, but he could still hardly hear himself. He hoped the others' ears were equally dulled, so he did not appear to be shouting at them.

"I wonder if I might have the honor of being first to land on the beach, once the cannonade is done?"

Toledo looked at him, scowled a bit, then said, "Yes, yes, certainly."

It was not at all clear to Alonso if the old bastard had heard him or not, or if he had understood the request, but it did not matter. He had granted Alonso his wish. Alonso and the others had heard it. The One Hundred's place was secured.

For another fifteen minutes or so the relentless barrage continued. Then an order was passed and the gunfire from the flagship stopped. A red pennant was hoisted to the top of the mainmast, and one by one the other ships stopped firing as well. There was a moment of relative silence, then Delgadillo appeared on the quarterdeck.

"Get the men ready," Alonso said. "The admiral has allowed we're to be the first ashore."

It did not take long. By the time the One Hundred were on deck, the sailors had hauled the ship's boats alongside and were seated on the thwarts, oars held straight up. Alonso stepped down to the waist where his servant was waiting with his helmet and breastplate. Once those were buckled on he crossed over to the boarding steps as Delgadillo got the men in order.

More of *Nuestra Señora de Seville*'s men-at-arms were assembling as well, ready to follow the One Hundred ashore. Alonso knew the bulk of Toledo's soldiers were on the transports, not the galleons. It would take them a while to join in the fight, which was fine by him. There was more glory to be had in fighting alone.

"Let us be off, then," Alonso said to the men behind him. He climbed down the high side of the ship and stepped with care into the waiting boat, the ship's longboat, thirty-five feet in length, manned by twenty men at the oars and a young officer aft at the tiller.

Alonso moved carefully to the stern, taking care to preserve his dignity as he did, then sat down opposite the officer.

One by one his men climbed down and found places on the thwarts until the boat was filled, lines of silver-helmeted soldiers seated between the sailors at the oars. The man in the bow pushed off and the sailors pulled a short distance from the ship, making room for the next boat at the flagship's side.

It took all the boats of any size that the galleon had on board, four in total, to carry all of Alonso's men. Alonso turned to the young man beside him at the tiller, ready to tell him to have his men row for shore, when a voice called across the water.

"Don Alonso!" It was the officer from the galleon's quarterdeck. "We have more men-at-arms here to go ashore. More boats coming from the other ships. Just back and fill here for a few moments, and you'll have men enough to make your landing."

Alonso looked back at the officer, but did not answer. He was not certain what to say. It made sense to wait for more men, but he also wanted it to be unambiguously clear that the One Hundred were the first ashore. Nor did he want to share command with the officers in charge of the other soldiers. He turned to the young man beside him.

"We won't wait for the others," he said, in a tone that suggested he would tolerate no arguments. "Tell your men to row for shore."

The young officer frowned, uncertain. He glanced back at the flagship's quarterdeck.

"You do as I tell you, or by God Admiral Toledo will hear of it!" Alonso snapped.

That seemed to do the trick. The young officer barked some orders forward, and the sailors, who seemed not to care one way or the other, dipped their oars and pulled.

"The rest of you," Alonso called to the other three boats, "follow us."

The small flotilla, the vanguard of an invading force, pulled for shore. Don Alonso looked back, past *Nuestra Señora de Seville*. He could see there were boats alongside the other ships, also loading soldiers aboard, and other empty boats heading for the flagship.

This will work well, he thought. He wanted himself and his men to be first into battle, though in truth he did not anticipate much resistance, not after the Biblical storm of shot they had unleashed. However, if there were enough of the bastards left to put up a real fight, the One Hundred would not fight alone for very long, not with the other men-at-arms coming behind.

It took only a few minutes for them to reach the shore. The longboat ground up on the beach and the sailors in the bow hopped out and hauled it farther up. Once they stopped hauling Alonso stood and stepped carefully over the side, into the warm, calf-deep water, and waded ashore. The rest of his men climbed out as well, just as the other three boats ran up on the sand on either side.

The dullness in Alonso's ears was starting to fade, and he could make out the crunch of his boots in the sand, the sound of the wind in the trees, the far off call of some exotic bird. He stopped fifty feet up the beach and listened, but he could hear nothing else. No human voices, no sign of an enemy near at hand.

He looked over the scattered debris strewn around the beach, the remains of the locals' ridiculous rampart. He shook his head, impressed at the work that the galleons' great guns had done. It put him in mind of the damage left in the wake of the hurricano that had hit when he first arrived in the West Indies.

Delgadillo stepped up beside him. For a moment the two men stood in silence, watching, listening, their eyes searching the town farther up the beach and the stands of trees and jungle that surrounded the clearing.

"No sign of anyone that I can see, Don Alonso," Delgadillo said.

"Cowards and villains. They've run off, no doubt."

Alonso was disgusted, though in truth it was hard to blame them. The Armada de Sotavento, and all the other ships in its company, were frightening enough. The demonstration of firepower that they had unleased on the town would convince any sane man to flee.

"Let us advance up the beach," Don Alonso said next. "See what sorry spoils we might lay claim to."

Delgadillo nodded. He turned to relay the orders to the others. And just as he did, a voice, some ways off, called out, just one word.

"*Maintenant!*"

Alonso frowned. It took him a second to register that the word was French, and another second to understand the significance of that. He stepped back and turned toward the sound just as the tree lines on either hand seemed to explode with small arms fire.

Chapter Twenty

It was all so familiar. Crouched in the foliage, musket in hand, ramrod stuck in the dirt by his side. His dog crouched beside him, all but quivering with frantic anticipation. LeBoeuf looking though the tall grass, unseen, ready, watching: it felt like putting on a well-worn glove.

But not watching pigs this time. Spaniards. A quarry that could shoot back.

He was not alone in thinking this, he imagined, the familiarity of it all. The others around him had plied that trade too, the pig-hunters, the *boucaniers*, until the hurricano and the Spaniards had dashed it all. And now they too were under arms and waiting.

It had been nearly twenty-four hours since LeBoeuf first saw the Spanish fleet closing in from the west and the east and ran his disabled ship aground. He gave his warning to the women and men at the makeshift wall, painting a picture of what the Spaniards' great guns would do, then he marched his own men up the road, heading for the cover of the jungle beyond.

He was all but certain that the rest of the people would follow, try as he might to ignore that truth. He did not want them to, did not want anyone beyond his own men to look to him for leadership. But he knew, even without thinking on it, that they would. Such would be the natural consequence of his warning.

And sure enough, he was not halfway to the scattering of odd buildings that made up the town of Cayona before he heard the rest behind, abandoning the wall, heading up the road in the wake of him and his men.

He continued on as far as the tavern, then stopped and turned around, and his men stopped as well. Other Dog sat on her haunches, tongue lolling. The townspeople were a hundred feet behind, and LeBoeuf let them catch up. They were an odd mix, maybe six score in total, mostly men, but not a small number of women as well. Some seemed to come from the ranks of the buccaneers, some were sailors, some wives, some whores, some just broken drunks. Some even seemed to be honest businessmen.

They gathered in a loose half-circle as they reached the place where LeBoeuf and his men were standing, and they stood in silence and waited. For what, it was not clear. Another warning? Orders? LeBoeuf figured he had better come up with something.

"I don't mean to tell a damned one of you what to do," LeBoeuf said in a voice loud enough to be heard by all who were there. "But I'll tell you what my men and I are going to do. And what I think you should do."

He looked around. They were listening, with various degrees of skepticism.

"My men and I are going to go into the jungle, yonder," he said, pointing over his shoulder with his thumb, "and we'll make ourselves comfortable. I don't reckon the Spaniards will come ashore today. Tide's low and starting to flood, and they won't want to come in with things in that state. They'll anchor out, and come in on the morrow.

"Once they're anchored in the harbor, they'll use their great guns, like I said. We'll keep out of the line of fire. Then, when the soldiers are in the boats and heading ashore, me and my men, we'll circle around, through the tree line. The bastards will be most vulnerable just as they're landing. Once their soldiers form up in regular order, we won't have men enough to stop them. So we'll do what hurt we can when the boats are landing."

That was, LeBoeuf realized, the most words he had strung together in a year at least. He looked around again. Some heads were nodding, but most faces remained expressionless. He wondered if anyone would think to ask the most obvious question. Then one did.

"Why?"

The question came from one of those whom LeBoeuf had reckoned for a broken drunk: clothes filthy and torn and mostly absent, splayed, bare feet, long and matted hair and beard. Former sailor, LeBoeuf suspected. He was a bit surprised. The wretch looked like he might drop dead directly.

"Why bother shooting the sons of whores?" the sailor followed up. "You ain't gonna stop 'em."

It was indeed the most obvious question, so it would make sense that LeBoeuf would have an answer ready. But he did not. He had been acting by instinct, like a wild beast. Not thinking. So he just started talking, as curious as anyone as to what would come out.

"Probably not worth the bother. No matter what we do, they're going to try to hunt us down, and if they catch us, then it's off to the silver mines. But we can kill some of them, and that's something. Kill as many as we can, put some fear into the rest. Make them think twice about coming after us. That's the most I'm hoping for."

That, or a Spanish bullet through the head, the easy way out, he thought, but he kept that to himself.

The ragged sailor nodded. "That's good enough for me. Anyone here got a firelock I can have the use of?"

LeBoeuf looked around at the others. Most, it seemed, would follow him in this pointless effort. *Like a hundred Sancho Panzas*, he thought, recalling a book he had read a few years back, about a Spanish fellow whose name he could not remember.

"And hear me," LeBoeuf continued. "No matter how many we kill, the Spaniards will take this town and everything in it, and they'll keep it as long as they like. If you have anything you don't want those dogs to take, I suggest you fetch it now. And recall, you'll likely have to carry it all over this God-forsaken island trying to keep away from those bastards, so choose with care."

It took a moment for that to sink in, then about half of the people there headed off in different directions to collect what they did not wish to lose to Spanish looters. The others, the penniless flotsam who had drifted to that place and carried on their persons whatever they possessed, remained where they were, leaning on muskets, drinking rum and brandy out of bottles hanging from cords over their shoulders.

LeBoeuf turned to his own men. "Some of you best go find some food and drink. We'll need it."

Soon the others came drifting back, carrying those things they considered too dear to let the Spanish have. A number of the men carried extra weapons, a good choice. Some carried haversacks, or bags over their backs, or blankets rolled and slung over shoulders with God knows what wrapped up inside. A woman carried two cats in her arms, which LeBoeuf thought was ridiculous, but he guessed it would not be a problem for long. Others carried musical instruments and wooden boxes of various sizes and even small pieces of furniture, things that would soon be no more than debris scattered along a jungle trail, making it easier still for the Spaniards to hunt them down.

The handful of LeBoeuf's men who had gone looking for food and drink returned as well, carry full sacks and bottles hanging from cords.

"Very well, let's go," LeBoeuf said. He headed up the road once again, Other Dog at his side, his men and then the people of Cayona following behind.

He passed the road that led off to his plantation, looking at it longingly as he did. A hundred yards beyond, the beaten ground faded into scrubby brush and then thicker jungle. It dipped down a bit before rising to the higher ground to the north, meaning any Spanish round shot aimed at the town would pass overhead. Perfect.

Once again LeBoeuf stopped and looked back at the people behind. The woman with the cats was already down by one, and that one was showing signs of restlessness. Near the back of the crowd he saw the tavern keeper, the man who had organized the wall-building. LeBoeuf was surprised to see him there; he had seemed understandably resentful of LeBoeuf's dismissing his strategic vision. LeBoeuf waved him over.

"When the Spaniards come ashore, it'll most likely be at the easiest spot, right on the beach," he said. "They'll think we've all run off. I mean to work my way down around the west side, keep hidden in the jungle. Hit them in the flank. It would be best if half of us attacked from the east side. Can you take the townspeople who want to fight, lead them down that way?"

The tavern keeper frowned, looked back toward the town, then toward the jungle to the east.

"Yes, I can do that," he said at last.

"Good," LeBoeuf said. "Name off the men you want. I'll take my men over there." He pointed to a place at the western edge of the clearing. "You take yours there." He pointed to the east. "I'll send you word when we're going to move. It'll be before the Spaniards land, some time on the morrow. We want to be in place before that. Hold your fire until a good number of the Don Diegos are onshore, and can't row away. I'll sing out loud when it's time for the first volley. Is that good?"

The tavern keeper nodded a bit, glanced around again. "Yes, good," he said.

They divided up, LeBoeuf and his men to the west, the tavern keeper and his people, the women included, to the east. The ragged sailor and a few others from the town joined with LeBoeuf's company, but that was fine. He marched them off across the open ground and then through the tall grass and the edge of the tree line, and then into the dark, cool of the jungle.

He stopped and looked back. He could not see the town for the trees, which meant the Spaniards would not see them, and none of the coming hail of iron would find them there.

"This is good," he said. "We'll wait here."

There was open ground enough for the men to find places to sit, to dig into their bags for the food and drink they had scavenged from the town. It was mid-afternoon, and getting late in the year, and it was cool in the jungle, with a bit of a breeze finding its way through the foliage. The air was pungent with the smell of vegetation and rich earth, and the quiet settled down on them, punctuated by the call of birds and insects and the occasional muttered conversation among the waiting buccaneers.

LeBoeuf found a parcel of forest floor large enough for him to lie down on. He rested his musket against a tree and settled himself on his back, hands folded on his chest, and Other Dog laid down beside him. He closed his eyes and took a deep breath and a minute later he was asleep.

He slept for exactly an hour, and then his eyes opened again. It was a skill he had developed over many years, when his life was regulated by the turning of a half-hour glass on a ship's quarterdeck, the regular striking of the ship's bell. One hour, two ringings of the bell, and he was awake. He did not always will himself to wake on the hour, only when vigilance was required. And it certainly was now.

He stood and arched his back, then took up his musket. Pierre Le Chasseur was sitting cross-legged nearby, thoughtfully chewing on a ship's biscuit.

"I'm going to go have a look around," LeBoeuf said. Le Chasseur nodded and kept chewing. LeBoeuf made his way through the trees, Other Dog at his heels. He stepped out into the clearing, into the sun, and the air felt noticeably warmer. He and Other Dog walked along the border between the beaten ground and the tall grass. To his left, and a hundred feet away, were the backs of the buildings of Cayona that lined the western side of the road.

On the ground between him and the buildings were various piles of debris that had been tossed out back doors, and a few sorry-looking kitchen gardens and compost heaps. A few chickens and pigs and dogs wandered listlessly around. He saw at least one human corpse, half hidden in the grass, and what he guessed was a second. Tortuga was not a place to look for sympathy.

He came at last to the end of the town. Stretched out before him was the beach, the harbor, and, far off on the southern horizon, the mountainous blue-green shape of Hispaniola. Closer in, a mile and a half or so distant, rode the Spanish fleet.

LeBoeuf stepped into the shade of the buildings, leaned on his musket and looked out over the water. The fleet was at anchor, sails hauled up, bows pointing east into the wind and tide. The nearest ship, the flagship, LeBoeuf assumed, was a big bastard, a galleon of forty guns or so, though he could not see for certain at that distance. However many guns she carried, he knew they would be big ones, and the ships would get in close enough that even the Spaniards were bound to hit something.

There were six other galleons of similar size anchored around the lead ship, and a clutch of smaller vessels that LeBoeuf guessed were serving as transports for the soldiers. At least a dozen other ships, from galleons to frigates and sloops, were underway in the open water beyond. There were so many ships in the Spanish fleet that they would not all find room to anchor in the harbor at Cayona.

"Mon Dieu, Other Dog, look how many ships and men the Don Diegos have sent. They must be terribly afraid of those teeth of yours."

Other Dog barked once, in recognition of the truth of that statement. Then she sat on her haunches and the two of them watched in silence, but there was not much to see. Some of the smaller ships were coming to anchor as well, and the frigates were keeping at sea, serving as pickets beyond the anchored fleet.

"Let's go," LeBoeuf said. "I don't think it gets any more interesting for a while."

He and Other Dog made their way back to where the men were sprawled out on the jungle floor, busy at various things: eating, drinking, cleaning weapons, gambling, sleeping. "Spaniards have come to anchor, about a mile to windward of the channel entrance."

"How many ships?" Levesque asked.

"Galleons? Twenty or so. Transports, frigates, sloops…a couple dozen, in all." Someone let out a low whistle.

"That would be the Armada de Sotavento," the old sailor said. "Toledo's fleet. They already done for St. Kitts and Nevis."

LeBoeuf nodded. He had never heard of this Armada de Sotavento, or an attack on St. Kitts and Nevis. He'd spent the better part of the past year hunting pigs in the wild country on Hispaniola's northern shore and making a point of not interacting with the world beyond. But he did know of Fadrique Álvarez de Toledo, Captain General of King Philip the Fourth's Ocean Sea Navy, and he knew he could be an unpleasant fellow.

"Huh," LeBoeuf said. "Well, I don't know what they want with this sorry little island. Guess we'll find out soon enough." He sat down on his former patch of ground, but Other Dog remained standing, keyed up now that there was some action in the offing.

In truth, LeBoeuf had a pretty good idea of what the Spanish wanted with Tortuga: they wanted it for themselves. All but worthless as the place might be, he knew that Seville would not tolerate any interlopers there or anywhere in their West Indies empire. Anyone who tried for a foothold had to be driven out. It was why they sent the *lanceros* to hunt down the pigs and cows that the boucaniers preyed on, and to hunt the boucaniers themselves. The disorganized and half-wild hunters were of little threat to the empire of Spain, but still Spain would not abide their presence.

For LeBoeuf, who, for the past few years, had wanted nothing more than to be left alone, the thought of it made him wildly angry. He reached into his haversack and pulled out a bottle of rum, pulled the cork and took a deep drink.

That's better, he thought as the liquid burned its way down his throat. Beside him, Other Dog was panting and looking at him expectantly.

"Not for you. You're as bad as Big Dog was, and look what happened to him," LeBoeuf said. "And you best sit down, we've a long wait ahead of us."

Other Dog made a whining sound but did in fact lay down as told. LeBoeuf corked the bottle, dug a biscuit and a chunk of cold beef out of his bag. He tore the meat in two and gave half to the dog, then stuck the other half in his mouth and laboriously chewed.

Night before battle, LeBoeuf thought, and shook his head at how ridiculous the notion was. It would not be much of a battle, he was pretty sure of that.

Once he and Other Dog had eaten most of the food they had, LeBoeuf spent some time cleaning and oiling his musket and checking his other arms and ammunition. Then he set them aside, close at hand, and stretched out again on the cool ground. He might as well sleep. There was nothing much else to do. He closed his eyes and made himself relax, willing the muscles in his arms and legs to loosen.

Don Quixote, he thought. It came back to him just then. *Don Quixote, that was the Spaniard's name.*

Chapter Twenty-One

LeBoeuf rose just after first light, made his way some distance through the jungle to relieve himself, then returned and took up his musket and sword. With his toe, he nudged Pierre Le Chasseur, who was sleeping nearby.

"I'm going to have a look at what the Spaniards are about," he said in a low voice, once he was certain Le Chasseur was sufficiently awake. "Keep the others here until I'm back."

He and Other Dog headed off, following the trail they had beaten the evening before. From the shelter of the buildings he could see the Spanish fleet, and from across the water he could hear the sounds of some activity. Rigging capstans, no doubt, preparing to weigh anchor.

He stood for some time, watching, as one by one the ships set their sails and hauled their anchor cables aboard. He was not curious as to what the Spaniards would do—he had a pretty good notion. He was more curious about the quality of their seamanship, which he had never held in very high regard.

"Please, God, let this bastard go hard aground," LeBoeuf muttered, as the lead ship made its cautious approach, barely making way under fore topsail alone. The beastly thing probably drew twenty-five feet. It was little wonder they were taking such care in the tricky shoals and sandbars. Grounding out would not inflict any damage on the ship, but it would throw the others into chaos, perhaps leading them to run into one another, and that might do real damage. At the very least it would be amusing to watch.

But it did not happen. The galleon in the vanguard made it as far into the harbor as she was likely to get, and LeBoeuf saw her massive best bower anchor plunge into the water again.

"So it goes," he said to Other Dog. "I don't think God sets much store by my requests."

He watched for a few moments more as the ship's longboat pulled around the stern and took a spring line that was handed down to them. So far, the fleet had done nothing LeBoeuf had not anticipated.

"Well, that was a tedious show," he said to the dog. He stood and they walked back the way they had come, stepping out of the brilliant morning sun and into the cool of the jungle, then made their way back to where the others were still sprawled out in the foliage. Some sat up on seeing LeBoeuf appear, some just opened their eyes. Some did neither.

"First of the Spaniards just came to anchor," LeBoeuf said. "Rigging a spring line. I'd reckon on it getting pretty hot around here by the turn of the next glass."

It was not long after that, twenty minutes, perhaps, when the first of the ordnance opened up, the dull boom of the galleon's broadside, the sound like distant thunder. It seemed to have substance behind it, deep and profound. Heads snapped up, turned in the direction of the harbor. The sound of the gunfire was still rolling over them when they heard the shot whistling by, somewhere off to the east, well clear of their position.

"Damn my eyes," Billy Solent said.

"Some big damned guns," Levesque observed.

"Spanish buggerers, they can't hit a thing even if it's standing in front of them, so they try to make up for it in weight of shot," Le Chasseur said.

LeBoeuf did not offer an opinion. He did not think any more of Spanish gunnery than he did of their seamanship, but he suspected they were hitting things now, and hitting them hard. He thought he could hear, under the sound of the guns and the whistling of the shot, the sharper crack of boats or buildings being torn apart by the heavy iron balls. It would not take too many hits from a gun firing a thirty-pound shot to do some real hurt.

It was quiet for a moment as the gunners reloaded, and then it started in again, gun by gun. The Spaniards were not firing broadsides now, just loading and firing as fast as each gun crew could manage, and the sound was more ragged, but impressive nonetheless.

It was not long before a second ship joined in, and then a third, and likely more, but by then the sound of the great guns was so continuous, the scream of the shot, the crush of balls hitting the nearby buildings so constant, that it all blended together into one grand symphony of destruction.

The buccaneers fell silent. It was not that it was difficult to talk over the gunfire—the ships were far enough off that their guns made only a muted sound. Rather, the power of the fleet felt like divine retribution, and it called for wordless respect.

How long the gunfire went on, LeBoeuf did not know. He, too, was silent, his mind drifting back to other fleet actions, other withering broadsides, and the crush of round shot tearing through bulwarks, and the look and sound of men whose limbs were flicked away like a crumb from a tablecloth.

He sighed. He felt like an old man. He had been alive now for all of about two and a half decades, and he felt like an old man.

And then the gunfire stopped.

They were not certain at first, thinking it might be one of those odd quirks, when, out of the dozens of guns firing, not one was ready in that particular moment. Men who had been growing dull with waiting suddenly sat up, ears cocked toward the harbor, eyes looking at nothing since there was nothing of importance that they could see.

A moment passed. Another. No guns.

"That's it," LeBoeuf said, standing, and the others stood as well. "Levesque, go find where the tavern keeper and the rest of them from the town are hunkered down. Tell them we're making our way toward the beach. Tell them to go around the east side of the town, work their way through the jungle, keep well out of sight. Get to a place where they have a clear shot at the beach. Tell them I'll call out before I open fire."

Levesque nodded, grabbed his musket and disappeared into the foliage. LeBoeuf looked around at the others. They had muskets in hand, bandoliers over shoulders, all their scant possessions secured. They were ready to move.

"Let's go," he said.

He turned and headed south, the way he had gone before, keeping just inside the tree line where the foliage was thick enough to hide them from even the closest scrutiny, but the going was not too difficult. He was being overly cautious, he knew: it would still be some time before the first Spaniard set foot on the beach, and there was little chance of being seen from the ships. But caution, LeBoeuf had found, was rarely a hindrance, and often very beneficial.

They moved quickly and silently, hunters that they were, and it was not long before they were near the water's edge, with the beach in sight through the trees and the tall grass. LeBoeuf could see the remains of the makeshift wall that the townsfolk had built. There was nothing about it that suggested a wall now: it was no more than a scattered field of debris. Long furrows had been cut in the sand by the passing shot, like claw marks left by some massive beast.

He looked to his right, out toward the harbor, where a few boats were pulling for the shore. The sun glinted off polished helmets and breastplates. This first wave would be picked men, elite troops, with the honor of leading the way. That was fine. Given a choice, LeBoeuf preferred to kill the elite.

"Here they come," D'Anton said. He kept his voice low, cautious, like LeBoeuf. A murmur ran through the watching men.

LeBoeuf kept his eyes on the boats. There were four of them, which surprised him. He would have expected the Spanish to fill a dozen before they headed for the beach.

"Just four?" Le Chasseur said, echoing LeBoeuf's thoughts. "Guess they don't reckon there's much fight left here."

"Figure they killed us all, or we run off," Billy Solent said. "Well, won't they be surprised."

"Let's move up, keep low in the grass," LeBoeuf said. "Pick your targets, wait for my word. They may charge us after the first volley, or they may stand there with their thumbs up their arses and let us drop them all. Just like hunting pigs."

"Just like pigs," D'Anton said.

"Just like pigs," LeBoeuf agreed. He eased forward, stepping with care, bending deep to keep hidden in the tall grass, and the others spread out and moved parallel to him. He moved as close to the beach as he dared, where he could still find cover from the grass. He pulled his ramrod out from under the barrel of his gun and stuck it in the sand, then knelt down on one knee, the musket cradled in his arms.

He could see nothing now, save for a wall of grass in front of him, Other Dog laying at his side, D'Anton to his left, Lessard to his right. The rest of the buccaneers, and the beach, were hidden by the vegetation. But he did not worry about what the others were doing, or what they would do. They were well used to this business.

He closed his eyes and listened. He could hear the breeze through the jungle, the lap of water on the beach. Other Dog's anticipatory panting. And farther off, the rhythmic creak of boats' oars against wooden thole pins, the splash of oar blades in water.

The sound grew louder, closer, and then came the unmistakable crunch of a boat's keel running up on the sand. LeBoeuf lifted his musket, extended it out in front of him, rested the butt against his shoulder, and parted the grass with the barrel. Through the narrow gap he could see the bow of a longboat on the sand, a half dozen sailors pulling it higher up the beach.

He swiveled right a few inches until he was able to see more of the boat. The sailors were coming over the sides and the soldiers after them, one of the latter on the beach already. He wore a steel helmet and breastplate that winked in the afternoon sun, a black tunic, high boots. Pistols and a sword hung from a shoulder strap.

More of the men-at-arms came up behind him and they were dressed in similar fashion, though they carried muskets and wore the accompanying bandoliers.

Fancy, LeBoeuf thought. Someone had spent a lot of money fitting this company out, making them look smart and uniform. He wondered if their fighting ability matched their appearance.

Reckon we'll find out directly.

He eased the hammer of his snaphance musket back, finessing the trigger so it made no clicking noise as it was cocked. The officer—he assumed the first man ashore, the one with no musket, was an officer—had advanced up the beach aways and was inspecting the damage done to the wall by the cannonade. Another soldier hurried up beside him, conferring, it seemed. Down at the edge of the water the other three boats had grounded out, and the men aboard them were now wading ashore.

LeBoeuf shifted the barrel of his gun over a few inches, until the muzzle was a bit above and to the left of the officer's chest, knowing from long experience that such aim would put the ball right through the man's breastplate. He flicked his eyes to the right. All of the soldiers had disembarked now and were halfway up the beach. They could not easily get back into the boats and row out of range.

"*Maintenant!*" he shouted, loud as he could, loud enough to be heard by the tavern keeper and the townsfolk on the far side of the beach, he hoped. He wanted a crossfire, bullets coming from all directions. He wanted the Spaniards to freeze in fear and confusion.

He waited a second, then pulled the trigger, and just as he squeezed he saw the officer step back and turn.

"*Merde!*" LeBoeuf shouted. The musket fired, the butt slammed against his shoulder, and everything in front of him was lost in a cloud of smoke. He was vaguely aware of D'Anton and Lessard's muskets going off as well. He stood up, the need to hide gone now. He grabbed a cartridge from his pouch and bit off the end, then dumped the powder, ball and paper down the barrel and snatched up his ramrod.

The smoke blew clear and he saw to his disappointment that the officer was still standing, though there seemed to be a crease across his breastplate where LeBoeuf's bullet had passed. But there were plenty of Spaniards who were not so lucky. Seven or eight were sprawled out and motionless, a few others down and thrashing. The rest seemed staggered and confused. Not pigs any longer. Sitting ducks.

LeBoeuf jammed the ramrod back into the sand and cocked the hammer. He heard the clicks of snaphances down the line. He looked over the barrel, sweeping it side to side, searching for a target.

The officer had his sword out and he was calling to his men and pointing with the weapon toward the tree line where LeBoeuf and his men stood. They had recovered quickly from the shocking volley, and the officer was rallying the men. Impressive.

"Hold your fire! Hold your fire!" LeBoeuf shouted. "They're making ready to charge us! Wait for it!"

Shoot at a boar and miss and the boar will do one of two things: run or charge. Spaniards, LeBoeuf reckoned, were the same. And now he knew which this one would do.

Other Dog was half laying at LeBoeuf's feet, her hindquarters elevated, ready to launch herself into an attack. She was making low growling noises, punctuated with high-pitched whining. She seemed like she might explode from the pressure boiling inside her.

"Steady, steady…" LeBoeuf said.

The Spanish officer had managed to rally his men, get the entire company into some semblance of a line, and they were running across the sand, charging directly at LeBoeuf and the others.

"Wait, wait," LeBoeuf called. "Let them come! And you bastards take care not to shoot my dog!"

The Spaniards were a hundred feet away now, running as fast as they could in the soft sand, muskets held across their chests, likely encouraged by the lack of opposition so far. Time for a surprise.

"*Allez! Allez!*" he shouted and Other Dog was gone before the second word was out of his mouth. She burst out of the tall grass and charged across the sand, barking maniacally as she hurled herself at the Spaniards. She was a massive creature, more than a hundred pounds of brown fur and black eyes, red mouth and white teeth, and the Spanish, shocked at her sudden and volatile appearance, stopped short in their headlong charge.

Some of the soldiers had the presence of mind to try to shoot this apparition, and they struggled to get their muskets' butts to their shoulders, to swing their barrels around, looking for the target, but there was no time for that. Other Dog was too fast. The first musket was not even level before she launched herself into the air at the man leading the Spaniard's charge.

The man tried to fend her off as she became airborne, but he failed completely. Her jaws went for his neck and LeBoeuf heard a strangled cry as man and dog went down in a spray of blood. They hit the sand, writhing. The soldier closest to them took two quick steps and aimed his musket at Other Dog, the muzzle just inches from her flank.

"Fire!" LeBoeuf called as he pulled the trigger of his own weapon. He could not see the result, lost behind the cloud of smoke, but he felt certain he had put a ball right through the chest of the man who was intending to shoot his dog.

Muskets fired all down the line. A wall of smoke, thick and ephemeral, formed and was whisked away. LeBoeuf's hands were already reloading, his eyes on the Spaniards just thirty yards distant. More were down, kicking in the sand: the second volley had been more deadly than the first.

Other Dog had finished with her victim and had another poor bastard down on the beach, arms flailing as he beat uselessly against the dog's back. But the others still had some fight in them: muskets were leveled, muzzles were aimed at the tall grass.

"Down!" LeBoeuf called. He dropped to a knee as the Spanish volley rippled along the line, the bullets buzzing overhead and thumping into trees and spraying his men with torn leaves.

LeBoeuf stood again. The Spaniards had resumed their charge. They would reach the tree line before LeBoeuf and the others could reload, and even with the casualties they had suffered, there were a lot more of them than there were buccaneers.

"Other Dog, come!" LeBoeuf shouted and, as if jerked by a rope, Other Dog left off tearing at the Spanish soldier and charged back toward the tree line. She looked for all the world as if she was joining the Spaniards in the charge as she broke through their line and raced on past, tongue lolling, blood slick around her muzzle and halfway down her neck.

She crashed back through the long grass and LeBoeuf shouted, "Back! Fall back, fall back!" He gestured for D'Anton and Lessard to move, pointing back the way they had come, and when the two men went charging off through the trees, LeBoeuf followed, Other Dog at his heels, calling to the rest and pushing them ahead.

LeBoeuf held his musket up vertically as he ran through the vegetation, using the gun to part the branches like the stem of a ship. Up ahead he caught glimpses of the others as they ran. Farther behind he could hear the Spanish soldiers crashing into the tree line, calling to one another in their foreign tongue.

This is pointless, LeBoeuf thought. *Like trying to stop the tide.* The Spanish would land, and they would take Tortuga, and he could not stop them. He knew that.

But he could at least make it damned hard for them, and make them pay the highest price possible for the real estate, and that made all this worth the effort. Now he hoped to dole out at least one chastisement more before they were overwhelmed.

Chapter Twenty-Two

Alonso heard the muffled sounds along the tree line, the *whuff* of primer, the sharp crack of a musket's charge going off, and then the roar of thirty more, all fired at once. He heard the buzz of bullets flying past, as if a beehive had been beat with a stick. He heard the strike of bullets on steel, bullets in bodies.

But mostly he heard a clang, like a broken bell, much closer than any of those other sounds. He felt as if he had been pushed sideways by some invisible hand against his chest. And he did not understand any of it.

He looked down and saw a long crease in the shining steel of his breastplate, a groove as if the metal had partially buckled. And still he did not understand.

For some time he stared at the crease, uncomprehending. How long he stared, he was not certain. It seemed a very long time, though later he realized it could not have been more than a second or two. Just until the first scream of the wounded cut through his reverie.

Bastards!

They had been hiding in the tree line, waiting for him and his men to come ashore. Cowardly swine.

He looked around, left and right. Ten men or so, tossed down on the sand, some still moving, some not. The others standing, wide-eyed, confused. They needed orders.

"There!" Alonso shouted, pointing with his sword toward the tree line from which the shots had come. They may have come from elsewhere, too, he did not know, but he knew for certain they had come from there. He had seen the muzzle flashes, the puffs of smoke.

"Form a line, and after them! Quickly, quickly, as they reload!"

Who they were, he did not know. The vermin infesting Tortuga, clearly, but who? French, English, Dutch? Broken drunks who could barely hold a gun, who would run in the face of the One Hundred? Or trained soldiers, or buccaneers, tough and unafraid, who could load fast and shoot well? They would find out.

Delgadillo was running back and forth, shouting at the men, pushing them in line. The men, in turn, had broken free of their surprised trance and were obeying, getting in some semblance of order.

Alonso watched the men fall in and he felt an odd calm settle over him, that calm that came when the fighting commenced and all the fear that went with waiting was swept away. He knew it well from his days campaigning in Europe. He was aware of his mind starting to work again. He felt clarity.

They could not stand there and be shot down, they had to get into the trees. But they needed to advance as a company, not run in like some panicked mob. Speed and discipline.

"Go!" Alonso shouted as he saw the men form up in reasonable order. He jogged off toward the trees, sword raised, two paces in front of his men.

How long since those cowardly dogs had fired? Long enough for them to reload, surely, if that was what they meant to do. Alonso felt himself bracing for the bullets to come, felt the fear creeping in around the edges. His breathing was coming harder as he jogged through the soft sand. He was not a soldier any longer, he was a government bureaucrat now, a functionary. He was no longer accustomed to this sort of thing.

And so it was not surprising when, to his annoyance, Delgadillo caught up with him as they ran, and in three steps was ahead, leading the way. Alonso opened his mouth to tell the man to slow down. It was humiliating to have to say it, but worse to not be the first into the fight.

"Delgadillo!" he called, but he was already near out of breath and the word came out as a strangled gasp. He doubted that Delgadillo even heard it. He gulped air, ready to try again, when he was startled by something bursting from the tall grass one hundred feet ahead of them.

Dios mío, what in hell is that? Alonso thought, and in the same instant he realized it was a huge dog, barking like it was raving mad and charging across the sand at them. He stopped running, shocked by this sudden apparition, and Delgadillo and the other stopped as well.

"Shoot that beast! Shoot it!" Alonso cried. He heard the rattle of muskets being raised, the click of hammers. He watched, immobilized with horror, as the animal closed the distance with stunning speed, leapt several feet into the air and sunk its teeth into Delgadillo's neck.

The two of them went down, twisting and flailing, blood spraying side to side as Delgadillo beat at the dog's flanks.

"Kill that thing!" Alonso shrieked, backing away. One of his men stepped up and aimed his musket at the animal that was tearing out Delgadillo's throat. He pulled the hammer back, and once again the tree line rippled with a volley of small arms, muzzle flashes, and jetting clouds of smoke.

The soldier, the one aiming at the dog, took a bullet in the center of his chest. The impact twisted him around and flung him back, and he dropped the musket as he fell.

Delgadillo was motionless now, his eyes wide, his throat nothing but torn flesh and a wash of blood. The dog left off its savage work, charged right and leapt up on another of Alonso's men who screamed and flailed at the beast as they fell to the ground.

Alonso was stunned, his mouth hanging open, as he looked with horror at what was left of Delgadillo. He could hear more cries of the wounded, men who had fallen in that last volley. How long until the men in the brush fired again? Seconds?

"Bastards!" Alonso shouted, as his mind came tumbling back to the present. He waved to the others as he started forward again. "Move! Move! At them!" They could not stand there in the open and be cut down. They had to get to the trees, get at the enemy, where they could see them and fight them.

He heard a voice call from somewhere ahead. He did not understand the words, but suddenly the dog came charging past him, racing for the tall grass. Alonso could see glimpses of them now, this hidden enemy, men like shadows back in the trees. They were moving, setting up a new ambush perhaps, but it did not alter his intentions. They had to get into the jungle.

Alonso reached the tall grass and crashed on through into the trees beyond. He held his sword in his right hand and pulled one of his pistols with his left. He stopped in the cool dark of the forest, tensed, and looked around. He could see no one, could hear nothing.

A second later the first of his men came through the grass and the scruffy vegetation and into the trees. "Hold! Hold here!" Alonso shouted. He had to keep the men together, and that would be hard in the jungle, where he could only see those immediately around him.

"Hold here!" he called again as more of his men entered the tree line. And then it was quiet once more as the men stopped where they were and waited for orders and Alonso wondered what he would do next. His eyes moved around the tangled vegetation in front: thick, but not impenetrable, the trees sparse enough that they could advance in some semblance of a line.

He listened. He could hear wind in the treetops, the water lapping on the beach, and some of his men, breathing hard. And behind them, the cries of the wounded. Beyond that, there was nothing.

We can stand here, Alonso thought, *or we can move forward, or we can go back*. If there were any more choices than that, he could not think of them. But going back was an admission of defeat, and standing there was an invitation to slaughter, so really there was no choice at all.

"Make certain your firelocks are loaded," Alonso called, speaking no louder than he needed to be heard. "Stay with me, as best you can. If you see anything moving, shoot it. We have no friends here."

He stepped off, moving slowly, placing each foot with care, then pausing to listen, his eyes everywhere. This was not at all the sort of fighting he was accustomed to. He was a stranger here, and he felt the uncertainty gnawing at him.

It was hard to judge how far they moved, advancing as carefully as they were, and with nothing obvious to mark their progress. A hundred yards at least, it seemed to Alonso, and they had seen nothing, heard nothing.

Cowardly dogs, have you run off? Alonso thought, and that in turn made him think of the dog, and Delgadillo, lying dead on the sand.

The dog. If this enemy was close, then so was that dog, somewhere, hidden in the undergrowth. Alonso felt his stomach twist up, felt his steps slow. He raised his sword higher, held the pistol straight out in front of him as he moved.

"Hold!" he called, stopping in his tracks, though he was not sure why. There was nothing he could see or hear that was different. But something did not feel right. He held his pistol under his arm and wiped his sweating palm on his trousers, then took the gun up again.

Suddenly a voice called out from somewhere ahead and not too far away. Two words—"Allez! Allez!"—and the silence of the jungle was broken by the manic barking of the dog off to his right, and a second later by the high-pitched scream of whoever it was attacking, a thrashing in the brush, shouts of surprise from the men around him.

"Level your firelocks! Level them!" Alonso shouted. If the dog was there, the enemy was, too. But there was nothing to aim at. They could see nothing but foliage.

Then from all around, from in front and from either side, the jungle erupted with the sound of musket fire, the buzz and tear of bullets whipping by, the thud of balls hitting trees, and here and there the grunt or scream of men as they went down.

"Fire! Fire!" Alonso yelled, the words coming out shrill and high-pitched. He leveled his pistol and shot at a thick clump of growth in front of him, and he hoped one of those bastards was concealed within, because he had no other target at which to shoot. All around him, and farther off where he could not see them, the remaining men of the One Hundred blasted away at…nothing. Trees and shrubs.

Alonso jammed the pistol back into its holster—no time to reload—and stood with sword ready. He was not worried about the men hidden in the trees, it was that hellish beast, somewhere out there in the undergrowth. He pulled his dagger and held it in his left hand. He could still hear the growling of the dog, the sick noise as it tore at one of his men.

"Find that damned beast!" he shrieked. He could hear the slightly hysterical tone in his voice. "Find it and kill the damned thing!" But he heard no one move. No one seemed eager to go hunting around for the creature.

Alonso felt his breath coming fast and shallow—he was breathing, but still he seemed to be struggling to get air into his lungs. He could hear other sounds now, clicking and rustling and the clang of steel on steel. It was his own men, reloading as they were trained to do, and, no doubt, their enemy off in the brush reloading as well. A musket fired, but who fired it, Alonso could not tell. Then two more, and then three, nearly at once.

This won't do, Alonso thought. These whores' sons who had ambushed them, they were most likely boucaniers, hunters. This was their theater. The Hundred were not trained for this. They were trained to fight in city streets, or on an open field of combat. It was not right, bringing them into this sort of combat.

And, more than anything, Alonso wanted to be out of that cursed jungle.

"Fall back!" Alonso shouted. "Keep up your fire, but fall back!" He stepped back and nearly tripped over a root, but caught himself before he went down. He could see about a dozen of his men around him, and they were moving back too, stepping carefully, loading as they did. Muskets went off, here and there.

Sure those bastards can't see any better than we can, Alonso thought. *How could they?* He and his men continued moving back, shooting as they went, a stubborn, fighting retreat.

Then once again the jungle was filled with the awful growling and barking of the manic dog, somewhere in the undergrowth, hidden, but close. Alonso felt his hands start to tremble, his arms twitch, felt waves of panic rolling up his spine. Every muscle in his body was poised to turn and run, just run, as fast as he could, thrashing his way through the jungle back to the beach. He had never in life experienced terror like this.

A man screamed, and Alonso jumped and gasped. He braced for the nightmare sound of the dog ripping his throat out, but he realized it was a cry of panic. Then another of his men shouted and crashed off through the brush; not retreating, but fleeing, just as Alonso was desperate to do. The man at Alonso's side turned and ran as well. Alonso had a glimpse of eyes wide with fright as the man threw his musket away and bolted back the way he had come.

It was a rout. All around him Alonso could hear the sound of men running through the undergrowth, a few even yelling in terror as they ran. Some of them he could see, others were lost from sight in the foliage. He opened his mouth to order them to stop, but no words would come.

Soon he was the only one left, as far as he could tell; just him and the enemy, out there in the brush.

And the dog.

Alonso tried to think, but all that came to him was an amorphous swirl of terror. His breath was coming even quicker now. He took a step back, and then another, his sword and dagger held out in front, his eyes sweeping the undergrowth around him. He could not see or hear a thing, but he knew the dog was close. He could feel it.

And then he was running, too. It was not by choice, not through any conscious decision. One moment he was standing, *en garde*, and the next he was running back through the jungle, slashing with his sword as he ran, aware of how exposed his back was, bracing for the feel of that horrible beast leaping up on him and bringing him down, like a wolf on a fleeing deer.

The jungle had been well-beaten by the men who had passed through that day, Spanish and buccaneers, and Alonso had no problem finding his way back. He ran, stumbling, branches whipping his face, until at last he saw the trees thin out and glimpses of the beach beyond. Then he stopped and doubled over and gasped, his sword hanging limp in his hand. His dagger was gone, but he did not recall dropping it.

He felt something warm and wet on his thighs, and his first thought was that he had been wounded somehow, that he was bleeding. And then he realized, to his horror, that he had pissed himself. He had no memory of doing so, but the thought of that humiliation set off a new wave of panic. He looked down, relieved to see that his black trousers hid the considerable wetness there.

At last he straightened and continued on. He saw the first of his men just ahead, three of them, squatting on the ground, helmets off, faces red and wet with perspiration.

He approached and stopped, then looked around. "The others?" he asked. He studied each man to see if they seemed to notice his soaked trousers, but none did.

One of the men nodded down the trail. "Sergeant Rodriguez told us to stay here, set up a picket," he said. He did not sound happy about it.

Alonso grunted. Juan Rodriguez was the company's sergeant, second to Delgadillo. He probably figured he was the captain now, and Alonso probably would not disagree. Rodriguez had told these men to set up some sort of line of defense, in case the boucaniers came in pursuit. Squatting on the ground, paying no attention, was certainly not what he had in mind, but Alonso was not going to argue. There was no fight left in these men, or in himself.

He walked off through the tree line and the tall grass and out onto the beach. Rodriguez had charge of the men. He was getting the dead laid out in a row and seeing the wounded tended to. When he saw Alonso he hurried over to him.

"Ah, Don Alonso! I looked for you. I feared that damned…I was afraid you did not make it. I was about to get a squad and go search."

"I made it," Alonso said. He wondered if Rodriguez really had intended to search for him. He doubted it. If he had, he seemed to be in no great hurry.

They were quiet for an awkward moment, then Rodriguez said, "I'm seeing to the dead and wounded. Trying to reckon who might be…still back in the trees…."

"Very good," Alonso said. He looked out toward the fleet. An armada of boats was pulling for the shore, each crowded with soldiers in helmets and breastplates, their muskets held upright like small groves of dead trees. The first of the boats, the largest, flew the Burgundy Cross on an ensign staff on the stern, Toledo's house flag at the bow. The boat was bright-painted, manned by sailors in matching outfits, and nearly up to the beach.

"Carry on, then, Rodriguez," Alonso said, his eyes still on Toledo's boat. He left Rodriguez there and walked down the beach to the water's edge. He stood on the wet sand as the boat ground ashore and the sailors laid their oars down, hopped over the sides, and hauled the boat up as far as they could.

The soldiers, Toledo's personal guard, came next, climbing over the gunnels as the sailors hauled the boat even farther onto the sand. In the stern sat Toledo, surrounded by his senior officers.

"Admiral Toledo!" Alonso said brightly, splashing out into the shallow water to get closer to the great man, and making sure to soak his trousers up to his thighs with sea water. "We've taken the beach, your grace, cleared the enemy away. There must have been a few hundred of the villains, and they put up a hard fight, I can tell you, but we drove them off in the end. My men behaved most gallantly. I'm proud of them."

Toledo looked at him and nodded and beyond that showed no reaction to Alonso's words, no suggestion that he cared in the least. But that did not matter. The important thing, Alonso knew, was that his version of events was the first to reach the admiral's ears.

Chapter Twenty-Three

"Other Dog, come!" LeBoeuf's voice sounded odd to him, after the quiet.

The first of the Spaniards had turned and run: LeBoeuf heard the unmistakable sound of a man plunging in terror through dense foliage. Then he heard another, and another, and then many of them at once. And then, to ears dulled by gunfire, it seemed as if there was no sound at all.

Other Dog answered the summons, bursting out of the undergrowth, her muzzle wet with fresh blood, and she sat down beside him. In a single attack she might only kill a few of the Don Diegos, but she could put terror into all of them, and LeBoeuf suspected that she had done just that.

"Good girl," he said. He spoke softly. He guessed that all the Spanish had run off by then, but he was not entirely certain. He stood motionless, listening, but he could hear nothing that caused him concern. He looked left and right. He could see a few of his men spread out among the trees, silent, like him. The rest were close, but lost from his sight in the jungle.

He let a few moments pass and still there was nothing; he did not think any living Spaniard could remain that silent for that long. He lowered the butt of his musket to the ground and breathed deep. He felt himself relax, as if he was setting down a heavy load.

"I reckon we're alone," he said in a voice that was just above a whisper. He heard the others moving, relaxing their vigilance. He gave them a moment, then said, "Follow me. Let's see what's acting."

He led the way toward the edge of the trees and the tall grass that yielded eventually to the open ground of Cayona. As the trees began to thin, LeBoeuf could see the backs of the dilapidated buildings—the tavern, a general merchant of sorts, a few others. There were gaping holes in roofs and great chunks blasted out of the walls. The Spanish guns had found their targets.

They came out of the tree line and into the grass. They could hear the raucous festivities from one of the buildings a couple hundred feet away: singing and shouting and hard things being smashed. LeBoeuf thought at first that the Spaniards had already swarmed over the town and were helping themselves to whatever they found, but that could not be it. The Spanish, the bulk of them, were just now coming ashore.

It was the people of Cayona, he realized, or some at least, who had decided to take advantage of the abandoned tavern and become insensibly drunk. Probably hoping to drink themselves to death before the Spanish arrived. LeBoeuf nodded to himself. It seemed an altogether sensible thing to do.

LeBoeuf continued on, bending low to give himself some cover in the grass, and behind him, and on either side, the others did the same, though he was not sure it was necessary. He doubted that the Spaniards were paying much attention.

They came to the edge of the grass, to a place where they could see across the open ground and down the sloping shore to the beach, and they went down on one knee.

"Damn my eyes," Billy Solent said, softly. That sentiment was met with various grunts and other forms of concurrence.

The beach was swarming. A dozen or more boats were pulled up on the sand, offloading foot soldiers who were advancing inland in a haphazard way. More boats, many more, also filled to the gunnels with men-at-arms, were pulling ashore from the fleet.

Central to all this, and farther up the sand, stood a cluster of men in brilliant breastplates and bright-colored tunics and sashes, great broad-brimmed hats festooned with plumes. They looked like birds of brilliant feather surrounded by lesser, duller breeds. Behind them, two flags waved from staffs held upright on the ground. One LeBoeuf recognized as the Burgundy Cross, the flag of Spain. The other he did not know. The house flag of the one in command, he imagined.

Who are you? he wondered. The clutch of gentlemen seemed to radiate power and authority. He wondered who it was who commanded such a massive armada.

Toledo?

That was what the old wreck of a mariner had said, and it made sense. LeBoeuf had heard rumors over the years that Fadrique Álvarez de Toledo, Captain General of King Philip the Fourth's Ocean Sea Navy, might be sent to the West Indies to reinforce Spanish rule over that increasingly chaotic. He wished them luck with that. Hundreds of leagues of ocean, thousands of islands, enormous wealth to be had…there was no chance that it would be contained, the interlopers kept out.

He considered the peacocks in command, standing in their little clutch. They were probably a hundred and fifty yards away. A long shot, but not an impossible one. He thought about it for a moment, then shook his head. Not worth it. Or they could move in closer, take down a few more of the soldiers, maybe even some of the peacocks, but the buccaneers would certainly be killed in the effort. There were some things worth dying for, but resisting the Spanish invasion of Tortuga was not one of them.

That was particularly true given that the Spanish would take the island no matter what they did. The best that LeBoeuf and his men could do was to make their conquest harder, put some fear into the Spaniards, make them wary of the renegades on the island, and they had done that. Time to go.

"I think we're finished here," LeBoeuf said. "Let's move."

"Where to?" Pierre Le Chasseur asked.

"The plantation," LeBoeuf said.

He spoke without thinking, and was not sure why he had said that. The smart thing to do was to disappear into the jungle, up into the high country, as far from the Spanish as they could get. Live off their skills at hunting, try to wait the Don Diegos out. He did not think the Spanish would stay on that sorry little island forever.

But LeBoeuf was not ready to do that. There was only so much defeat he was willing to take. And he had a bad habit, readily acknowledged, of acting on impulse, and without thinking, when the spirit moved him sufficiently. That tendency had already created great problems in his life, and likely would again.

"You think they'll leave us be, if we're off on the plantation?" Le Chasseur asked. He did not try to hide his skepticism.

"Don't know," LeBoeuf said, which was true, though he had a pretty good idea, and it was not an optimistic one. "We'll see."

He stood and headed back through the trees, with the others following behind. They could still hear the singing and shouting coming from the tavern, but it grew dim as they made their way deeper into the jungle. LeBoeuf led the way north, keeping just out of sight in the tree line, knowing that the Spaniards were bound to send out patrols, at least on foot. They probably had horses with them as well, since the Spanish did not like to go anywhere without horses, but it would be some time before they were offloaded.

The buccaneers made their way around the northern end of the town, hidden from sight by the same rise that had hidden them from the Spanish broadsides. The ground was littered with leaves and broken branches, and the tops of dozens of trees were shattered and splayed. To the east they found the road that led off to the Tortuga plantation.

There, rather than keep to the trees, they walked down the center of the road, since they could not be seen from the beach and they did not think the Spanish would come in pursuit anytime soon. The old sailor was with them still, carrying a musket he had picked up from somewhere. He seemed determined to join them, and that was fine. LeBoeuf did not much care who was in their company.

It was about a mile and a half to the plantation and they walked in silence. LeBoeuf wondered what the others were thinking, what they expected of him. He wondered what he could expect from them.

Men looked for leaders, it was just the way of things, and they were looking to him now to play that role. None of these men wanted to be in command. Of all the buccaneers in that company, Van Loudersong had been the only one who yearned for supremacy, and that had played out pretty much as LeBoeuf would have expected.

It's your own fault, you great fool, LeBoeuf thought. When he needed those men to sail his ship and take his plantation he had manipulated them into following his command. Now, with their world in flux and confusion, they would continue to turn to him for leadership.

So be it. He was comfortable enough in that office.

They were getting closer to the plantation—LeBoeuf recognized the landmarks that were just starting to become familiar to him. He looked off down the road. A column of smoke was rising over the trees. Not enough smoke to be alarming, not like a building engulfed in flames, but more like a brush pile put to the torch, or a smith getting the forge up to temperature.

No cause for worry… The servants should still be there, and the smoke was likely from some work they were doing.

Other Dog, eager for home, bounded off ahead, and a moment later was lost from sight around a bend in the road walled in by trees on either side. The buccaneers marched on, their weariness evident.

"Gin and a bed, that's all I'm looking for now," Levasseur said. That was met with sounds of agreement. LeBoeuf remained silent, but he felt the same.

Then Other Dog was back, tearing down the road, tongue out. She came to a halt in front of LeBoeuf, turned in a circle, ran two steps up the road again, then made another frenetic circle where she stood.

Merde…

"Your dog's gone mad, LeBoeuf," Levesque offered.

"No," LeBoeuf said. "She says something's amiss." He stopped and rested the butt of his musket on the ground and the others did the same. He frowned and looked off down the road. Every bone in him, every muscle and sinew and God knows what else inside his over-large body ached with exhaustion. He was not in the mood for further nonsense.

He remained like that for a moment, wrestling with indecision, then he sighed and hefted his gun. "Whatever it is, let's not blunder into it," he said, and led the others off the road and once again into the trees, where they might approach unseen.

They made their way through a hundred yards or so of jungle before they reached the edge of the cleared land and stood just inside the tree line, hidden enough that they were unlikely to be seen. They looked out at the plantation house, about fifty paces away, and the estate that LeBoeuf claimed for his own.

The smoke they had observed was coming from a roasting pit, a circle of flame and embers on the ground with what looked to be the carcass of a pig turning on a spit above. The breeze carried the smell of the cooking meat down to them, and it made LeBoeuf realize how terribly hungry he was. Judging by the soft, guttural noises a few of the others were making, he guessed he was not the only one.

A few men were gathered around the pit, tending to the cooking, turning the spit and poking at the flames. Two black men and one white; no one LeBoeuf recognized, not any of the servants they had left behind. But the servants were there as well, at least some of them. Beyond the fire pit, near one of the out-buildings, LeBoeuf was all but certain he could make out Vassy and a couple of the others, and they did not seem to be in any great distress.

He searched every bit of the ground he could see, looking for Henriette, but she was not there. He felt an uneasy twist in his stomach. If they had done her any harm, then a lot of blood was going to spill, and soon.

"These are just folks who run when the Spaniards showed up, I'd wager," Le Chasseur offered. "Getting the hell away from the Don Diegos."

"There's not too many of them," Lessard said.

"Not so many that they won't have plenty of that pig to share," said Billy Solent, and the truth of that, and the growling in his stomach, decided the matter for LeBoeuf.

"See that your firelocks are primed and loaded," he said, "but hold them easy. Not threatening. We don't want to fight if we don't have to."

He waited as the others did a perfunctory check of their weapons, though none of them would have been walking around with an unloaded musket, or not been entirely aware of the state of their firearms. When they were done, LeBoeuf rested his own musket on his shoulder and said, "Let's go."

He stepped out of the trees and into the warm afternoon sun, and behind him he heard the soft footfalls of his men's rawhide shoes on the grass. Other Dog, as usual, was on his right flank, tongue hanging out as she walked. Despite LeBoeuf's particularly long stride, he had the distinct impression that she was frustrated by the slow pace he set.

"You calm yourself and behave," he said to the dog. "And don't kill anyone that I don't tell you to kill."

They crossed the open ground and were halfway to the fire pit before anyone noticed their approach. The man turning the spit looked over in their direction and LeBoeuf thought he saw him jump in surprise. He said something to the others, and one of the men tending the fire bolted off toward the house.

"There's more here than just that lot at the fire pit," LeBoeuf said.

"How do you know that?" Lessard asked.

"That one, he went to tell someone that we're coming," LeBoeuf said. And that probably meant there was someone in charge there, someone who had to be informed when armed strangers were heading their way. If there was someone in charge, then there were enough men there to warrant having someone in charge. This changed things.

"Be ready," LeBoeuf said. "But stay calm." He walked steadily on, head up and eyes searching left and right. No sign of an ambush or any such unpleasant surprise. No sign of Henriette.

They were forty feet from the plantation house when the men came around the corner. There was about three dozen of them, about the same number of men following LeBoeuf. They were white men, and black, and brown. Most were dressed like sailors, with slop trousers and cassocks and clothes tied around their necks, though a few looked more the part of pirates than honest mariners.

They were armed with muskets and pistols and cutlasses, though they held their weapons easy, in a way that presented no threat, just as LeBoeuf's men were doing. Whoever was leading these men, he seemed to be thinking the same way LeBoeuf was, and that was good.

Two men stood in front of the others. One was heavyset, with a thick beard, the other slighter, dark-skinned, with a leather jerkin and a red cloth bound around his head. The whore's sons who had been sailing the other ship. Van Loudersong's ship.

Oh, dear Lord, why do you toy with me like this? LeBoeuf wondered. He looked around. He did not see Van Loudersong.

He stopped ten feet from where the two men stood. His musket was still on his shoulder as he looked at them and they looked at him. Other Dog made a growling noise. The heavy man with the beard looked at her with concern and shifted his palm to rest on the butt of the pistol in his belt. The dark-faced man glanced down, vaguely annoyed, then up at LeBoeuf.

"There was a woman here," LeBoeuf said. "What's become of her?"

The fat man opened his mouth to speak, but got no further than that. Henriette came storming around the corner of the building, talking at hurricane force as she did.

"Oh, so you decided to come wandering back did you, you great ox? Where in all hell have you been? The Spanish have invaded here, in case you didn't know, and me, left all alone to defend myself!"

Other Dog gave a loud bark and ran up to her, pressing her head against Henriette's thigh, looking for a good scratching.

"Oh, wonderful, you've brought this damned beast back with you as well! This day just gets better and better."

"I see you are well, Henriette," LeBoeuf said.

"Well? How do you know I'm well? How do you know these beasts didn't rape me, each and every one of them?"

"If they'd tried to rape you, there'd be dead men all over the ground. Men with their balls cut off. It would be a dreadful sight."

Henriette scowled and folded her arms. She did not reply, which gave the fat man leave to speak at last. "You're the one called LeBoeuf, ain't you?" He spoke English, which was clearly his native tongue. And that was fine, since LeBoeuf, despite his obfuscation, spoke English as well.

"I am," LeBoeuf said. "And this is my plantation."

"Your…" At that the fat man smiled and even laughed a bit. "Your plantation, is it? Lord of the manor?"

LeBoeuf nodded. "That's right."

"Well, I'm sure I don't know how that works," the fat man said. "On Tortuga ownership goes to them who has the most men and guns."

"Which is not you."

"No, it's not," the dark man with the leather jerkin said, in an accent as ambiguous as his look: part Spanish, part French, part Carib. "That would be the Spanish."

LeBoeuf nodded. "You make a good point." He looked around. It must have been Van Loudersong who told these men about the plantation, but the bastard was nowhere to be seen.

"Where's Van Loudersong?"

"Who?" the fat man asked.

"Van Loudersong. The Dutchman. I thought you worked for him."

"Oh, the Dutchman. Yes, it seems he thought that, too," the fat man said. "It got bloody tiresome, I can tell you. So we…parted company."

Parted company.... LeBoeuf wondered what that meant, exactly. In any case, Van Loudersong was not there, which made this situation less complicated.

"Very well," LeBoeuf said. "I'm sure you've enjoyed your time here. Now you may leave."

The dark man's face still showed no expression, but the fat man's split into a wide grin. "Giving us leave to be on our way, are you? Most kind, m'lord!" His hand slid down the butt of his pistol, his finger an inch closer to the trigger. Behind him, and on either side, men lowered guns off their shoulders, or lifted them higher. Level. Behind him, LeBoeuf heard the rustle of his own men doing the same.

"Oh, for the love of our Dear Lord!" Henriette exclaimed. "Are you idiots truly going to shoot one another? Well, you'd better be quick about it, because the Spaniards will be here soon enough, and they'll drag all you sorry bastards off to the silver mines. And don't think I'll cry to see you go."

LeBoeuf looked over at her, as did the bearded man, and the dark man with the red head-cloth, and most of the others. Henriette glared back at them, arms folded, eyebrows knitted. The man in the red-head cloth spoke softly to the bearded man: translating Henriette's words, LeBoeuf guessed.

The bearded man laughed out loud and turned back to LeBoeuf. "I recall we were trying to kill each other yesterday," he said, "but that was such a damned long time ago. I'm not sure I'm feeling that urge just now."

"It was Van Loudersong I meant to kill," LeBoeuf said. "I care not if you lot live or die."

"Well, that's very considerate of you," the fat man said.

Le Chasseur stepped up to LeBoeuf's side. "What's this buggerer saying?" They had been conversing in English, which most of LeBoeuf's men could not understand.

"He was wondering if we should resume our fight, take up where we left off yesterday," LeBoeuf said. "I told him Van Loudersong's the only one I had a mind to kill, that I don't care about them. And they don't seem much interested in killing us, either."

"I ain't killing anyone until I've had some rum, or gin, and some damned sleep," said Levasseur. Heads nodded, men muttered.

"Some of that pig would not be amiss," Billy Solent added.

"Very well, then," LeBoeuf said to the fat man and the one in the red head-cloth. He spoke English, which apparently they both understood. "You can take your share of our rum and gin, which I reckon you already have. We'll take our share of that pig you're roasting. The master bedchamber is for me and Henriette alone. Rest of you can bunk down where you like. Everyone keeps the peace, and beyond that, I don't give a rat's arse what any of you lot do."

The man in the red head cloth translated for his men. LeBoeuf translated for his. Heads nodded all around. Men grunted in agreement.

Very well, LeBoeuf said. He was back. Back in the peaceful embrace of his plantation. His Tortuga plantation. Which he would relish until the moment that the Spaniards came and took it away.

Chapter Twenty-Four

The day after LeBoeuf's return to the plantation, the Spaniards did not come and take it from him. They were nowhere to be seen. Nor did they come the following day, or the day after that.

On the third day, he and Henriette were sitting at a small table set up just outside the front door of the big house. They each had a glass of wine, the bottle being a gift from D'Anton, who had pilfered it and a few others from the tavern in Cayona on the day the Spanish had arrived.

"So, when do the Spaniards come?" Henriette asked.

"I don't know," LeBoeuf said. It was evening, warm and soft. The last of the day's breeze carried on it the heavy scent of jungle flowers and vegetation and warm earth. LeBoeuf made a contented sound in his throat, almost imperceptibly.

"And when they do come, what will we do?" Henriette demanded next.

"I don't know," LeBoeuf said. Which was true. It was also true that he did not want to think about it just then. He doubted that the Spaniards would launch any sort of attack that late in the day, so he reckoned they were safe until dawn, at least.

Still, he was surprised they had not come yet. He figured on a day or so to offload the ships, to set up camp and secure the area around the town. Three days, at most, before the first of the Spanish troops began spreading out over the interior, running down the miserable handful of men and women they saw as a threat to their sovereignty.

But no. And each day felt to LeBoeuf like a gift from heaven: not an unalloyed gift, but one mixed with strands of worry, since he knew that at any moment he could find himself fighting for possession of the place, and losing. He questioned the point of remaining there, of making any sort of stand at all. It was a losing proposition, particularly when he and his men and the women and Henriette could be in the jungle, establishing some sort of stronghold higher up in the mountains. A place they might actually defend.

It made little sense to remain, but still he could not leave. Since he first found that letter patent, and seen in the words a vision of a place that might be his, a place where he might, for once in many years, stop and breath, it had become, for Jean-Baptiste LeBoeuf, more than just a hundred acres of cleared jungle with a battered manor house and a few outbuildings.

What it had become, he did not know. It was still more a vision than an actual place, despite his being there, feet on the dark soil. He did not bother to look that deeply into it. He just knew he would not abandon it to the Spanish. He would make them take it.

"Humph," Henriette said. "Well, I don't know why I expected anything else. You've always been frightfully ignorant, ever since I've known you."

"It's better that way, trust me," he said. He picked up the bottle and refilled Henriette's glass and his own. "This is good wine, methinks. Did they serve wine such as this at the Tuileries?"

"Such as this?" Henriette snorted in disdain, though she still took up her glass and took a deep swallow. "No, this would not be given to the servants. Nor to the swine."

"No?" LeBoeuf said. "Tell me about the wine you had, then. Tell me about the Tuileries."

Henriette sighed. "Very well." She thought for a moment, then said, "M'lady loved to entertain, all her ladies, she loved to have the most lavish parties, but intimate ones…"

Prior to being shipped to the West Indies to be sold as a wife to some buccaneer, Henriette had been in the court of Louis the Thirteenth of France, a lady in waiting to the queen, Anne d'Autriche. That, at least, was the tale that she told. Based on her descriptions, LeBoeuf, who knew the Tuileries quite well, was all but certain she had never set foot inside the palace.

Still, he loved to hear her talk about the times she supposedly had there. He was always astounded at her inventiveness when it came to describing people and rooms and gardens, artwork and food and wine and music. She spoke with authority and knowledge, which suggested to LeBoeuf that she was no stranger to wealth and nobility, even if that did not actually include the royal court.

LeBoeuf loved the melodic, rapturous way she described her supposed former life. There was a genuinely lovely tone to her voice, which was usually lost in the harsh words coming out of her mouth, but which shone when she was speaking of the finer things. And such talk put her in a good mood. It made her happy, one of the few things that did, and that in turn made LeBoeuf happy.

He closed his eyes and listened as Henriette spoke of wines and candied fruits and pastries as light as air, of elaborate wigs piled on ladies' heads and men in suits embroidered in gold and silver. She talked about lunches with the queen and her lady's maids, where they recounted the copious palace gossip, the frailty of the king, the treachery of Cardinal Richelieu.

When at last she wound her story down LeBoeuf felt more relaxed than he had in some time, at least since he had discovered Van Loudersong's crime. Henriette, too, seemed buoyed by the telling. He looked at her and smiled and she smiled back.

He was not sure what next to say. If he said the wrong words, no matter his intention, even if he did not realize they were the wrong words, then the whole thing would shatter like crystal.

"Thank you," LeBoeuf said.

"You're welcome," Henriette said. LeBoeuf poured the last of the wine into their glasses, and they sat a while in silence before making their way up to the bedchamber.

And so it went, day after day, in relative peace. The heavy, bearded Englishman—whose name, LeBoeuf later learned, was Benjamin Graves—and the dark man with the red head-cloth, whose name was Maja, and their villainous band, caused no trouble. And that was good, because LeBoeuf knew they were a dangerous lot, and could have caused a considerable amount of trouble, if they so chose.

LeBoeuf and Maja had fought back on Hispaniola, on the deck of his old ship, the ship that had been blown by the hurricano into the bay. Man to man, sword, cutlass, and the club, the *boutou* that was always in Maja's belt. LeBoeuf could not recall a harder fight, or one he came so close to losing.

His fight with Graves was less intimate—ship to ship—but Graves, he discovered, could work a vessel with as much skill as Maja could work his boutou. LeBoeuf had been impressed with both of them, and impressing LeBoeuf was not an easy thing to do.

But for all that combat, there had been nothing personal to it, and LeBoeuf felt no animosity toward the men. Circumstances had made them enemies then, and allies now. It was the way of things.

Nor did there appear to be any lingering ill will between their crews, LeBoeuf's or Maja's. There was even a grudging sort of comradeship. These men, after all, were not too different from one another. Outcast, lawless, not much given to respecting those whom God had placed over them in the great hierarchy of being. They were natural comrades, particularly with the specter of the Spanish haunting them.

It was two weeks after LeBoeuf's return to the Tortuga plantation that the threat of the Spanish finally materialized. D'Anton reported their approach. LeBoeuf had been sending men out along the road, a mile or so distant, watching. He did not intend to be surprised, not when surprise was perfectly avoidable.

LeBoeuf was in the tobacco barn with Vassy, and Vassy was explaining how the dried tobacco leaves were bundled and pressed—"prized"—into the hogsheads for shipping, when D'Anton rushed in through the big door. He was breathing hard, wet with perspiration, his shirt soaked through, but he was the most skilled hunter of all of them, the fastest runner, and LeBoeuf was happy it had been him on patrol.

"Lanceros," D'Anton said. His voice was admirably strong despite his having just finished a mile run. "Two dozen or so. Coming this way."

"How far off?"

"A mile and a half? I was up a tree, saw them from a distance."

Up a tree…good man, LeBoeuf thought.

"How fast are they moving?"

"Slow," D'Anton said. "A walk, sometimes a trot. No more. I think they're frightened."

"They should be. Very well, let's make ready to greet them." LeBoeuf wiped the dust from the dried tobacco leaves off on his trousers. He stepped out of the dark interior of the barn and into the brilliant late-morning sun.

"Maja! Graves!" he called. The two men were sitting on benches outside the tents they had set up on the far side of the open ground. There was a small table between them, an open bottle of rum and two pewter tankards. LeBoeuf crossed the yard. The two men looked up at him as he approached, but they did not move otherwise.

"D'Anton says there are lanceros, coming up the road. Two dozen, about a mile and a half away. By the sound of it, they'll be here in the turn of a glass."

"About bloody time," Graves said.

Maja stood, the move fluid and effortless, as if he was being lifted by some unseen hand. It was the way he always moved, LeBoeuf had noticed. Graves, in turn, grunted and pushed himself to his feet.

"We'll get our men in place. The way we spoke of," Maja said.

LeBoeuf nodded. "With any luck these whore's sons will be no great trouble."

"With any luck," Maja said.

They went off in different directions, calling to their men, sending them to collect up small arms and powder and shot. In the week they had been waiting for this moment they had spent some time discussing what they would do when it came, how they would work together, LeBoeuf's men and Maja's. There was no thought of either LeBoeuf or Maja taking overall command; no one would tolerate such an arrangement. But cooperation, that was conceivable.

LeBoeuf's men were positioned in the plantation house, in the windows. The former pig hunters were the surest shots, with the fastest rates of fire, so they set up where they could best employ those skills. Others were in the tree line on the north side of the road.

Maja's men took to the trees at the south side, or behind the outbuildings, or concealed behind wagons and barrels and such in the yard. Let the Spanish approach, let them find what would seem to be a deserted plantation. Let them spread out over the open ground, searching. And once they had advanced into the yard, like fish in a trap, the musket fire would come from every direction.

It did not take long for the men to get where they needed to be. Five minutes of noisy rushing, crashing through brush, feet on stairs, the clack and snap of weapons being loaded, and then it was quiet again.

LeBoeuf stood in the middle of the open ground, his musket in his hand, Other Dog at his side, the last living things still visible. He stood very still and listened for the sound of hoofbeats, or the call of Spanish voices, but he could hear nothing beyond the birds and the wind in the branches and fronds. He looked along the tree line, looked over the plantation house and the outbuildings. He could see no one, and neither would the lanceros, at least until it was too late for them.

"Come," he said to Other Dog. "We'll see what mischief you are able to get up to today."

Together they crossed the open ground and went up the two front steps and through the door of the big house. Sunlight streamed in through the windows, illuminated the dust in the air, and made bright squares on the unpainted wooden floors. Half hidden in the shadows by the walls, flanking each of the windows, LeBoeuf's men sat on the floor, backs to the wall, muskets cradled in their arms. LeBoeuf ran his eyes around the room, nodding to the men, and they nodded back. All was ready.

He and Other Dog climbed the stairs to the second floor. LeBoeuf went first into the master bedchamber. Henriette was seated in one of the wing chairs by the cold and little-used fireplace, arms folded, an angry look on her face, though what she was angry about now, LeBoeuf could not guess. Other Dog, panting, raced over for a scratch.

"Nasty, filthy cur!" Henriette spat and kicked Other Dog in the flanks, but that only encouraged Other Dog to be more assertive in her approach, and finally Henriette, cursing, relented and scratched the dog behind the ears.

Once again LeBoeuf looked around, nodding to the men crouched by the windows, and the men nodded back. He left the master bedchamber and crossed over to the smaller room on the other side of the landing at the head of the stairs.

There was only one man there, that room being least likely to present a good, clean shot, and that man was the old sailor who had attached himself to LeBoeuf's band back at Cayona and had accompanied them to the plantation. LeBoeuf had always thought of him simply as the broken one; a man, a sailor, who, by the look of him was laid low by a fondness for drink. He did not know the man's name, and had never cared enough to ask. LeBoeuf had seen plenty of his sort.

Now he crossed the room to the window under which the man was sitting, leaned on the sill and looked out. Nothing to see. He stepped back and said to the man, "Are you well? Ready for this?" The man did not look as if he had the strength to lift his musket, never mind aim and fire, but LeBoeuf knew that could be deceptive. These scraggly wrecks, cast-away sailors, were often a lot stronger than they seemed.

"Oh, aye, ready," the man said.

LeBoeuf nodded, and started to turn away.

"With you here…and a fight in the offing," the sailor added. "It puts me in mind of those days on board the old *Neptune*. And a fine ship she was."

LeBoeuf stopped, mid-stride. *Neptune*. One word, and it was like a knife in his gut. He felt…he was not sure what he felt. So many things at once, it added up to nothing he could discern.

He turned and looked down at the ragged man leaning against the wall. He had a hint of a smile on his face, seemed perfectly aware of the effect his words would have. He seemed to know they could cost him his life, and he did not care.

LeBoeuf took a step closer, looked into the man's face, past the hard lines etched by weather and drink and hard use, the uneven, patchy beard, the gray and brown strands of hair hanging down like vines. He squinted.

"Le Roux?"

The man grinned. "Oh, aye. When last you saw me, I was not so miserable a specimen as I am now. And you, *Capitaine*…well, the scar is something new." He nodded to indicate the scar that ran along LeBoeuf's cheek and disappeared into his beard. "But the rough clothes and that great hedge of a beard and the tangle of hair, it does not disguise you. You are not a forgettable man."

They were silent, looking at one another. Jacques Le Roux. Fore topman, until he grew too old, then captain of the forecastle on the frigate *Neptune*, a small part of the French navy expanded under orders from Armand Jean du Plessis, Cardinal Richelieu.

LeBoeuf still did not know how to react. Embrace the man? Shoot him? Le Roux seemed to understand the conflict.

"Do as you will, Capitaine. Matters not to me. I'm long past caring a fig about this life. You can see that, I'll wager. But I'll promise you this…if you are now 'Jean-Baptiste LeBoeuf,' then that is who you are, and no man will ever hear me say otherwise."

LeBoeuf realized he had raised his musket to chest height and set his thumb on the hammer, a prelude to swinging the barrel around and firing. Now he took his thumb off the hammer and lowered the gun again.

Jacques Le Roux. A good man, an honest man. Or he had been, anyway, back in the day.

"How do you come to be here?" LeBoeuf asked.

Le Roux lifted his hands, a gesture that suggested he was not sure himself. "When you…left *Neptune*, Lieutenant Perrin was elevated to command. That was not so good. I was twenty-three years in the navy by then. I could tolerate pretty near anything. But that was not so good. Particularly not for us who had been fond of you. Perrin took it out on us. When the fleet was in Brest I reckoned it was my time to leave."

LeBoeuf felt as if he had sprung a plank in his head and this was all rushing in. He was suddenly aware of his breathing. "Why here? Why the West Indies? Tortuga?"

Le Roux smiled and shrugged. "This is where a man goes if he wishes to disappear. To become a new man. Is it not?"

LeBoeuf nodded. "Yes, it is."

"You recall Capitaine Pierre Lepers, I imagine," Le Roux continued. "He gave up command of *Saint Christopher*, and he was said to be coming to Tortuga, to take charge of a plantation. This plantation, as it happened. Took some of his men with him. I had no great love for Lepers, but he didn't know me. So I thought, an old man-of-war's man, I might find some welcome here."

"Lepers was here. I took this plantation from him, but he recognized me, too. It seems the West Indies is not so good a place for a man to disappear."

"You're not old, Capitaine, but you've crossed paths with many men," Le Roux said. "And that makes it more likely you'll cross paths with them again. What's more, you are a sailor, and this is where us broken sailors go."

"Do you know why I…left, as you say? Left *Neptune*? France?"

Le Roux shrugged. "I heard rumors. We all heard rumors. There was talk of an *affaire d'honneur*. Involving a young woman. Some gentleman of great import was killed. But I do not know. Such things are not for the likes of me."

An affair of honor. It did not seem so honorable now. He had let his fury blind him, killed his dearest friend in the world. Spent years running from it, pushing the memory down. He had nearly succeeded in losing it in the muck, but here it was rising again.

LeBoeuf looked at Le Roux, wondered if he truly did not know. Wondered if it mattered. He was Jean-Baptiste LeBoeuf now, regardless of who he had once been.

He was thinking of what he might say next, or if he had to say anything at all, when he heard, faint but unmistakable, the sound of horses' footfalls on soft earth. He stood perfectly still, an ear cocked toward the open window. He heard the jangle of tack and weapons. He heard a voice speak, a single word, and though he could not make it out, it had a very Spanish flavor to it.

He looked down at Le Roux. "Our suitors have come to call," he said, his voice soft as a breath. "You know what to do?"

Le Roux nodded. LeBoeuf nodded back, then turned and moved out of the room and across the landing to the master bedchamber, walking on the balls of his feet in order to make as little sound as a man his size could. He stepped through the door and he could sense the changed atmosphere, like the approach of a lightning storm. The men were tensed, weapons raised. Henriette was staring at the window, her eyes wide, the anger in her face gone.

LeBoeuf stepped close to the wall and moved along its face until he reached the nearest window, then leaned over a bit until he could peek around the frame. Two dozen riders, just as D'Anton had said. They wore crested helmets and bright polished breast

plates and held long lances upright, so they looked like a grove of saplings in the wake of a forest fire. They were riding slowly, no more than a walk, their eyes everywhere. Suspicious, as well they should be. Even Spaniards would see how well this situation lent itself to an ambush.

Too much discipline in your ranks, LeBoeuf thought as he looked at the riders. These were not new recruits; they seemed to know their business, staying in formation, not giving over to the temptation to dismount and see if there was anything of value in the apparently deserted plantation house. If they maintained that sort of order they might well ride out of the trap largely unharmed. If even one of them made it back to Cayona, they would alert the men-at-arms there, who would return with overwhelming force.

The dogs of war…methinks I'll let them slip. He looked over at Other Dog. The animal was crouched low, teeth bared. She was quivering.

One dog of war, anyway… LeBoeuf corrected himself.

"Allez! Allez!" he said. He spoke in a whisper, but the effect was as if he had shouted the words with all the force of his lungs. She shot to her feet, her nails scraping on the floor as she struggled to gain traction, then bolted out the door. LeBoeuf could hear her feet on the stairs as she raced down to the lower floor and out the main entrance. And only then did she begin to bark.

LeBoeuf was smiling as he stepped over to the window and looked out. No need to conceal himself now; with Other Dog racing across the yard, barking like something let loose from Hell, the lanceros had all the distraction they needed.

The horses began to shy and prance and the lanceros struggled to control them. But the soldiers did not panic, and they did not lose their discipline. They lowered their lances, thrusting at Other Dog as she came at them, wheeling and spurring their horses.

Other Dog, in turn, twisted left and right, avoiding the wicked points of the polearms, running barking between the horses, spreading panic among the mounts, if not the men. The carefully ordered column of riders had broken down now, their attention all on this hellhound that had come tearing out of the main house, and LeBoeuf figured that was as good as he was going to get.

"Take aim and fire!" he said to the men in the room as he lifted his musket to his shoulder and held the barrel out through the open window. He swung the muzzle to the left, sighting down the length of the weapon. Beside him, a buccaneer named Berthelot did the same, swinging his musket to the right.

LeBoeuf lined up one of the lanceros, adjusting his aim until the man was directly where he knew the musket ball would go. The rider turned his horse to one side and LeBoeuf tracked him for a second, then squeezed the trigger.

The Spaniards were lost in the burst of smoke from LeBoeuf's gun, and from Berthelot's, and from the half dozen other muskets that had been fired from the three windows in the room. LeBoeuf did not even bother trying to see what damage they had done. A fair bit, he reckoned. They must have dropped a few of the lanceros, or wounded them at least, and now the panic would really be sweeping through as they realized they were indeed in a trap.

From the floor below LeBoeuf could hear other small arms going off, and from across the yard as well, as Maja's men joined in from behind the outbuildings. He poured priming in the pan of his snaphance, stepped up to the window and looked out as he raised his musket. Panic, as he thought. The horses were racing off in every direction around the yard, the lanceros were shouting and pointing this way and that. Other Dog added to the madness, charging back and forth through the riders, barking and snapping at the horses' legs.

LeBoeuf lined his muzzle up with a shining breastplate and pulled the trigger again, then stepped back from the smoke, his hands reaching for another cartridge. He heard shouting in the yard below, orders called out in a voice of command. He looked out the window. The captain of the lanceros had managed to organize a charge, and a dozen horses were pounding toward the outbuildings and the other places where Maja's men were hiding.

"Shoot those bastards on the charge! Shoot them!" LeBoeuf called to the men in the room as he reloaded his weapon. Maja's men, flushed out from hiding, were running from the lanceros. LeBoeuf watched, helpless, as one was cut down with the tip of a lance, another trampled underfoot. He raised his gun, primed and cocked, and stuck the muzzle out the window. He swept it across the grounds, found his target, and squeezed off another shot.

He could see, when the smoke cleared, that the volley had failed to break the lanceros' charge and Maja's men were getting the worst of it.

This won't do, LeBoeuf thought. Shooting from the big house and the tree line would not drive the Spaniards off, not with them concentrating on Maja's men. They had to confront the riders on the ground.

"Come along, come along with me!" LeBoeuf shouted. He raced for the door with the others running behind him, and called to the men in the lower rooms as he charged down the stairs.

He burst out the door and into the yard, shouting as loud as he could. He hoped to get the lanceros' attention, and he succeeded. Heads turned, horses turned, at the sound of his voice, and the rest of the men from the house came piling out the door and formed a line on either side.

"Fire as you can! Take them down!" LeBoeuf called, and his men took a knee and raised their guns, or stood with muskets to shoulders. A few of the lanceros had been knocked from their horses, others were hunched over, wounded. But more were turning their way, spurring their horses, taking up the charge, lances lowered.

LeBoeuf primed his weapon, raised it, as he thumbed back the hammer. He found a rider who seemed to have chosen him as a target, his horse gathering speed as it closed the distance between them, his lance lowered, the point coming for LeBoeuf's chest.

He squeezed the trigger and saw the rider jerk back in his saddle. His horse twisted sideways, collided with the horse beside him, and that horse in turn shied and bucked as its rider tried to stay in the saddle.

We can't stand here for long, LeBoeuf thought. Foot soldiers stood little chance against cavalry in open field combat, he knew that much. *We'll have to go back inside the house, unless…*

More shots came from the far side of the open ground, more shouting. Through the chaos of horses and smoke LeBoeuf could see men coming out of the trees: his men and Maja's men who had been positioned there. They were advancing over the open ground, shooting and reloading as they did. A new threat on the lanceros' flanks. LeBoeuf could see the surprise on the Spaniards' faces, the shadow of panic.

Then, from behind the tobacco barn, came more men, Maja's men, who had been driven back by the riders. They, too, were shouting as they charged, small arms blazing, with the Spaniards under fire now from three directions. And that was the end of their resolve.

If an order was given, LeBoeuf did not hear it, but suddenly all the lanceros who were still in the saddle—those hunched over with agonizing gunshots wounds and those miraculously still intact—turned their horses as one and charged off toward the road from which they had come. LeBoeuf rammed his shot home, primed his pan, raised his gun, looking for a target in the fleeing crowd of men and horses. He found one, and pulled the trigger just as the man's horse moved sideways.

Merde… He could not see for certain, but he felt sure the bullet had gone wide.

More shots went off as the lanceros charged through the gauntlet of LeBoeuf's men and Maja's, and then the gunfire stopped as the targets disappeared down the road, hemmed in here and there by jungle.

"Ha!" Lessard shouted after them. "Run, you bastards!"

Yes, run, LeBoeuf thought. *Run and tell the other five thousand Spaniards that we are here.*

Chapter Twenty-Five

Something was broken inside Don Alonso Menéndez, something deep inside, too deep for him to see. He could feel it, certainly, but he did not try to examine it or understand it. It frightened him. He did not want to look at it directly.

It was the brutality of their fight with the buccaneers that had done it. It staggered him, as if he had been hit on the head, recalling that short time in the jungle (it seemed like hours, days, when he thought back on it), and before that, on the beach. The blinding, all-consuming, bladder-loosening terror. He might forget for a moment the image of that beast tearing into Delgadillo, and then he would remember, and he would feel sick with rage and fear all over again.

He would picture himself back in the jungle, knowing the creature was out there. *They* were out there. He would see himself running in blind panic. He remembered it all. Over and over again. He could not make it stop.

The odd part of it all was that Alonso was no stranger to battle, to death in a hundred violent ways. He had stood on the field of combat at Breda and Groenlo, felt the iron flying around him, seen men die as great armies took to the field. But somehow the jungle was different, the claustrophobic uncertainty, death hidden and close where all he could do was wait for it to come at him out of the foliage. And not the clean death of a bullet. The blood-sprayed death of being torn apart. The moment had been brief, but it had done something to him, something profound.

Until then, things had been unfolding as he intended: the great, humiliating ruse he played on Don Nicolás, securing a place for the One Hundred in the invasion of Tortuga, manipulating things so that he and his men had the honor to be first ashore. The Tortuga plantation, within his grasp.

But the heretics and whoremongers in the jungle had snatched it all away, showing Alonso a level of horror he had never known, even after years of campaigning on the Continent. Horror, and on its heels, fury.

The fury was kindled while greeting Admiral Fadrique Álvarez de Toledo at the water's edge. He expected some word of praise from Toledo, some acknowledgement at least of the bold effort he and his men had made in securing the beach. Questions about the losses they had suffered. But there had been nothing. Alonso was still not certain Toledo knew who he was.

Worse, perhaps, was the way Toledo and his officers did nothing at all to build on the sacrifice that the One Hundred had made. Instead of moving to secure the town and the island, they just stood about, dithering, posing, as more and more troops were landed. They discussed their accommodations aboard the ships, and whether it would be preferable to remain there rather than in pavilion tents ashore. Servants arrived with wine and glasses of Venetian crystal.

And all the while the bastards who had ambushed Alonso's men, who had turned the dog loose on them, were disappearing deeper into the jungle, farther up into the high country. Beyond the reach of Spanish vengeance. Alonso felt the fury start to build: storm clouds, great mounting anvils on the horizon.

For a short while Alonso remained with Toledo and his officers, knowing that it was in his best interest to be part of that company, but soon the thunderheads of anger and disgust grew so ominous that he had to walk away. He trudged back up the beach to where Rodriguez had a few men digging graves for those of the One Hundred who had died in the fight.

"Did you bury Delgadillo?" he asked.

"No, Don Alonso. I did not know…was not certain what your instructions would be."

"Wrap his body well. We'll find a cask of spirits. He deserves better than an unmarked grave on this miserable, dung-heap island."

"Yes, señor."

The afternoon was filled with the tumult of soldiers coming ashore, the yelling of sailors at the oars, the shouting of sergeants and captains, the crunch of boots in the sand. Yet there was another sound as well, an incongruent sound, beneath it all, that was working on Alonso like a pebble in his shoe. And then he realized what it was.

It was the people in the tavern. Drinking, carousing. Singing. They were still at it. While his men lay dead, or bleeding their lives out, while Toledo and his bejeweled flock stood idle on the beach, those whore's sons had the gall to drink and act as if they had not a care in the world. As if there was no proximate threat at all, as if nothing in their world had changed.

"Leave this off," Alonso said to Rodriguez, nodding toward the men digging. "Get the men under arms, muskets and pistols loaded. Immediately."

"Yes, señor," Rodriguez said, then turned and began shouting orders. He might not know what Alonso had in mind, but he knew enough to respond instantly and without question, and Alonso was pleased to see it. As the men rushed to obey, Alonso began loading his pistols, and by the time he was done the men were in line.

"Follow me," Alonso said. He headed across the sand to where the beach gave way to a road of sorts, a wide, well-beaten stretch running between dilapidated and poorly constructed buildings on either side. They must have been sorry things even before the Spanish fleet arrived, and the broadsides from the galleons had done nothing to improve them.

There was no doubt as to which of the buildings was the tavern: the singing and shouting grew louder as Alonso led his men down the road. He stopped outside the open door from which the noise was pouring out like smoke, and pulled a brace of his pistols from their holsters.

"Come," he said.

He mounted the two steps to the porch that fronted the tavern and then walked through the open door. The large windows facing the street left the room dim, but not dark, and the tobacco smoke was not as thick as Alonso would have expected. But the rest was just as he imagined: a scattering of tables and benches, a filthy bar with bottles and glasses behind it, two dozen men, well drunk, sitting, standing, sprawled on the floor. A half dozen or so women.

The people were so far gone in drink that they did not even notice Alonso at first, and it was only when the One Hundred began filing in behind him that one man, at least, looked their way. He was a big man with a big beard, a long, filthy, ripped coat and equally filthy slop trouser. No shirt or waistcoat, just a bare chest covered in dark, matted hair.

Alonso could see the man's expression change as the fog of brandy and gin parted and he realized who the newcomers were. He pushed himself to his feet, struggling to pull a pistol from his belt as he shouted, "Ah! Spanish bastards! You've come now, have you!"

He spoke French, which Alonso spoke as well, fluently.

"*Oui,*" Alonso said as he raised his pistol and put a ball right through the man's broad, hirsute chest.

The Frenchman was flung back onto the two men seated behind him, who leapt clear of their falling *camarade*. Others in the room stood as well, knocking chairs and tables aside as they reached for weapons. Some simply remained where they were. A woman screamed, the sound piercing and feral. Alonso turned to Rodriguez and the rest of his men who were pushing their way inside.

"Kill all the men. Kill them all."

"Señor," Rodriguez protested, "Surely Admiral Toledo will want…"

"Kill them all!" Alonso shouted, the fury, the siren song of vengeance, throbbing in his head. He raised his second pistol and put a ball through the head of a man ten feet away who was pulling a cutlass.

Rodriguez and the One Hundred needed to hear or see no more than that. Muskets fired in a wicked volley, lead shot ripping through the close-packed men, men who had nowhere to run. The buccaneers managed to get off five or six shots in return, all of which went into the ceiling or the wall behind Alonso's men.

And that was it. Fifteen seconds, twenty, perhaps, and it was over. Tables overturned, smoke thick in the air, dead men laying in heaps on the floor or against the back wall.

Alonso stood there, silent, looking at the carnage, his hearing dulled from the gunfire in the small room. He could hear something toward the back wall, but only just, some soft groaning, a thumping. He moved across the room, stepping over sprawled bodies.

It was the shirtless buccaneer, the one who had first reacted to their coming in the room. He was not dead, despite the gaping wound in his chest. He was lying half-propped up against the wall, moaning and thumping his hand on the floor. Somehow the bullet had missed anything that might have ended him instantly.

Amazing…

The man looked up at Alonso, rage and hatred in his eyes, emotions that Alonso recognized well. He tried to spit on Alonso but lacked the strength, and the spittle ran down his lips and into his beard. Alonso pulled his one remaining loaded pistol and pointed it at the man's head, four feet away. But he did not shoot.

Rather, he stood there and looked into the man's eyes as the man looked back at his. Alonso savored the moment, relished the sensation of watching this man, this Frenchman, this buccaneer, as he saw his own death approach.

"*Bâtarde…*" the bearded man said, as emphatically as he could. He grimaced, and Alonso guessed he thought the bullet would come at that moment, but Alonso's finger remained resting on the trigger, caressing it. He could see the confusion on the man's face, and the pain. But he did not see fear, and that disappointed him. He pulled the trigger.

An ugly hole appeared in the man's forehead and, in the same instant, a great splash of blood and brains against the wall. The body jerked once, then seemed to collapse in on itself, motionless. Alonso considered his work for a moment, then turned and looked at the other dead around him. This slaughter did not make up for what had been done to his men, but it helped. He felt the rage subside, just a bit; a temporary salve. He would need more, he knew that. But more could be found, he knew that, too.

Alonso holstered his pistol and walked back toward Rodriguez and the others, glancing around as he did. Taking inventory. Of the women, four remained alive, huddled in the back of the room.

"That was well done," he said, speaking to all his men. "There are rooms above stairs, I'll wager. You may take the women and do as you will. Any plunder you find is yours."

With that he turned and walked back out the door, into the bright sun of the afternoon. He barely heard the shouting and screaming in the tavern room behind him. He walked back down the road, toward the water, with an odd, hollow feeling inside.

What next? he wondered. *What next?*

For all the violence of the morning there was not much that came on its heels. The whole thing, from the flagship's first broadsides to Alonso's greeting Toledo on the beach to the slaughter in the tavern, had been madness, like a boulder tumbling uncontrollably downhill.

But now the boulder had reached the bottom of the hill and rolled quickly to a stop.

The rest of that day, and the next, were spent in ferrying the remainder of the army ashore, the field artillery, the supplies, the horses, the tents. The miserable town was quickly and thoroughly sacked, though there would have been little worth taking even if Alonso's men had not sacked it first. This was not Naarden or Antwerp, after all.

With the town plundered and the dead cleared away, the lesser officers found rooms where they could in the various deserted homes and inns and brothels. Toledo and most of those immediately under him elected to stay in their pavilion tents, which were much more opulent than any quarters that might be found on Tortuga. Others lodged back aboard the ships, where the quarters, at least for the senior-most officers, were more opulent still.

All this arranging and organizing took the better part of a week, and beyond posting guards around the perimeter of the town, nothing was done in the military line. The only battle taking place, as far as Alonso could tell, was the one inside himself.

He ached to lead the One Hundred out into the countryside, to hunt down the men who had ambushed them, to kill them all in the same way they had killed the men in the tavern. He wanted to send out patrols in all direction, lanceros and columns of men, and swift-moving bands of hunters. He wanted to subjugate the island and anyone foolish enough to remain there.

Alonso wanted to do these things because he was terrified by the thought of doing them. Images of being in the cool, silent forest once again, knowing death could be feet away, but not knowing if it was, made him physically ill. He had to confront that fear, and he was deeply, deeply afraid to do so.

Don Alonso Menéndez wanted Tortuga brought to heel. He wanted it for the greater glory of Spain and His Most Catholic Majesty. He wanted it in order to further Spain's iron grip on the West Indies, and as a lesson to those who would try to encroach on his country's dominion. But far more than that, he wanted the island brought under control so he could find the plantation he had worked so hard to secure, and finally claim it for his own. To start bringing to fruition the plans he had first imagined years ago and a few thousand miles away.

On some evenings, councils of officers were held near Toledo's pavilion, where a vast oak table was set up, with plush chairs whose legs sank into the soft ground. The discussions were far-ranging, concerning the benefits to Spain of taking Tortuga (few, it was decided) and to Toledo personally and those men in his entourage (even fewer, to the greater disappointment of all). There was talk of feeding the army and its horses, housing the men, how many men would be required to complete the work of conquest, and whether those present would be enough.

They talked about how taking the island might be regarded back in Seville, if it would be seen as a tolerably impressive military action, and if any titles or other royal gifts might be distributed as a result. And, on occasion, they discussed what they might do next to bring Tortuga under control.

There was a great deal that Alonso wished to say. He wanted to point out that only a handful of the villainous buccaneers on Tortuga had been killed or captured, and that there must certainly be bands of them wandering the jungle, preparing some sort of mischief against the invaders. He wanted to suggest that they send armed patrols out in every direction to hunt these people down, that they could never truly occupy the island until that unknown threat had been met and eliminated, which was why they had come there in the first place. He wanted to insist they get off their arses and do something.

But he did not. In Santo Domingo he was the second highest ranking official, and had done much to cement his position. But in this company he was nothing, he was unknown, and his mere hundred men, less those killed or wounded in the cowardly ambush, were meaningless. The only reason he was even at the table was because he had some minor influence in Seville, was the one who had supplied beef to the fleet, and, more to the point, was husband to a woman who called Admiral Toledo "Tío Fadrique".

So he sat and listened and fumed and, after a week and a half, when he could bear no more, he spoke up. He suggested sending foot patrols and mounted lanceros into the countryside to see about rounding up the renegades, or killing them. He talked about how effective such action had been against the boucaniers on the north coast of Hispaniola, how they had almost entirely driven those savage men off the island, which was not quite true—actually, not even close to being true—but still it made the point.

He offered that same suggestion several more times, at subsequent councils, and every time the idea was met with nods of approval and even additional thoughts as to how to effectively run the enemy to ground, but nothing was ever done. Then, one evening, just as Alonso was trying to work up the nerve to say it one more time, Don Ramón Calderón, Toledo's second in command, announced that the following morning a column of lanceros would be sent out along the road leading east to see what might be found there, and two columns of foot sent off down trails in the jungle to the north and west.

The road leading east, Alonso thought. He had been eyeing that road, thinking about the words on the letter patent, a copy of which he had in his possession, and which he had read many times.

Half a league to the east of the chiefmost harbor of said Island of Tortuga…

He did not know if the road he had seen led to the plantation, but it seemed reasonable to think it did. He had no notion of what the plantation looked like, what size it might be, what buildings might be there, but if it was significant enough for the king of France to give away in a letter patent it most likely had some sort of road leading to it, and he had not seen any other road leading east.

Alonso rose the next morning after a night of hellish dreams, one after the other, from which he woke gasping or screaming. His body ached, his eyes burned. He smelled of dried sweat. He stumbled over to his washbasin, splashed water on his face, ran wet fingers through his hair.

The pavilion tent he occupied was to the northeast of the town, close to the head of the road leading east, where he had ordered the One Hundred to pitch their tents. He pushed back the flap and stepped out into the cool morning. The sky was the light blue of the early hours, the air heavy with jungle and sea. A hundred yards south, the lanceros were assembled on the road that cut through the town, some mounted, some attending to last minute business. Alonso watched as the last of them climbed into their saddles and fell into line, following the barked commands of their sergeant.

Alonso wondered if he should speak to the officer in command of the column, tell him what to look for. He wondered if he should have found mounts for the One Hundred and accompanied the lanceros. But in the end he dismissed both ideas. He did not want to show undue interest in the plantation. And when he did finally make his way there, he did not want any witness to his actions besides the One Hundred.

So he stood there as the mounted troops walked their horses through the town and then veered off to the road leading east, watching until the last of them was lost from sight. His face was expressionless, his feelings similarly neutral. He was tired. That was all he was. So many torments, so many crosscurrents over the fortnight past. He was weary.

For the rest of the morning and into the afternoon he kept to his pavilion as Rodriguez drilled the men or had them service their weapons or some sort of thing. Alonso did not know what. He gave Rodriguez just one instruction, and that was that he, Alonso, was to be immediately alerted if the lanceros returned.

He spent the day brooding, drinking wine, sleeping on and off. He could hear through the canvas walls the mundane sounds of the day; soldiers drilling, officers yelling, horses snorting and clomping about, food being cooked and served. Life rolled along as if this was home, the town in which they had always lived, and their fathers and grandfathers before them. As if they were not an invading army, camped on a foreign shore, with an enemy lurking in the hills at their back.

It was late in the day, and Alonso had drifted off to sleep sitting upright in his chair, when a voice outside the tent finally woke him.

"Don Alonso! Don Alonso!"

He startled awake, unsure where he was. He looked around in the half light of the pavilion. "What is it?"

"The lanceros, señor. They have returned."

Alonso felt a pulse of energy shoot through him and the weariness was gone. He snatched up his hat, pushed his way through the flap of the tent, and walked quickly toward the head of the road. The first of the lanceros was just coming into sight, a quarter mile away. The column was still too far off to see exactly how many there were. Two dozen had ridden out. Alonso did not think there were two dozen coming back.

He stood a bit to the side of the road, not blocking it, but enough in the way to make it clear he meant to speak to the returning men. Even if the captain of the lanceros did not know who he was, his clothing and sword and pistols would mark him for a man to be obeyed.

The riders were moving at a walking pace, their lances not held upright in a show of discipline, but resting on shoulders, or crosswise on saddles. Most sat upright on their mounts, but others were slumped over to various degrees.

"*Dios mío*," Alonso whispered as the lanceros came closer, as he was able to see them better. He made the Sign of the Cross.

The men were blood- and dirt-streaked and wore makeshift bandages around arms and legs. Some were white, ghost-like, from loss of blood, bent nearly double, ready to fall from their saddles. The sergeant leading them had an ear that was no more than a bloody wreck of flesh. Alonso could not see the captain.

He stepped up as the sergeant approached, held up a hand. "Hold a moment," he said, and the sergeant, too well trained and perhaps too beyond caring to object, held up a hand as he reined his horse to a stop.

"Where is your captain?"

The sergeant took a deep breath. He nodded with his head back over his shoulder. "Back there, señor. Tied to his horse. Dead."

"Tell me…briefly…what befell you?"

The sergeant stared at Alonso, wordless, for a moment. "We saw no one on the road, señor, for the first few miles. Then we came upon a farm or plantation or such. Seemed to be deserted as we rode in, but they were lying in ambush for us. They fired at us from the windows of the big house, and from the trees."

"Why did you not ride away?"

"There was a dog, señor."

Dog. Just the word made Alonso's stomach twist. "A dog?" he asked.

"Yes, señor. They let a dog loose and it frightened the horses, turned all into confusion. We fought as best as we could. We killed some. I don't know how many. But they made a great slaughter amongst us."

"How many of them were there?"

The sergeant shook his head. "Forty? Fifty? It was hard to tell. Our captain…he was a good man. The bastards."

Alonso nodded. He could think of nothing more to ask, and did not think there was anything more he needed to know.

"Very well, sergeant. See that your men are tended to."

The sergeant flicked his reins and the bloody parade of riders continued on past in their weary pace, making for the town, where some would find succor and others a more comfortable place to die. Alonso watched them as they rode away, but his mind was elsewhere.

A dog…

The foreign villains who had settled on Tortuga, many of them, most of them, perhaps, were the hunters whom Spain had driven out of Hispaniola. And those bastards all had dogs. It was the way they hunted. The lanceros might have encountered a band of men with a dog, but there was no certainty at all that they were the same men, the same dog, who had ambushed the One Hundred in the jungle.

On the other hand, there was no reason to think they were not. A murderous band with a vicious dog, springing yet another ambush on a column of Spanish troops? Was it possible that the very bastards whom Alonso most wanted to kill were now occupying the plantation Alonso most wanted to possess?

He walked quickly back toward his pavilion and the field of tents that the One Hundred occupied. He called for Rodriguez as he approached, and Rodriguez came running over.

"We're marching at first light," he said, his words more certain, his voice more confident than any time since he had fled from the jungle in terror. "See the men have their weapons in order, and all the powder and shot they can carry. Find a wagon to carry more powder and shot. And food as well. As much as will fit. I don't know how long we'll be gone."

He could see the hesitation on Rodriguez's face, just a hint. Alonso had not been given orders or permission to lead his column out of town, and Rodriguez knew it perfectly well. But Rodriguez also knew perfectly well not to question Alonso's instructions.

"*Sí,* señor," he said. "And will we break camp on the morrow, and bring the tents?"

Alonso considered it. "No. Where we are going, there will be quarters better than tents."

"Sí, señor," Rodriguez said, and hurried off.

It might be true that Alonso did not have orders or permission, but he did not care, and he had come to realize at long last that Toledo did not care either. The Admiral would subdue the island at his own petty pace, and he was not much concerned with the particulars of how it was done.

Alonso would, of course, request permission, though it would be mostly a formality, more telling Toledo what he meant to do rather than asking if he could do it. He had witnessed enough of Toledo's decision making to know that the old man would simply nod and say, "Yes, fine, fine..." and think no more of it.

And then Alonso would be free to do whatever he wished. Not what would do the most good for Spain, perhaps, but whatever would bring him, Alonso, the most wealth, power, and position.

Chapter Twenty-Six

Henriette de Labonté stood on the edge of the gathering, arms folded, scowling. Unsure what to do.

She knew what she wanted to do: she wanted to wade in and start slapping faces, just slap and slap, left and right. Maybe throw a punch or two. A few kicks. Keep hitting and kicking until she had knocked some sense into this collection of idiots that plagued her.

LeBoeuf's stupid dog was pressed up against her, tongue lolling, oblivious to the ridiculous spectacle taking place. The beast kept looking up at Henriette with expectant eyes, hoping to be scratched, which made Henriette's fury flash like a fistful of gunpowder tossed on an open flame.

She cocked her leg and kicked the dog hard in the flank, but it was like kicking a sack of grain, and had about as much effect. Worse, the dog seemed to like it, thought it was an expression of affection. It looked up at Henriette again, panting, waiting for more.

Stupid cur, she thought. It was no wonder LeBoeuf loved the thing so much. They were one of a kind. Kick either of them as hard as you could and they'd just come panting back for more.

Still, the dog was the least of Henriette's worries.

They had enjoyed two weeks of peace, the lot of them there on the plantation, but it was over now. From the moment LeBoeuf's men and Maja's men had tacitly agreed to not kill each other, right up until the moment the Spanish lanceros had come riding in, things had been mostly calm. But no more.

It was a bloody show, the fight with the Spaniards, what little Henriette had seen of it. She had remained in the master bedchamber throughout, trying to maintain her veneer of bold disinterest, masking fear with anger as she was so accustomed to doing. The riders were driven off in the end, but they left fury and distrust in their wake, a volatile mix.

Now, as LeBoeuf and Maja and Graves faced off once again, Henriette debated whether or not to insert herself a second time, to step in and try to slap some sense into these men as she had done before.

In her gut she knew she would not. Passions were burning hotter now, the anger was fresh and real. LeBoeuf was leaning on his musket, facing Graves, with ten feet between them. The Englishman had voiced the hint of an accusation, touching on the anger that had been simmering since the Spanish rode off. It was enough to get LeBoeuf's blood up, and to get his men and Maja's facing off.

This would be an ideal time for LeBoeuf to reply, Henriette knew, for him to say something that might cool things down. But she also knew that he would not. It was exactly this sort of situation where he was bound to say the least.

The silence stretched on, well beyond the point of discomfort. Finally, LeBoeuf spoke.

"Speak. If you will."

Graves spit on the ground. "What I'm saying is that things played out damn well for you and your men, didn't they? Hiding in the house, while them Spaniards rode us down. My men, and Maja's. Skewered 'em."

LeBoeuf was frowning now, his eyes narrow. Henriette had seen him wear that expression before. Not often, but she had seen it, and it generally meant something bad was about to happen. She saw his fingers spreading over the barrel of his gun, and she had a vision of LeBoeuf jerking the weapon up and slamming the butt into Graves's face, a vision so clear it was as if she was watching it happen.

"LeBoeuf…" Henriette said, taking a step forward. She had to speak now; they were seconds away from a bloody slaughter. Then Pierre Le Chasseur broke in.

"*Your men*," Le Chasseur said, derisively. "Your men would not know which end of the musket the ball comes out. That's why you were cowering here at the plantation while we fought the Spaniards in the town."

"Fought the Spaniards, did you? How'd that go?" Graves asked. "You win? Send 'em back to Santo Domingo?"

"Killed our share of them," Le Chasseur said. "That's good enough for me."

Graves looked back at LeBoeuf, as if waiting for him to add something, but Henriette knew he would not. LeBoeuf had already said more than she would have expected.

She felt herself tense. If the words were done and the shooting was about to start, it was LeBoeuf or Graves or Maja who would make the first move, and she had to be ready to step in if need be. She did not actually care if they blew each other to Hell, but if they did, it might go very hard on her. Who knows what the others would do with her, or to her? And LeBoeuf so far remained her best hope for getting back to Paris.

It was Maja who next broke the silence, prefacing his words with a grunting sound. "We're done here," he said. He lifted his musket, which set off a sudden flurry of motion as sixty men swung their weapons up and leveled them at an enemy a dozen feet away.

But Maja did not level his gun. Rather, he rested it on his shoulder, turned his back on LeBoeuf, and walked off toward the tobacco fields and the jungle beyond. One by one his men did the same, following after him, muskets on shoulders or held at their sides.

"Where are they going?" Henriette asked. She had no idea as to what just happened, and she wondered if she was the only one.

"Off to the jungle, I'd reckon," LeBoeuf said.

"Why?"

"Because the Spaniards will be back soon. And those whores' sons don't care to stand up to them. So they're going to hide out."

"Damn lot of cowards," Le Chasseur said.

"Mayhaps," said Levasseur. "But now we have half the men we had before. And when them Spaniards do come back, it won't just be just a company of lanceros, I can tell you."

Henriette looked around at the others. Heads were nodding. Levasseur's words, apparently, did not come as a surprise. Every man there seemed to believe the same thing. And with that understanding came a strange sort of mood, which soon settled like mist on the plantation; a quiet and subdued air, quite unlike the drunken revelry that usually marked the buccaneers' camp. It seemed more like the somber attitude of men waiting for the dawn, when they would be hanged by the neck until dead.

For the rest of the afternoon the men occupied themselves in eating, drinking, lounging around, their usual day's work, but with none of the enthusiasm they usually showed for such things. Henriette went through her now well-established routine as well, directing the servants, seeing that the cleaning and mending and sundry chores were done, the few animals put away, cursing at Other Dog. But it seemed different for her as well. She could feel the presence of the Spaniards, some ways away to the west, a looming threat, a hurricano building on the horizon. A force of nature that would assuredly fall on them, even if they did not know when.

It was dark when she climbed the stairs at last, weary, wearier than she could recall being in a very long time. The bedchamber was empty and she was glad of it because she was in no mood to speak to anyone. She stripped off her apron and her overbody and her petticoats, stripped down to her linen smock. She washed her face in the basin then climbed into bed and blew out the candle.

She was nearly asleep when she heard LeBoeuf coming up the stairs, his tread light, which always surprised her. He was a great beast of a man, but still he managed to move with an unexpected grace most of the time. He opened the door slowly, and the light from his candle partially illuminated the far side of the bedchamber as he set the holder down on the wash basin and began to undress.

Will he want me tonight? she wondered, and then wondered if she would acquiesce if he did. She was certainly not feeling very amorous just then. But there were times enough that she had felt uninspired in that way, only to warm up quickly to LeBoeuf's advances.

She had been with many men over the course of her life, and she had become quite adept at pretending to like it, but with LeBoeuf she genuinely did. It was not something that she would admit, or even think very much about, but she knew that it was true. LeBoeuf's light touch and grace of motion applied to more than just his climbing the stairs.

Henriette lay perfectly still, feigning sleep, eyes partially open as she watched LeBoeuf undress. He no longer wore the bloodstained and filthy clothing of his pig-hunting days, and she was grateful for that. Early on, when she first came to live with him in the hunting camp, when she realized that he truly meant to make no demands of her, she had taken it upon herself to do his washing. It seemed a reasonable exchange. He had, after all, saved her from whatever horror would have otherwise been her fate.

She was no laundress, and had done very little of that sort of thing, but she understood how it was done. Still, try as she might, she could never get LeBoeuf's clothes anywhere near what she might call clean. LeBoeuf seemed more than satisfied with her efforts, but she still found it all quite revolting.

Happily, those clothes had since been consigned to the flames. Now he generally wore slop trousers and a light canvas cassock, new-made by some of the seamstresses among the buccaneers' wives, the same ones who had stitched up his ridiculous suit of many colors.

Henriette watched as he pulled the new clothing off, leaving only his long linen shirt over his great bulk.

Who are you? she wondered.

Jean-Baptiste LeBoeuf did not speak much, but Henriette had observed enough to know that he was not the man he claimed to be. She had figured out, for one thing, that he could read, despite his claims that he could not. He spoke English, apparently. That was no great feat, to be sure—plenty of people, sailors in particular, spoke languages other than their own native tongue—but it was still something to which he had never admitted.

And there was something else: a layer of gentility, like a coat of fine paint that he tried to cover over with uglier, cruder colors. To anyone else, LeBoeuf seemed every bit the man he said he was; a pig-hunter, a buccaneer, a common sailor. Unrefined, uncouth, and uncaring. But on occasion Henriette caught glimpses of something else. She had spent most of her life in the company of the finer sort, the titled, the wealthy, and the connected, and she recognized that *je ne sais quoi.*

LeBoeuf still thought he had her fooled. Henriette was sure of that. He still thought she considered him some miserable wretch who had crawled out of a ship's scupper. But she was not as dumb as he believed her to be. And she was starting to wonder if the same was true of him, if he was not so dumb either, this rogue whom she had always considered some great stubborn ox.

LeBoeuf leaned over and blew out the candle, and the yellow light of the flame was replaced by the softer bluish light of the moon coming in through the open windows. She could make out his large form as he stepped across the room. He was walking with care, trying not to disturb her, but she could tell from the way he moved that he had been drinking, even more than was his wont. Earlier, he had wandered off toward the tobacco fields, just him and his cursed dog and a bottle of rumbullion. She had not seen him for the rest of the evening, until now.

He stopped by the edge of the bed and pulled the bedclothes back. He lay down, easy as he could, but still the mattress heaved like an ocean swell. He stretched out, full length, his feet projecting out over the end of the bed. He pulled in a deep breath, held it, then let it out in a soft sigh.

Henriette's eyes were open now and she was looking at his profile in the moonlight, the vaguely beak-like nose, the massive beard. His eyes were closed and he did not seem much interested in love-making, not with the stress of the day and all the rumbullion he had consumed. Just as well. She would let him sleep.

"Pray, LeBoeuf…what will happen on the morrow?" The words came unbidden, and they surprised her. She had not intended to speak. But LeBoeuf did not seem surprised. For a moment she was not even sure he had heard.

"The Spaniards will come," LeBoeuf said at last. He was still lying on his back, his eyes still closed. "Tomorrow, or the day after. They'll come in strength, like Levasseur said."

"And what will you do?"

Again LeBoeuf was silent for so long that Henriette thought perhaps he had not heard, or had fallen asleep. He answered at last, though it was not much of an answer.

"I don't know," he said. "Maybe fight them. Maybe die here."

Now it was Henriette's turn to be quiet as she considered LeBoeuf's words. "Why would you die for this place?" she asked, finally. "Why do you love it so?"

LeBoeuf shrugged, a gesture that was less effective when seen from Henriette's perspective, lying beside him, but it conveyed what he wished to convey.

"When I saw that letter patent, and the great seal, something inside of me changed. And I thought this place could be my home. I have not had a home in a long time. Then you read it for me, the account of what this place was, and I saw what it might be."

"You read it yourself. I might have read it first, but you read it as well. Because you could."

Again LeBoeuf was quiet for a long time, as if debating how much to admit. "Yes," he said at last. "I read it myself."

Who are you? Henriette had no idea. Just as he had no idea who she was. She spun her tales of life in the Tuileries, of kings and queens and courtiers, and LeBoeuf seemed to relish them, and seemed to have no notion that she was making it up from whole cloth.

Henriette de Labonté, born Henriette Sauveur, daughter of a Parisian wigmaker, a precocious child, and by twelve years old already a remarkable beauty. Orphaned at thirteen when the smallpox swept through their part of the city, killing her parents and half the people on the street where she lived, but somehow leaving her unscathed.

Sent to a workhouse after her uncle claimed for himself all of her parents' earthly possessions, she was soon adopted by François d'Albert, le Comte de Labonté, who took her in for reasons that had nothing to do with kindness or paternal affection. Raised to the elegance of le Comte's grand household, instructed in the habits and manners of a courtier, and in the skills and expectations of a courtesan.

Henriette enjoyed a life of elegance and leisure, and in exchange she was available to le Comte de Labonté whenever he wished, for whatever he wished, an arrangement that included accommodating his friends, and those to whom he owed favors, or those he wished to have in his debt.

It was not an idyllic life, but Paris offered endless examples of fates much worse, so Henriette endured it and hid her seething fury under a patina of well-rehearsed grace and charm. And all was well, until her twentieth year, by which time she was too old to hold le Comte's interest anymore.

Out on the street, unable to secure a position of any sort, she turned, for a brief and nightmarish spell, to whoredom of the basest kind: a streetwalking, filthy-rented-room-on-a-third-floor sort of whoredom. But, for better or worse, it did not last long. She was soon swept up in an effort to rid Paris of her sort, and sent off to the West Indies, where it was hoped the presence of women might help tame the growing population of wild men who were spreading like a disease from island to island.

She was prepared from the outset to kill any of the filthy swine who tried to lay a hand on her, and then kill herself. She was done with the humiliation and the abuse. But it had never come to that, because the captain of the ship she was put aboard wished to keep her as unsoiled as he could. She was not like the other whores—fat, poxed, mostly toothless—and it was worth resisting temptation for the price she would fetch.

So Henriette kept her stolen knife hidden in her stocking and waited for the moment when it would be needed. And then, on that beach on the north shore of Hispaniola, amid the leering, shouting beasts who called themselves *boucaniers*, LeBoeuf appeared.

"Who are you?" Henriette asked, and again LeBoeuf did not answer for some time.

"I was a pig hunter. Now I am lord of the manor," he said. "And I might remain so for another day. Two, mayhaps."

Henriette propped herself up on her elbow. "You were not always a pig hunter," she said. "And you were not always a filthy, unlettered sailor. You were something else."

"Yes, I was."

"What were you? Were you wealthy? Were you titled?"

LeBoeuf sighed, long and deep. He stared up at the ceiling, then his head lolled over until he was looking at her. "Yes," he said. "Perhaps. And I'll say no more." And with that he rolled over, turning his back on Henriette, and on any further revelations.

Moments later he was asleep, his breathing deep and rhythmic. Henriette stared at his broad back, his massive shoulders, and tried to tamp down her irritation and frustration. She wondered why he felt the need for such mystery, if he truly had some great and terrible secret, or if he was just trying to play the man of intrigue. Or if he was just lying about it all.

With a sigh of disgust she lay back down, and, soon after, she was asleep as well. Then, the next day, the Spaniards came.

Genet saw them first. He had the watch out on the road, a half a mile from the plantation. He had climbed D'Anton's tree, which the men had dubbed "the mainmast," and that gave him an unobstructed view for another half mile before the road bent from view. He came running back into the dooryard, red-faced and heaving, struggling to get the words out. Not that it was so necessary for him to speak. Everyone there knew what he was going to say.

When Genet's breath returned he made his brief report, and the men grabbed up their muskets and powder and shot. It did not take long, since they had been ready for this.

Henriette stood leaning against the big house, watching as they gathered outside. LeBoeuf, as usual, was rushing here and there, snapping orders. But there was something different about the others, some lack of enthusiasm. They moved slower, exchanged glances as they fell into rough order. LeBoeuf seemed not to notice, but Henriette did.

"I reckon these Spaniards heard from the lanceros about how we ambushed 'em," LeBoeuf said, once the buccaneers had gathered again. "They won't let that happen a second time. So we need to position ourselves in a different way, some way that—"

"Here, LeBoeuf," Pierre Le Chasseur said, interrupting. LeBoeuf stopped talking, scowled. "Genet, he said he saw a hundred of them Spaniards coming on foot," Le Chasseur continued. "And there could be more. There's no saying."

"So?"

"So, we're less than thirty men, here. And we got women with us. And only so much powder and shot. And we won't surprise them this time."

"What of it?" LeBoeuf asked, and Henriette wondered if he was being purposely obtuse. It was pretty obvious where Le Chasseur was going with this. It was the only reasonable place to go. She realized that the others had discussed this before, out of LeBoeuf's hearing, and had already made their decision.

"I'll tell you what of it," Le Chasseur said. "None of us much cares to die right here on this shit-heap island, for your silly plantation. That's what of it. Not worth it, not by a long shot."

LeBoeuf looked around at the men in front of him, and he actually seemed surprised at what he was hearing.

What in God's name did you expect? she wondered. *You think these bastards want to die for this sorry tobacco plantation, just because you think it's paradise?*

Perhaps she had been right about LeBoeuf's intelligence, or lack thereof, all along.

"All of you, you all think this?" LeBoeuf asked. Only a few heads nodded. Most remained silent. But no one offered to stay and fight.

"Then what would you do now?" LeBoeuf demanded.

Levasseur spoke next, and again it was clear to Henriette that he was not making this up in the moment. They had talked this all out amongst themselves.

"We'll take to the jungle. We know how to hunt, how to live there. We can keep moving, keep ahead of any Spaniard patrols.

Ambush them now and again. The Don Diegos can't stay here forever." Heads were nodding again, more of them this time.

For a long moment LeBoeuf did not speak, just glared out over the men, and Henriette was struck by a sudden insight. The others, the buccaneers, owed LeBoeuf nothing. He had no authority over them. They did not have to argue this point. Yet he had such a natural aura of command that they mostly did as he said, despite their self-professed rejection of authority.

Even now, as he was asking them to die in defense of his miserable plantation, they could not simply reject him outright.

But they would reject him. Henriette could see that too. And so could LeBoeuf.

"Very well," LeBoeuf said. "But give me this. Let us take to the jungle just there." He pointed to a spot north of the plantation house, where the tree line marked the edge of the forest that stretched away up into the high county. "We'll hide ourselves, watch the Spaniards as they come. If they're of no great force, we'll attack them. But if they're too much for us, we'll make off into the mountains, as you say."

The buccaneers looked at one another, silently debating this proposition. There was more nodding.

"Very well," Levasseur said. "We'll wait and see. But don't count on us volunteering for your forlorn hope."

They did not have much time, twenty minutes perhaps, before the Spanish column reached the plantation, so they scrambled to collect up as much food and strong drink and powder and shot as they could carry. Then, with LeBoeuf in the lead, the buccaneers headed north, with Vassy and the other servants trailing behind.

They did not go far beyond the tree line, twenty feet or so, just enough to be swallowed up by the foliage. There they took a knee or stood half hidden behind a trunk and looked back a hundred yards toward the plantation, LeBoeuf's plantation, their idyllic home for so brief a time.

LeBoeuf had been right about the Spaniards: they were not about to walk into an ambush again. They did not even come by way of the road. At some point before reaching the plantation grounds they had taken to the jungle, and now, as the buccaneers watched, they began to emerge from the tree line to the south. Just a few at first, black-clad and holding muskets at the ready, they stepped tentatively into the open from the cover of the dense green vegetation, advancing with great caution toward the house.

"Are those the same sorry turds we took on back at the beach?" Lessard asked, his voice low.

"They're dressed in black," Billy Solent said. "Never seen any other Don Diego soldiers dressed in black, except those we met on the beach."

Henriette watched, fascinated, as the soldiers slowly emerged from the trees, more and more of them, and moved out across the dooryard. Others came from around the house and carefully climbed the steps to the front door. Those in the open found cover and aimed their muskets at the windows above.

How many of these sons of bitches are there? she wondered. There were close to a hundred, at least, all fitted out in black trousers and tunics, swords at their sides, helmets and breastplates gleaming. She knew little about soldiering, but it seemed to her these were not the rag-and-tag sort she had often seen. This was some elite crowd, some well-outfitted company.

A few horses appeared now, coming around the house, coming from the road, she guessed. She could see sunlight flash off the silver of the horses' tack, and off boot buckles and swords and armor. Some of the men on foot ran over to the horsemen to report, and one of the mounted men pointed here and there, giving orders. The man in charge of these well-appointed soldiers, apparently.

Was he the one who paid for the men's gear, she wondered, the breastplates and the swords and such? Soldiers such as these, they were not led by guttersnipes or men of low birth.

You must be some sort of gentleman, Henriette thought. *Titled, no doubt. A man of means. Influence.*

Henriette was aware of a strange sensation in her gut, feelings that swirled around like a column of smoke in the breeze. LeBoeuf had been her protector, but the men were no longer following him. What might that mean for her? That uncertainty made her nervous. Frightened her, actually.

When she first arrived on Hispaniola, LeBoeuf had saved her life, she knew that. And she had repaid him well with her kindness, and her domestic help, and her carnal efforts. She had always considered him to be her best chance at getting back to France. He had, after all, a fortune in gold, half of which she considered hers, sitting in his burned and sunken wreck of a ship.

But for all his promises, he had shown little real interest in retrieving it. All he cared about, it seemed, was his ridiculous plantation, and now even that had been taken from him.

So what did Henriette have to look forward to? Living in the jungle like an animal, starving to death, or being killed by some beast, or felled by disease? The very thought of spending a night in that godless wilderness terrified her. And if she and the others did not die quickly, then the Spaniards would see they were killed in the end, or enslaved, or worse.

Her eyes were still on the man mounted on the fine horse. He was there, on Tortuga, to hunt down the buccaneers, to kill them or round them up for labor in the silver mines. But what would such a man—a man of good breeding, no doubt, a gentleman—what would such a man do to a woman in distress? A Frenchwoman, to be sure, but still a woman of status and high birth? A victim of the wicked buccaneers?

She had no good choices left, but of those that were available to her, which was the least bad?

With no more thought behind it, she stood. And then she was running, running through the trees, through the tall grass, out into the open ground, running with arms up, toward this mounted Spaniard with his fine horse and silver buckles, this man of honor, or so she hoped.

Chapter Twenty-Seven

"What the devil is she doing?"

Levesque said the words, but they were exactly the words that LeBoeuf was thinking as he watched Henriette racing away over the open ground.

He stood straight up, and beside him, Other Dog stood as well, growling, panting, completely unsure as to what was happening or what she should do. Like Levesque's words, a perfect mirror of LeBoeuf's own thoughts.

"Silence!" LeBoeuf snarled.

The first thought to come to mind was that she was trying to distract the Spaniards, mislead them, give LeBoeuf and his men a better chance at escape. But that notion was no more than a flash in the pan. He knew what she was doing.

Damn you, LeBoeuf thought, his eyes on Henriette's dark hair, tossing as she ran. There were feelings churning up in his guts, ones that he did not care to consider.

"Is she going over to the Don Diegos?" Lessard asked.

"Quiet!" LeBoeuf barked, angrier and more emphatic than he meant to sound. "She's not chattel," he added, trying to strike a more reasonable tone. "She can do whatever she damned well pleases."

They continued to watch in silence as Henriette neared the plantation house and slowed to a stumbling walk. The soldiers had muskets raised and pointed vaguely in her direction, ready for some sort of trap. The men on horseback slid to the ground as she approached.

"Will she give us up?" Pierre Le Chasseur asked. "Send them after us?"

"No," LeBoeuf said. He did not believe her treachery would extend so far. But then, he would not have thought she would do what she was doing now. "She won't give us up, no," he said again.

He was trying to convince himself as much as the others, and he knew it.

They were too far to hear anything that was said, but they could see Henriette waving her arms for emphasis, see her pointing—not toward them, but off to the east—then waving her arms some more. They saw her collapse against the officer's chest, saw him put a protective arm around her.

LeBoeuf set his musket over his shoulder and turned his back on the scene. "Too many of those Spanish bastards for us to fight. Let us away."

He pushed his way through the line of watching men and headed north, through the trees and the ground cover. He shifted his musket to his left shoulder and drew his fine sword to cut a path through the worst of it. Other Dog remained at his side, and behind him he heard the rest beating a path, heard birds screeching in the trees, and other creatures, unseen, chattering away. He heard them all and paid them not the least bit of mind. His thoughts were elsewhere.

He knew why she had done what she had done, of course. Self-preservation, keeping an eye out for the main chance, that was what Henriette was about. Always looking for who, or what, would give her the best odds of getting what she needed, and what she wanted.

Just now those desires were pretty simple. Survival. Freedom from the wretched company of the buccaneers. A way back to France, ideally with gold, silver, or specie, in her purse.

And what did he have to offer her, miserable creature that he was? Nothing, because once again the Spaniards had taken it all from him. There was nothing ahead for any of them, save living like the beasts of the forest, scrambling for what food or shelter they could find, always moving, always hunted.

Henriette had guessed right about that prating toad of a Spaniard, LeBoeuf suspected. If the garlic-eating don was the same cur who had led the soldiers on the beach—and LeBoeuf was fairly certain that he was—then he was a man of wealth and influence. You did not get the honor of spearheading an invasion, even one as insignificant as the taking of Tortuga, unless you were a man of some importance. You did not outfit your company in that manner if you were just some low-born knave.

"Bitch!" LeBoeuf spoke out loud. He had not meant to—the word come out unbidden—but no one seemed to hear. He took a powerful swing at a tangle of vines in his way.

Damn that bitch!

He kept the words confined to his head that time, and he chastised himself even as he thought them.

What do you expect? What does she owe to you?

To be sure, he had saved her from some uncertain but certainly unpleasant fate when she had first arrived on Hispaniola. But she had not asked him to do it, and he had not necessarily done it out of any sense of expectation or gallantry. He was not entirely sure why he had saved her, other than his natural impulsiveness and visceral objection to the destruction of something so beautiful.

Like many of the decisions he had made over the past few years, and often enough before that, it was not really a decision at all. He had simply acted. It was that unfortunate tendency that had brought him to the place where he was now.

Henriette had remained with him not out of loyalty or gratitude but because she had no choice, really. And he had become accustomed to her company. He had never considered the possibility of her leaving, or thought that he would care if she did, and now he was embarrassed by his reaction.

There is no reason that I should care a damned fig whether she comes or goes, some silly bunter from the streets of Paris, and not a particularly pleasant one at that. Wandered into my life…now she's wandered out. No reason to ever think on her again. And so he did not.

Until a few minutes later, when he did.

Damn it, damn her… He put her out of his mind once more.

They continued on, higher and higher up into the hills, sometimes cutting their way through foliage, sometimes walking across meadows of tall grass, and sometimes over scattered, rocky terrain. LeBoeuf hope that those at the tail end of the line were listening for the sound of pursuit. He himself heard nothing. But then, he was not really paying attention.

It was early evening when they stopped on the edge of an open field, with the mountains at their back and the ocean off in the distance to the south, and the long, blue, ragged outline of Hispaniola beyond that. They ate some of the rations they had brought with them from the plantation. They did not light a fire for fear of being seen, though there was no sign that anyone was looking for them. They did not set a watch because LeBoeuf could not be bothered to suggest it, and it did not occur to anyone else.

The next morning they awoke and broke their fast with more cold rations and debated as to what they would do next. Some thought they should move higher into the mountains. Some thought they should go south. Some north. A few felt they were fine right where they were.

LeBoeuf took no part in the discussion. He did not care where they went, or what they did. He felt hollowed out, like the shell of something that had died and rotted away, or whose soft innards had been devoured by betrayal and misfortune.

He recognized the feeling, like a taste from long ago. Recognized it from years before, from the last time he had, through his own stupidity, turned his life inside out.

He shook his head, as if he could shake those thoughts clean out of it.

"Well, LeBoeuf, what do you think?" Pierre Le Chasseur asked.

LeBoeuf shrugged, by way of an answer. The buccaneers were accustomed to him saying very little. Not so long ago they would not have even asked his opinion. And now when they did ask, he had nothing to offer.

He looked around, out at the ocean, then back over the faces of the men and women there. They were waiting for him to speak, but still he had nothing of any real value to say.

"Keep moving, I reckon," he said at last. "They'll send out patrols. Not looking for us, necessarily, but they mean to clear out everyone from the island. Everyone who ain't a Spaniard, that is. We'll be easier to find if we stay put. We'll need to hunt. Soon. We can have cook fires at night, if we keep the flames hidden."

Heads nodded. More discussion followed. LeBoeuf stared out at the flickering blue water of the Canal de la Tortue, and he took comfort in the sight of the ocean, as he often did.

Eventually it was decided they would head west, get as far from Cayona as they could. They settled on some amorphous plan that involved keeping clear of the Spaniards and waiting until they eventually abandoned the island. They repacked the gear and rations they had pulled out for the night, and by midmorning they were moving again, following the line of mountains to the north of them.

LeBoeuf did not lead this time. No one did. They just acted by mutual consent, wandering west in a long, slow-moving, straggling line. They stopped for the evening by a stand of candlewood trees and ate cold rations and drank gin and rumbullion. LeBoeuf wondered what would happen when those things ran out. Food was not so much of a problem: there was plenty of fruit growing wild and game on the island. But once the hard liquor was gone, there was no hunting or gathering that. Things might degenerate quickly.

On the following day, an hour or so after resuming their march west, they encountered their first Spanish patrol. Other Dog sensed them first, bristling and giving off a low growl, reacting to their scent, LeBoeuf guessed, since there was nothing to be seen.

"Spaniard patrol," LeBoeuf said, and he said no more, just turned and trotted off across the meadow they were traversing to a grove of trees higher up the slope. He made his way into the cool cover of the foliage, crouched down and turned, looking back. The rest were following behind, all nearly running, and one by one they, too, found cover in the trees.

They were silent and motionless as they waited. Only Other Dog could not keep still, standing and sitting and growing until LeBoeuf told her to calm herself, which she did, mostly.

They did not wait long before the Spaniards appeared, coming out from behind some trees to the east, a mounted patrol riding slowly across the open, grassy country. There were two dozen of them: not the same men who had taken the plantation, not dressed in those damned black tunics and trousers with the silver breastplates. These soldiers were something less than elite, some equipped with breastplates, some with leather jerkins, all with crested helmets on their heads.

They carried long lances held upright as they rode. They looked cautiously around, heads swiveling, alert, even if their horses seemed bored and tired. They were wary, perhaps even afraid.

You are well to be afraid, LeBoeuf thought as he rubbed his thumb gently over the hammer of his snaphance.

He wondered if this was natural caution that the riders were showing, or if this patrol had been ambushed by another band of refugees. Even if they had not, any soldier was bound to be nervous, riding through such open country, that offered so many places for an enemy to hide.

But the Spaniards were in no immediate danger. LeBoeuf and the buccaneers around him were not interested in fighting any patrols, just avoiding them. That much they had concluded the day before. So they remained silent, hidden in the trees, and watched as the riders passed by, fifty yards away. Several times one soldier or another looked straight at them but seemed not to see them in the deep shadows of the woods.

Or, if they did see them, they were not much interested in fighting, either.

LeBoeuf and the others remained hidden in the trees for another half hour after the Spaniards rode out of sight, then continued on their way. Later that afternoon they shot two wild goats, and after dark, when the smoke would not be seen and the fire was hidden by a stand of trees, they cooked them and feasted on the fresh meat. They had cold roasted goat for breakfast the following day.

And thus it went for the next day and the next. The buccaneers had only fourteen miles to traverse before they ran out of island, but they felt no sense of hurry, since they had no particular reason for going where they were going, and nothing much to do once they got there. So they took their time breaking camp in the mornings, and when they did at last get underway they moved with caution, keeping away from open ground, scouting ahead as best they could, and stopping and hiding when they thought a patrol might be near.

At last they reached the western end of the island, which was low country, covered in scrubby vegetation that ran down to stretches of brilliant white sand beach. It was lovely, and it would have made an excellent place to locate a new buccaneers' encampment if there had been wild pigs or cattle to hunt, and no Spaniards hunting them. Unfortunately there were none of the former, and sooner or later the latter was bound to appear, so the best they could do was find some spot that was somewhat hidden and somewhat defensible and set up their new temporary home there.

And that was what they did.

For the next week or so the buccaneers made a desultory effort at building a redoubt of sorts, enclosed by short walls made of the coral blocks that were found in abundance. From behind those walls they would be able to hold off multiple assaults from Spanish troops, dropping the attackers at a distance with their superior musketry. Or that, at least, was the idea.

LeBoeuf did his share of hauling and stacking stones. More than his share, in fact. But he took no part in the planning of the thing. It all seemed absurdly silly to him. He wondered if any of the others truly believed that their efforts would do the least bit of good if it actually came to a pitched battle. If they thought about it, they too would see how pointless this was. But he was fairly certain that none of them had really thought about it.

At least it gave them all something to do, and working through most of the day meant their liquor supply was not depleted as quickly as it would have been were they just lounging around the camp. But even with that distraction, the bottles seemed to be emptying at an alarming rate.

Another week passed. The walls were built up to about four feet, as high as anyone felt compelled to make them. Hunting parties went out and brought back goats and the occasional wild boar. Scouting parties went out and reported sighting Spanish patrols off in the distance, but no Spaniards ever came closer than a few miles from the encampment.

LeBoeuf guessed that the Spanish troops were not searching very hard, making just enough effort to satisfy their orders, and no more. Not hunting so diligently that it might bring them *face à face* with the enemy. No one seemed too interested in fighting, save for the gentlemen officers safely back on the beach.

But that would not last. Eventually one of those gentlemen would insist that the soldiers return from the field with prisoners or with corpses.

LeBoeuf kept to himself, mostly, as had always been his wont. He walked along the beach, scrutinized the sails that he saw passing on the horizon, or closer in. He brooded. He tried not to think about anything, but he was not very successful with that. And then, finally, one evening, he realized that he was done.

He walked back to where the rest of the buccaneers and their women and the servants from the plantation were roasting the latest kill over a driftwood fire. They had given up on the precaution of lighting fires only at night, and now the column of dark smoke roiled up into the sky, as if taunting any Spaniards out looking for them.

LeBoeuf stopped by the fire, let his eyes rest on the roasting meat. He debated whether or not to say anything, and decided he would not. He had come to dislike speaking.

He turned from the fire and headed over to the place where he stowed his sword, musket, bandolier, bedding, and the leather bag containing his few remaining worldly goods. Other Dog was lying close by, protecting their possessions. LeBoeuf picked up his bandolier and slung it over his shoulder. Over the other shoulder he slung the strap of the leather bag with his bedding rolled and bound to it. He lifted his musket. He nodded to Other Dog, and Other Dog got to her feet, panting, tongue out.

I should have waited until dark, LeBoeuf thought. He had hoped to get away without explaining himself, but now he realized it was foolish to think he could do so in the daylight. And he was right.

"Here, LeBoeuf, what say you? What are you about?" It was D'Anton who had noticed him gathering up his gear.

LeBoeuf looked up. The former slave was staring at him, expressionless, as were most of the others. They had all become accustomed to his oddities, LeBoeuf realized, his unpredictability, and now they were just waiting to see what he was planning to do next. He was not sure if that was good or bad.

"I'm leaving," LeBoeuf said. "I'm done."

"Leaving?" Levesque asked. "Leaving the encampment?"

"Leaving Tortuga. I'm done here."

They were expressionless no more. Now there were looks of surprise. Confusion.

"Where are you going?" Levesque asked next.

"Someplace that isn't Tortuga," LeBoeuf said. "Not sure where that is."

"I thought we were planning on waiting out the Spaniards," Pierre Le Chasseur protested. "Staying here until they leave."

"That's what you lot were planning," LeBoeuf said. "But the Spaniards, they aren't leaving. At least not soon enough for me. I'm done."

He could see the uncertainty growing on their faces. They thought a decision had been made and agreed to. They did not like to make decisions. It was a relief for them to settle on a plan, even if it was a stupid one. But now LeBoeuf was doing something else, and it called everything into question once again.

"How are you getting off the island?" Billy Solent asked.

"Boat."

Another pause. LeBoeuf wanted desperately to just leave, just walk away, but he knew that doing so would cause even more chaos than if he just stayed and answered their questions. Besides that, these men and women had been loyal to him. Loyal after a fashion, and for their own reasons, to be sure, but loyal nonetheless. He owed them an explanation.

"You're just going to row away?"

"It's not but three or four miles to Hispaniola. I've rowed farther than that."

People were glancing at one another. There was a low murmuring, and it was building. "You don't reckon the Spaniards will be going soon?" D'Anton asked.

"Most will go. After a while. They'll leave a garrison behind. Hard to say how strong of one. But either way, I'm done with Spaniards, and I'm done with Tortuga."

LeBoeuf had no idea where his peripatetic life would lead next, but he knew it was time to find out. He lifted his musket and rested it on his shoulder.

"Don't have to go on a boat," a voice said, soft, from the edge of the fire. Jacques le Roux, whose health seemed to be improving in proportion to his limited access to gin. Heads turned, men frowned at Le Roux's seemingly absurd statement.

"You could take a ship," Le Roux continued. "There's a lot of them at anchor, and out in the channel. You could take one of them, if you had men enough to do it."

Damn your eyes, LeBoeuf thought. He had considered this plan already, and dismissed it. He wanted to strike off on his own, him and Other Dog, and damn the rest of humanity.

"Take a ship?" Pierre Le Chasseur said. "You mean…board one? Be off with it? Like we did on Hispaniola?"

Le Roux nodded.

"On Hispaniola the crew abandoned their ship without a fight," LeBoeuf said. "No crew here will do that."

"Sure, but we got, what? Thirty good men?" Le Chasseur said. "And like Le Roux said, there's all sorts of ships. We pick one of the small ones, one of the transports. That crew won't have much fight in them."

LeBoeuf closed his eyes, briefly. He drew a long breath. He knew already where this would end up, but still he fought back. "You're welcome to take any ship you wish," he said. "Me, I'll stay with my boat."

"But see here, LeBoeuf," Levesque said. "There's any number of reasons you won't make it in a boat. But in a ship…"

"Not a thing stopping you from trying," LeBoeuf said. "You don't need me." He watched them glance around, glance down at their feet, screw their faces up in expressions of deep thought.

Who will say it? he wondered.

"The thing of it is, LeBoeuf…." It was Levesque who spoke. "Back when we were fighting Van Loudersong and that lot, well, you've got some skill as master of a ship. A lot of us here, we're able-bodied, we can hand, reef, and steer. But what you done…." He let the words trail off. The others nodded.

LeBoeuf glanced over at Le Roux. The old fore topman, of all the people on that beach, was the only one who knew just how qualified LeBoeuf was to take command of a stolen ship, or any ship for that matter. More qualified than any refugee on Tortuga, most likely. He wondered if Le Roux would tell the tale, give his secret away. But the old sailor just stood there with arms folded and lips shut.

And in that instant, LeBoeuf made a decision, though deep down he understood that he had made it already. He set the butt of his musket back on the ground.

"I have business to attend to first," he said. "If you'd have me take the lead in cutting out a ship…" he paused, did some calculations of time and distance, "…then meet me in three days' time in the jungle just north of where we left the boats. Stay out of sight until I arrive." Experienced hunters that they were, LeBoeuf knew they would have no problem doing either.

"If you're not there I'll reckon the Spaniards got you. If I don't show up by the fourth day, then the Spaniards got me. Understood?"

He looked around. Heads nodded. He saw a wide range of reactions: uncertainty, relief, confusion.

"And what of us?" Vassy asked. He gestured toward the other servants from the plantation who were standing in a rough group.

"Yes, you lot as well, if you wish. You may live to regret it, but you may come." He looked around at the others. "Three days."

He lifted his musket back on his shoulder again and walked off into the growing dark of the evening, the dog at his side.

"Well," he said to Other Dog, once they were far enough from the fire that he would not be heard. "It looks like we get company whether we want it or no."

Chapter Twenty-Eight

Don Alonso Menéndez did not know what the time was, he just knew that it was very early. The witching hour, he guessed. Three o'clock. Well before dawn. And he was awake.

He leaned on the windowsill in the master bedchamber and looked over at the bed pushed up against the wall opposite. Despite the late hour, there was a single candle burning on the nightstand because Alonso seemed to have developed an aversion to the dark. The light from the small flame cast deep shadows over Henriette, sleeping under the covers. The shape of her thigh and hip and shoulder was like a series of miniature rolling hills. Alonso could hear her gentle, rhythmic breathing.

Generally, post-coitus, he fell easily into a deep and relaxed sleep. That was true whether it was after marital relations with his wife or fornicating with the various women he had enjoyed before and after marriage. But not this time.

He sighed, softly, so as not to wake her. Not out of concern for her sleep, but because he was in no mood to speak to her. Or anyone. But mostly her.

Sleep had eluded him of late. Ever since the jungle, the ambush, the dog. He resisted sleep. He feared it. He feared the nightmares that came when he did manage to drift off; amorphous visions, indistinct creatures that carried on their hellish backs wave after wave of pure terror.

He cursed himself for a weakling. He turned and looked out the window and rested his shoulder against the frame. There was no moon and he could see very little, just the dark shapes of the outbuildings: the barn and the smith's shop, and the others, and the jungle beyond that. A handful of his men were out there, too. The night watch. Guarding. Patrolling. But were they awake?

Lazy villains…

In truth he did not know whether they were neglecting their duties or maintaining perfect vigilance. If Delgadillo had been overseeing things, then everyone would most certainly be attentive and alert. But Delgadillo…he could not think about it.

He pushed himself off the window frame and crossed the room to where his weapons were hanging from hooks on the wall. He could hear, from two floors down, the beastly snoring of those of the One Hundred who had found a place to sleep in the plantation house. He gently lifted the shoulder belt that held his sword and his pistols, draped it over his nightshirt, and adjusted the way it hung. Unlike those below stairs, there was no chance he would be sleeping anytime soon, so he might as well have a look around, see if his men were still up to the task of guarding him.

He crossed the room and stepped out of the door to the landing at the top of the stairs, the wooden planks, worn smooth, cool under his bare feet. It was very dark after the small light from the candle. He paused and let his eyes adjust, then found the banister with his hand and found the step with his foot and made his way down. There was a gentle squeak every few steps or so, but beyond that it was silent.

By the time Alonso reached the bottom of the stairs, the sound of the snoring had grown considerably louder and more revolting, and he was able to see tolerably well. There may have been no moon but there was an astounding sweep of stars across the sky, as there was nearly every night, and the light of those thousands of tiny points came in through the windows and faintly illuminated the imperfectly sealed front door. Alonso crossed the foyer, opened the door and stepped out into the cool night.

"Señor Don Alonso!" The guard just outside the door sounded surprised to see him, as well he might be. He spoke a bit louder than one might expect, and Alonso wondered if it was to warn the others that their master was out and about. He looked off to his left. There were supposed to be two guards there, but this man was alone. Was the other off taking a nap?

"Bárba has gone to do a sweep around the perimeter, Don Alonso," the guard said, guessing Alonso's thoughts. "We take turns, on the hour."

Alonso nodded. He was not in the mood for further inquiry or excuses. He left the guard standing there and stepped down the beaten path from the front door to the open ground beyond the plantation house. He took a deep breath of the cool night air, rich with the scent of damp earth and thick vegetation and the smell of the horses staked out nearby, which, to Alonso, was a pleasing and comforting smell.

He loved this place, this Tortuga plantation. He had to admit it. At first he thought his affection was due just to the difficulty he had gone through to claim it, all the plans he had made that were centered on his possessing this piece of land. He thought he loved it only because he had worked so hard to get it. But it did not take him long to understand that it was more than that. Much more than that.

When he came to take the plantation from the rogues who had so mauled the lanceros, he had expected a bloody fight, the sort of fight—like their foray into the jungle—that was not at all what he was accustomed to. He had tried to be smart about it, though after the jungle his confidence was not high.

But it turned out there was no fight at all. The vermin who infested the place had scurried off at the first sign of the Spanish troops, who were clearly superior fighting men in every way.

His thoughts were just moving onto the girl when he heard the sound of feet on the soft ground. He turned. Captain Rodriguez was hurrying toward him. Like Alonso, he was wearing his night shirt with his sword and pistols draped over it. His hair was wild. The guard at the door must have sent word to tell him that his commanding officer was, for some reason, up and wandering in the dark: a cause for concern.

Rodriguez gave a quick bow of his head as he approached. "Don Alonso, is all well?"

"It seems that way, captain," Alonso said, taking an exaggerated look around. "But I keep my eye on things, you know. At any time of day or night."

"Of course, Don Alonso." Rodriguez clearly did not know what to make of that, if he should consider it a rebuke or a warning. That was good. Alonso liked to keep his underlings on edge.

"The night has been quiet, señor," Rodriguez hurried on, trying to show competence and mastery of the situation. "I have men around the perimeter, as usual. They report nothing."

"Good, good." Alonso looked out into the dark and wondered if that was true. Rodriguez had proven himself to be able enough in his new office. He lacked Delgadillo's brains and initiative, but he showed tolerable ability. He would grow into the office, Alonso knew, or he would prove himself to be totally out of his depth and be sent back to the ranks. Either way.

"You have a guard for the morrow?" Alonso asked next.

"Yes, señor. They'll be ready to ride at first light."

Alonso nodded his approval. He himself would not be ready until well after first light, but that was fine. They could wait. Wait for him to have a leisurely breakfast, and perhaps another go at the French girl, if he felt so motivated.

Since taking the Tortuga plantation weeks before, Alonso had made regular trips back to the main town to report to Admiral Toledo. It was not good to be away from the seat of power for too long, Alonso knew, away from the gossiping and the intrigue. Bad things could happen to someone who was not there to defend his reputation and his place in the hierarchy.

On the other hand, Alonso did not care so much about the hierarchy surrounding Admiral Toledo. Admiral Toledo and his entourage would not be around forever. Alonso was far more interested in establishing his hold on the plantation, and the more time he spent on that blessed plot of land, the less he wanted to be anywhere else.

So he convinced Toledo that he had established a military outpost of sorts, from which he was sending out patrols to scour the countryside and hunt down the refugees from the town who had run off in the face of the Spanish invasion.

That was even true, to some degree. He did send men out to sweep the area thereabouts, to make sure there was no threat to his new estate. They might not go as far afield as Alonso implied, but they did go out. They had even managed to catch a handful of the French scoundrels, a sorry bunch of half-dead drunks whom Alonso had sent back to Toledo in chains. That had done much to bolster his reputation and reinforce the importance of what he was doing. Now it was time to report to the admiral again.

"We have no prisoners to bring this time?" Alonso asked.

"No, señor. I think most of the French and the others who were here, they've gone off into the mountains."

"Very well. We'll let Toledo worry about them." He considered sending Henriette in as a prisoner, so Toledo's officers, if not Toledo himself, could make use of her. That would certainly boost his good name. But no. He was enjoying her too much himself, and he did not care to give that up just yet.

"You may return to your duties, Captain Rodriguez," Alonso said next. "I will off to bed here in a moment."

"Yes, Don Alonso."

Rodriguez hesitated. He was not sure what to do, that was clear. He was smart enough to know that he had been dismissed, but cautious enough to wonder what this was all about. Anything out of the ordinary with regard to the captain general was cause for concern.

Finally he bowed once more, then turned and hurried off, guessing, correctly, that he was better off leaving Alonso in peace than remaining there and trying to ingratiate himself.

Alonso turned and stared off into the dark, out toward the stand of trees that stood like a living wall at the edge of the open ground. He thought, as he often did, about the morning, a bit more than two weeks earlier, when he had first set eyes on the plantation.

The memory brought with it a strong whiff of tension and uncertainty. Alonso, having heard firsthand the story of how the lanceros were brutally handled, was not about to send his men blundering into the open, just to be shot down. Or worse. The mounted soldiers had told him about the dog.

On his orders, the One Hundred had worked their way through the trees to the south and west of the plantation, emerging slowly into the open, muskets in hand. They met with no resistance. There was no one there. But finding the place deserted was not a relief to Alonso. It made him even more on edge. Where were they?

She had come running out of the jungle a hundred yards away, as unexpected as a ghost. Had she been closer it's quite possible that one of Alonso's men would have shot her down, so ready were they to fire on anything that moved. But she was too far distant to hit, and by the time she was close enough, Alonso could see that she was just a woman alone, no more.

"Hold your fire! Hold your fire!" Alonso called, then, "Look around! Look around! This might be a distraction!" She was about the last thing he would have expected to see. He was not at all convinced she was not part of some trick.

He watched, and his men watched, as she came running over the open ground, her pace dropping to a stumbling jog as she came closer. Her clothes were plain but clean, not those of a woman of means, but not those of an indentured servant or a whore, either. From a distance she seemed to be attractive, and the closer she came, the more that impression was confirmed. Young, dark hair hanging in soft curls, a lovely face just slightly kissed by the sun, a shapely figure under her overbody and petticoats.

Alonso felt his curiosity becoming aroused.

Her face was streaked with tears, her eyes red-rimmed, and she was gasping with sobs and the effort of running as she stumbled to a halt and Alonso moved forward to meet her.

The first words she spoke came out in a breath of anguish and relief. "*Monsieur, monsieur…*"

French, Alonso thought, and that put him on his guard again. It was the French vermin, mostly, that they had come to eradicate. But she did not look or sound like the filth they had met and captured or killed back in the town, or in the jungle.

"Do you speak French?" the girl asked through desperate and pathetic sobs.

"Yes," Alonso said. He was quite fluent in French, though he had not spoken it in some time. "Who are you? What are you doing here?"

"Oh, monsieur, I am Henriette…Henriette de Labonté. I have been a prisoner, monsieur, of those wicked buccaneers! For many weeks, monsieur, and I have been used most cruelly!"

"Buccaneers?" Alonso was reminded why he and his men were there. "Are they still here? At the plantation?"

"No, monsieur, they've run off. That way." Henriette pointed to the east, where the beaten path ran off toward some fields some distance away, and the jungle beyond.

"Run off?"

"Yes, monsieur. They had men watching the road. They knew you were coming, so they ran off rather than fight. They are a cowardly lot, monsieur. I managed to get free of them, and they were too afraid of you…too eager to get away…to chase after me. I hid in the trees until I could see that you were not such as them, that you were civilized men. Men of honor. And then I came out. Oh, monsieur!"

With that she flung herself against him, pressing her face into his breastplate, heaving with sobs, and there was nothing Alonso could do but put a protective arm around her and whisper a few comforting words.

"There, now, there…" he said, softly. "You are safe now." Which might be the case, if he decided that she was telling the truth, or it might not be the case at all. Either way, he had no time just then to waste on such things. He turned to the two men nearest him.

"Take her back by the horses and keep her there. I'll attend to her when our business here is done."

Alonso explained to Henriette that she was to go with his men, that they would look after her until he could attend to her. She smiled through the tears and thanked him again and again as they led her away.

We'll see if you're still thanking me on the morrow, Alonso thought, and then had no more thoughts to spare for the mysterious French girl. At least not then.

He had Rodriguez send a company of men to check the plantation house and the outbuildings, and another to move east along the path, following the direction the girl said the buccaneers had fled. Alonso warned Rodriguez to have the men proceed with great caution. He would rather the vermin escape than the One Hundred suffer the sort of mauling they had received before.

Two hours later it was determined that the buccaneers were indeed gone, disappeared into the jungle as far as anyone could tell, but Alonso knew it would be some time before he truly believed that. He set pickets all around the perimeter of the grounds and some ways into the jungle, keeping a careful eye out for any sign of a surprise assault.

The day was growing late by the time Alonso had business well enough in hand that he felt he could talk with the girl and give her the attention that his mounting curiosity required. There was a small table and chairs set up just outside the door to the plantation house, a surprisingly civilized touch, in Alonso's opinion. He ordered his steward to fetch wine and bread and cheese, which they carried with them in the supply wagon, and ordered that the girl be brought to him.

Alonso was pouring the wine when the two guards approached with the girl between them. Any trace of her earlier tears was gone, her red-rimmed and puffy eyes returned to normal, and he could see she was even lovelier than he had thought at first. He gestured for her to sit and handed her a glass.

"So, pray, tell me…Henriette…how you came to be in these dire straits?" He was pleased with how quickly his French was coming back to him.

"I shudder to think back on it, monsieur…"

"Please, I should have said…I am Don Alonso Menéndez de Aviles, knight of the Order of Santiago, and lieutenant governor of Santo Domingo. But I would be honored if you would call me simply Alonso."

"Yes…thank you…Alonso." She spoke the name as if she was tasting it, and her voice was rich with gratitude. "I knew you were a gentleman. I am accustomed to the company of the better sort, and I could tell, even from a distance, that you were no mere foot soldier. And so I knew you would come to the aid of a woman of quality."

"A woman of quality?"

"I think you can see, Alonso, that I'm not some bonded servant, or wife to some miserable shopkeeper. I am a lady in waiting to Anne d'Autriche, queen to our Most Christian King Louis."

"Indeed?" Alonso said, and he could not quite keep the note of amusement out of his voice.

"Oh, yes, indeed," Henriette continued, and if she had picked up on his skepticism she gave no hint of it. "We were on a pilgrimage to Rome…not the queen, but some of us ladies and gentlemen of the court, and we were beset by a wicked storm that blew our ship very far to the south. At least that's what the master said. And there we were taken by pirates…most of the crew were butchered…oh, monsieur, the things I have seen!"

She paused, fighting back the tears, composing herself. Part of Alonso was sympathetic with her plight, part of him was impressed by her performance, and he was not sure which way to lean.

"And these pirates?"

"They did not hurt me, my dear Alonso, but they carried me off. Me and some of the other women. If they meant to ransom me or…something unthinkable, I do not know. But I was brought here, and made to live among them. I had nearly despaired of a chance to escape. Until you arrived."

"I see," Alonso said. His mind toyed with the obvious questions: had she genuinely been forced to live with the pirates, or had she done so willingly? If the latter, what else was she was willing to do?

And, of course, how much of this was simply fiction?

"These villains who took you, were they salt-sea pirates, or the buccaneers who plague us here in the West Indies?"

"Pirates? Buccaneers? I have no idea, monsieur, what manner of rogue these people were. I know nothing of such things."

Alonso saw a flash of irritation, even anger, in Henriette's face as she spoke. She tried to keep it tamped down, but she could not, entirely. Like trying to stop a reflex.

There's some spirit in this one, he thought, though he was not so sure that was a good thing.

Still, he found her intriguing, and he could not dismiss her claims out of hand. She had not spent her life doing servile labor, or labor of any sort, that was clear, and she did carry an air of titled wealth about her. Her manners were courtly, and her speech seemed refined, not the coarse utterances of the lower sort. But Alonso was not a native French speaker, and so could not tell with any certainty how genuine her way of speaking was.

"So, you will help me, won't you, Alonso?" she said, and again her words were served up like a fine dish, with subtle flavors: eagerness, gratitude, promise. "Help me get back to Paris? I know you are a gentleman of Spain, and I am from the court of France, but our countries are not at war."

Alonso nodded. Strictly speaking this was true, though in reality a semi-permanent state of enmity existed between France and Spain, near-constant war with occasional bouts of peace breaking out. But certainly he could help her. If he chose.

"Of course, my dear Henriette," he said, with his most ingratiating smile. "I'm sure we can find some arrangement that will work for all."

It turned out, by Henriette's telling, that the buccaneers had allowed her to sleep in the master bedchamber. That seemed to Alonso a suspiciously accommodating way for such rogues to treat a prisoner. On the other hand, if they were holding her for ransom, or meant to sell her, they would want to keep her as unsullied as possible, so it might make sense. Alonso let it go, and he took one of the other bedchambers on that upper floor for himself, and had his men housed wherever they could find space.

The next day Alonso had his men search the entire plantation, and what they discovered encouraged him greatly. There was food and drink enough in the stores to maintain the One Hundred for weeks before they would need to look to the main army for supplies. The tobacco fields were planted and seemed to be growing nicely. Walls on the plantation house had been recently repaired, and fresh boards in the barn and the outbuildings marked where maintenance was ongoing.

"You say these buccaneers were lazy creatures," Alonso said one morning as he and Henriette strolled along the path from the house to the fields. It had become their habit to spend several hours a day together, and take meals in one another's company. "But I see signs of considerable activity."

"Much of that was done before those curs took this place," Henriette explained. "And what was done after was done by the servants who were here. Those villainous rogues forced those poor people to work while they all laid about, idle. That's why they made the servants to go with them when they fled. They could not bear the thought of having to work for themselves."

"I see," Alonso said. "Well, this seems a fine property. I'm glad it has not fallen to disrepair."

In truth, Alonso was more than glad that the plantation was not the ruin he feared it would be. He was delighted by the sight of it. He wanted only to continue the work begun by whoever had been there before him, so he set some of the One Hundred to furthering the improvements, and he had some laborers sent from Toledo's main camp to help as well, and soon the plantation was hive-like with activity.

They fell quickly into a routine; Alonso, Henriette, Rodriguez, the One Hundred, the laborers. The workers would see to repairs, or undertake new building, or weed the tobacco. The One Hundred would stand guard duty, or go out on patrol into the countryside, or lend a hand with the work. Rodriguez would oversee it all. Alonso would stroll the grounds, and keep an eye on things, and plan other things. Often Henriette would accompany him.

It was, in Alonso's opinion, an altogether pleasant way of life.

Then finally, one night, a week earlier, he had stopped by Henriette's bedchamber to make certain that she was well, as was his custom. And this time her greeting and her manner suggested that he did not have to retire to his own room. That he was, in fact, welcome to share her room, and her bed.

It was a development he had been hoping for, knowing as he did that grateful women were often pliant women. And that place, that Tortuga plantation, which had long existed in his imagination alone, took another step toward becoming his paradise on earth.

But still he would wake at the witching hour, sweating, shaking, mouth dry as dust. Still, for all his outward calm, he knew there was something frightened inside him, something cringing and squatting in a corner of his mind, near broken. Terrified.

He pulled his eyes from the dark tree line. The grass was wet under his bare feet, and the breeze was cool. He turned and headed back toward the plantation house, thinking that now at least he might sleep again.

He made his way up the stairs, feeling the rail with his hand as he did, and stepped through the half-open door to the master bedchamber. Henriette was still asleep, still in the same position as before. Alonso crossed to the far side of the room, lifted the belt off his shoulder and hung it back on the hook, carefully, so as not to make a sound. Then he made his way to the edge of the bed and sat.

He was about to swing his legs up and stretch out when he heard a sound from below stairs that was not snoring, and it caught his ear for that reason. It was a single thump, just the faintest of noises. It might have been any of a hundred different and innocuous things, and he never would have heard it if he had not been so keyed up and alert. But he did hear it, and he sat straight upright and cocked his ear toward the door.

Nothing had changed. He could still hear the faint sound of insects out in the tall grass, and the hiss of the breeze in the branches. He was starting to relax again when he caught a tiny creaking sound, as faint and meaningless as the thump. No doubt just the sound of a wood-frame house settling, but Alonso was up off the bed and across the room before he even considered that.

His hands went for the wheellock pistols first, but he recalled that they were not cocked, and finding the spanner and fitting it in the wheels and cranking the wheels would take time and make noise. No good. Instead, his fingers wrapped around the hilt of his sword and he drew the blade as quietly as he could. The grip was familiar, and the weapon felt good in his hands. It gave him a flood of confidence, which a second before was starting to ebb.

Sword in hand, standing loosely *en garde*, Don Alonso Menéndez eased back into the shadows, remained perfectly still, and waited.

Chapter Twenty-Nine

From the far western end of Tortuga, it was sixteen miles back to what Jean-Baptiste LeBoeuf still considered his plantation, and he and Other Dog covered the distance quickly.

They left the buccaneers' camp in early evening and made about five miles over the uneven ground before it grew too dark to carry on. They bedded down for the night, relishing the ease of movement that a single man and his dog enjoyed. It was quite different from traveling with women, servants, and more than two dozen buccaneers who were not much inclined toward cooperation.

LeBoeuf and Other Dog broke their fast the next day with cold boar and biscuit and, for LeBoeuf, a solid jolt of rumbullion, and then they were on their way once more. By midafternoon LeBoeuf could see smoke rising up from several fires that had to be coming from the plantation's grounds: cook fires, or a smithy, or fire to boil water for washing, or any of a number of reasons such a thing would be lit.

They approached cautiously after that, walking along a semi-beaten trail, the same one the buccaneers had followed on their retreat weeks before. LeBoeuf had no idea what was going on at the Tortuga plantation, whether the Spaniards were still there, or if they had looted the place and abandoned it, or gone and left a small garrison behind, or if the fires had been lit by the next band of interlopers to show up there.

He had to assume, however, that at least some of the Spanish troops were still there. And though he did not think much of Spanish vigilance, he knew better than to ever underestimate an enemy. And once again that proved to be wise policy.

The plantation was still a mile off when they heard men moving toward them, not so far away, and getting closer. He and Other Dog stopped, listened, then moved off the trail and ducked into a thicket of brush, crouching down, peering out through the leaves.

It was just a few minutes later when the men appeared: soldiers, just as LeBoeuf had guessed they would be. They were the black-clad troops with the shining breastplates, the same who had taken the plantation from him, and apparently still held it.

Who are these whores' sons? LeBoeuf wondered. They seemed to be a regiment separate from the powerful army that remained back at the harbor landing.

He and Other Dog kept low, silent, and largely motionless as the men approached to within twenty feet of their hiding place. Other Dog was trembling in her eagerness to be at them, but she would not move or make a noise unless LeBoeuf told her to. Which he most certainly did not.

The soldiers passed them by, never even looking in their direction. They remained hidden for another quarter of an hour, just to be sure, then emerged from the brush and continued on down the trail, to the place where the jungle thinned out at the edge of the open ground. They could catch glimpses of the plantation house and the outbuildings through the trees and the tall grass. They could see men moving around.

LeBoeuf led the way off the path, and they moved as quietly as they could through the brush along the edge of the tree line. They came to a small open patch where they could make themselves comfortable, remain unseen, and observe the plantation as they wished.

"Sit, relax," LeBoeuf said in a whisper. "But keep your mouth shut." Then LeBoeuf sat as well, stretched out on the soft ground, and closed his eyes.

He was up again a short while later, moving slowly through the grass until he could see the plantation stretched out in front of him. All around the place men were working at various tasks, some standing guard, some working on construction, some tending to the horses, some manning a big cooking fire. There were near a hundred men that he could see, the entire regiment that had taken the plantation weeks before. Apparently once they had come, they had not left.

For the rest of the daylight hours LeBoeuf moved back and forth from his resting place to his place of observation. He studied the men and where they stood guard and how alert they seemed to be. He saw the man who commanded them, dressed in black tunic and wide-brimmed black hat, feather jutting aft, walking around the open ground, conferring with his second in command, giving orders.

He saw Henriette. She stepped from the front door of the plantation house and walked down the path to the dooryard. She did not seem to be under guard of any sort. In fact, no one seemed to pay her any attention, at least not until the commanding officer noticed her. When he did, he left off the conversation he was having and walked over to her, arm extended, and she took his hand and held it briefly, then let it drop.

She's playing him well, LeBoeuf thought. *Using her wiles…she thinks she'll charm her way clear back to Paris.*

Whether or not the Spaniard was taken in by Henriette, LeBoeuf reckoned he must have made some sort of promise to help her. She would not be showing him such obvious favor otherwise. But LeBoeuf understood something that Henriette apparently did not: any "help" the Spaniard had in mind for her would not be anything that she would find very helpful.

That was why he had come.

Once evening began to settle down on the plantation, LeBoeuf moved back to the edge of the grass, and with the darkness hiding him ventured farther out into the open. He watched the Spaniards go through their routine as they settled in for the night. He watched the cooking and the eating and the cleaning up after, the horses tended to, the guards posted. One by one the men turned in, some off to sleep in the plantation house, others to the various tents they had pitched around the grounds.

Finally it was full night, with no moon and only the stars to illuminate the grounds, though they did a tolerably good job in that office. LeBoeuf watched the guards as they made their rounds and were changed out periodically. He noted how often their captain came around to check on them. And still he waited.

He waited for the witching hour. Dead of night, the inverse of the Hour of Mercy, when vigilance was at its lowest ebb. He waited until it was as still as it was going to get.

"You stay here," he whispered to Other Dog, and Other Dog made a small whimpering sound. LeBoeuf was glad that in the dark he could not see her disappointed expression and accusatory stare.

He left her there in their little clearing along with his musket and bandolier, which were too awkward for the work he had to do. He moved over his now well-beaten trail to the edge of the grass.

He paused there, partially concealed by the vegetation, enveloped in the dark, and took one last look around. All was quiet, as far as he could see. Two guards by the front door of the big house, but one would soon make a sweep around the grounds, which would include a short nap behind the tobacco barn. A couple other men were out in the dark somewhere, keeping an eye on the wider perimeter, but they would not interfere with LeBoeuf's business.

He left the tall grass and hurried along the edge of the tree line toward the plantation house, keeping to the open ground where his steps would make no rustling sound. He stayed hunched over as he moved so that his outline would be as small as possible, though it was still not terribly small.

It took a few minutes of cautious jogging for him to reach the place where the jungle came closest to the house. He stopped there and went down on one knee and looked around again. About fifty yards of open ground separated him from the north side of the building. Crossing it would put him at serious risk of being seen, but there was no other option. He waited another minute, until he was sure nothing was out of the ordinary, that no alarm had been raised, then he stood and stepped away from the cover of the trees.

He walked upright this time, and he moved at a brisk pace, but he did not run. Running meant louder footfalls on the soft ground. And if someone did look in his direction and happened to see his dark form, they would be more concerned by the sight of a running man than one who was walking.

But no one looked in his direction, as far as he could tell, no one yelled out or challenged him. He reached the side of the plantation house and stepped gratefully into the shadows, pressing his back against the wall. He stood motionless and listened, and still he heard nothing beyond the normal sounds of the night.

He moved down the wall to the corner of the house, where a rain barrel stood under a downspout. He half hid behind the barrel, then eased himself around it toward the front side of the house. He tensed, took a deep breath, and as he readied himself to step out around the corner he heard the front door of the plantation house creak open.

Merde! He ducked back behind the barrel and crouched down. He heard soft padding like bare feet on the front stairs, and then a voice that said, "Señor Don Alonso!" or some such thing. It was not entirely clear to LeBoeuf.

What the devil? he thought. He could hear two men conversing, and though his Spanish was certainly good enough that he would have understood them, he could not make out the words.

He tried to imagine what this could be about at such an hour. The captain checking up on the guards' vigilance? Possibly, but it would have taken a damned conscientious officer to be making the rounds just then.

LeBoeuf straightened a bit and looked over the top of the barrel. He could see someone moving down the path from the front of the big house out toward the dooryard and beyond: an odd, spectral figure, silent, white, and of indistinct shape. A more superstitious man might have found it unnerving, but LeBoeuf guessed it was a man in a night shirt.

And who is this? he wondered. The one in command of these troops? The one with the wide brimmed hat he had seen earlier, the one who had been strolling with Henriette? Perhaps.

LeBoeuf watched from his hiding place as the man walked slowly across the open ground, his white clothes leaving him just barely visible in the dark. Had he been wearing the black tunic and trousers of earlier LeBoeuf would not have been able to see him at all.

The man stopped, and a moment later another came hurrying over to him, and he seemed to be clad in the same sort of white nightshirt. LeBoeuf knew then that they were not expecting any trouble that night. Had they been, they would surely have dressed more appropriately for it.

The two men seemed to confer for a few minutes, which reinforced LeBoeuf's notion that the first man was the officer commanding this lot. The one who had taken the Tortuga plantation from him and seemed eager to keep it for himself. The one to whom Henriette had stupidly gone running for help.

Whatever the two men were discussing, it did not take long. The second man took his leave and walked quickly back the way he had come, and an odd sort of stasis seemed to settle over the night. LeBoeuf crouched behind his rain barrel, looking out at the ghostly figure who seemed to be staring off into the distance. It seemed like there was nothing else living in that dark world.

The Spaniard remained standing, motionless, for what seemed a very long time, long enough for LeBoeuf to start growing impatient and wonder what he could possibly be doing. Then, at last, the man turned and walked back toward the plantation house and disappeared from LeBoeuf's view. A moment later LeBoeuf heard the front door open and then close again.

He took a step around the rain barrel. He knew he would be better off waiting until everything settled down again, but he did not have that luxury. Dawn would come soon, and no doubt the cooks and servants and such would be moving about even before that. As it was, what he had in mind was all but suicidal. He had to go now.

He peeked quickly around the corner of the house, long enough to see that there was a single guard standing beside the front steps, the butt of his musket resting on the ground. LeBoeuf took a deep breath and balled his hand into a fist. He had one chance at this, and if he made a hash of it he would not get another.

He stepped around the corner of the house and walked toward the guard, not quickly, but not leisurely either. He was twenty feet away before the man noticed him. He half turned toward LeBoeuf, and though his face was lost in shadow his movements seemed to suggest uncertainty.

"Bárba?" the man said.

"*Sí*," LeBoeuf said. He did not know what the man had asked, but he figured he had better agree. Still, the guard did not seem mollified by that answer. He started to raise his musket, but by then it was too late for him.

LeBoeuf all but ran the last five feet. He could see the man's face now, the dark moustache, the eyes wide with surprise and the first inkling of panic, mouth open, ready to shout. The guard was raising his musket as LeBoeuf swung his fist around in a wide arc and slammed it into the side of the man's head. An explosion of pain rippled up LeBoeuf's right arm as the guard fell sideways and dropped with a soft thud onto the damp grass.

LeBoeuf shook out his hand, then grabbed the man by the coat and dragged him back into the shadow of the building. He picked up the guard's musket and leaned it against the wall, then pressed himself into the shadows as well and listened. He could hear the faint sound of snoring from the plantation house—a good part of the garrison was sleeping there—but he heard nothing else, nothing out of place.

He moved along the wall and then up the two stairs to the front door. He lifted the latch carefully, swung the door open, and stepped inside. The ugly sound of snoring was considerably louder in there, but LeBoeuf was happy for it, as it would mask the sound of his footsteps.

He crossed the foyer, his steps making small creaking sounds, loud to his ears but not enough to wake any of the sleepers. He reached the stairs and began climbing as quickly as he dared, pausing every few steps to listen. Nothing, besides the cacophony of sleeping men.

At the top of the stairs he paused again and looked at the doors of the bedchambers there. To the right was the bedchamber that he and Henriette had shared. He could see a faint light around the bottom edge of the door, a candle burning within, most likely. Henriette? Would whoever had taken possession of the plantation have allowed her to remain in the master bedchamber?

He might, if he genuinely thought she was a woman in need of rescue, and if he truly fancied himself a gentleman.

LeBoeuf looked at the door to the left. No light that he could see, no sign of occupancy, or at least no sign of anyone awake. The same was true of the other doors. A one in four chance of getting the right room. Maybe better than that, if this Spaniard had allowed Henriette to stay where she was. He put his hand on the latch of the door to the right, then slowly, and with great care, he lifted the latch, swung the door open, and stepped partway through.

A single candle stood on the nightstand beside the bed, illuminating the room in a small pool of light. He could see the shape of Henriette's body under the bed clothes, her back toward him, her dark, soft hair spilling over the pillow. He looked left and right. The bedchamber appeared unchanged.

He took another step toward the bed, and then another. He wondered if he should clap his hand over Henriette's mouth. He did not recall her ever shouting when startled awake, but it was still possible that she might. The bastard who had taken the plantation was most likely in the bedchamber right next to them, and LeBoeuf knew that he was almost certainly awake.

Five feet away Henriette shifted a bit in her sleep and LeBoeuf froze. His eyes flicked over to the table near the window, at the familiar sight of the wash basin and the pitcher. And sitting on the edge of the basin, something that he did not recognize. He stared at it for a heartbeat before he realized what it was: a straight razor.

It took him another second to grasp the implication of what he was seeing, and then to chastise himself for his stupidity. He had not considered the possibility that the Spaniard was sharing Henriette's room, and her bed. And just as that realization broke through, he heard the movement behind him.

LeBoeuf whirled around, and instinctively he lashed out with his left arm, sweeping it sideways as he turned. He saw a blur of motion, the white nightshirt rendered a muted yellow in the candlelight, the glint of the sword coming at him.

His forearm hit the flat of the blade and knocked it aside and he continued to turn, bringing his right hand up in a fist, stepping forward, and taking a wild swing at the dark-haired, moustached, and goateed head. But the Spaniard was fast, leaping back with a fencer's grace, bringing the sword up, *en garde*.

LeBoeuf leapt back as well and drew his own sword. He held it before him and assumed an awkward stance, that of a man who had no training or skill. The Spaniard advanced quickly, recklessly, with little caution, flicking the tip of his sword left and right, a gesture meant to confuse his hapless opponent.

LeBoeuf let the blade get close, perilously close, and then in a flurry of motion he parried the Spaniard's thrust and moved it, one step, then lunged full out. The tip of his blade drove at the Spaniard's exposed chest, but the man leapt clear again.

"LeBoeuf!" Henriette hissed his name, emphatic, but low enough to not be heard beyond the confines of the room. "LeBoeuf! What do you think you're doing, you great, stupid beast?"

LeBoeuf held up his hand, gesturing for her to stay quiet. He had no time to reply. He could not take his eyes from the man in front of him, because the Spaniard was skilled with a sword and was not cowed by LeBoeuf's size or his speed.

LeBoeuf stepped a bit to the right, away from the bed, sword held straight in front like an accusatory finger, and the Spaniard matched his move. The tension seemed to pulse like blood as each waited for the other to commit.

The Spaniard moved first. He stepped in, made a halfhearted thrust, and when LeBoeuf parried he circled his blade around LeBoeuf's and came in for the real attack. LeBoeuf twisted sideways and the Spaniard's blade tore through his upper arm. The laceration burned as if the edge was hot iron but LeBoeuf could tell it was not deep. He pushed the Spaniard's blade aside with his left arm, lunged with his right, but once again the Spaniard leapt clear.

"LeBoeuf! Don't! What are you doing? Don't do this!"

The words rippled through LeBoeuf's head. They struck something deep inside him and reverberated off, and he froze where he stood. All those memories that he had pushed down, pushed down further than he realized, now came rushing up.

It was Henriette's voice, but the words were from a different woman, in a different room. Not a rundown room on some dung-heap island. It was a bedchamber, certainly, but one as big as the entire upper floor of the plantation house. A bedchamber in le Chateau de Garamond, the finest estate in Roumois, France. The ancient home of *la famille Garamond.*

His family.

Him, Jean-Baptiste Charles de Garamond, Chevalier de Roumois.

Him. LeBoeuf.

He took a step back. He could feel the sweat standing out on his forehead, despite the cool evening. The grip of his sword was slick in his hand and the point was shaking like a luffing sail.

He could see it all again. Facing him: François Guiton, captain of the frigate *Saint Guirec*, sister ship to his own *Neptune.* LeBoeuf's best friend. They had been raised together, gone to sea together, served out their midshipman's berths and lieutenancies together. Then, in the time it took to throw open a door and draw a sword, he became a man LeBoeuf intended to kill.

Guiton stood before him, absurdly naked, save for the sword in his hand. LeBoeuf in his fury, eyes flooded with tears, could barely make him out. LeBoeuf's sister, Genevieve, on the bed, naked as well, bedclothes pulled up around her, crying, screaming.

François Guiton, the man LeBoeuf had trusted more than any on earth, and now caught in the act of raping his sister, in her own home, where he was LeBoeuf's guest. LeBoeuf, walking past, hearing Genevieve cry out. Bursting in, Guiton on top of his sister, rutting away.

Jean-Baptiste! Don't! What are you doing? Don't do this! Genevieve's words echoed through the years.

Two passes of the swords, that was it. LeBoeuf's rage gave him a strength beyond even that which he normally possessed. And, as he would later realize, François Guiton, his friend, was not really fighting back. He did not want to kill LeBoeuf, or harm him. He just wanted to make him stop.

But LeBoeuf had not stopped, not until François lay bleeding out on the floor, and Genevieve, on the bed, was shrieking and flinging invectives at him, and LeBoeuf's mind was a whirl of revulsion and anger and confusion and fear.

François Guiton had not been raping Genevieve. She told LeBoeuf as much that night, but it was not until the following day that he genuinely understood it. They were in love. François had proposed that they marry, and Genevieve had accepted. Happily, elatedly. She had given herself to François that night, the both of them too eager to wait.

LeBoeuf had ended it all. Ended François with a thrust of his sword. Ended, for Genevieve, any desire to live. Ended his own life for all practical purposes.

So, lacking the guts to take that last full measure, as Genevieve had done, drowning herself days later, lacking the guts to face the executioner for his crimes, he had run to the one place on earth he knew that he could disappear and live out the rest of his miserable life as a pig hunter named LeBoeuf.

Or so he thought.

How long LeBoeuf stood there in that state of shocked recall he did not know. Half a lifetime, it seemed, but it must have been seconds, no more, and then the Spaniard attacked once again. LeBoeuf's spirit was quite ready to let the sword take him right through the heart, but his reflexes, honed by hundreds of hours of practice under the careful eye of his fencing master, were not.

He caught the Spaniard's blade with his own, stepped closer, let the weapons slide against one another until they were hand guard to hand guard. Two feet separated the men, blades locked, when the Spaniard realized his danger. His eyes went wide and he began to step back, but that only brought him into more perfect range for LeBoeuf's left fist, which shot out like a striking snake and hit the man hard in the mouth.

The Spaniard's head jerked backwards and he stumbled as LeBoeuf cocked his sword arm like the hammer of a flintlock ready to strike sparks. Nothing but open space between the point of his sword and the Spaniard's chest, the man too staggered to defend himself, too stunned to even see death coming.

"LeBoeuf! No! Don't kill him, damn you!"

Henriette again, and this time he heard her. He paused, unsure, shaken. He looked over at her. She was on the bed, on her knees, her eyes wide, soft hair falling around her shoulders. Pleading.

He looked back at the Spaniard. The man's senses were returning, he was finding his footing, lifting his sword. LeBoeuf took half a step forward and hit the man hard on the side of the head with his right hand, which was still wrapped in the hand guard of his sword. The Spaniard went careening sideways, hit the wall and slumped to the floor, his sword, impressively, still in his hand.

"Damn it, I said—" Henriette began but LeBoeuf cut her off.

"He's not dead. Come on, we have to go now, quickly."

Henriette did not move. "Go where?"

LeBoeuf frowned. That was not the response he had expected. "Away from here."

"Why should I do that?"

LeBoeuf shook his head. The past minutes had been dreamlike, nightmarish, but still it seemed he could not wake up. It made no sense, any of it.

"Because now you can escape this Spanish whore's son," he said.

"I don't want to escape him."

"But…"

"You think I'm better off running through the jungle with you and your damned dog and your filthy pirates? Hunted like one of your pigs?"

"But…this bastard…" LeBoeuf pointed with his sword at the body slumped against the wall. "He's just using you. You're nothing to him. Can't you see that?"

"Every man is just using me. That I saw years ago," Henriette hissed. "So I must choose which is likely to do me the most good. And it sure as hell is not you."

"I said I would get you back to France."

"Yes, you did," Henriette said. "And here I am. And Alonso says he'll get me back to France and he's probably a lying pile of shit as well, but at least he has the means to do it, if he chooses, unlike some penniless stinking pig hunter."

Alonso...LeBoeuf thought. He did not know what else to think, what to say.

"Get out of here now, you great ox," Henriette said in a harsh whisper. "I hear no sound of alarm. They're all still asleep. Go, while you can!"

LeBoeuf hesitated. He still could not grasp what was happening, what he should do. Grab her, throw her over his shoulder? Her weight would be nothing to him, he could easily run off carrying her.

But she might scream. She might not want to go.

She doesn't want to go... It broke through like a ship coming out of the fog, and he realized, fool that he was, that he had not considered that possibility, even after she made it clear. He nodded, slowly, his eyes on her pretty, scowling face. He turned and hurried out the door.

The snoring was still loud and filling the lower floor. LeBoeuf was aware of it as he moved quickly down the stairs. Incredibly, the fighting above stairs had disturbed no one's slumber.

With three long strides he was across the foyer and out the door. He could just make out the shape of the guard he had left unconscious in the shadows. He snatched up the man's musket, which he had left propped against the wall, and hurried off into the night.

Chapter Thirty

LeBoeuf had no sense for how long it took him to reach the rendezvous with the others, or how he got there, or what had happened en route. It was daylight when he arrived, so he knew he had walked for one night at least. Maybe two. He could not remember.

He did remember that Other Dog was at his side some of the time, at other times running ahead then circling back. He could picture the two of them walking on trails and through dense forest. The sword wound on his arm was bandaged, so he must have done that at some point.

His thoughts, if such they could be called, had been little more than a chaotic swirl in his head, unfocused fireworks of memories and emotions and desires, all of them hellish and brutal. That much he knew.

He knew that he fell asleep, because he recalled waking to Other Dog poking at him with her nose and making soft, whining sounds, as if pleading for him to stand, to carry on, when all he wanted to do was lie there and rot away into the earth. Which he might well have done if not for the dog's persistence.

Instead, he groaned and pushed himself to hands and knees and then, with what seemed to be more effort than he had ever expended before, and using his musket as a crutch, he stood and stumbled on.

The sun was starting to rise and his mind was starting to clear by the time he found himself north of Cayona, far enough inland to avoid any Spanish patrols or pickets. He thought of Henriette. He pictured her there on the bed, her face set in that familiar scowl.

What did I expect? he thought. *How great a fool am I, to think she'd want to come with me?*

Self-preservation was Henriette's *raison d'être.* Love of anyone, loyalty to anyone, or anything, those were not a part of who she was.

Her choice had been between a fellow Frenchman with nothing—not a ship, not a home, not a sou in his purse, nothing but a dog and a gun—and a Spaniard rich enough to fit out a hundred men in the finest clothes and armaments, and influence enough to command a place of respect in the fleet of Admiral Toledo.

Choice? No, there was no choice.

Alonso… It was like a thorn in his shoe. And that led to the next obvious question. *Why do you care so much about that silly tart?*

He sat down on the trunk of a fallen palm at the edge of a clearing and looked south toward the line of trees there. Columns of smoke were rising up beyond the stands of candlewood and *lignum sanctum* and LeBoeuf knew that on the far side of those trees was the settlement of Cayona, its population increased tenfold or more with the arrival of Toledo's fleet.

Why do I care?

He was a gentleman. A chevalier. Son of a noble family. It was incumbent on a man of his station to help others. To help women.

Man of my station. He looked down at his filthy canvas trousers, his rawhide shoes, his bare, sockless calves, and he smiled.

You did not help your sister.

The thought came from some ugly place inside him, a blow he did not see coming. If another man had said that, LeBoeuf would have called him out and killed him. But such defense of honor did not apply to himself. He did not have the courage to end his own life. He had learned that long ago, and the self-torment was starting to grow old. He sighed and stood and walked on.

Why?

Henriette was lovely, to be sure. Desirable. But when he had saved her from the flesh dealer, he had done so with no thought of enjoying her sweet favors himself. He knew that to be the honest truth. Later, when she offered herself, he did not refuse, but that was not what had motivated him at first. He simply could not see so beautiful and spirited a thing crushed.

Was that why he had gone to the Tortuga plantation to fetch her back? Because he did not want to see her crushed?

Or had more complicated feelings bubbled up through the muck of his tortured mind?

"Bah!" he said out loud. "*C'est de la merde.*" Other Dog barked her agreement.

Soon they were in the trees again, moving cautiously along a trail some ways from Cayona, skirting the lions' den. Once, Other Dog gave a low growl of warning, and they found a clump of thick brush and secreted themselves as a Spanish foot patrol marched past them, bored and inattentive. The Spaniards had been on the island for weeks now, and likely had met with no real opposition. They were growing slack and complacent. Good.

Once the patrol was well past, LeBoeuf and Other Dog pulled themselves from the thicket and continued on. LeBoeuf was moving though unfamiliar territory now, but he had spent time enough hunting on Hispaniola to have a good sense for navigating overland.

For the better part of the afternoon, he and Other Dog worked their way to the south and west, sometimes hacking through thick jungle, sometimes skirting around open fields. They were in the trees, not too far from the shore by LeBoeuf's best guess, when Other Dog made a sound in her throat, a warning, but not the same sound that she made when the Spanish were near.

LeBoeuf went down on one knee and kept perfectly still. And suddenly, from nowhere, a thought flashed into his head.

She could have screamed…

Back at the plantation house, in his standoff with Henriette. He realized now that she could have screamed, she could have shouted for help, and then the men sleeping below stairs would have come running to her aid and LeBoeuf would have been taken, or died fighting them off. Either way he would have been out of her life for good.

She could have done that. But she did not.

Guess she's not so eager to see me dead. LeBoeuf felt oddly satisfied by that realization, which irritated him, but he could not deny the feeling.

"LeBoeuf?" The voice came from his right, *sotto voce*, the speaker lost in the trees.

"Yes," LeBoeuf replied. He gave Other Dog an accusatory look, annoyed by her negligence, but she remained flat on her belly with her tongue hanging out. He heard the crunch of underbrush and a moment later Lessard appeared through the trees, musket in hand.

"There you are," Lessard said. "We thought the damned Spaniards had gutted you."

"Not yet. Are the others close?"

Lessard nodded. He led LeBoeuf another hundred yards through the trees to a small clearing where the rest were gathered. Heads turned as they came out of the brush and into the open, people made sundry gestures of greeting. No one asked LeBoeuf where he had been, what he had been doing, and LeBoeuf was grateful for that.

"Very well," LeBoeuf said after the brief reunion was over. "Let us leave this damned island in our wake."

"Might be a problem with that," Pierre Le Chasseur said. LeBoeuf saw grim expressions all around. "The boats are gone."

"Gone?"

"We went down to check on them, right off," Le Chasseur said. "They're gone. Not so long ago. You can still see the marks in the sand where they were dragged to the water."

LeBoeuf scowled as he thought about that. *Gone?* They had been well hidden, and there was little reason that the Spaniards would go searching around for them. And even if the Spanish had found them, they would most likely have smashed holes in them, rather than go to the effort of taking them off.

"Graves…son of a bitch," LeBoeuf said out loud.

"Graves?"

"That bastard Graves. And Maja. Who were with us at the plantation. The ones who ran off with tails between their legs. They knew where the boats were. Walked right past them, after they beached their ship. Must have seen the drag marks. Son of a bitch."

"Why would they do that?" Billy Solent asked. "They had boats of their own."

"Don't know," LeBoeuf said. "Maybe their boats were shot up. Maybe they wanted to make sure we stayed put at this place. Doesn't matter."

There was silence in the clearing as the others digested this. He could see men shaking their heads in disgust at such a thing. But in truth LeBoeuf knew he would have done the same thing, were he in Graves's shoes.

"Never mind about that," LeBoeuf said at last. "It's no concern. The Don Diegos have boats aplenty. I'm sure they'll be happy enough to part with a few."

There was silence, and then Levesque said, "Reckon they'll just give them to us?"

"No," LeBoeuf said. "I reckon we'll have to take them." How they would do that, he was not sure, nor was he sure what they would do after. But he did know that none of it was going to happen in the light of day, so he told the others to relax, to eat, to rest. With any luck they were looking at a long night ahead.

LeBoeuf lay down, closed his eyes, but sleep did not come. His thoughts were like eddies and ebb tides and surging water. Boats. Spaniards. His men. The women. Henriette. It was all churning in his mind.

He stood after a while and made his way south out of the clearing until he could see the ocean through the trees, then continued on carefully to where the trees yielded to the sandy beach. He paused there and looked in both directions. There was no one around. The harbor of Cayona was a couple hundred yards to the east, too far for anyone there to pay much attention to a lone figure on the shore. He stepped out of the trees and walked down to the water's edge.

A couple hundred yards off, his old ship was still run up on the sand, or the charred remains of it, anyway. The Spaniards had apparently not thought it worth the effort to haul it off, and had burned it instead. To the west he could see that Graves's ship had suffered the same fate. LeBoeuf wondered if the Spaniards had even bothered to remove the great guns before putting the ships to the torch. He doubted it.

To the east, the great Spanish galleons that had cannonaded the town were still riding at anchor, looking as if they had not moved in decades. Boats pulled between them, and between them and the shore, carrying orders, men, supplies, all of it, the blood of the army and the fleet. A few other galleons were anchored farther out, but LeBoeuf could see that maybe half of the initial fleet was gone, off on other business of the Spanish empire.

There were still plenty of ships, however: supply ships anchored among the galleons or working their way on or offshore, frigates patrolling the water between Tortuga and Hispaniola, little sloops and brigs racing off to Santo Domingo with dispatches and requisitions.

"It's like a banquet, no?" LeBoeuf said to Other Dog. "So many ships to choose from. Which shall we have?"

He looked from one to the other, trying to gauge its seaworthiness, armament, the number of men it might have aboard.

He looked longingly at a trim frigate anchored near the outer edge of the harbor.

"I know, I know, I'm getting greedy," he said. "Very well, we'll leave that one for now."

He looked out over the ships, the boats, the sea beyond, the beach with its dozens of men going back and forth, and he tried to conjure up a plan. So many variables, so many considerations. And then, as abrupt as blowing out a candle, he was done. Done with thinking, done with planning. It was time to act, and then see what happened, and then act again.

LeBoeuf walked back up the beach, into the trees and back to where the others were waiting.

"What did you see?" Levasseur asked.

"Ships," LeBoeuf said. "Boats. Plenty for us."

He looked around at the assembled men. They each of them had some experience on shipboard, but a handful, like LeBoeuf, had spent considerable time at sea, and had the inimitable look and swagger of sailors. Their clothes, too—canvas breeches and rough linen shirts, faded and patched, knives hanging from thick leather belts, an odd assortment of hats and caps—were no different from the dress of seamen the world over.

"Once it's full dark we'll go get a boat," LeBoeuf said next. "Not all of us. Le Chasseur, Levesque, you're with me. Billy Solent." He looked from man to man, naming off the more seasoned mariners, the one who would not give themselves away with poor oar handling or some other lubberly gaff. He considered D'Anton. A good man in a fight, but with his black skin and tribal tattoos and scarring he was unlikely to pass for a Spanish sailor.

"The rest of you will make your way to the beach. We'll fetch you there."

It was several hours later, after the sun was well down, that LeBoeuf rose from his seated position, stretched and yawned.

"The lot of you who I named off, it's time to go," he said. Pierre Le Chasseur and the other stood and reached for bandoliers and muskets.

"No, no. No muskets," LeBoeuf said. His words were greeted with looks of confusion and protest. "We're supposed to look like Spanish sailors. Have you ever seen a Spanish sailor walking about with a long hunting musket?"

The men nodded. They set the weapons down again. They did not look happy about it.

There's a thousand of the Spanish bastards on the beach, LeBoeuf thought. *A dozen muskets will do you precious little good in any event.*

LeBoeuf told Other Dog to stay, ignored her look of dismay, and led his little band back toward the beach. There was no moon, which was good for the work they had to do, but it made the going harder. They stepped out onto the sand and walked east, keeping close to the tree line, invisible in the night.

When they reached the place where the jungle yielded to the beach fronting the harbor they stepped back into the shelter of the trees and looked out over the scene before them. There was little activity at that time of night, and all of it farther up toward the town. The shoreline was deserted, with half a dozen boats pulled up on the sand. Perfect.

"Come along," LeBoeuf said in a low voice. "And no one says a word but me, understand?"

He stepped out of the trees and led the way across the sandy ground, walking with the easy confidence of a man who was where he was supposed to be, doing what he was supposed to do. He headed down toward the water's edge. From the trees, the boats had appeared as little more than dark shapes, but as he drew closer he could make out more detail. His eyes fell on two halfway down the beach: ship's barges, twenty feet long, light enough to be rowed by the men he had with him, big enough to carry all of the buccaneers, their women and gear. Perfect.

LeBoeuf led the men to where the boats were pulled up on the sand and gestured that these were the vessels they would take. He turned casually and looked around. No one nearby, no one paying any attention.

"Shove them off," he said in a whisper. "Let's go."

He stepped up to the boat closest to him, put his hands on the gunnel, pushed, and the boat moved a bit with a grinding sound of keel on sand. The bottom of the boat was lost in shadow, but suddenly LeBoeuf saw a flurry of movement there, heard the thump of hands and feet hitting wood, and a face appeared out of the dark. A man, apparently sleeping in the boat, startled awake.

"What the devil?" the man all but shouted in rapid Spanish.

"Silence!" LeBoeuf said, speaking Spanish as well. He was nearly fluent in the language, and his accent, if not perfect, was passable, particularly in the heterogeneous world of sailors. "Who are you?" he demanded.

"Who am…?" the Spaniard sputtered. "I'm watching the boats. Who the devil are you?"

As the man spoke LeBoeuf took two small steps in his direction, trying not to seem threatening, or not overly threatening, at least.

"The captain sent us for the boats," LeBoeuf said, softly.

"Captain? What cap…"

The man got no further. LeBoeuf's left hand shot out and grabbed him by the shirt and jerked him over the gunnel. His right hand drew the long hunting knife from the sheath on his belt. He held the dagger point under the man's chin, the steel just barely pressing into the skin of his throat.

"Not another word, not another sound. Understood?" LeBoeuf whispered. In the faint light he could see the man's eyes go wide as his anger turned to surprise and then fear. He nodded, as much as he as able without stabbing himself on LeBoeuf's knife.

"Down in the bottom of the boat," LeBoeuf said next, half shoving the Spaniard down. He turned to the others. "Let's go."

They pushed the boats off and climbed over the gunnels and set the oars in the tholes. With no word spoken, and with practiced skill, they pulled together, and the boats gathered way, leaving the beach behind in the dark.

LeBoeuf sat at the tiller of the lead boat, the terrified Spaniard at his feet, huddled in the bottom, motionless, either from fear or a desire to not be noticed. The men at the oars kept up an easy, unhurried stroke as LeBoeuf set a course out toward the anchored fleet. He glanced over his shoulder. The second boat was right in his wake, and farther back the beach was growing indistinct in the dark. LeBoeuf pushed the tiller over, swinging the bow of the boat west.

It took considerably less time to make the return trip by boat than it had to get to the town on foot, and soon the bows of the two purloined barges were run up on the sand and the men hopped out and pulled them farther ashore. LeBoeuf grabbed the Spaniard and lifted him to his feet and all but threw him into the water.

"You go sit there," he said, pointing to a spot a dozen feet away. "Stay there, stay quiet, and I might let you live." The Spaniard, eyes still wide, retreated to where LeBoeuf had indicated and sat, cross-legged, and said not a word.

Figures, dark and indistinct, emerged from the trees on the far side of the sand, and a moment later the rest of the buccaneers and the women appeared at the water's edge. They carried with them all of their possessions and weapons, as well as those of LeBoeuf and the men who had gone with him. Other Dog came bounding up, tongue hanging out. She rubbed against LeBoeuf's leg, apparently willing to forgive the insult of his leaving her behind.

"Should we get in the boats now?" Vassy asked.

"No," LeBoeuf said. "Now, we wait."

"Tide's flooding," Levesque said, answering Vassy's question before he could ask it.

"Oh," Vassy said. "Well, I reckon we can wait. We're well practiced at it."

They were certainly that, as was LeBoeuf, and he was happy to wait in this instance. Stealing a ship was best done in the predawn hours, when vigilance was at its nadir. Board her in silence, overwhelm the crew, slip the anchor cable and let the ship drift off on the ebbing tide. Easy as could be.

It was some hours later, with most of the folks on the beach fast asleep, including the captive Spaniard, when LeBoeuf grabbed a nearby stick, pushed himself to his feet, and walked down to the water's edge. He tossed the stick into the water, ten feet from shore, and before he could react Other Dog leapt into the ocean and half ran, half swam out, grabbed the stick and brought it back, dropping it at LeBoeuf's feet like an offering.

Stupid dog, LeBoeuf thought. "You, stay put, now. Sit."

Other Dog sat momentarily, then stood again.

"Stay. I'm not joking, stupid dog," LeBoeuf said. He tossed the stick out again and this time Other Dog stayed put, despite her clear and burning desire to fetch it. LeBoeuf kept his eyes on the wood, bobbing in the water, as the ebbing tide drew it away from the beach. Time to go.

He walked back up the sand and roused the others. He told them to load their gear into the boats, then told the women to climb in and take their places on the thwarts, amidships.

"What's your plan, LeBoeuf?" Levasseur asked. "What are we to do?"

"We'll row out to the fleet. I'll decide what ship we take. When I do, we go alongside, go aboard. I go first. No one say a thing, just like when we took the boats. Hopefully we catch them all asleep. Anyone we find, we take him silently. No guns. Understood?"

He looked around. The men were nodding.

"Good. Let's shove off." He turned to the Spaniard, who had woken up with the commotion. "You stay here until daybreak."

The Spaniard nodded vigorously. LeBoeuf could not imagine he would actually do it, but it was worth a try.

The men grabbed the gunnels and pushed the boats into the water, then climbed over the sides, the sailors at the oars, the others inboard. With only the faintest of sounds the blades dipped into the water and the boats pulled away from the beach. Off to the southeast the lights of the anchored fleet made a discrete constellation low in the sky. LeBoeuf set his course for a light toward the western side of the anchorage, where he had seen a likely-looking ship earlier in the day.

They pulled on through the dark, and as they drew closer the ships began to reveal themselves, the massive galleons and the smaller transports and supply vessels. A few had lanterns hanging from the rigging, illuminating their decks. They would most likely have anchor watches set, a handful of men on each ship keeping an eye out for anything of concern. But nothing of concern had happened for weeks, and LeBoeuf did not think the men on watch would be terribly vigilant. He did not think they would notice two boats pulling quietly past.

Then he saw it, right ahead, barely visible, a dark outline on a dark night, a single lantern hanging from the mainstay: the ship he had been eyeing earlier in the light of day. One hundred tons or so, barque-rigged, trim and fast-looking. She was a transport of some sort, but seemed well-armed, at least judging by the gunports that LeBoeuf could make out along her side.

From his vantage point standing on the beach he could tell nothing of her qualities, or her seaworthiness, or the condition of her fabric or rigging, of course, but there was something about her that caught his eye. He had a feeling, and until he stepped aboard that was as good as he was going to get.

He pushed the tiller over a bit and headed toward the anchored ship. "That's our prey there," he said softly. "Get ready with the boat hook."

As they drew closer, more and more of the ship resolved itself, and nothing LeBoeuf saw suggested he had been wrong: she seemed like a fine ship, not too big, not too small, not too old. Two more strokes and he called, softly, "Toss oars!"

Starboard and larboard the oars came up in two vertical rows and the boat glided the last twenty feet to the side of the ship. In the bow, Billy Solent hooked the main chains with the boat hook and pulled the boat up under the boarding steps. LeBoeuf looked up just as a head appeared over the gunnel looking down, lantern held at arm's length over the water, casting a weak light into the boat.

"Who the hell are you? What do you want?" the man asked in coarse Spanish.

"I've brought the women," LeBoeuf replied, nodding forward. The man looked where LeBoeuf indicated, at the half dozen women sitting amidships. He looked back at LeBoeuf.

"What women?"

"These women."

"Why are you bringing women?"

LeBoeuf sighed, as if this was the stupidest of questions. "The women the captain called for."

"The captain? Our captain? Called for women?"

LeBoeuf sighed again. "Here, let me come aboard so we can sort this out without yelling at each other."

In truth they were speaking in normal tones, but LeBoeuf, not waiting for a reply, stood and climbed quickly up the boarding steps and through the entry port onto the deck.

The sailor with the lantern stepped aside, but only a foot or so. "Very well, what do you mean by this?" he demanded, but he had not even finished speaking before LeBoeuf's knife was out and at the man's throat.

"Quiet, quiet," LeBoeuf said. "You are the only one on watch?"

The sailor nodded.

"How many aboard?"

"Captain and the mates down below, aft. Ten others. Most are topside." He nodded forward and LeBoeuf noticed the dark, irregular shapes of men sleeping on deck.

"Good," he said. "You make any noise at all, you're a dead man. You understand?"

The sailor nodded again. LeBoeuf leaned over the rail. "Everyone aboard, quiet as you can."

One by one the men came up and through the entry port, their rawhide shoes or bare feet silent on the wooden deck, muskets in hand, what edged weapons they had hanging from belts. Vassy handed LeBoeuf his sword belt and musket. LeBoeuf leaned the musket against the rail, strapped the belt around his waist.

Someone gave Other Dog a boost and she came bounding through the entry port. LeBoeuf tensed, ready for her to start in barking, but she seemed to understand that silence was the order of the day and she made no noise at all, save for her nails gently tapping on the deck.

LeBoeuf nodded toward the sailors sleeping on the deck, and his men needed no more instruction than that. They spread out, clapped hands over mouths, knelt on chests, held knives to throats as the sleepers woke in surprise.

It was over before LeBoeuf's men had even finished boarding. Ten Spanish sailors sprawled out where they had been sleeping, held motionless at knifepoint. LeBoeuf gestured to a half dozen men standing near him. "Take the lantern, go down through the 'tween decks and the hold, see if there's anyone else there. Secure them, silent as you can. Le Roux, D'Anton and me, we'll go aft, get the captain and the officers."

The men nodded, took the lantern and headed for the main hatch. LeBoeuf looked down at Other Dog.

"Stay," he ordered, then led D'Anton and Le Roux aft and down the scuttle forward of the tiller, stepping with care, silent as they could. They moved carefully aft, peering into the dark for any sign of movement.

The bottom of the ladder led to a narrow passage aft, and in the dim light they could just make out a door on either side of the passage and one at the far end: the mates' cabins, and the captain's in the stern.

LeBoeuf paused and turned to the men behind. He pointed at the two doors and the men nodded. He held up a finger to indicate that they should wait, then eased himself aft until he was within a few feet of the captain's cabin.

He paused a second, then lifted his leg and kicked in the flimsy door, bursting into the great cabin. Behind him he heard D'Anton and Le Roux kick their own doors in, heard shouts of surprise, but his eyes were on the space in front of him, searching for the captain, searching to see if the man was waiting with pistol in hand, loaded and cocked.

A lantern was hanging from the overhead beams, its candle burned down to a stub, giving off just the merest hint of light, but enough to somewhat illuminate the place. The great cabin of a middling merchant vessel, pretty much what LeBoeuf would have expected: a table, settees aft, a wardrobe of some sort, windows in the transom, black in the night.

On the larboard side there was a bunk, and LeBoeuf could just make out a figure thrashing its way out from under the covers: the captain, who had been asleep and was now awake, after a fashion. In two steps LeBoeuf was across the cabin. The captain was just sitting up, just getting off a strangled cry of surprise, when LeBoeuf grabbed him by the collar of his shirt, jerked him to his feet, and clapped his hand down on the man's open mouth, moustache, and goatee.

"You be quiet, understand?" LeBoeuf said. The captain nodded despite LeBoeuf's firm grip on his jaw. LeBoeuf pulled his hand away. The captain looked more furious than afraid.

"Good," LeBoeuf said. "Now..."

That was it. Before LeBoeuf could even think of what he would say next he heard a shout from the deck above, then another, and then small arms fire, four shots in ragged succession, and Other Dog barking madly.

Oh, mon Dieu, what now? he wondered.

Chapter Thirty-One

LeBoeuf let go of the captain's shirt, turned, and raced for the door. D'Anton and Le Roux were in the narrow passageway, each holding a prisoner by the arm: the mates they had roused from sleep and pulled to their feet.

"What is…" D'Anton began but LeBoeuf pushed past him and called, "The captain's in the aft cabin. Bring the lot of them topside!"

Then he was past the men and onto the ladder. He came head and shoulders through the scuttle and looked around the weather deck, where the lantern was casting a bit of light on the scene. His men were forward, huddled behind the masts or the windlass or below the hatch combings. He could see the muzzles of their muskets poking out, the deck now a makeshift fort. He could see Levesque holding Other Dog back with a length of rope around her neck.

He looked to the starboard side. More men, but not his. They, too, were finding shelter where they could, muzzles pointed across the open space. A stand-off, a stalemate. But who were they, this second boarding party?

LeBoeuf tried to peer into the shadows, to see who these men were who had ruined his otherwise perfectly-executed plan. He could make out Black men, and white men, and in between. He could see heads bound in cloth, cutlasses hanging from shoulder belts.

"*Oh, mon Dieu*!" LeBoeuf shouted. He climbed the rest of the way up the ladder and walked out onto the open deck, stepping up onto the main hatch. He held his hands up over his head, and called, in French, "Put up your guns! Hold your fire!" and then again, in English, "Graves! Maja! Do you plague us still? Show yourselves!"

He looked around. He saw Maja step out of the shadows, Benjamin Graves at his side. Behind them, their men stood and spread out along the starboard side. Forward, LeBoeuf's men also emerged from their defensive positions, guns still leveled, and took places along the larboard rail.

"LeBoeuf," Maja said, nodding.

"LeBoeuf," Graves said. "Fancy running into you here."

"Not so surprising," LeBoeuf said. "It seems whenever I take something for my own, you poxed scavengers appear."

"Your own?" Maja said. "How do you figure that? I've reckoned on taking this ship for two days now."

"You might have reckoned on it for two years, for all I care. I still took her first." He heard a shuffling, a low muttering aft, and the mates and the captain stepped through the scuttle, with D'Anton and Le Roux behind.

"See, here," LeBoeuf said, pointing with his thumb at the men. "Captain's my prisoner. So, pray, round up your men and get your miserable selves off my ship."

Maja shrugged. "I planned to take the ship from the Spaniards. I can take it from you just the same."

This whole situation felt familiar to LeBoeuf, like being in a ship's magazine, surrounded by barrels and cartridges and horns and loose gunpowder — the feeling of being a single spark away from utter and bloody destruction. He could almost hear the sound of muscles tensing around him, of fingers caressing triggers.

"You can take this ship from me. Or try, at least," LeBoeuf said. "But see here, I'm no savage like you, Maja. Don't care to see men butchered for no cause. And we have women with us."

He lowered his hands and stepped toward the center of the main hatch. "Just you and me, Maja," he continued. "We fight until one of us is dead or calls for quarter. Winner keeps possession of the ship, loser's men go free. Agreed?"

Maja gave a hint of a smile, just the subtlest flicker of what might be called amusement. "Until one of us calls for quarter?" he asked.

"Yes," LeBoeuf said, and he could not help smiling a bit himself. Maja clearly understood, as he did, that the agreement was a formality. No one was going to call for quarter.

"Very good," Maja said. He pulled his cutlass with his left hand. With his right he drew his *boutou*, his squared-off club, two and a half feet long and covered with intricate carvings, a native weapon, elegant and lethal. LeBoeuf remembered it well.

Maja stepped up onto the main hatch, ten feet from where LeBoeuf stood. He turned to Graves. "We'll slip the cable once I've killed this one," he said, nodding toward LeBoeuf. "His men can take to their boats. We'll keep the women."

"Keep the women, aye," Graves said.

LeBoeuf smiled a bit wider. Maja's bravado was admirable, his attempt at getting under his opponent's skin clever, if futile. He turned and stepped down off the hatch. He pulled his pistols from his belt and handed them to Le Roux. He glanced out across the water. He could see lanterns moving around the decks of the galleons, and he thought he could hear the distant sound of voices, the rattle of gear. The hornet's nest had been disturbed. The shouting and gunshots that had just rung out in an ostensibly peaceful harbor could not have gone unnoticed.

"Listen here," LeBoeuf said to Le Roux, his voice low. "The Don Diegos will be here soon enough. Tell the others. Keep your mouths shut until they're aboard. Don't try to fight them, it's back in the boats for us, and off we go. Understood?"

"Aye, captain, understood," Le Roux said, and in his voice LeBoeuf heard the sound of an old man-of-war's man, smart and disciplined. He turned and walked back to the main hatch, pulling his sword with his right hand, his hunting knife as a *main gauche* with his left.

And there they were, LeBoeuf and Maja. Flames had driven them from the deck of the last ship where they had faced one another, but here, rare as it might be, was a second chance. LeBoeuf hoped there would be time and opportunity to make proper use of it.

He swiped the air with his blade, the fine sword that had been in the De Garamond family for three generations. He took a stance — feet at right angles, right foot pointed forward, weight slightly on the back leg — that was as familiar to him as lying in bed. But he kept it loose, less formal, so he could bring the main gauche into play.

Maja took no particular stance. Rather, he stood easy, arms at his side, weapons down, as if he was not sure what to do. Vulnerable. Or so he wanted to appear. LeBoeuf did not doubt that it was purposeful: let your opponent think there was an opening to exploit, let him move in bold and reckless, and then that snake-fast boutou would do its work.

But two could play at make-believe.

LeBoeuf moved forward, one step, two steps, nearly within the arc of the wicked club. Maja did not move, did not flinch, but LeBoeuf could see the muscles in his arms tighten as he made ready to strike. Another half a step and LeBoeuf lunged with his sword, then leapt back clear as the boutou came swinging around, the hard wood whipping past his face so close he could feel the air of its passing.

Then he was moving in again as Maja twisted, off balance, with the momentum of his swing. It was dark on deck, just the light of the one weak lantern. Maja, with his dark clothes, his dark skin, was hard to see, but LeBoeuf drove his point as best he could, lunging with determination this time.

He did not find his mark. Maja continued to twist around, and in the heartbeat it took LeBoeuf to thrust straight out, Maja had spun and brought the cutlass to bear, parrying LeBoeuf's blade. LeBoeuf leapt back again, clear of another swipe from the boutou, then retreated back two more steps.

Bâtarde…he thought. He would not have guessed that any man could move as fast as Maja had just done.

Have a care, Jean-Baptiste, or you're a dead man.

He stood a bit more upright, let his weapons hang loose from his arms. Inviting an attack. And Maja accepted the invitation, after a fashion. He took a step closer. With his lean body and aura of strength and speed he put LeBoeuf in mind of a jaguar he had once seen.

LeBoeuf tensed, tightened his grip, stood stock-still and waited for Maja's move. His eyes were everywhere: on Maja's hands, his weapons, his eyes, which he could see only when they caught the glint of the lantern.

Maja led with the cutlass. LeBoeuf knew he would. They had taken two passes so far, and on Hispaniola they had nearly fought to the death, and that gave LeBoeuf a decent understanding of how Maja did this sort of thing. No doubt it worked on the brutes who Maja was accustomed to fighting, but it would not work on LeBoeuf.

The cutlass was in Maja's left hand. He drew it back over his shoulder and swung, backhand, at LeBoeuf's head. But LeBoeuf did not retreat. Rather, as the blade started coming around, he stepped closer, brought the hand guard of his sword across and stopped the cutlass in mid-swing.

That was a surprise. Maja did not expect LeBoeuf to step in like that, he expected to have room to swing. The boutou in Maja's right hand whipped around, but LeBoeuf was too close now for Maja to hit him a proper blow. The lower part of the club hit LeBoeuf's side — solid, but not so hard as to do much hurt. And just as the boutou struck LeBoeuf, LeBoeuf brought his hunting knife up from under and drove it into Maja's gut.

Maja made a grunting sound and staggered back quickly, his left hand, which was still holding the cutlass, pressed against the wound. He kept as straight as he could, his eyes never leaving LeBoeuf's, the boutou ready if LeBoeuf tried to exploit this advantage.

LeBoeuf stepped back too, well clear of any danger from club or cutlass, and held his weapons easy. He could see blood soaking into Maja's shirt and running over his fingers, but he could not tell if the wound was profound at all. From the feel of it, he did not think the knife had driven in too deep. Certainly Maja did not seem *hors de combat.*

"You can dress that," LeBoeuf said, pointing with his sword at Maja's wound.

"What?"

"Your wound. You can get one of your men to dress it. I'll wait." LeBoeuf was in no hurry. In fact, he would have been happy to wait.

Maja stood a little straighter and squinted at LeBoeuf. "I wouldn't call it a wound, and it don't need dressing."

"Are you quite certain? It seems to be bleeding with some vigor. I don't covet a victory here just because you bleed out."

Maja frowned. He spit on the hatch cover. "Ain't going to bleed out."

LeBoeuf shrugged. "As you wish." He refreshed his grip on his weapons, took a step closer, eyes studying every move that Maja made. His wound, it seemed, was not fatal, but neither was it inconsequential. He seemed to be struggling to stand upright, to raise his arms. But was that just subterfuge?

LeBoeuf reckoned he was about to find out.

He took a step closer, then another, no longer in his fencer's stance, but coming at Maja straight on, leading with both sword and knife. He made small, tentative movements with his weapons, as did Maja, both men feeling their opponents out, both more wary than they had been at the onset of this.

LeBoeuf held his knife low and slowly brought his sword up to striking position. Maja was nearly still, and he seemed to be fighting down the pain from his wound. Then suddenly his right arm was a blur of motion, whipping the boutou around, but once again LeBoeuf was ready for it. The knife came up and the hard wood club embedded itself in the blade. LeBoeuf held the handle with a death grip, but still the force of the blow nearly knocked the knife from his hand.

With the knife holding the boutou at bay, LeBoeuf lunged with the sword, but still Maja was too fast for him. His cutlass knocked LeBoeuf's blade aside, and he lifted his right foot and drove it into LeBoeuf's gut, sending him stumbling back to the edge of the hatch.

Incroyable… Even a knife wound in the belly did not slow the son of a bitch down. Apparently Maja was not as injured as he pretended to be, or as LeBoeuf had hoped that he was.

LeBoeuf was still recovering his footing when Maja moved in again, holding his cutlass and boutou straight out, chest height, as if he was leveling some accusation. Five feet away and Maja began to windmill the weapons it a confusing, chaotic way, depriving LeBoeuf of an easy parry.

LeBoeuf let him approach, four feet, three feet, then he lunged, forcing Maja to react. Maja brought the boutou back over his shoulder, a distraction, then lunged with the cutlass.

It nearly worked. LeBoeuf's eyes flickered to the boutou, but on the edge of his vision he saw the cutlass coming in. He swiped it aside with his sword and lunged again, this time with the hunting knife, as Maja jumped clear.

And then the shouting started.

It came from the larboard side; loud, bellicose, and emphatic. Who shouted first, and in what language, LeBoeuf could not tell, but instantly the voices were accompanied by the sound of a pistol firing, a scream, more shouting, Other Dog barking furiously, then more pistol shots.

LeBoeuf's eyes were on Maja, Maja's eyes were on him, neither man daring to look away. Then, by unspoken and mutual consent, they moved back from one another, three steps, four steps each. LeBoeuf spun around to the sound of the fighting.

The Spanish had arrived.

All along the larboard side men were swarming up over the bulwark, pistols in hand, cutlasses hanging from shoulder belts — sailors from the galleons, come ready for battle. Dark-haired, moustached, and the first over the rail, sword raised, was the officer leading them, distinctive in his shining breastplate. Distracted by the duel, no one had seen them coming. But LeBoeuf, at least, had guessed that they would.

As the Spaniards swarmed aboard, LeBoeuf's men met them with cutlasses and pistols and muskets, and Other Dog raced wildly around, barking and snapping and biting. D'Anton raised his long pig-hunting musket to waist height and swung it around, pointing at the officer leading the attack. He pulled the trigger, the twin ignition of priming and powder bright in the dark night. The blast of lead shot slammed into the man's breastplate from five feet away, knocking him back against the other boarders, but if the ball pierced the metal or no, LeBoeuf could not tell.

"Give quarter! Give quarter! Let's go! Let's go!" LeBoeuf shouted. He hoped Le Roux had passed the word. His men did not seem taken by surprise, but the real test of the plan would come now.

Maja and Graves and the men with them were pushing their way across the deck, getting into the melee with cutlasses raised, pistols firing left and right. LeBoeuf saw one of the boarders, a single leg over the rail, blown back over the side, the look of shocked surprise on his face illuminated by the muzzle flash. Others lay in the scuppers, but some of Maja's men were down too, and some of his own.

"Let's go! Let's go! Other Dog, come!"

Other Dog was the first to obey, letting go of a screaming Spaniard's calf and racing across the deck to LeBoeuf's side.

"Let's go! Let's go!" LeBoeuf shouted again. He took three steps across the deck, grabbed Levesque by the shoulder, spun him around and shoved him toward the entry port on the starboard side. He grabbed Pierre Le Chasseur and then Billy Solent and did the same with them, and soon the rest of them were moving as well. Falling back, yielding to the Spaniards who had gained the deck, leaving the fighting to Maja and his men.

LeBoeuf was the last to go, stepping backward across the deck in a fighting retreat, Other Dog leaping and racing around his legs, assisting in keeping any attackers back. A pistol went off just feet away and LeBoeuf felt the ball pluck at his sleeve as if trying to get his attention. And it did. Time to go.

He turned and he and Other Dog raced the last five feet to the mizzen shrouds. They were alone on that patch of deck. Maja and Graves and that lot were still fighting the Spaniards, and the Spaniards had their hands full driving them back. LeBoeuf and his men were of no concern to anyone.

LeBoeuf leaned over the rail. One of the long boats they had stolen from the beach was floating just below the mizzen channel, the thwarts crowded with men, the women sitting along the centerline.

"Catch this!" LeBoeuf called and tossed his musket and bandolier the six feet down to the boat. He turned and hefted Other Dog up in his arms and held her over the side. "And this!"

He heard a voice from below shout, "Son of a bitch!" in a tone of surprise, and he dropped the dog down into the boat as the occupants scrambled to get clear. Then he threw a leg over the rail and climbed out onto the channel and hopped down into the boat, stepping into the space that Other Dog's impact had cleared. He sat down in the sternsheets and took up the tiller.

"Shove off! Give way!" he called and someone in the bow pushed off the ship's side and as the boat drifted clear the oars came down and took up the stroke. LeBoeuf pushed the tiller over.

They did not have far to go. The boat pulled away into the dark, making a wide circle as the ship receded behind them, the deck illuminated here and there with the flash of a gunshot. The night was filled with the sounds of shouting and screaming and the clash of steel on steel, but it grew fainter as they drew farther from the ship, until an odd sort of calm settled over them.

LeBoeuf shifted the tiller just slightly, bringing the boat around until it was headed for a place astern of the ship they had just abandoned. The sound of the fighting was starting to taper off, but it was difficult to know what was happening on deck.

"Let's pick it up, double time," LeBoeuf said. The men had been pulling easy, but LeBoeuf was afraid now they had left it too late. Timing was crucial here.

Pierre Le Chasseur bent forward quickly and pulled back hard, and the rest followed his stroke. The looms of the oars squeaked louder and more rhythmically in the thole pins and the sound of the water running along the side rose in pitch and volume. The boat continued to describe a wide circle until at last its bow was pointed directly at the stern of the ship, aboard which Maja and his men were still fighting.

"Pull easy," LeBoeuf said. Le Chasseur and the others eased their stroke and the speed of the boat fell off again. Ahead, the stern of the ship rose up above them, blocking even what little they might have been able to see on deck.

"Toss oars," LeBoeuf said and the two banks of oars came straight up as the boat glided the last thirty feet until the ship's transom loomed overhead. Two darker shapes seemed to materialize in front of them; the second boat they had stolen from the beach, and a third, one of Maja's, borrowed as well. The boats, crowded with the rest of LeBoeuf's men and the remainder of the women, were tied off to the chains on the ship's rudder.

LeBoeuf's boat drifted into the gap between the two, thumping gently against their gunnels, and hands from the other boats pulled it in closer.

"Halloa, the boats," LeBoeuf called in a low voice. "All's well?"

"Some wounded, but well enough," Billy Solent's voice came out of the dark.

"All's well, captain," Le Roux called from the other boat.

"Good," LeBoeuf said. "Now we wait."

They did not wait long. They could hear well enough what was happening on deck, even if they could not see it, and what they heard told them the fight was near its end. The predominance of voices shouting in Spanish made it clear who had won.

And then, the sound LeBoeuf had been anticipating; men climbing into boats, the thump of oars lifted off thwarts, the slightly panicked cries of fighting men in retreat. Maja's company were good hands in a fight, LeBoeuf did not doubt that, but they had been surprised and overwhelmed by the Spaniards, and left to fight alone. It came as no shock to him that they were fleeing back to their boats, giving up the fight.

"Wait…wait…" LeBoeuf said, just loud enough to be heard over the chaos. In the dim light of the stars they could just make out the dark shapes of Maja's boats pulling away. A musket went off, fired from the deck of the ship, and then two more, and for an instant the handful of boats moving directly away from the ship's side were illuminated in the flash.

Maja and Graves would have to find a different means of leaving Tortuga.

There was more shouting in Spanish from overhead, a few more muskets were fired at the retreating boats, but soon Maja and his men were swallowed up in the dark, and the shouting died away. LeBoeuf could hear nothing, save for the lap of the water on the hull and little bits of unintelligible conversation above.

"Now, LeBoeuf?" Pierre Le Chasseur asked. "Shall we go now?"

"No, no. We wait some more."

LeBoeuf understood well the rhythms of a fight. Men were tensed in the immediate aftermath, like springs under pressure. The energy was coursing through them. And when they were victorious, as the Spaniards had been, their spirits were raised and they were ready for more. But it would not last. Soon the ardor would ebb, the spirit would fade, and in its place would come weariness and ennui.

For long minutes the boats floated in their strange netherworld under the ship's stern as the shouting abated and the night grew quieter. LeBoeuf could still hear jubilant voices, and urgent voices, and the cries of the wounded, and slowly all that too began to fade.

More minutes passed, and the voices became more subdued, with no further loud and enthusiastic talk. A handful of the Spaniards climbed back over the rail and down into the boats. Soon they were pulling away from the side, a contingent of sailors returning victorious to their own ships, LeBoeuf's men unnoticed in the dark under the stern.

LeBoeuf watched until the Spanish boats were swallowed up in the dark. "Prithee, listen," he said, his voice just loud enough to be heard. "Now we go. Quietly. No shouting, and no pistols unless you must. Fight with cold steel only, if you can. Understood?"

All around him he heard murmurs of agreement, though he could not make out a single man in the dark.

"Follow my boat," he said, then to the men on the thwarts, "Ship oars. Back water."

Somewhere forward the bowman cast off the painter and the oars came down. The rowers pushed them forward and LeBoeuf's boat backed slowly out of the shadow of the ship's stern.

"Give way," he whispered and the men leaned into the oars and the boat stopped dead, then began to move slowly ahead. LeBoeuf kept the tiller over and the boat crept around the ship's starboard side, which earlier had been crowded with his and Maja's boats, but was now deserted.

He looked up. He could see no one on the deck above, no one looking over the side. Whoever was still on board was likely sitting down now, or collapsed on the deck, or nursing their own wounds, or those of their shipmates. The spirit of battle had deserted them, and it would not soon return.

"Ship oars," LeBoeuf said, his words barely audible, and just as quietly the oars came in and the boat glided the last dozen feet alongside, until the entry port was right above LeBoeuf's head. He let go of the tiller and stood, then bent over and scooped up Other Dog who was sitting on the bottom of the boat at his feet.

He grunted as he lifted her and whispered in her ear, "You know what to do, *oui?*" Then he all but tossed her up and through the gap in the bulwark, her claws scratching his chest as she kicked her way up. A second later she disappeared from sight, and less than a second after that the night seemed to explode with the terrible sound of her manic barking, followed close behind by shouts of surprise and terror and screams of pain as Other Dog went to work.

"Let's go! Follow me!" LeBoeuf cried, putting a foot on the boarding step and climbing quickly to the deck. He came through the entry port, pulled his knife and sword, and looked out over as strange a sight as he had ever seen.

There were dead and wounded strewn around, in the scuppers and on the main hatch and draped over the deck guns. A dozen Spaniards were on their feet, eyes bulging with surprise, their attention entirely on the crazed beast that was tearing around the deck, sinking its teeth into one man, then darting off to attack the next. Another dozen men were struggling to get to their feet

A pistol fired, the ball splintering the deck where Other Dog had been a second before. The shooter lowered the spent gun, raised a second, aimed at the dog. In three long strides LeBoeuf crossed the deck and slashed his arm before he could pull the trigger.

He felt someone push past, and Le Chasseur appeared, cutlass in hand as he raced at the Spaniards. D'Anton came around LeBoeuf's other side, his cutlass swinging like a scythe. Then LeBoeuf plunged forward into the fight, even as he was pushed from behind by the press of his own men coming up the ladder and bursting onto the deck.

The battle, if such it was, was short and strange, with LeBoeuf's men fighting in silence, and the only sound that of steel on steel, and the occasional Spanish exclamation, and Other Dog's barking. There was little gunfire. The Spaniards, in the wake of their victory, seemed not to have reloaded their weapons. Now some of them turned and fled over the larboard rail and down into their boats. Some flung their weapons away and held their arms up. Some dropped to their knees. A few kept fighting, but that, too, ended quickly.

"Put up your arms! Put up your arms!" LeBoeuf called and one by one his men heeded and gave up the slaughter. "Other Dog, come! Sit!"

It was quiet again, a strange quiet, almost otherworldly. No sound but the lap of water and men gasping for breath, the low moans of the wounded, now too far gone to cry out. LeBoeuf looked up and outboard. The ship's bow was still pointed toward the island of Tortuga, the tide still ebbing, still strong enough to bear them away. He turned to his men, spread out over the deck.

"Get the women onboard, and let us have hands aloft to loosen off the topsails. Billy Solent, forward and make ready to cut the anchor cable on my word."

The men moved off in various directions to obey. LeBoeuf walked aft, Other Dog at his side. The tiller was lashed amidships and he left it that way. With little wind blowing they would be carried out on the tide, and the rudder would have no effect on where they were going.

He walked forward again. The last of the women were coming up through the entry port, and overhead LeBoeuf could just make out the shape of the topsails as they were untied and pushed in bundles out of the tops to hang in big folds from the yards.

"Go ahead, Billy! Cut us free!" he called forward, and immediately he heard the chop, chop, chop of what he guessed was Billy Solent's cutlass hacking away at the thick anchor cable.

It took a dozen or so blows with the sharp blade and suddenly the ship was moving under them, the bow turning slightly, the lights of the distant fleet of galleons sweeping past as the current pulled them out to sea. LeBoeuf felt a flush of relief, a renewed sense of hope.

And then he thought of Henriette, somewhere back there, in their bed on his plantation, and the good feeling was swept away.

"We'll leave this cursed island well astern," he said out loud. Other Dog made a soft, whining sound, the only one who heard LeBoeuf's words.

Epilogue

Witching hour. Or thereabouts. And once again Don Alonso Menéndez was fully awake.

He stood in the open window of his bed chamber and stared out into the dark, letting the soft, tropical breeze, the rich jungle smells, wrap around him. There was no moon, but the stars were brilliant, and they cast a faint light over the yard below and the outbuildings, rendering them just visible in the night.

His left cheek throbbed under the big, ugly bruise where that great beast of a man had struck him with the hand guard of his sword. Why the villain had not simply killed him, Alonso did not know. He had a vague memory of Henriette calling out, but he could not recall what she had said. He was not really certain if she had spoken at all.

But the bruise was real, and the fight was real. The beast had knocked out the sentry, walked right past his men who were sleeping below stairs, and come into his and Henriette's bed chamber. Those were not the actions of a man who was just looking for some opportunity to rob or make mischief. They were deliberate and planned.

But why? Henriette claimed she had no notion of who the brute was, or what he might have wanted. Her protestations sounded genuine enough, but then Alonso had come to believe that she was a particularly skilled liar.

He could hear her breathing in her sleep, in the bed they shared, just a few feet away. She was an amusement he had not anticipated when he first made plans for Tortuga. How could he have? But she made a nice diversion nonetheless. She even did a tolerable job of overseeing the household and keeping the prisoners-cum-servants at their tasks.

Alonso's plans had begun to solidify. He could see it: dividing his time between Santo Domingo and Tortuga, strengthening his place and power in government, building his illicit empire here on this lawless island. He had even started working Henriette into those plans. How nice it would be to have Francisca in the one place and Henriette in the other. Henriette was by far a more energetic and willing lover than his wife, which was no surprise, given that Henriette had been part of the French court.

But now he was having second thoughts. This business with the intruder, and Henriette's apparent dissembling about the whole thing, made him question the wisdom of having her around. He wondered who she really was.

All that he knew for certain was that she was from France and wished to return there, and he knew that because her subtle and infrequent reminders about his promise to help her return were becoming far less subtle and far less infrequent. In truth, she was starting to annoy him. It would not be long before that annoyance outweighed even the carnal pleasure she provided.

Alonso stared out the window. The night was dark, but it was not quiet. The air was filled with the buzz of insects, the rustle of unseen creatures in the bush, and the soft breeze in the branches. Sometimes, the sounds from the ships anchored in the harbor a few miles away would make their way over the water to the plantation.

Earlier, Alonso had heard the evening guns as the ships took in their colors at sunset. Now, as he stared out into the dark, he heard another sound, faint and far off, so soft he was not sure of what he was hearing. It sounded like gunfire, small arms fire, pistols and muskets. And he thought he heard shouting as well.

He cocked an ear in that direction and listened. He picked up snatches of noise, and it did indeed sound like gunfire. But it was so faint he could not be sure, and when a few insects started up again in earnest it drowned out whatever he was hearing.

Now what the devil could be happening at this hour? he wondered. *Drunken sailors, no doubt, the miserable dogs.*

And then there was more commotion, not far off now, but from the yard below. A shouted word, what seemed to be a door slammed shut. Loud voices. Alonso stood straighter and looked down at the dim-lit ground. He felt the sweat on his palms, the sudden tension in his shoulders. He wondered if he should take up his sword, or his pistols.

Then he saw figures coming out from behind one of the small outbuildings: three men, two of them were his guards, with a third held between them, struggling against their grip. As he watched, two more men, one carrying a lantern, came running across the lawn to help. Since the incident of the night before, and the brutal dressing down and punishment that Alonso had given his men for letting the beast get past them, vigilance had become considerably heightened, and the number of guards patrolling the grounds much increased.

The five men converged in the middle of the lawn and Alonso could hear the buzz of their voices though he could not make out what they were saying.

Very well… Alonso thought. Whatever was going on, it would no doubt be brought to his attention soon, so he figured he might as well go investigate now.

He turned from the window and saw that Henriette was sitting up in bed, her long, unbound hair tumbling around her shoulders in a most provocative way.

"What's happening?" she asked, her voice groggy.

"I don't know. Nothing to concern you, *ma chère*. But I must see what's acting."

"Pray, take care, my dear Alonso," Henriette said. Alonso smiled. Her tones of concern and affection were damned convincing.

He grabbed his sword and shoulder belt as he crossed the room, slipped them over his shoulder on the landing, and headed down the stairs. He heard the snoring that was his nightly symphony and he wondered if he should turn the men out to meet whatever threat this might be. But from what he had seen from the window, it did not appear to be any great concern, so he let them sleep on.

Out the door and down the steps, he could see the lumbering form of Captain Rodriguez heading toward the house. Beyond him, the four men were still holding the prisoner, who seemed to have ceased struggling.

"Don Alonso, I was just coming to wake you," Rodriguez said as they drew within speaking distance. "We found this man breaking into the storeroom." He pointed with his thumb back over his shoulder.

Alonso looked at the prisoner, dimly lit by the single lantern. "Who is he?"

"I don't know, señor. Not a Spaniard. I'd guess one of these sorry dogs who was living in the town. Half starved, he looks. He was probably looking for food."

Alonso made a grunting sound of acknowledgement. "Let's go have a word with the cur."

He led the way over to where his guards held the prisoner, and he took the measure of the man as they approached. A *boucanier*, he seemed, by the look of him, one of the wretched hunters the Spanish were driving like vermin from Hispaniola, and now from Tortuga. But this one wore a jerkin and a wide-brimmed hat that Alonso could see had once been decent articles of clothing. And now that he had ceased struggling there was a certain quality to the way he held himself; pride and defiance.

Alonso stopped ten feet short and gestured for the guard to hold the lantern higher. In the light Alonso could see the moustache and sharp-pointed goatee on the man's chin, though much of the rest of his beard had also grown in. His clothes were torn and filthy and there was a gaunt, hunted took on his face. He looked like a man who had been living in the jungle for weeks, hiding from patrols, eating what he could. Which, most likely, was exactly his situation.

"Did he have weapons?" Alonso asked. "Musket, sword?"

"Just this, señor." One of the guards held up a hunting knife, a wicked looking thing with a ten-inch blade. Impressive, but still just a knife. Not an easy thing with which to feed one's self.

Alonso looked the man in the eyes, and the man met his gaze, like one who was willing to accept his fate.

"Who are you?" Alonso asked in Spanish, but the man just shook his head.

"Who are you?" Alonso tried again in French.

"My name is Hendrick Harmansz Van Lauwersoog," he said. His French was decent, but his accent was certainly not that of a native speaker.

"Dutchman?"

"Yes."

Alonso nodded. "There are all sorts who live and die in Spain's silver mines," he said. "I'm sure you'll find some of your countrymen there." He considered asking this — whatever his damned name was — what he was doing sneaking around at that hour, but by the look of him, Alonso had a pretty good idea. And he did not really care all that much. He turned to Rodriguez.

"Put him in irons, under guard. On the morrow we'll take him to the town, turn him over to the fleet." With that he turned and headed back toward the house, but he did not take two steps before the Dutchman spoke again.

"Pray, give my regards to Henriette," he said.

Alonso stopped. He turned back. The Dutchman's face was expressionless. "Henriette?"

"Yes. She still goes by that name, no? I saw her earlier."

Alonso retraced his steps. "Who are you?"

"I told you. My name is Van Lauwersoog. I was with that bastard LeBoeuf and the others when they took this plantation."

For a long moment Alonso just studied the Dutchman's face. "LeBoeuf?"

"A buccaneer. Big whore's son. Plays it dumb, but he's not so dumb as he'd have one believe. The others seem to be following him now. He and Henriette were lovers. But now apparently she's deserted to the enemy."

"Big?"

"Very big. Better than six feet tall. Seventeen, eighteen stone. But quick with a sword. Have you met with him?" A hint of a smile appeared on the Dutchman's lips. "That's quite the bruise you have on your face."

Alonso's mind was tumbling in this flood of information. Henriette? LeBoeuf? Lovers? Is that why he had come? This Van Lauwersoog seemed to know a great deal, and that made him possibly quite valuable.

"You and these others, you were boucaniers? Pig-hunters?"

"Yes. But I'm not such garbage as them. I was rebuilding a fortune lost. I was an officer in the Dutch Navy. A privateer captain after that. I am a gentleman, señor. A seeker of fortune."

Alonso cocked an eyebrow, and it said as clearly as words, *you do not look like a gentleman.* But for all that, he knew the Dutchman was not lying, not entirely. His clothes and his speech and his bearing suggested that he was indeed not such scum as these pig hunters.

"You are friends with this LeBoeuf?"

"We were fellows. Now we are enemies. He tried to kill me. I mean to kill him."

The flood in Alonso's mind was growing deeper, stronger, his thoughts swirling in those murky waters. So much to consider. This man was a privateersman. A Dutchman, not a Spaniard. He was a sworn enemy of the villain LeBoeuf. And Alonso held his life in his hands.

He could make great use of this man. Van Lauwersoog might fit into his plans like a hand in a glove. He was not sure how. He had to think. But he knew there was opportunity here. He could feel it, deep down. Once again he turned to Rodriguez.

"Put him in irons, as I said. Keep two men on him. He's a slippery one, I'll warrant. In the morning I'll have further word with him."

With that he turned and headed back to the house, and Van Lauwersoog did not call out again. So much to consider, so much to weigh and decide. But Don Alonso had an odd feeling now. A feeling that somehow God or fate or the devil was presenting him with a grand opportunity here, a key to unlocking his iron chest of ambitions.

It was Alonso's intent to be the sculptor of his own fate. Now Hendrick Harmansz Van Lauwersoog could be the sharp edge of his chisel.

The ebb tide, the faithful ebb tide, carried LeBoeuf and the others miles away from the Tortuga coast, and there was no reaction from the Spanish fleet. It seemed that no one even noticed.

LeBoeuf was surprised. More than surprised. That last, sharp fight to take the ship must have been heard all over the harbor, even without much small arms fire. But if it had been, no one seemed moved to do anything about it.

They watched intently for some sign of pursuit, LeBoeuf and his men, some indication that one of the powerful ships was getting underway, coming after them. But none did. It seemed an incredible stroke of good luck, and that was not something LeBoeuf was accustomed to. It made him wary.

"The shooting," Levasseur observed, "they probably reckoned it was the Spanish crew executing prisoners."

That seemed as reasonable an explanation as any, though LeBoeuf doubted it. He suspected the Spanish simply could not be bothered getting a man-of-war underway to stop the theft of some insubstantial merchant ship.

Even without evading pursuit, there was plenty to do as they drifted through the dark. The women were sent to look after the wounded. The Spanish prisoners who were still whole enough to pose a threat were rounded up and held at gunpoint up in the bow.

There were nine men dead; Spanish, and Maja's men, and a few of LeBoeuf's. Those were wrapped and bound in canvas with a round shot at their feet and tossed overboard. It was a lot of effort, but had they not done so, the corpses would have floated and remained alongside, drifting out to sea with the ship, and LeBoeuf did not think that would do much for the men's spirits.

Once they were well away from the land, LeBoeuf ordered the Spaniards, both hale and wounded, down into the boats. He gave each boat's crew a single pair of oars; enough to get them back to Tortuga, but not quickly.

As the boats were pulling away, disappearing into the night, LeBoeuf felt the first hint of a breeze on his cheek, and heard the gentle rustle of canvas overhead.

"Hands to set the topsails!" he said and the men moved to the lines; clewlines, buntlines, sheets, braces. "Le Chasseur, take the helm."

A moment later the topsails came spilling out of the lines that had held them bundled aloft. A moment after that the yards were hoisted up the topmasts, the sails snapped and filled, and the dull, drifting vessel became a living thing.

LeBoeuf walked aft. Le Chasseur was standing at the tiller, his eyes moving from the sails above, to the compass in front of him, to some point out to weather, then back again, the way a real sailor's eyes should move.

"What heading?" he asked. It still sounded odd to LeBoeuf to have such a question posed that did not end in "sir" or "captain," but such things would not be countenanced by the buccaneers, and he let it go.

"West," LeBoeuf said. "For now." They would run before the trade wind. He had no destination in mind, save for leaving Tortuga astern.

They sailed on through the dark hours and LeBoeuf resisted the temptation to set more sail. He did not want to run too far to leeward until he had made a decision as to where they were bound, and he had no notion as to when that decision would be made.

Dawn came, with the sun rising dead astern and illuminating the upper rigging and the sails in a brilliant red-orange light. Slowly it crept down the masts to the deck and cast a long shadow out ahead, so it seemed as if the ship was making a futile effort to overtake that dark image of itself.

LeBoeuf breathed deep, leaned back on the rail, ran his eyes around the horizon, which was now visible in every direction. To the north and well astern, Tortuga could still be seen, a low, blue-green shape against the pale blue sky, too far away now to look menacing or insidious. To the south and stretched out ahead of the ship was the western end of Hispaniola. And beyond that…nothing. Open sea.

But that was not true, as LeBoeuf well knew. About twenty-five leagues to the west was the great island of Cuba. Twenty leagues to the north, the islands of Great and Little Inagua. To the southwest and seventy leagues distant, Jamaica. Islands everywhere, and to the west of it all, the Spanish Main. So many places for a ship to run, so many places to hide. It was what drew men such as him to those waters.

LeBoeuf smiled, grim and ironic. He was leaving Tortuga the same way he had left Hispaniola: on a ship stolen from the Spanish. So be it. If Spain would insist on harrying him and his men, depriving them of their livelihoods, taking from them what little scraps of land they laid claim to, then they would take to the sea. The sea was their element, where they most belonged. It was where they could inflict the most hurt, where they could most efficiently exact vengeance.

If the buccaneers could not be hunters of pigs, they would be hunters of men. And they would take from Spain much more than a few miserable ships. They would take the very foundations of empire.

Visit our web site to sign up for our (occasional) e-mail newsletter for information about new titles as well as preview sample chapters and other good stuff cheap (actually free):

www.jameslnelson.com

Other Fiction by

James L. Nelson:

The Norsemen Saga: Novels of the Vikings in Ireland

Fin Gall
Dubh-linn
The Lord of Vík-ló
Glendalough Fair
Night Wolf
Raider's Wake
Loch Garman
A Vengeful Wind
Kings and Pawns
The Midgard Serpent
The Narrow Seas

The Brethren of the Coast: Piracy in Colonial America

The Guardship
The Blackbirder
The Pirate Round

The Only Life that Mattered:

The Story of Ann Bonny, Mary Read and Calico Jack Rackham

Glossary

Aft: toward the back end of a ship
After: behind, toward the stern or aft end
Amidships: around the middle of a ship
Astern: outside a ship and behind it
Barque: a three-masted vessel with square sails on the fore and main mast and fore and aft sails on the mizzen; generally refers to any small ship
Batten: long strips of wood secured to the edges of tarpaulins to keep the tarpaulins in place, often used to secure hatches
Beam ends: a vessel lying on her side is said to be on her beam ends, i.e. the ends of the deck beams are perpendicular to the water
Belaying pin: a club-shaped wooden pin, generally about eighteen inches in length, to which ropes are tied
Bend: to attach one thing to another; a sailor "bends" a sail to a **yard**
Binnacle: a cabinet just forward of the **helm** in which the compass is housed
Bitts: a heavy vertical structure near the bow to which the anchor cable is made fast
Block: nautical term for a pulley
Boatswain's chair: a seat attached to a rope sling by which a person can be hoisted up.
Bonaventure: in 16th and 17th century vessels, the fourth mast
Bow: the forward end of a ship's hull
Bowsprit: a sort of mast that extends up from the bow
Brace: a rope attached to the end of a yard and used to swing the yard on a horizontal plane to adjust the sail to the wind
Brace of pistols: a pair of pistols
Bulwark: the "walls," generally waist-high, that surround a ship's deck.
Burthen: the carrying capacity of a ship, expressed in tons

Butt: a large cask holding 126 gallons, roughly equal to two **hogsheads**
Cable length: two hundred yards
Capstan: a vertical wooden drum turned by means of men pushing on wooden bars that project horizontally from the top of the drum; used to lift anchors and other heavy weights
Capstan bar: wooden bars that are inserted into holes in the head of the capstan.
Chains: metalwork attaching the **deadeyes** to the sides of a ship; also used to mean the platform to which the deadeyes are attached, which is more correctly called the chain-wale, or channel
Combing: a raised frame surrounding a hatch or other opening in the deck.
Come about: to change a ship's heading by turning the bow through the wind; same meaning as to **tack**
Cunning: archaic word for conning, to oversee the direction of a ship by giving orders to the helmsman
Deadeye: a thick wooden disk with three holes attached to the end of a length of rigging; a rope passed through the holes is used to tighten the rigging
Fall: the rope from a block and tackle which is hauled upon
Fall off: to turn a ship's bow away from the direction of the wind
Fid: a wooden block that fits in a square hole in the base of an upper mast on which the upper mast rests
Fife rail: a horizontal rail at the base of a mast in which **belaying pins** are mounted
Firkin: a small cask, about a quarter of a barrel
Flemish eye: a type of eye splice, or fixed loop in the end of a rope
Flush-decked: a ship whose deck runs at one level from bow to stern, with no raised deck fore of aft
Fore: toward the front or bow of a ship.
Full and by: sailing with the bow pointed as close to the direction from which the wind is blowing as possible with the sails full
Gasket: a short rope used for tying a sail in place
Grapeshot: ordnance fired from a cannon consisting of a cluster of small iron balls; used as an anti-personnel weapon
Grating: a **hatch** cover made up of wooden slates arranged like a heavy wooden screen
Hatch: an opening in the deck to give access below

Headed: said of a ship when the wind shifts to come more directly over her bow
Hogshead: a cask holding approximately sixty-five gallons
Keel: a long timber that forms the very bottom of a ship and upon which the rest of a ship is built
Keelson: an internal keel that sits above the main keel
Larboard: the left side of a ship when looking forward; archaic term for *port*
Leeward: down-wind
Lift: a rope attached to the end of a yard to support the yard in a horizontal position
Line: any rope that serves a specific function on shipboard
Marline: a type of heavy-duty twine
Martnet: a series of ropes used to haul up the edges of a sail.
Mast: a vertical wooden pole used to support the **yards** and sails; on larger ships the masts were made in sections: the lower mast, topmast and topgallant mast
Mast rope: a rope used for lowering a topmast or topgallant mast down to the deck
Mizzen: the third mast back from the front of a ship.
Overbody: an article of women's clothing, similar to a bodice, generally made of wool or canvas and laced up the front
Painter: a rope attached to the bow of a boat, used for towing or tying the boat off
Parceling: old cloth wrapped around a rope to shield the rope from chafe or to keep water out
Periagua: a large canoe made up of the hollowed trunks of two trees; indigenous to the West Indies
Pinrail: a wooden rail mounted inside a ship's **bulwarks** in which **belaying pins** are inserted
Pounder: term used to describe the size of a cannon by the weight of the cannonball it fires; a four-pounder gun fires a ball that weighs four pounds, etc.
Ratline: pronounced *ratlin*; a rope tied horizontally across the **shrouds** to form a sort of rope ladder for climbing up a mast
***Real Audiencia*:** the first court of the Spanish crown in America
Rigging: cumulative term for all the ropes and other gear used to control a ship's sails

Ringbolt: an iron ring mounted on the deck to which rigging or gun tackle is attached
Rose lashing: a type of knot used to fix a **block** to a **spar**
Round shot: a round iron ball; a cannon ball
Scuttle (noun): a small opening in the deck or side of a ship
Scuttle (verb): to deliberately make an opening in the hull of a ship to allow water in
Seizing: a lashing of small line used to bind two larger lines together
Sheet: a rope used to hold the corner or edge of a sail down so it can catch the wind
Shrouds: heavy ropes leading from the side of a ship to the top of the mast; used to prevent the mast from falling
Spar: general term for any of the wooden poles that support a ship's sails
Spritsail: a square sail mounted under the **bowsprit**
Starboard: the right side of a ship when looking forward from the stern
Stay: a heavy rope used to prevent a mast from falling backward
Stay tackle: a block and tackle hanging from a ship's **stay**: mostly for lifting things in and out of the hold
Stern: the back end of a ship's hull
Stern sheets: the back end of a boat
Sweep (noun): a long oar
Sweep (verb): to propel a vessel with sweeps
Tack (noun): a rope attached to the corner of a lower square sail and used to pull the corner forward.
Tack (verb): to change the direction in which a ship is sailing by turning her bow through the wind
Tackle: any combination of ropes and **blocks** arranged to achieve mechanical advantage
Tarpaulin: canvas treated with tar or something similar to make it waterproof; used to cover hatches, boats, etc.
Thole: a wooden pin mounted vertically on the side of a boat to hold an oar in place
Thwart: the seat in a boat on which the rowers sit
Tiller: horizontal bar attached to a rudder by which a vessel is steered
Top: a platform located at the top of a lower mast, often erroneously called a "crow's nest"

Top hamper: general term for all the masts, spars, rigging and sails
Topmast: the mast mounted above the lower mast
Topmast stay: a rope that extends from the top of the topmast to some secure point lower down to prevent the topmast from falling backward
Tun: a very large cask, the equal of two **butts**
Waist: the middle section of a ship's upper deck
Weather (adj.): an object "to weather" is to windward
Weather (verb): to "weather" something such as a point of land is to pass to windward of it
Whipstaff: a vertical handle attached to a tiller and used to steer a ship; in use before the advent of the ship's wheel
Windlass: a machine for lifting heavy objects consisting of a horizontal barrel supported by vertical posts and rotated through the use of bars inserted into holes in the barrel
Windward: upwind
Worming: a rigging technique that involves laying small lines in the grooves between the strands of a rope
Yard: the horizontal **spars** from which square sails are hung
Yardarm: the very end of the yard, beyond the point where the sail is tied off
Yard tackle: a tackle hung from the end of a yard, used for hoisting boats and other heavy objects onboard

Acknowledgements

I am grateful, as ever, to all the folks who helped lift this book up from the watery depths of my imagination. Thank you to Nat Sobel for his insights and his excellent representation these past three decades(!). Thanks to Nathaniel Nelson and Stephanie Nelson for their proofreading and suggestions. Thank you to Catrin Russell of Subtle Touch Creations for the excellent cover, and to Christopher Boyle for the maps.

And, of course, to Lisa Nelson, admiral and first mate…underway and making way.

Printed in Dunstable, United Kingdom

68940040R00201